JUSTICE

THE LOST WARSHIP BOOK FOUR

DANIEL GIBBS

Justice by Daniel Gibbs

Copyright © 2023 by Daniel Gibbs

Visit Daniel Gibbs website at

www.danielgibbsauthor.com

Cover by Jeff Brown Graphics—www.jeffbrowngraphics.com

Additional Illustrations by Joel Steudler—www.joelsteudler.com

This book is a work of fiction, the characters, incidents and dialogues are products of the author's imagination and are not to be construed as real. Any resemblance to actual persons, living or dead, is entirely coincidental.

All rights reserved. This book or any portion thereof may not be reproduced in any form or by any electronic or mechanical means, including information storage and retrieval systems, or used in any manner whatsoever without the express written permission of the author, except for the use of brief quotations in a book review. For permissions please contact info@eotp.net.

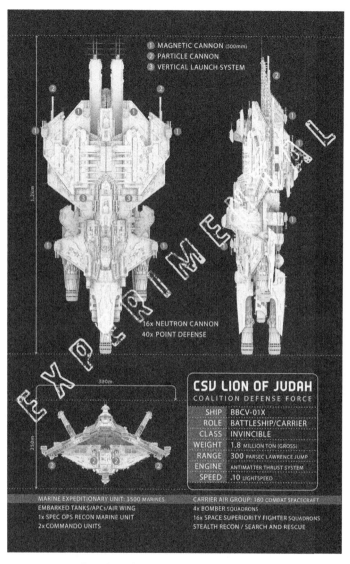

For more detailed specifications, visit http://www.danielgibbsauthor.com/universe/ships/lion-of-judah/

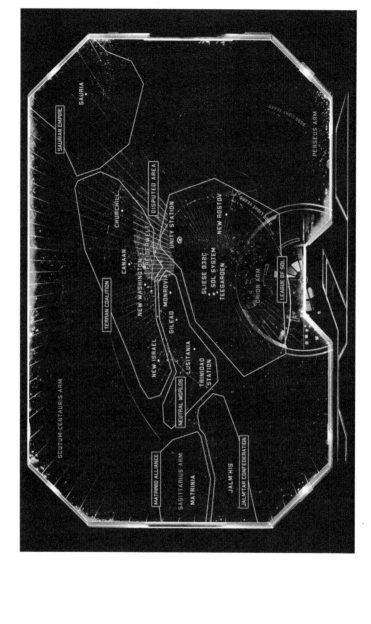

ALSO AVAILABLE FROM DANIEL GIBBS

Battlegroup Z

Book 1 - Weapons Free

Book 2 - Hostile Spike

Book 3 - Sol Strike

Book 4 - Bandits Engaged

Book 5 - Iron Hand

Book 6 - Final Flight

Echoes of War

Book 1 - Fight the Good Fight

Book 2 - Strong and Courageous

Book 3 - So Fight I

Book 4 - Gates of Hell

Book 5 - Keep the Faith

Book 6 - Run the Gauntlet

Book 7 - Finish the Fight

The Lost Warship

Book 1 - Adrift

Book 2 - Mercy

Book 3 - Valor

Book 4 - Justice

Book 5 - Resolve

Book 6 - Faith (Coming in 2023)

Breach of Faith

(With Gary T. Stevens)

Book 1 - Breach of Peace

Book 2 - Breach of Faith

Book 3 - Breach of Duty

Book 4 - Breach of Trust

Book 5 - Spacer's Luck

Book 6 - Fortune's Favor

Book 7 - The Iron Dice

Deception Fleet

(With Steve Rzasa)

Book 1 - Victory's Wake

Book 2 - Cold Conflict

Book 3 - Hazards Near

Book 4 - Liberty's Price

Book 5 - Ecliptic Flight

Book 6 - Collision Vector

Courage, Commitment, Faith: Tales from the Coalition Defense Force

(Anthology Series)

Volume One

1

Military Administration and Command Center
Zeivlot
8 September 2464

DAVID COHEN SUCKED in a breath as ornate twin doors with hand-carved reliefs of martial images from a time gone by opened in front of him. He and a dozen officers along with a small Terran Coalition Marine Corps honor guard strode into the massive chamber. Scores of alien military officers and civilian staffers lined the room, while Zupan Vog't was seated at a circular table in its center.

Everyone wore somber expressions, which was to be expected, since David had transmitted a briefing with everything they'd learned so far about the nanites, including real-time sensor data on the swarm devouring an inhabited planet.

In the week it had taken the *Lion of Judah* to return to the Zeivlots' solar system, preparations for what to do next had been nonstop. David barely slept between strategy sessions, while the scientific personnel, led by Dr. Hayworth and Major Arthur Hanson, searched for a technological solution. Little progress had been made, but he held out hope they would find a breakthrough. *Time. We have time.* The words did little to comfort David's spirit.

Vog't stood as the humans came to a stop. "General Cohen. I would have welcomed you with joy and celebration, but in light of the current events..."

"Of course," David replied. Since everyone had an ear-mounted device to quickly translate English into Zeivlot and vice versa there was a slight delay. After almost six months, they were used to it.

"Please, sit."

They all did so. The other seats were taken by Zeivlot military officers and several rather severe-looking civilians.

Attired in dress whites, David felt uncomfortable, as he usually did in formal uniforms. With all his campaign ribbons, a dozen medals for various acts of bravery dating back twenty years, and command-in-space pins, his shirt was colorful, to say the least. David put his cover on the table before laying a tablet in front of him. A knot formed in the pit of his stomach.

"Do you have any further updates for us, General?"

"Little progress has been made in the last week, Zupan," David replied. He kept his voice carefully neutral.

One of the Zeivlots said something under his breath that didn't translate before snarling. "You humans. You brought this monstrosity down on us, and you have nothing to say besides 'No progress.' How long until we die, and you fly away in your ship?"

David forced himself to meet the man's hateful stare. "I won't shy away from our culpability." He glanced at

Hayworth. "We didn't know what the nanites were, nor do we fully understand them. But what I *will not* do is fly away."

Vog't cleared her throat. "Then what do you propose, General?"

It seemed as if she'd aged twenty years since they arrived. *I suppose aliens showing up on your doorstep, narrowly avoiding Armageddon—twice now—will do that to a person.* Calvin Demood's reports had been quite colorful reading. *I'll deal with the colonel and his rampant ignoring of direct orders later.*

"You have two options." David stared. "Fight or run."

"How can we possibly do either? We might be able to build a few generational ships to get a small portion of our population off. Still, we know of no other habitable worlds, nor can we build military vessels in enough numbers to matter." Her voice rose as she spoke.

There's no going back from this. HaShem, help me. "We... I am prepared to transfer all needed technology for building ships capable of moving large numbers of your citizens or combat vessels."

Silence swept the room, and several Zeivlot military officers' jaws dropped.

Vog't swallowed and licked her lips. "Did I hear you right? You are prepared to give us FTL, fusion reactor, and weapons tech?"

"Everything except our antimatter reactor plans. The supply chains for building more exceed what your world is capable of at this point."

"And you wouldn't want to empower a species to be a threat against yours."

David smiled thinly. "Always on point, Madam Zupan."

"There's got to be a *but* in there."

"Yes. Both Zeivlot and Zavlot must agree to the same

terms, and all work will be conducted under the watchful eye of CDF personnel. And... both planets must join the Terran Coalition."

Vog't's eyes widened. "*What?*"

"The only legal method I can find to transfer technology is between member worlds of the Coalition." David shrugged. "I'm probably exceeding my authority, but this situation isn't in the rules-and-regs manual."

"Now the truth comes out," the same Zeivlot officer spat. "The humans wish to rule us."

David almost slammed his hand down on the table. Instead, he made a fist under it before relaxing it. "Stow the nativist propaganda. I am trying to help save your world, and I certainly have no desire to rule it. Your system of government will continue without any influence from us. I will maintain complete control of all CDF military assets and take overall command of any fleet constructed. And before you object, War Leader, no one on either planet has experience with interstellar warfare."

"And what of the rest of our military force—"

Vog't held up her hand. "We agree to your terms, General. There will, of course, be a vote in the parliament. But I do not foresee it receiving less than nearly unanimous support."

That was the easy part. "Then you need to decide whether the Zeivlot people would prefer to fight, or evacuating as many as possible is the better goal."

"That... thing destroyed an entire planet in less than a rotation," the war leader snapped. "How can we hope to prevail?"

"By building enough warships with a new weapon that neutralizes the bonds between the atoms that make up the nanites or in some other way impedes their function. Dr.

Hayworth believes we're dealing with a hive mind. If he's right, breaking the bonds should cause enough impediment to its function that we can destroy what's left." *Well, that's not entirely what the doctor believes, but they need hope. And that's all I can give them right now.*

Raucous chatter broke out between the Zeivlots. The translators didn't pick up everything, but David could make out enough to realize that most of the civilians wanted to flee.

Vog't barked something in her native tongue that brought the room to a standstill and held up her hand again. "General Cohen, what do *you* think we should do?"

Everyone turned toward David. In their eyes, he saw fear, anger, and in more than might be expected, hope. *We saved them before. At least some think we can do it again.* In that moment, David knew why Hayworth stuck to his non-interference beliefs so tightly. "Humans have a long history with fighting against impossible and overwhelming odds. It's easy to advocate for dying on your feet rather than living on your knees. But this is a unique dilemma. At least, in the last major war my people fought, surrender *was* an option. It would've meant slavery to a communist government, but some of us would've survived and lived to resist from within, had total defeat come."

The weight of the universe seemed to descend on his shoulders. He'd been prepared for Vog't to ask for his advice, but actually giving it was different. *HaShem, guide my steps, and give me wisdom.* "If you flee, it may be decades before a suitable planet can be found, and it also runs the risk of being destroyed by the nanites. We encountered a race that had taken to living in the void. After hundreds of years, their existence was so horrific that they'd rather commit collective suicide than continue. I advise fighting, with a small number of people movers to ensure that if the worst happens, your race doesn't vanish from the galaxy."

"Then we will fight." Vog't's voice echoed loudly.

David nodded. "Very well." *Here goes nothing.*

"Where do we begin?"

Hanson leaned forward with an almost imperceptible raise of his right eyebrow at David. After David nodded, he spoke. "It's essential for all of you to understand this isn't the kind of goal your planet has ever executed, Madam Zupan. We're talking all hands on deck, in short order. Creating a series of factories to fabricate the required components, building zero-G construction facilities in low orbit, training the personnel to run them... It will be an around-the-clock, no-days-off, do-or-die effort."

"Total mobilization."

"Yes, ma'am," David said. "And it will take the Zavlots too. Major Hanson has prepared a detailed program-management plan to get things going."

Vog't turned toward a female Zeivlot behind her. "We'll have to get emergency powers to redirect all manufacturing concerns toward the war effort."

"Only one thing matters now. Making enough warships to fight the nanites effectively. Defense platforms... mines... space-superiority fighters. In numbers that will make a difference." David crossed his arms.

"I assure you, General, we're up for the challenge." Vog't seemed almost serene. "When do we start?"

"How soon can you arrange a summit with Olgasin?" He was the Zavlot leader.

"Is tomorrow too late?"

David shook his head. "No, that'll be fine, and it'll give me time to meet with Colonel Demood. Any other questions?"

Justice

7

"No."

"Then I will take my leave and hope that further discussions will be productive."

Vog't pursed her lips. "Thank you, General. May the Maker bless your steps."

David stood. "And yours as well." As he and the rest of the *Lion*'s crew filed out, the next problem slotted into view. *Calvin's disregard of my orders to stay out of the fighting between the Zeivlots and the Zavlots.*

————

COLONEL CALVIN DEMOOD had taken extra care to ensure his uniform was in perfect condition before David's arrival, partly because it was how a Marine functioned, but he also worried about what the day would bring. While every action Calvin had taken felt wholly justified under Coalition law, he couldn't set aside that he'd knowingly exceeded his mandate to provide training, advice, and intelligence to the indigenous population.

Since David had explicitly requested a private meeting before touring the joint intelligence task force facility, Calvin thought he would probably get a tongue-lashing at best. *Or dismissal from command.* Still, he was proud of his actions and those of everyone who'd served on Zeivlot. *The general is a fair man. I know he'll see what we did here was the right thing.*

The door to the small meeting area swung open, and David strode in.

Calvin sprang to his feet and came to attention. "Sir. Wasn't expecting you for another twenty minutes. Apologies."

David flashed a smile. "To my immense surprise, it took

less time than I expected to discuss the nanite situation with Zupan Vog't and come to an agreement. Now, at ease." He dropped into a chair.

Calvin counted off a couple of seconds before he sat as well. "I'm fully prepared for any punishment you wish to hand out, sir. All I ask is that you consider our actions' effects."

"A few weeks ago, I might've had a different outlook on your actions." David stroked his chin. "And perhaps you went too far in going all in on direct combat against the terrorist cells. But I remember times in my career when I disobeyed orders because it was the right thing to do."

"I remember doing that with you." Calvin leaned back and let out a sigh. "We had to help, sir. The Zeivlots were getting their asses handed to them, and I lost good men to those terrorists."

David took a moment before responding. "Yes, I read the report. And probably would've done the same thing. What's the situation now?"

"Who knows, sir." Calvin shrugged. "We stopped the asteroid attacks and helped Zeivlot and Zavlot security forces round up nearly anyone who's ever tried to use violence, espoused violence, or supported terrorist groups. Something tells me plenty of people out there are willing to try to kill one another, though."

"You can't change the heart with force." David bit his lip. "That comes from HaShem. But to your point, we can stop the worst of them from harming others. I'm recalling you to the *Lion*, effective immediately. We'll have Major Almeida take over here."

Calvin's chest tightened. "Is this a punishment, sir?"

"Absolutely not." David seemed to stare through him. "I

need my best Marine to help deal with these nanites. You read the briefing?"

"Yes, sir. Horrific things. But killable with Saurian plasma weapons."

"Which we're in short supply of. I want your best people on the problem. Perhaps working with Hayworth and the other scientists, we can figure out something else that works."

Calvin nodded. "Of course, sir. What about the others?"

"We'll see. I'm hopeful that the threat of impending doom on both worlds will force a truce, at least for the time being."

"You'd think multiple brushes with planet-wide disaster would've had the same effect."

David rose and held out his hand. "Unorthodox, as usual, Colonel. But that's how we both roll. Oh, I noticed in your report how you dealt with prisoner questioning, and I commend you for keeping it within the confines of the UCMJ."

"It wasn't always easy, sir."

"Doing right isn't. That's kind of the point, my friend."

Calvin shook his hand. "Thank you."

David grinned. "Now get out of here before I change my mind."

"Yes, sir." Calvin smiled in return before turning to go, pleased he hadn't misjudged the situation and that the stars on David's shoulders hadn't gone to his head. *Too many good officers get messed up by those higher ranks. Good thing our skipper isn't one of them. And now, we get to fight microrobots that can shapeshift at will. What I wouldn't do to be back fighting the damn Leaguers.*

2

SELENA BO'HAI SMOOTHED her dress one last time, feeling out of place in the halls of government. She'd been summoned to the zupan's residence for what had been described as an informal discussion. *A year ago, I'd never been in the same city as our leader. Now, I've been alone with her thrice.* For a linguist who had been part of a fringe scientific group searching for extra-solar life, it was a strange twist of fate.

Her escort, a close-protection officer clad in a smart-looking suit with a sidearm in a hip holster, opened the door to the zupan's private office.

Bo'hai walked through it and took in the room. The décor ranged from dozens to hundreds of years old. Virtually everything except the electronics was an antique, and she recognized a few sculptures from art textbooks she'd devoured as a child. *I think that one is from before the last calamity.* Works dating to a previous cycle were highly prized.

"Thank you for coming," Vog't said as she stood behind

the ornate desk. "I realize being called here can be disconcerting."

"I live to serve my people, Zupan." Bo'hai gave a traditional curtsy. "Thank you for placing trust in me."

"Please, join me." Vog't gestured to a couch.

Bo'hai waited for the zupan to sit before doing so. Her heart pounded as she wondered what the purpose of the meeting was.

"Before we begin, how aware of the situation with these... nanites... are you?" Vog't struggled to pronounce the word the humans used. Zeivlot had no equivalent.

"General Cohen briefed me the same night the swarm of them consumed the inhabited planet, and the *Lion of Judah*'s crew determined they were headed toward our home."

"Did you feel he held anything back?"

Bo'hai's eyebrows rose. "What are you suggesting, ma'am?"

Vog't kept her inscrutable expression. "While I generally believe the humans want to help us, I must examine all motivations for their actions. What they ask for is not easy, and if the threat is somehow exaggerated—"

"Ma'am, I saw the video, and moreover, I observed first-hand the reactions of every member of the *Lion*'s crew. They were utterly crushed in a way I've never seen before."

"So you believe everything they've said?"

"Unequivocally."

"Is there any chance they have coopted you, or personal feelings have somehow influenced your opinions and thoughts?"

Bo'hai pursed her lips. "Are you suggesting I would put the interests of another species above mine if they were doing something to harm us?"

"I believe that being in the presence of beings who are clearly far more advanced than us after they collectively saved our world might induce mixed emotions in such a situation."

For a moment, Bo'hai wanted to bite Vog't's head off. Though the zupan was the most powerful political figure on Zeivlot, the question did more than offend her. It made her *angry*. "I am objective, ma'am." She forced her tone to remain civil.

Vog't stared even more forcefully for a few seconds. "I've read your reports. They contain a tremendous amount of detail. Would you agree with that?"

"Yes. I'm a scientist. Detail is what we do, Zupan."

She held up a piece of paper. Some words were circled in bright blue. "Do you see those?"

Bo'hai looked through the markings before returning her gaze to Vog't. "You highlighted wherever I used the name David."

"It is telling to me that you went from General Cohen to David. The human military personnel address each other by their last names almost exclusively. Why deviate from this convention?"

In the piercing silence that followed, Bo'hai heard herself breathing. "Because we became friends. And it is our custom and theirs to use given names when addressing a friend." The leader of Bo'hai's planet had forced her to acknowledge a reality she'd refused to so far: she had developed feelings for David. Not that she would reveal that to anyone. *I wonder if interspecies relations are possible.* From a purely mechanical perspective, she had no idea. But the feelings remained.

Bo'hai continued, "I have an incredible amount of

respect for General Cohen... David. He is the one who was prophesized to save us from the cycle. *He did it.* The Maker has blessed him and the *Lion of Judah.* That is plain to see. And he has been gracious enough to treat me as an equal, with respect, and we've become friends. It is impossible for him or the other humans to lie and deceive us."

"What makes it impossible?"

"Do not the ancient texts say that the one who stops the cycle will bring peace to us all?"

Vog't shrugged. "Perhaps. But I am unwilling to put my future and the future of Zeivlot itself in the hands of documents from eons ago. Facts are demanded."

"Then accept this as fact. In every situation, the humans have tried to do what they regard as religiously and morally right. Actions that conform to what *we* think is morally right because of the Maker's instructions to us. I have observed closely. None of them deviate from this."

"What of the ones who do not place their faith in the Maker?"

Bo'hai shook her head. "They have similar ethics. I cannot speak of every human being in the universe, but *these* are good people. *All of them.*"

"And if you were in my place, you would risk our entire world based on their word?"

"Yes." The word tumbled out of Bo'hai's mouth without a second thought. She blinked, surprised at herself.

"That is a strong conviction."

"It comes from watching people who repeatedly do what is right, even when it's the most difficult option." Bo'hai pursed her lips. "That is a rare quality. Even for those most committed to the Maker."

"You should know that every member of our delegation

agrees with your assessment, if not in quite so animated a manner."

"Then you will heed General Cohen's words?"

Vog't nodded. "Yes. And I expect you to remain the head of our scientific delegation. In the event any... doubts may surface, report them immediately."

Bo'hai fought to keep her expression neutral despite the anger that exploded in her heart. "Yes, Zupan."

Vog't smiled. "You have served our people well. Once this is all over, I hope to be able to repay the debt."

"There is nothing to repay, Zupan. I've gained a lifetime of knowledge in these last few months, and I hope to continue my education."

"Of course." Vog't stood. "If you will excuse me, there are many matters of state to attend to."

Bo'hai rose and bowed her head. "I live but to serve the Maker."

"May He go with you."

It took some time after the meeting for Bo'hai to fully realize how disturbed the discussion with Vog't had made her—or the outrage she felt at anyone questioning David's morality. She couldn't share it with anyone. Instead, it would be bottled up inside, sealed for eternity.

CSV *Lion of Judah*
Midway between Zeivlot and Zavlot
15 September 2464

Justice 15

SOME SAID the wheels of government moved slowly. *At least, they do on Canaan.* In the last week, the speed at which both alien worlds had changed previous policies, broken the news of the impending nanite threat to their populations, and worked to come together had surprised him. While he'd suspected Vog't would come around quickly, as they had more of a personal relationship, Olgasin, the Zavlot chief of state, seemed to be just as eager.

Though there were sticking points. Part of the reason for the joint summit David was about to walk into was to address some significant areas of disagreement that still remained. But he had some ideas on how to get over the impasses.

The gravlift opened only a few sections down from the VIP reception area where they had gathered after shuttle rides to *Lion.* David took one last glance at the polished metal surface to make sure all his insignia, ribbon bars, medals, and pins were in the right places. He had his dress whites on, and their wear was infrequent enough to make lining everything up a chore. *Besides, can't have the master chief mentally assigning me demerits for my uniform.*

As he moved through the passageway, memories of Sheila Thompson, his old friend and former executive officer, who had died in the Second Battle of Canaan, flashed into his mind. She'd always kidded him about getting dressed up and preening over it. *I really wish you were still here, Sheila. You'd have insight into something I was missing.*

Then the richly appointed VIP wing came into view. He had no time for ruminations, only a steely resolve to handle the here and now.

Two Marine sentries wearing full combat armor and carrying short-barreled rifles came to attention as David approached. He acknowledged them with a nod before stepping through the hatch into a conference room roughly three times the size of the one off the bridge.

"Thank you all for coming," David said as the hatch slid shut behind him. He walked up to Vog't and shook hands with her. "Zupan, always a pleasure."

Olgasin extended his hand. "General, it's good to see you once more, and may the Maker illuminate your path."

David shook with him. "And yours, Chairman."

Clustered around the room were groups of Zeivlots and Zavlots along with most of the *Lion*'s senior staff, including Aibek, Ruth, Hanson, Dr. Tural, and Amir. Calvin and another group of Marine sentries provided security.

"Let's get settled in," David said as he gestured to the long table then waited a few moments as most took their seats before he slid into his chair. "Before we begin, I'd like to take a moment to recognize how far we've all come here. Just a few months ago, Zeivlot and Zavlot were ready to destroy each other. Now, the leaders of both worlds sit in the same space, having a civil conversation. That's something that hasn't happened in thousands of years. You're now on the precipice of an even bigger leap."

"Flowery words, General Cohen, from an alien species who wants to arm us to fight its war," a Zavlot military officer replied.

Before Olgasin could interject, David held up his hand. "No. He's only voicing what many think. I'd rather address it head-on. War Leader Deiba, this isn't our war. These nanites seem to only exist to devour worlds with minerals they desire... or in this case, technology."

"Which, by your own admission, is on *Zeivlot*."

David ran his teeth over his lip, wanting to verbally rip the man from limb from limb. *But that won't solve the problem or win hearts and minds.* "Did you watch the visual

Justice 17

recording of what happened to the planet this thing destroyed?"

"Well—"

"Yes or no."

"I did."

"Then why do you think it's going to eradicate all life on Zeivlot and not come to your home next?"

They stared each other down for several seconds.

"Even if that's true, it wouldn't have found us if it hadn't encountered *you*."

David placed his hands on the table. "It would have eventually. Not as soon, but one day, it would've arrived."

Olgasin interjected, "General Cohen, my government feels it owes the Terran Coalition a debt, specifically to you and your personnel. The heroic efforts to save our worlds from destruction and the space-elevator projects have radically changed our outlook on life."

"They want us to crew ships side by side with heretics!"

Well, I suppose it's all the better to rip the bandage off and deal with this now. "War Leader, I have examined the main differences between your two people's religious beliefs. You know what I found? They're virtually identical outside disagreements over a few books from your ancient texts and the definitions of specific prophecies. You worship the same deity, have nearly the same rules, and follow the same scripture."

"Your religions have similar differences?"

David chuckled and gestured to the small flag emblem on his left in the country position. It consisted of a blue Star of David on a white background with a blue stripe above and below it. "That symbol denotes that I'm from New Israel. I am a Jew. Captain Goldberg was a conservative Jew and converted to Christianity a year ago. Major

Hanson is also a Christian. Colonel Amir is a Muslim, as are Dr. Tural and many other members of my crew. Dr. Hayworth is an atheist. He doesn't believe in any higher powers."

"Your point?"

"We have radical differences. Religious. Political. Cultural. Yet we are able to come together and serve as one unit because we represent a united humanity. This wasn't something that just happened overnight, nor was it simple. Humans used to be at one another's throats over the smallest things."

When no one else spoke, David turned toward his old fighter pilot friend, who served as the *Lion*'s CAG. "Colonel Amir and I have known each other for more than a decade. He's saved my life more times than I can count and vice versa. We have wildly different beliefs about God, how God interacts with us, what His law is, and how we should conduct our lives. Oh, sure, there're similarities. But we respect each other's beliefs and believe that every person has the right to determine what he or she worships, if anything at all."

"There was a time when Muslims and Jews hated each other," Amir added. "How and why doesn't really matter. But our people were incapable of peace. Until we were faced with a communist entity that sought to subjugate our countries and rule the planet. At that moment, Jew, Muslim, Christian, Hindu, atheist—all had to set aside their different cultures, religions, and countries to fight as one. I doubt those people started off liking the arrangement, but I know from the history books that they realized over time how silly the old hatreds were."

"Now we stand united. We focus on what we have in common and agree to disagree on things we don't." David flashed a smile at Amir. "And together, we're unstoppable. Just ask the League of Sol."

Silence filled the room.

Vog't licked her lips. "General Cohen, do I understand you believe that the external threat we now face is something that could unite Zeivlot and Zavlot?"

David knew she'd stated her argument for effect and hoped the purpose was pure, but it was hard to tell. While he believed Vog't was a decent person, she was still a politician.

"Yes, I do. If there is anything positive to come out of this crisis, let it be that it draws your worlds closer together and helps heal the horrific rift from thousands of years of conflict. What better way for Zeivlot and Zavlot to stand up and let their voices be heard than by doing it *united?*"

Olgasin cleared his throat. "On my world, I was something of an outcast. A man who advocated for peace with our brothers on Zeivlot. That's why my people chose me, I think, to represent them after we came so close to destroying ourselves. Despite that, I went into this summit believing that a fully integrated military service was too much of a stretch. But after hearing General Cohen and Colonel Amir's testimonies, I realize how wrong that was. Things will never change unless we take the first step. Zavlot supports the proposal as stated."

"As does Zeivlot."

David allowed himself to smile. "Then we have an agreement."

Vog't gave him what seemed to cross between a grin and a smirk. "Not quite, General. There is the matter of who controls these warships and their purpose."

"The purpose is simple. Defeat and destroy the nanites."

"But as I understand it from the reviews my senior military advisors have completed, you do not yet have a weapon capable of defeating the nanite swarm. Is that not correct?"

David turned to Hanson.

"Ah, well, actually, Zupan, our neutron beams, with modifications, are effective against the enemy. It's a matter of heat output. They're susceptible to extremely high temperatures."

"Forgive me... Major Hanson, is it?" Vog't waited for a nod before she continued. "Your after-action reports state those modifications destroyed the... emitters?"

Hanson pursed his lips. "We're redesigning the beam emitters to avoid that problem, ma'am. But to your point, even with a hundred or two hundred Ajax-class destroyers, neutron beams aren't stopping the entire swarm. That's why Dr. Hayworth, your scientists, and our top engineers will work together to create a weapon that is effective against the nanites."

"That's a large unknown," Olgasin said. He tilted his head. "What good are space-going vessels if they can't defeat the enemy?"

"If our efforts are unsuccessful, they can be used to escort civilian ships in an attempt to save some number of your species," David interjected.

The room once again went deathly silent.

David gritted his teeth. "That's not the outcome we're looking for, but it's one we must acknowledge. Both of you indicated you'd rather fight than gear up to remove as much of your population as possible. So we're proceeding with a contingency plan to ensure someone escapes if it comes down to the worst possible scenario."

"And what are your plans, General Cohen, if that worst case happens?" Olgasin asked softly.

David felt everyone staring at him as if they were

looking into his soul. "In the event we're unable to come up with a weapon capable of defeating the nanites, I will evacuate the *Lion of Judah*, except for a small group of volunteers. We along with whatever other military force is allocated will buy the rest of the fleet as much time as possible."

A few Zeivlots and Zavlots gasped as they heard the translation of his words. Vog't inclined her head. "I pray to the Maker it will not come to that, General."

"As do I, Zupan."

The alien leaders glanced at each other and seemed to share a moment of clarity.

Olgasin turned back to David. "Then we are all in agreement. That leaves one major item for discussion."

"Who controls the fleet once it's built." David flashed a thin smile.

"Zeivlot and Zavlot civilian leadership must have control over assets we build," Vog't said.

David knew a hard bargaining line when he heard it and had come prepared. The initial proposal was that the Terran Coalition, through his command, have complete operational authority. He'd made it hoping to get them to agree to a compromise. "Zupan, Chairman, if I may. I must maintain a cohesive command structure. Your people will be trained in CDF procedures and technology to become interchangeable crewmen on the destroyers built over the next two years. To your point, you must also have input on decisions that put the lives of Zeivlots and Zavlots in harm's way. While the *Lion of Judah* and her battlegroup will remain under my sole leadership, would you accept a three-person advisory council consisting of each head of state and me that will review fleet battle plans before implementation?"

Olgasin and Vog't exchanged glances again before both nodded.

"That is acceptable, General," Vog't replied.

"By my people as well, General Cohen," Olgasin said.

"Then I think we have what we need to get—"

Dieba abruptly stood, ripped his rank insignia off, and threw it at the conference table. "No! I will not be a part of this... heresy. You cannot erase what these *creatures* did to my people with your flowery words, human. They may work on others but not on true Zavlots." With that, he turned on his heel and stormed out.

I suppose I can't win them all. "How many do you think will agree with his take on integration?"

"Too many," Vog't replied. Her face hardened, and she furrowed her brow. "But more will side with the light, because we *must* to survive."

"I pray you are right, Zupan."

David glanced around the room, taking a moment to make eye contact with several back-bencher personnel from both worlds. "We will do our best, and it'll have to be enough. Back in our home galaxy, when the CDF went out to fight, often outnumbered, against the League, we delivered this exhortation: fight the good fight, no matter the cost."

Emotion welled within David as he thought of how many times he'd heard or uttered those words and the losses that inevitably followed. "We knew the League of Sol had far more ships and personnel than us, but we were equally determined to defend our homes. Today, our three species stand united to defend Zeivlot and Zavlot against a similar implacable foe. We will protect these planets, no matter the cost. And with blessing and support from HaShem, *we will not fail.*"

Applause erupted from several Zeivlot civilians and quickly spread to the entire alien delegations. Within moments, everyone was clapping, including the *Lion*'s senior officers.

David beamed and joined in with the rest of them. It felt like they could overcome any obstacle. *HaShem, help me to make this happen and follow Your will, whatever it may be.*

3

FROM HER PERCH in the back of the *Lion of Judah*'s bridge, Master Chief Rebecca Tinetariro kept a careful watch over every enlisted rating and the ship's disposition at all times. She'd kept the deck force in line for fifteen years as the senior enlisted soldier on a parade of different vessels, but the *Lion* was special. While Tinetariro had taken pride in every combat assignment she'd ever had, her four years aboard the *Lion* were a part of history. To be present at the Second and Third Battles of Canaan along with signing the peace treaty was something she would tell her children and grandchildren about. *Well, if I ever have any.*

The Coalition Defense Force and thirty-three years of service to it had consumed most of her life. *I was ready to leave, but we ended up here.* Part of her, though, welcomed the additional time in uniform. *Because really, what other skills do I have besides kicking youngsters in the rear to make them do their jobs?*

"Master Chief?"

First Lieutenant Robert Taylor brought her out of her thoughts. He was the vessel's communications officer, and

Tinetariro had grown to respect him, even though she still thought of him as a kid. *Most of them are so young. I barely remember being that young.*

"Yes?"

"General Cohen is requesting your presence in his day cabin immediately."

She nodded. "Thank you."

It didn't take long to walk from the back of the *Lion's* bridge through the portal, which was guarded at all times by Terran Coalition Marine Corps sentries, and arrive at the commanding officer's day cabin a few steps down the passageway. She rang the buzzer.

"Come!"

She pushed the hatch open and came to a stop in front of David's desk before pulling herself to a ramrod-straight position. "Master Chief Tinetariro reports as ordered, sir."

"At ease. Please, sit." David flashed a smile.

Tinetariro had grown to greatly respect her CO. In the beginning, she hadn't been sure that an officer without gray hair should be commanding the largest warship in the Coalition's arsenal, but David had proven himself time and again. More than that, he'd consistently proven his primary goal was to get the crew home safely while winning the war. She dropped into one of the chairs in front of his desk and put her hands in her lap. "What's on your mind, sir?"

"I've got a job for you, Master Chief."

"Oh, that sounds dangerous, sir." Tinetariro grinned. "Have you figured out a new addition to the Order of Jupiter for crossing galaxies?"

David laughed. "Not quite, Master Chief."

One of the more ribald customs in the CDF, new soldiers who completed a Lawrence drive jump were inducted into the Order of Jupiter. A good bit of hazing was involved, but most saw it as being in good fun. Tinetariro certainly did.

"In evaluating how to crew all these new ships we're going to build with our Zeivlot and Zavlot partners, I've concluded we will have to create a new training program."

Ah. He wants me to push boots.

"Along those lines, out of everyone's in this fleet, your service jacket has the most time as a drill instructor and senior drill instructor, and you're the only soldier I've got with a master training specialist designation."

Tinetariro grinned again. "I enjoyed my time wearing the red ropes, sir."

"Think you could stand up a new, joint OCS in the next two weeks?"

"For the purpose of training Zeivlots and Zavlots in the ways of the CDF?"

"More than that, I'm afraid. Both planets have a pretty decent military in terms of structure, professionalism, and ability. But—"

"They can't work together," Tinetariro finished.

"Exactly, Master Chief. We're not going to have ships crewed by separate species. The only way this succeeds is if we're *all* the same."

"Dark green... light green."

David grinned. "We are all green."

Tinetariro was quite familiar with the mantra. While she fell into the dark-green side of things, the Coalition as a society that treated everyone equally was a concept that just *was* to her. Seeing a species so closely related hate one another over what seemed to be trivial matters was challenging to process. "How do we impart that to the Zeivlots and Zavlots, sir?"

"I'm not entirely sure, but... Master Chief, I have no

doubt I'd be terrified of you, should I be under your tender care in boot camp. Inflicting that on these species ought to make them come together."

She laughed. "Oh, I'm tough. But fair, I like to think. The objective is to produce soldiers who won't freeze up in battle and get everyone around them killed. It's a tough process."

David nodded. "Quite. Are you up for this? I'll give you carte blanche on picking a team of twenty."

"I set the curriculum?"

"Yes. All of it. Your objective is to mold them into Coalition soldiers who can work as a unit. We'll set up additional A schools for engineering, weapons... and our various pieces of technology."

"So break down their biases, force them to treat one another as equals, and get them to work with us." Tinetariro snickered. "Anything else, sir?"

"That about sums it up." David pursed his lips. "I realize I'm asking a lot, but we must find a way to make this work. They've got to understand that beneath our skin, we're all the same."

"I'll get it done, sir. Or make them wish they'd never been born." Tinetariro grinned. Her mind was already racing on how she could adjust existing CDF training methods for the alien species.

"Glad to hear it, Master Chief. Leave me a few qualified bosun's mates, eh?"

"Of course. I couldn't have the *Lion of Judah*'s enlisted contingent getting soft, now, could I?"

David chuckled. "No, that would never do."

"I'd like Senior Chief Antonio Silva to serve as my temporary replacement."

"Does he warrant a promotion?"

"A temporary one, for respect. There's no real way to run the boards out here."

"Yes, that's a problem for officers too." David shook his head. "Who would've thought being stuck in a different galaxy would generate so many paperwork issues."

They both laughed.

"I have a feeling this assignment will be the hardest of my life." Tinetariro crossed her arms. "But my mother used to say anything worth doing is difficult."

"Smart woman. Mine said something similar."

Tinetariro considered for a moment. "I wonder how they got to where they are now. Oh, I fully understand hating a group of people who nuked you back to the stone age, but... what's the root cause?"

"It's been going on so long that no one knows." David shook his head. "I'd like to believe humanity has evolved beyond such behavior, but I know it hasn't."

She recalled the last few years of the war against the League of Sol and how elements of the Terran Coalition had turned against the CDF, driven by social media demagoguery and extreme politicians. *A stain on our nation.* "We didn't quite get to the point of hurling racial or religious epithets at one another."

"But too close for comfort." David snarled. "I'll never forgive Jezebel Rhodes."

"Nor will I." Tinetariro weighed her words carefully, as technically, military officers were not to discuss politics in uniform. *Though we're four and a half million light-years away from the nearest polling place.* "Or Fuentes. President Spencer felt he had to create a unity government, I know... and I respect him for it."

"But that doesn't change the fact that Fuentes cost tens of thousands of good men and women their lives," David replied. "Yet Spencer was dead on that we had to move on as a nation and try to heal. So do the Zeivlots and Zavlots. If there's anything positive to come out of this debacle, let it be that."

"From your lips to God's ears, sir."

"Amen."

Tinetariro stared at him for a moment. "Are you okay, sir?"

David tilted his head. "In what way, Master Chief?"

"This has to be a lot for you."

"I suppose it is, but... it comes with the job."

He's not being entirely honest, though I can respect a stiff upper lip in a leader. She hoped David had someone he fully confided in, because no one should have to shoulder their burdens alone. "That, it does, sir."

"All right, Master Chief. I'll let you get to picking your team. Good luck, and Godspeed."

Tinetariro sprang up and came to attention. "Yes, sir. You'll have the names and proper paperwork within the hour."

"Very well. Dismissed."

As she reached the hatch, she looked back at David. "Fight the good fight, sir. No matter the odds."

"No matter the odds," he replied.

Tinetariro flashed a smile then strode out of the day cabin. While her time as a drill instructor had long since passed, it would be a new challenge to dust off that knowledge and impart wisdom to a new group of recruits. She relished the opportunity.

———

"THE SPACE ELEVATORS won't be nearly enough!" Hanson said. "I've run the math several times. The amount of cargo tonnage required per day justifies an entire fleet of purpose-built shuttles with large bays for hauling ship components."

"And how are they supposed to build enough of them to make a difference in the time we have?" Merriweather shot back.

David felt a headache coming on. He was many things, but an engineer, he was not. Though like every CDF space-warfare officer, he'd completed a rotation in engineering, it had been more to round out his knowledge. He'd known a week into the duty station there was zero chance of switching tracks. "Okay, people. We're getting overheated here. What can we do to increase the cargo-carrying capability of the space elevators until shuttles are built?"

Hanson and Merriweather stared at each other for a moment before she spoke. "How many gondolas are on the spire at any given time?"

"Ten, I think," Hanson replied.

She pulled up something on her tablet and tapped at it then raised her eyes again. "We could add at least double that without endangering the structural stability of the cable."

"Still not enough, but it'll help."

David nodded. He'd called a staff meeting of all department heads to talk through how to facilitate building Ajax-class destroyers on both Zeivlot and Zavlot, and it had quickly become obvious how difficult a task was in front of them. "Something else I want you all to remember is that the leaders of both worlds have pledged to run this as a whole-population effort."

"That's hard to get my head around," Merriweather said.

"We didn't even do that in the Terran Coalition during the war against the League."

"Yeah. I saw something where Vog't gave a speech saying not to expect to buy a new aircar anytime soon. Hanson, you should take that into account when looking for factories to build things, whatever they may be. I bet you can find plants that make spacecraft parts or fabricate alloys. Piecemeal it together until we can get new, purpose-built facilities up."

"Engineers don't care for eighty percent solutions, sir, but I see your point."

David grinned. "There's a reason I've got the stars on, Major. Generals *love* eighty percent solutions."

Chuckles swept the room.

"You wanted a report on how many personnel we can keep our ships running with, sir?" Silva asked. He appeared at ease and wore the insignia of a master chief, as befitted his temporary rank.

"Yes, that's going to be important as we bleed off people to man these new ships and cross-train our allies."

"Sir, if we take more than a third of each vessel's enlisted and officer complement, I believe we'd compromise our ability to maintain combat readiness to a dangerous level."

David did some quick mental arithmetic. While the *Lion of Judah* had a nominal crew of ten thousand, thirty-five hundred of those were embarked Marine Expeditionary Unit, while another twenty-two hundred consisted of the aviation ratings. *Meaning we could only take a thousand to maybe fifteen hundred soldiers.* "We'll be lucky to get twenty CDF trained human personnel per new Ajax, assuming one hundred fifty of them are made."

"Put another way, five percent of the crew. Officers, even less," Hanson interjected. He crossed his arms. "Are we comfortable with that?"

"I don't see that we have a choice," David replied. "Furthermore, we're going to have to really look for qualified commanding officers among our field-grade officers, with battlefield promotions granted."

"Zeivlots and Zavlots will end up in command. That is the only mathematically possible outcome." Aibek raised an eye scale. "The longer we peer into this hole, the deeper it becomes."

"Anyone got a better idea?" David asked.

"Install kill switches in the primary reactor circuits of each ship that's built."

A chill swept through David's body as he turned to Hayworth. "For what purpose, Doctor?"

"Isn't it obvious? To have control over them. If they were to turn those ships against one another or another civilization, we could destroy them. Or just vent the reactor fuel into space, if you prefer a less violent solution."

A curtain of silence descended over the conference room.

"Doctor, down on the surface of both these planets, there are people in uniforms telling their leaders that they don't trust us. You know why? Because that's what professional military officers do. They exist to protect their citizens, and we are a big fat unknown. Maybe we're what we say we are. Maybe we're not. For all they know, we're working a long con to take over their worlds. I can tell you this—they're not stupid. We put something either hardware or software based into those ships that gives us the ultimate power without telling them... they'll find it. And when they do, this entire alliance goes up in smoke."

Aibek hissed loudly. "General Cohen is right. Such a thing would be dishonorable and is the way of the serpent."

"I think the doctor has a point," Hanson said. "We're

talking about a lot of Coalition knowhow and technology. Having a way to stop them if something got out of hand seems prudent."

"No. Unequivocally no," Ruth interjected. "The general's right. It would be seen as a massive betrayal."

"What if we told them the kill switches were there?" Merriweather asked. "That way, it's not a surprise."

"How would you react, Major?" Amir shook his head. "I would immediately believe it was a trick."

"We could take a vote." Hayworth smirked. "Though I suspect most of you disagree."

"This isn't a democracy, Doctor. We're not installing kill switches. End of story. Next topic." David rarely pulled the "I'm the supreme authority here" card, as he felt it was counterproductive and generally a poor leadership technique. But he was sure the road to hell lay in lying to either alien species. *I hope I'm right.*

"Hanson, prepare a personnel list for transfer in conjunction with Master Chief Silva. We won't execute immediately, but as the ships are completed and begin shakedown cruises, we'll be ready. Oh, and start putting an asterisk next to the names of younger enlisted personnel who go above and beyond. They'll be trained to step up."

"Yes, sir." Silva seemed incapable of relaxing in the conference room.

"Okay. What else, if that wasn't enough?"

Hayworth grumbled and crossed his arms. "I have something."

"By all means, Doctor."

"After careful review, I believe the science team has identified a new advanced civilization from last week's sensor sweeps."

David raised an eyebrow. "You are *master* at burying the lede, Doctor."

Hayworth smirked. "Blame Eliza and her efforts to tone down my *ego*."

"How do we know they're advanced? Did you get an FTL signature?" Ruth asked. Her eyes had lit up.

Didn't think she'd be all that interested in new aliens.

"Particle emissions consistent with large-scale antimatter refinement."

David's eyes widened, and he fought the urge to rip Hayworth a new one for not bringing that to his attention immediately upon discovery. "I'd say that's *quite* the find, Doctor. Any further details?"

"No trace of FTL detected. And I looked for the Albecure drive too. Nothing. It's possible they have something we're not familiar with or found a way to stealth a Lawrence drive jump. But it's more likely that this race, for whatever reason, doesn't leave its home planet."

"But they have antimatter reactors."

Hayworth shrugged. "It's plausible that the entire species has a genetically ingrained fear of space travel."

Several people snickered.

"No offense, Doctor, but that seems highly unlikely," Ruth said.

"Who knows? I don't bother speculating about things I have no facts to draw conclusions against. But I suggest that a race capable of such technology might be advanced enough for us to talk to without causing them to implode. You know, like the Zeivlots and Zavlots."

He's got a bee up his bonnet today. David forced a thin smile to his lips. "Perhaps. I think we just discovered our next mission, unless someone here can give me a good reason why we shouldn't pay these guys a visit."

Justice

"To not at least try would be foolhardy," Aibek said in a low hiss. "Though why would this race have any reason to help us? They could have planetary defenses powered by their reactors that render them invulnerable."

David pursed his lips. "Maybe. Maybe not. But if we don't ask, the answer is always no." He turned to Hanson. "How long will it take you to coordinate all engineering staff requests with the *Salinan*?"

"Three days, sir."

"You've got two. Doctor, how far away is this mystery planet?"

"About a week, if we're careful. Three days if minimal cooldowns are observed."

David harrumphed. "A week it'll be, then. Let's get to it, people, if there's nothing else."

Silence was the only response.

"Dismissed," David said. "Doctor, stay behind for a minute."

Everyone stood and headed for the hatch.

Once they were alone, David asked, "So, is there something I should be aware of?"

Hayworth eyed him. "Oh, did I hurt someone's *feelings*?"

David stared down his nose. "Doctor, you're wound tighter than a pissed-off Saurian looking for revenge. What's up?"

After a pregnant pause, Hayworth sighed and put his hands on the table. "I'm not having as much success with my research into the nanites as I'd like."

"And?"

Hayworth's face clouded. "There's a bond between the microscopic machines that make up the whole. I can't tell you exactly what it is or how it works, but that is the only explanation for the behavior we saw. After examining our weapons and, frankly, their lack of effectiveness, I've come to believe the only viable solution is an EMP-like pulse that disrupts that bond."

"That sounds like progress to me."

"Not if I can't get past step one in building such a device."

"You've been working on it for two weeks, Doctor. No one expects you to solve it overnight. I'm sure with the proper research equipment, personnel, and data, the solution will present itself."

"I don't think you understand, General. I'm the smartest human on this ship. Probably one out of fifty in the Coalition. If I falter, it'll kill morale in everyone."

"Welcome to my world, Doctor. You're the one who invented a usable antimatter reactor for humanity, and you've made *very* sure that *everyone* knows how brilliant you are."

"How is that your world?"

"Since I'm the commanding officer of this ship, everyone looks to me. I've won over and over when, honestly, I shouldn't have. The Third Battle of Canaan being the most obvious example. Those kinds of expectations become difficult to live up to. At some point, impossible."

"Then why bother with it?"

"For the same reason you push yourself to the limit in science. Because the people under us must believe. If they lose hope, they'll give up, and we'll *never* get home or defeat this nanite monster."

Hayworth leaned back. "I don't ask for advice often, General. But I will this once. How do you deal with it?"

"I try to have a couple of people I can confide in, I pray often for wisdom and guidance, and I force myself to portray the happy warrior, even when I'm not."

Justice

"That's difficult."

"Yes, it is. That's what being the smartest man in the room or the tactical genius or the tier-one commando that never fails or excellence period gets you. So man up, put your head down, and ah, fake it till you make it."

Hayworth nodded. "Direct, as always, General."

"It's good advice."

"Yes, it is. Well, except that part about praying."

David grinned and stood. "I'm no scientist, but if you ever want to talk about what's troubling you, my hatch is open."

"Thank you." The way Hayworth said the words, they seemed to have real meaning behind them.

"Good day, Doctor."

4

_____

CAPTAIN RUTH GOLDBERG gingerly set a tray of food down in front of her along with a cup of water. Dozens of other officers milled about the mess, as it was the prime lunchtime of about eleven thirty hours. While she'd stood a four-hour watch already, most of Ruth's energy was going into examining sensor data from their last engagement with the nanites.

The grueling part of the job was detailing the power output and method by which the swarm dismantled a planet. Viewing the same data over and over weighed heavily on her soul.

She said a prayer over the meal before taking a bite.

"Hey," First Lieutenant Robert Taylor, her fiancé and the _Lion of Judah_'s communications officer, said as he slid into the chair across from her.

Ruth pursed her lips and swallowed. "Straw."

"Oh cute. In a mood?" Taylor snickered.

"No. Yes. Ugh." She let out a sigh. "I hate watching that planet die over and over. But I have to in hopes of pulling some information Hayworth and the eggheads can use."

Taylor put his hand on her arm. "It's okay to take a break. Do something else."

"Kinda hard to plan date night, you know?"

"I'm up for a quiet night in, reading something."

"You would be, Mr. Homebody." Ruth forced a smile. "How are you doing?"

"Eh, you know. Another day, another credit. Well, if we ever get home to get our back pay. You wonder what's going to happen to all our stuff and apartments."

Ruth stared at him for a moment before bursting into laughter. *God, sometimes I need him.*

A couple of lieutenants from engineering at the next table stared at them before resuming their meals.

"It wasn't that funny."

"Oh, I'm just trying to imagine everyone's respective families cleaning out their houses or apartments or, in my case, a storage unit."

"Storage unit?"

"I don't have a lot of stuff." Ruth shrugged. "I normally live on base, so I keep a standard CDF storage pod with a few mementos and such in it. They'll probably trash the thing. Dang it, I've got some stuff I want to keep in there."

Taylor scrunched his nose. "Maybe they'll keep it all active for seven years... until we're declared legally dead."

"If we're not back in seven years, I might not want to go back," Ruth replied darkly.

"Hey, we're getting home. Okay?"

Ruth took another bite of food and chewed it. "I don't know how we're going to defeat this entity. General Cohen seems to think we can, but..."

"We beat the League."

"Big difference."

Taylor shrugged. "Really? Quantity over quality—they

threw unending streams of ships at us filled with communist conscripts. Sounds similar to me."

"Except these, ah, nanites have far superior technology to us."

"We'll figure it out."

She put her fork down and stared at him. "You are ever the optimist."

"Somebody around here's gotta be. Besides, haven't we always won in the end?"

Ruth considered his words before begrudgingly nodding. "Yes, but some of those victories had a rather steep cost."

"And we never forget it, but we'll also pay that cost. Because it's *worth* paying."

She knew as he spoke that she'd forever see him as a Boy Scout who always tried to do the right thing because that was who Robert Taylor was. And she loved him for it. "Let's hope I can help us avoid some of it."

"That's the spirit." He took a bite of some root vegetable and nearly spit it out. "Good grief, that stuff sucks."

Ruth smirked. "I wish I could say it's the worst food I've eaten. Sadly, it's not."

"C-rats would be an improvement over this slop."

"You're probably right. Hear any good rumors lately?"

"Such as?"

"You're the communications officer," Ruth replied with a dazzling smile.

"Hmm. Some of the junior Zavlot scientists tried to punk Hayworth by flipping his computer screen upside down, but he caught them in the act."

Ruth nearly sprayed water out of her mouth. "Oh, that would've been great to watch."

"And we're shutting down half a deck of berthing

compartments. The master chief ordered for power-save mode to go into effect."

"Because of all the personnel we're transferring off to help build ships and shipyards?"

Taylor nodded. "Yeah. That's going to be weird."

"Maybe the deck will become haunted."

"Seriously? Come on. There's no such thing as ghosts."

"Speak for yourself."

"You pulling my leg?"

Ruth grinned. "Maybe. Though I think there're plenty of things we don't understand."

"Now, that, I would agree with."

After a few more bites, Ruth could barely stand the vegetables. At least the meat was more appetizing. The last couple of hydroponics harvests hadn't been as bountiful as they should've been, so more and more Zeivlot food was making it onto their plates. *The higher the ratio, the worse it tastes. I should just be thankful to have something edible that will give me strength.*

"You okay?"

"Hmm?" Ruth looked up from her plate.

"You're a million light-years away."

"Oh, just thinking we should be thankful for what we have."

Taylor took a bite and said between chews, "Maybe these new aliens Dr. Hayworth found will have better food."

"It won't matter unless they're willing to share."

"Humans share."

"Correction: some of us do." Ruth smirked. "Though we could probably all stand to be better at that."

"No argument from me. So, what do you think they'll be like?"

"If they have antimatter, probably powerful. I hope that

power means they don't fear others, and the general can do a deal."

Taylor put his hand on hers and squeezed. "Hey. I know you're having a bad day, but it's going to be okay."

"Promise?"

"Promise." Taylor grinned. "Now, why don't we get our work finished in time for a dinner back in our quarters?"

"Deal," Ruth replied. While she projected a happy exterior as best as possible, going back to study the nanites was the last thing she wanted to do. *But it must be done.* In the back of Ruth's mind, a voice said she should've done more, but she pushed it down with all her might.

———

DINNER with fellow officers and friends had become a highlight of David's life. In truth, it always had been. The peaceful moments of breaking bread and sharing thoughts on a better life after the war had been a staple during the war. In Sextans B, they were one of the few normal things left.

David shared his table with Aibek, Amir, and Calvin. As always, the tough Marine was getting a lot of laughs with his combat stories.

"So I'm standing there, my sidearm runs dry, and all I've got left is my battle rifle to use as a club," Calvin said, gesturing wildly.

"Then what? Close air support saved the day?" Amir replied with a grin.

"No, brother, I used my rifle like a pugil stick and beat every last one of those six Leaguers to a pulp."

David had heard a variation of the story before but still laughed. Something about how Calvin delivered the lines

Justice

made them come alive. "I think the moral here is to carry more ammo."

"Hoo-rah." Calvin took a swig of tea. "Or make sure you've got some close air lined up. But not those CDF pukes. No, sir, Marine pilots all the way."

Amir *tsk*ed. "Let's see if you say that when the Marines are all hungover, and I'm all you've got."

"I think he's got you there, Cal." David snickered.

"Maybe back in the Milky Way. We don't even have any beer left." Calvin grumbled. "I'm getting really tired of that."

All four men laughed loudly.

"You and every enlisted soldier on this ship," David said. "Me, I could take or leave a glass of wine every once in a while."

Calvin stared down his nose. "If I hadn't personally witnessed you smoke a few dozen Leaguers, I'd question whether you were a real soldier." A few moments afterward, he added, "Sir."

David was about to send a smart-aleck comment back when a new entrant into the mess caught his eye. Dr. Hayworth's white lab coat was ubiquitous on the ship. *It's pretty much his uniform.* He waved at him and got a curt head nod in reply.

"Doctor, join us, please."

Hayworth ambled over to the table, while Amir stood, grabbed another chair, and set it at the edge.

"Too kind," Hayworth mumbled as he eased himself into the chair. "You're all here a bit late."

"Long day," David replied. "For you as well, by the looks of it."

"When you get to be my age, they're *all* long."

"Don't usually see you around these parts, Doc." Calvin winked. "Tired of hanging out with all those eggheads?"

"Ah yes, the Marine mentality of insulting higher intelligence with needlessly dismissive terms."

Calvin smirked. "I'll send a hurt-feelings report your way, Doc."

"Oh, *please* do." Hayworth grunted. "The officers' mess down by my lab is out of most human food and has switched mostly to Zeivlot fare."

Aibek twitched his nose. "I agree with the doctor. Zeivlot meat is most unappetizing. But I must remember to thank the Prophet for sustenance."

"That's almost as bad as Hanson bragging about getting two breakfasts on a circuit," Calvin groused. "But yeah, Doc. I don't care for this alien grub either. Still better than C-rats."

"I've had combat rations that taste better than anktar roots," Amir replied.

Amused, David listened to them all complain about the food. A maxim of warfare was that an army marched on its stomach. *At least they're full.* "I thought the Otyran food was pretty tasty."

Calvin nodded. "Yeah, valid point. It's better than some of the rest, anyway."

A mess steward appeared at the table and deposited a plate in front of Hayworth along with a glass of water.

"Thank you," the doctor said as the young man hurried off. He took a bite of the grilled anktar and chewed then grinned after he swallowed. "The trick is to get it down quickly and not let the flavor linger in your mouth."

"Good advice, Doc," Calvin replied. "Though I think not eating it is superior."

"Yes, well, we require sustenance, as Colonel Aibek put it." Hayworth cracked his neck. "Any special occasion tonight?"

David shook his head. "Just talking about what life used to be like and how it's changed out here."

"Yeah, I used to have a definable enemy to put down. Now, there's a new species every couple of weeks." Calvin snorted. "Makes it hard for this old Marine to keep up."

"You're not old," David deadpanned.

"Not as lean, twice as mean, still a Marine," Amir interjected, barely holding his laughter till the end. Everyone else joined in.

"A purpose does make life simpler." Hayworth took a sip of water.

"What about you, Doctor? Miss the Milky Way?"

Hayworth shrugged. "Of course, but not as much as I thought I would. When I was a young man, I dreamed of seeing the universe and exploring the cosmos. Now we are."

"Why didn't you join the Far Survey Corps?" Amir asked. "They let you do that and pay you to boot."

"Because I don't do well with top-down organizational structures where I'm expected to obey all commands given without question. Not to mention that the idea of being yelled at for eight weeks in a boot camp never appealed to me."

David sat back. Sometimes, he wondered how Hayworth had survived working for the military as long as he had. "It may shock you to hear this, but I, too, didn't care much for how things worked when I was drafted."

Hayworth raised an eyebrow. "I had the impression you came out of the factory preset to follow orders."

"Cheap shot, Doctor. You know I've questioned and disobeyed orders."

"Perhaps. But you obey most without a second thought."

"That's how it works. Without good discipline and order, the CDF breaks down. Which is one of the reasons why being out here is so challenging, because I'm the ultimate authority. It gives me a new appreciation for COMSPACE-FLT's job."

"Science is so vastly different. We question *everything*. It's the only way new knowledge is unlocked."

David flashed a grin. "There's a need for both, don't you think?"

"Yes. Though now, I wish we'd done a bit less exploring. Empowering these nanites to kill more innocent life-forms isn't what I wanted on my memorial."

"That's why we're going to erase their evil from the universe before they commit any further genocide," Amir interjected.

"I normally dislike applying the term *evil* to something. It's so fraught with judgments that encourage us to treat the opponent as something beneath us and therefore worthy of death." Hayworth blew out a breath. "But there are some that deserve the label. These nanites, while most likely unfeeling killing machines, are certainly one of the closest examples I've seen."

David, too, resisted referring to a species or government as evil, even when deserved. *If we dehumanize our opponent, killing them—their civilians and the innocents—becomes very easy.* He decided to move on. "At least for now, we can focus on contacting this race that's built its own antimatter reactors."

Aibek raised an eye scale. "I still question the lack of FTL activity around their planet." He'd remained silent so far, seemingly watching the interplay.

"What's so odd about that? Not every species has the desire to leave its home world. Or a desire to explore." Hayworth took a bite of food. "Or in the Saurians' case, conquer others."

Justice

47

"We no longer engage in that behavior, Doctor."

Hayworth smirked. "Your government doesn't do it openly, but Saurians are a proud warrior race. It's nothing to be ashamed of, simply a reminder that we all have different cultures and that different things motivate species. Humanity all too often thinks everything else behaves as it does."

"Any individual is capable of growth. As are cultures and species," Aibek replied. "Would you not agree?"

"Yes, clearly, that's true. I simply counsel against assumptions. We could easily get to this system and find that the antimatter reactors are automated and protect a microbial life-form from destruction by solar rays."

"That's a bit far-fetched," David said. "Even for us."

"So is traveling 4.4 million light-years on one Lawrence drive jump."

Calvin snickered. "You oughtta come down here more often, Doc."

"Technically, this deck is higher than the ones I normally inhabit."

"Touché." Calvin downed the rest of his drink. "It's nice having a partner in acerbic repartee to deal with these touchy-feely space-warfare officers."

Amir cleared his throat. "The CAG isn't an SWO. Eating too many crayons mess up your mind?"

"Nah, just a few these days. They've got extra fiber."

Everyone roared with laughter, except for Hayworth, who politely chuckled.

"Demood's right, Doctor. It's good to have you break bread with us. You should make it a weekly thing."

Hayworth nodded. "I'll consider it, General." He peered at Aibek. "There's something different about you. Your scale tones are darker."

"The discovery of the nanite swarm has given me purpose. Defeating them is honorable and a better objective than trying to get home."

David had noticed the scale shift, too, but hadn't put two and two together. *Am I losing touch with my senior officers... and friends?* "Having a purpose is positive."

Conversation waned for a few minutes as Hayworth finished his food. When he was done, he pushed the plate forward and dropped his napkin on top. "I don't want to appear rude, but at my age, sleep comes at a premium. Another day of research awaits."

"We're all in that craft, Doc," Calvin replied. "Think I'll hit the rack myself."

"Same." David stood. "Let's get some rest and get back with it at oh four thirty."

As the group departed, David wondered how Master Chief Tinetariro was faring back on Zeivlot and reminded himself to include her in his evening prayers. He hoped they would rapidly make first contact with the new alien species, gain their help, and get back in time to see the graduation of the first joint class of new CDF soldiers. *What was it my mother used to say? If wishes were horses, beggars would ride.*

5

MASTER CHIEF REBECCA TINETARIRO stood in the scorching heat, which was made worse by her khaki service uniform decked out with numerous ribbons, medals, pins, and insignia. She wore a campaign cover that was reserved for drill instructors. *It's been a long time since I pushed boots. Nearly fifteen years, in fact.* But she'd enjoyed it as both a company commander and later a senior drill instructor over multiple sets of recruits. And for reasons she couldn't explain, she *relished* what was coming next.

Three buses came into view around the bend of the spartan military installation Tinetariro had named Recruit Depot Sextans B. It had a couple of prefab buildings with plasticrete walls and actual roofs, but everything else was a polymer tent, including all barracks. They had enough room for six hundred recruits, but the first group was only a hundred twenty. She'd decided to figure out what worked on them then replicate it once they'd hammered out the kinks.

The transports were Zeivlot in design and were wheeled. While the alien species had many hover vehicles, most of their population movers still relied on tried-and-true older technology. The buses also used internal combustion engines instead of the Zeivlot military's hydrogen-powered designs.

Tinetariro had decided to go with a full-on new-recruit experience. She would give no credit for prior military service, even though every person walking off the incoming buses was a veteran, and virtually all of them were the elite of the elite—commandos, special operators, senior enlisted technicians, and engineers. They represented the cream of the crop, and if Tinetariro couldn't whip them into shape, she probably couldn't get the lower echelons there either.

With a roar and a burst of noxious fumes, the three buses came to a halt in front of a line of DIs. The side doors opened, and junior drill instructors, most of whom were senior or master chiefs themselves, charged inside.

Moments later, a stream of Zeivlots and Zavlots in civilian clothing filed out and lined up on a series of yellow footprints painted onto the rapid-set plasticrete surface.

Tinetariro had insisted on the nonmilitary attire to have as much effect as possible on her new charges. Uniformed personnel snatched any personal belongings, including hats, sunglasses, and jewelry, away before tossing them into a pile to the side. All the while, they screamed at anyone and everyone.

Thirty seconds later, she strolled up and down the neatly formed ranks. *Proper posture is one thing I won't have to teach them, anyway.* She shouted so that all could hear, "I am Master Chief Rebecca Tinetariro of the Coalition Defense Force. Though you represent your respective militaries and serve in uniform with distinction, you are no more than recruits here."

She stopped and faced one of the three groups. "You

have no rank. No privileges. You are no more skilled to me than an eighteen-year-old draftee back on Canaan. Do you understand me?"

"Yes, ma'am" echoed in the wind.

"I thought you were soldiers! The best your world has to offer. I've seen children who have more vigor! Try it again!"

"Ma'am, yes, ma'am!" they shouted.

"Better. But not good enough!" She marched down to the next group. "It is a privilege to serve the Coalition Defense Force. One you may earn if you follow the instructions of my drill instructors and me, never quit, and strive as hard as you can." Her voice took on a raspy quality as she barked at the recruits. *Just like riding a bike. Pushing boots comes back to you.*

A small commotion in the final group caught Tinetariro's attention. She closed the few steps rapidly and yelled, "Get back into formation now!"

A Zeivlot said, "I won't stand next to this—" The translator cut the last word off as he shoved the man next to him.

Tinetariro assumed whatever he'd said was a curse or racial epithet. Whatever it was, it had no place on her drill field. She stepped into the line and got a few centimeters from the offender's face. "You will never strike another recruit again, and if you do, I will drum you out immediately. Do you get me?"

"Yes, ma'am."

"*I didn't hear you!*"

"Yes, ma'am!"

"*Drop down, and give me one hundred push-ups right now, maggot!*"

The Zeivlot lay down on his belly and started pushing.

Tinetariro provided a cadence. "One, two, three, four, I love the Coalition Defense Force!" *I suppose they have a word for push-up, since he seemed to know what I wanted.* As the man kept pushing, another DI took over the count, and she turned to face the rest of them.

"From here on out, there are no more distinctions between Zeivlot and Zavlot. You are *all* green!" She stopped in front of a dark-skinned Zavlot. "Some of are you *dark green*! Some are *light green*! All are green! There will be no division by religion, race, creed, or physical characteristics. The only thing I care about is your devotion to the Coalition Defense Force and whether you deserve to be accepted into it!" Spit flew from her mouth.

One of the recruits in another group snickered just loudly enough to carry.

Once again, Tinetariro got several centimeters from the female Zavlot's face. "Do you think I'm amusing, maggot?"

"No, ma'am!"

"In that case, I'll have to work on my material." Her eyes glinted. "Drop down, and give me fifty now!"

As the woman had the good sense to comply without further comment, Tinetariro turned her attention back to the group at large. "You will fall in with the drill instructors to processing, where you will be stripped of all civilian clothing, have your heads shaved, and get proper attire issued. You will obey all commands given to you by me and my fellow instructors at all times. Failure to do so will result in harsh punishment. Now move!"

Unlike a civilian recruit formation, those before her had the good sense to try to form an orderly line. Tinetariro had planned for that too. Drill instructors screamed obscenities at anyone who didn't run at double-quick toward the processing tent, and within moments, the entire group was running at full speed.

"I'm getting the impression you're having some fun, Master Chief."

Tinetariro turned to see Senior Chief Carson Freeman smirking. A bosun's mate from the *Lion of Judah*, Freeman had been one of her top deck-force leaders. He had a reputation for motivating his soldiers with creative tactics and was one of the chief instigators for Order of Jupiter initiations. "And what gave you that idea?"

"Since we got here, your expression has been similar to that of a cat who realized she's found a whole group of mice to hunt down."

"I suppose I do. Pushing boots was an activity I enjoyed and was good at. And these beings need attitude adjustments."

Freeman grunted. "Amen to that, Master Chief."

She eyed him. "You have the same look about you."

"Oh, I do. The *Lion*'s crew is polished enough that I have to really look for something to get on them about. These guys, on the other hand, are walking demerit generators." His expression hardened. "And they need to get their prejudices drilled out of them yesterday."

"Just remember we'll have to do more than PT them until their feet bleed. They've got to buy in to what we're selling."

"Yes, Master Chief. I've worked out a whole set of activities in which they will be forced to rely on one another."

"Make sure you force Zeivlots and Zavlots to do everything *together*."

Freeman grinned. "Oh, I'm *planning* on it. I had to dive deep into the database for training materials back when the CDF fully integrated itself with different races and religions. Found a few things to help."

"Good. Let's get ready for the next phase."

"Yes, Master Chief."

Tinetariro took off toward the other side of the processing tent. In about fifteen minutes, the recruits would exit, and she would be waiting. Their day was far from over.

———

CSV *Salinan*
Docked with Zeivlot Space Elevator
3 October 2464

FLIPPING through the day's repair reports, Major John Wilson was disheartened over the status of his ship. It had been a couple of weeks since the *Salinan*, under his command, had stopped the asteroid attacks on Zeivlot. Unfortunately, doing so had nearly broken the back of the Achomawi-class deep-space rescue vessel. He updated a series of color-coded tabs on a spreadsheet using his tablet's drawing interface, notching the dorsal tractor beams twenty percent further toward fully restored.

I'll need to get out there tomorrow and see if I can't motivate the crews. As Wilson had served as a bosun's mate while an enlisted soldier, he knew how to repair virtually anything that wasn't electronic on a ship.

Should probably head down to the wardroom and get some grub before I hit the rack. Sixteen hours a day of nonstop work had worn him down, though it came with the territory.

Wilson stood and went to the bathroom to ensure he was remotely presentable. As he combed his hair, his tablet buzzed incessantly. He returned to the living space and picked up the device. An incoming vidlink read as gold priority. *Uh, only one flag officer around these parts.*

After pressing the accept button, Wilson waited a few moments for David's face to appear.

"Major, I hope I didn't wake you."

"Not at all, sir."

"With the newly installed comm relay, we've actually got some range on FTL communications now. I apologize for not meeting with you in person."

Wilson grinned. "With all that's going on, my little ship is a long way down the line, General."

David chuckled. "Your 'little ship' outperformed itself, as did her crew. I'm authorizing a battle star to be displayed under your bridge."

"Thank you, sir. The crew will be thrilled." Wilson brimmed with pride.

"I also need something from you."

"Ah, buttering us up before the ask, of course, sir."

"Well... not quite that mercenary."

Wilson smirked. "It's okay, sir. I'd rather do something besides lament the poor state of my ship and its repairs. What can we do for you?"

"It's more a matter of what you can do personally. I noticed in the field reports that you've been overseeing the refit efforts yourself and submitting these wonderfully built-out Gantt charts as to when the *Salinan* will be ready to go back into the void."

"Been doing that for years, sir. I like to know when my ship's going to be done, and you know how shipyard workers are. Always milking the system."

"Tell me about it. Defense contractors," David nearly growled. "Only met a few worth anything in my time."

"Same, sir."

"Well, I'd like you to produce an integrated master schedule for building an Ajax-class destroyer from scratch. Once we start building, you can run herd on the shipyards."

Wilson's eyes widened. He relished that sort of challenge. "Yes, sir."

"Also, I'll need you to do this in addition to keeping the *Salinan* running."

"Ah, wouldn't want to make the task easy, would you?"

David chuckled. "No."

"All right, I'm in. With one caveat. You give me carte blanche to kick the ass of anyone who doesn't pull their weight. CDF, Zeivlot, Zavlot, civilian, military."

"Wouldn't have it any other way, Major. You've got a rep for keeping things on track, according to your service jacket."

Wilson grinned. "Glad to see that preceded me."

"All right, Major. I'll let you get back to it. Good luck, and Godspeed."

"Godspeed, sir."

The screen went blank, and a few moments later, a series of files appeared in Wilson's fleet-link application. He took a quick look through the proposed schedule for building out the shipyards and immediately identified several time-saving measures. *I'd better get Senior Chief Stokes to review these with me. So much for a quiet bite to eat before sacking out.* Wilson's mind felt alive, however, and that made him happy. The ever-present desire to return home was always in the background, but he and he suspected most of the others in the fleet had a new directive. *And people to save.* It felt good to have a purpose.

6

System XEI-313
CSV *Lion of Judah*
15 October 2464

A VORTEX TORE itself open at the edge of an otherwise-nondescript solar system, and moments later, the *Lion of Judah* emerged. It had been two weeks since they reached their target and had spent the time decoding the language of the new race. As far as Bo'hai and Bodell could tell, they called themselves the Mifreen. Covert scans using the scientific sensor suite confirmed multiple antimatter reactors scattered across the fourth planet's surface, and Hayworth postulated the entire civilization was powered by them.

David wondered if, fifty years in the future, the Terran Coalition would similarly use large-scale antimatter reactors. *Fusion reactors work well, but reducing infrastructure and energy costs would improve lives across the board.*

"Conn, TAO. Sensors online. No contacts within five hundred thousand kilometers."

The bridge was even more packed than it usually was. Hayworth manned what had come to be officially known as the science station. The ratings called it the "head seat," and David felt sure Hayworth would've hated the nickname if he knew of it. Bo'hai and Bodell also occupied communications substations to assist with translation efforts.

"No surprises, it would seem," Aibek said with a slight hiss. "What now?"

"Let's see if we can all be friends." David chuckled. "Communications, send greetings in all languages, and tie in our rudimentary translation matrix for the Mifreen."

"Aye, aye, sir."

David expected to wait for hours for a response. Since the Mifreen had no apparent FTL capabilities or orbital infrastructure beyond satellites, it was unlikely they had FTL comm tech. He was about to transfer the conn to Aibek and go do some paperwork when Taylor interjected.

"Conn, Communications. I've got a transmission back from the planet, sir. Text only. Using one of our comms bands too."

"That was fast," David replied. "What's it say?"

"They're requesting our dictionary. The syntax is garbled, but that's the only thing that makes sense to me."

David turned to Hayworth. "Doctor, thoughts?"

"There's nothing to be lost by giving them what they're asking for." Hayworth furrowed his brow. "It's possible they have better technology than we do, at least in some applied science areas. It would be unusual without faster-than-light travel, but stranger things have happened."

"Do it, Lieutenant."

"Aye, aye, sir," Taylor replied.

Justice

Minutes ticked by. David played out various possibilities on how the meeting would go. From interception of their media broadcasts, he already knew roughly what the aliens looked like. They were humanoid in appearance, though at least some of them had thick body hair. *I wonder if that's a trait all share or only a few.*

"Sir, they're sending us a video transmission on the proper carrier wave for us to receive and process."

David raised an eyebrow. "Okay. Put them on my viewer."

"Aye, aye, sir."

The monitor above his head came alive with an idyllic scene of a long beach—crystal-clear water, not a cloud in the blue sky, framed by what looked like an outdoor office. David felt envious for a moment. *Nice digs.* Three humanoids of varying skin colors were seated on stools. By David's estimation, two were male, and one was female.

"Greetings. I am Hes Diran Sansan," the darker-skinned male said with a smile. "And my colleagues, Hes Nutar and Hes Quosan of Mifreen."

"Major General David Cohen, Coalition Defense Force."

"What solar system do you come from?" Sansan's face contained a dizzying smile and an almost childlike sense of wonder.

"We're from a different galaxy from yours, roughly 4.4 million light-years away, and our home world is Canaan."

Sansan's jaw dropped. "Incredible. Beings from an entirely different galaxy. This will be the event of the cycle."

"From your wording, I assume you've encountered other species before?"

"We're aware of others, but they were not deemed advanced enough for us to communicate with."

Interesting. David pursed his lips. "What would you like me to call you? I gather that Hes is a title?"

Sansan paused for a moment and touched a small device on his ear. "Ah, yes. A title. Yes, Hes is my title. It means leader in your tongue. By the same token, what may I refer to you as?"

"General Cohen works fine."

"That is a rank, according to your language library."

"Yes," David replied.

"So your species still uses a hierarchical command structure?"

The way the Mifreen uttered the words led David to suspect they looked down on such things, but he wasn't quite sure how to reply other than with the truth. "Yes, we do."

"I would've expected a species as advanced as yours is to have done away with such trappings." Sansan sucked in a breath. "No matter. It is still a joyous day. Tell me, does your netsim have the ability to interface with others?"

David exchanged glances with Aibek. "I'm sorry, Hes Sansan. What is a netsim?"

"Well, we use a different word, but I assumed you would call yours something to the equivalent of networked simulation." Sansan tilted his head. "Surely you are aware of neural simulators."

What the heck is he talking about? David ran it through his mind, and the only thing he could come up with was some sort of VR game. "Aside from entertainment and training, we rarely use simulators."

"I am... You mean to say that what I'm seeing is a physical construct?"

"Yes." *What else would we be?*

The Mifreen spoke among themselves for a few

Justice 61

moments before Sansan turned his head back toward the camera. "We always assumed any other advanced species would use the same methods as us."

David flashed a grin. "Humans used to think the same way until we started running into all sorts of different types of life in the universe, Hes Sansan."

"It must be so hard for you, to be cut off from your digital environment."

"I'm not sure I understand," David replied. "Could you explain a bit more what you're talking about?"

Sansan tilted his head, and his eyes widened. "You truly do not have a netsim?"

"We might, but I don't know what it is. Break it down for me." David forced a thin smile.

"Our netsim is an advanced simulation environment where most of our population lives in complete happiness. Anyone is free to pursue anything they wish inside it."

The hair on the back of David's neck stood up. *That sounds beyond creepy.* "Is this in addition to your daily obligations and jobs?"

Sansan stared and blinked. "We... No. Ah, we have no structured lives inside the netsim. Only what each person wants to do with their lives. It is paradise."

"Do people wear VR suits or something to log in?"

"Nothing so primitive. Our bodies and minds are linked to the netsim with various biomedical feedback systems. It is entirely self-contained, so we never have to leave."

"You mean you're in—" David closed his mouth before the word *pod* came out.

"Yes, we're in the netsim now. This is simply a projection of our shared reality. Our physical shells are housed in biohousing centers. How are you not aware of this? I am astounded, truly."

David felt like he'd walked into a real-life production of *Alice in Wonderland*, and everything was flipped upside down. *They exist inside pods.* He imagined what such a place would look like and suppressed a shudder. *Yet this is their culture, and it is not for me to pass judgment.* He carefully tried for a neutral expression and tone. "Humans have interactive simulations but nowhere near as complex as what you describe. Primarily for entertainment."

"Fascinating."

Going on endlessly about this netsim thing won't get us anywhere. David opted for a different tack. "We'd love to speak with you in person, introduce our species, and perhaps open diplomatic contacts. Would you and your government be open to this?"

Sansan stared for a moment. "We would be unable to do this, as we do not remove ourselves from biohousing. But for the portion of our population that lives outside the netsim, there is a similar government system. They could meet with you."

"Not all of your civilization is in the simulation?"

"No. Someone has to keep the lights on, after all. More than seventy percent of us live inside. The rest are the Outers. They have our eternal thanks and gratitude for ensuring our survival. That is with whom you would meet."

"By all means," David replied. "Would you object to us moving into orbit?"

"You may do so. All five of your vessels."

Shrewd. He's letting me know they have us under surveillance. "Thank you, Hes Sansan."

"We will inform you when a meeting is set. May you walk in peace." He put his hands together and bowed slightly before the image blinked off.

Silence filled the *Lion*'s bridge, which Ruth broke. "So,

Justice

63

let me get this straight. Somehow, we showed up at the pod-people planet?"

Chuckles and guffaws swept around the room, and even David was amused.

"I have seen many things in the universe, but this takes the steak," Aibek hissed.

"Cake," David replied. "Takes the cake."

"Ah. I am still working on my human idioms." Aibek crossed his arms. "This society is most strange."

"And we're odd to them," Hayworth said as he appeared next to the CO's chair. "What do you plan to do?"

"Meet with them."

"Try to obtain more information on how this netsim works."

David raised an eyebrow. "Why, Doctor? It's not like we want to take it for a spin." The idea of being confined in some sort of life-support pod was nauseating.

"Think bigger. The processing power required to make something of that magnitude work... It's got to be better than ours. Perhaps even an advanced quantum computer. They're clearly more advanced than we are in several areas, and most of them point to better electronic systems."

"I'll make sure I inquire. But you're coming with us, of course."

"Naturally."

David blew out a breath. "Okay. Navigation, plot a Lawrence drive jump for their L5 LaGrange point."

"Aye, aye, sir," Hammond replied.

"Still, pod people? Doesn't anyone read science fiction?" Ruth asked. "That never ends well."

Hayworth harrumphed. "Jokes aside, you cannot prejudge their civilization based on our culture. This may be how they have evolved."

"But, Doctor, simulations are by definition not real."

"If you couldn't tell the difference between reality and a simulation, wouldn't that tend to make it real?"

Aibek shook his head. "Not to me."

"Because of your culture and probably religious influences."

"The doctor is right," David interjected. "All that matters here is making some friends. But I'm still not going inside some weird bio pod, to Captain Goldberg's point."

"Jump coordinates plotted, sir."

David set his jaw. "Let's get on with it. Communications, signal our escorts to follow us in." A lot had been thrown at David in the last ten minutes, but he was determined to press forward and see where the path led. *Not being shot at and avoiding offending an alien species in the first ten minutes of contact is a welcome change. I hope that will hold.*

———

DAVID HAD MET ENOUGH new alien species in Sextans B that it had become if not routine then something that no longer inspired awe. That probably had something to do with the dozens of species known in the Milky Way. Depending on the planet, seeing Saurians, Matrinids, or any of a dozen others wouldn't be remotely out of place. While the more rural worlds rarely saw nonhuman visitors, unless they specifically catered to tourism, it was common knowledge to every kindergarten-aged child in the Terran Coalition that humanity wasn't alone in the universe.

Nevertheless, listening to Bo'hai as she gushed about her experiences with the Mifreen linguist assigned to interface with her was endearing. He loved her almost childlike wonder at the universe. *It's something we could all use a dose of.*

"Do you think they are more technologically advanced than the Coalition?"

David tilted his head. "I'm not sure. Perhaps in some areas. This whole netsim thing, for one."

"A fascinating thing to meet a species that can best even humanity in anything."

"Oh, I'm sure there're plenty out there. It wouldn't take much, just one that's been starfaring longer than we have by a few centuries."

Bo'hai took a sip of her tea. They had eaten a light dinner together and were sitting in the officer's mess alone, watching the planet below. "What about in the Milky Way?"

"I'm unaware of a species that's much more advanced than us. The Matrinids have superior shields and muon-based weapons, but we have antimatter power generation, and *no* one else has that."

"Ah." Bo'hai set her mug down and furrowed her brow. "I need to tell you something."

"You've decided to leave the *Lion of Judah* and join the Mifreen because of their stupendous translation systems?"

"No." She smoothed out her dress, and it was clear the jest hadn't landed the way David hoped it would. "Zupan Vog't asked me to monitor you and the fleet for any signs of dishonesty."

His cheeks heated. "*What?*" The first reaction David felt was anger, but when he stopped to ponder the situation for a moment, it seemed only prudent that the leader of a world would want to make sure a fleet of alien beings who'd shown up out of nowhere less than a year before were what they claimed to be.

"I... I won't. I know you, and the others are only trying to help us."

David blinked. He immediately went back to the kill-switch conversation only a few days ago. *And here's exhibit A as to why that would've been a horrible idea. We're all only a decision or two away from doing highly unethical and immoral things.* "Why tell me?"

"Because I didn't want it to come between us. Or affect my feelings or how I act toward you."

Silence filled the mess, and David gazed at the void and the blueish-green world they orbited. *I owe it to her to be honest. As she was with me.* He turned back and put a hand on top of Bo'hai's. "I have feelings for you too. I've known that for a while now."

"Is this not a good thing?" Her unique accent shone through even more.

"It is, and it isn't." David ran his tongue along his lips. "Someday, the *Lion of Judah* is going home. You're in the prime of your life, and you shouldn't waste it on me. Because once this nanite situation is dealt with, if an opportunity to return arises, I've got to take it. I owe it to my crew."

Bo'hai swallowed, and tears came to her eyes. "Is there someone waiting for you back there you haven't told me about?"

"No."

"Then why not try... us?"

"Because..." David sighed. "I'm a soldier, Salena. I fought in a war for twenty-two years and never knew if I would live to see the next day. It didn't seem right to put another person, especially someone I loved, through that kind of hell. I've certainly had relationships, one that even lasted a bit and seemed like it might end up in marriage. But in the end, I owe my allegiance to the Coalition Defense Force. The service has always come first."

She sniffed and wiped her eyes. "It's up to me to decide whether something is fair. Would you agree?"

"Well, sure."

"I am drawn to you and have been since I met you. If we feel the same way toward each other, then why not explore it further? Is it not better to feel something and lose it than never have it at all?"

David squeezed her hand. "Probably. But my father died defending the Coalition. I saw what it did to my mother. She never could move on."

"And you don't want to inflict that on another?"

"No." David shook his head.

"I promise that if you decided to return to your home galaxy, and I chose to remain here, I would, as you say, move on. But I want us to have a chance. You deserve to be something other than lonely."

"Kinda accepted that as my lot in life."

Bo'hai made a show of rolling her eyes. "I see men are the same regardless of species."

David chuckled. "And so are women. Okay, so what are we here?"

"In Zeivlot society, it is typical for a male to court the female to determine whether they are compatible for mating."

That's a sterile way of putting it. David laughed again. "Well, that's kind of how we do it too. But there are different... levels of human relationships."

"How does that work?"

"When two people are dating each other, courting, if you will, they're free to end the relationship at any point. It progresses from there to being engaged and, finally, married. Marriage is a serious matter and commitment. It's challenging to dissolve legally, and from a religious perspective, at least for an Orthodox Jew, divorce is the last resort."

"Is there a name for dating?"

"Besides dating? When it's between two adults and exclusive... we usually call that boyfriend and girlfriend." David smirked. "I'm over forty years old. Saying that makes me sound like I'm back in high school."

Bo'hai giggled. "Listening to you explain this is cute."

David's cheeks heated yet again. "I'm glad *you're* enjoying it." He sucked in a breath. "I suppose this means you're my, ah, girlfriend?"

The way Bo'hai stared into his eyes was all at once endearing and electrifying. She smiled. "Yes. Tell me, how do humans show affection?"

"Hmm. We hug, hold hands, and kiss on the lips. There are other ways too." *Okay, my cheeks are fire-engine red by now.*

She moved closer to him, nuzzling her more petite body against his.

David put his arm around her. "This would be considered showing affection too."

"I like this."

As Bo'hai made herself at home under his arm, David felt as if a weight had lifted off him, and for a few moments, there was peace in his soul.

"Now what?"

He glanced at her. "We hope no one comes in looking for a snack and busts us."

She giggled once more. "Why? Would it be bad for them to see the *great* General Cohen enjoying the company of another?"

"You've got a singular way of making things I'm

Justice 69

concerned about seem trivial. It's more that I have to lead by example. This is still a warship."

"Many of your crew have, ah, paired up."

David shrugged. "I'm aware."

"Do you not approve?"

"I'm concerned that it'll cause issues with good conduct and discipline at some point. But on the whole, without some human interaction, morale will end up in the head. I feel there's no good solution, so I picked the least bad."

Bo'hai stared at him, her head tilted and one eyebrow raised. "Why would morale be in the head?"

"Idiom. Sorry." David grinned sheepishly. "CDF soldiers call the toilets a head. It's an old tradition."

"Ah." Bo'hai ran her fingers through her hair and pushed a strand out of her eyes. "That's one human saying I've haven't heard."

"It's considered ungentlemanlike behavior to talk about the bathroom in front of a lady."

"On Zeivlot, kissing means that we lock our lips together. What does it mean for humans?"

David's cheeks heated yet again. "Same thing."

"We could do that."

He frowned. "You should know that my religious beliefs put some... shall we say limitations on physical contact I'm able to have before marriage."

"Oh?"

"No kissing, and obviously no..."

Bo'hai gave him a dazzling smile. "I'm not the kind of woman who goes for intercourse before bonding either. But I don't understand the other part."

"Some Orthodox practitioners of Judaism would say that merely holding hands is unacceptable and a violation of the

Mitzvot. Those tend to be my ultra-orthodox brethren, though."

"Your beliefs have a lot of rules."

David glared but couldn't keep a grin off his face. "And yours doesn't?"

She giggled. "This is enough for now," Bo'hai said dreamily. "Do you have an early day tomorrow?"

"Every day starts at oh-four-thirty hours." David yawned. "We have the meeting with the Mifreen council. I'm not sure what that will lead to, but if you don't ask—"

"The answer is always no."

"Finishing each other's sentences already," David replied.

"Not the worst thing we could do."

David found it easy to forget all the other things around him, like his responsibilities and what the next day would bring. He focused solely on being with her. Reality would return soon enough.

7

HURTLING toward the planet in a shuttle traveling at nearly thirty-six thousand kilometers an hour, David reviewed the xenoanthropology notes on the Mifreen. They were a humanoid race, and the planet's atmosphere was well within expected tolerances. The world was larger than Canaan and therefore had a higher gravity rating. *I'll feel a good ten percent heavier down there.* It wouldn't be enough to affect his health, at least not for the amount of time they would be on the surface.

"Have a good night, sir?"

David put down the tablet and turned to Calvin. "Why, yes, I did."

"Good. We all need some R and R every now and then."

Something about the way Calvin had put it made David cock his head. "I feel like I should be reading more into that."

Calvin snickered. "Scuttlebutt has it that you and a certain purple-haired alien linguist hung out in the deck-two officers' mess until nearly twenty-three thirty hours."

How small is this ship anyway? David felt annoyed at first but smirked. "Yes, well. We're, ah, friends."

Hanson looked up from his own tablet. "As long as you don't start getting your shirt ripped off in fistfights with other aliens."

"Oh, come on. This is real life, not some lame *War Patrol* holovid."

Hayworth had apparently realized what the conversation was about and put his reading material down. "Our esteemed leader is human, after all. In need of some companionship, eh?"

Yeah, I probably deserve being ribbed for this one. "Okay, we're friends. We care about each other, and that's the last I want to hear about it. Clear?"

"Uh-huh. So, that purple hair, is it limited to her head, or is it found elsewhere?"

"We're not having this conversation, Demood."

Everyone on the shuttle, including the enlisted Marines that made up their security detail, burst into laughter.

"Anything you say, sir," Calvin replied with a smirk.

"Subject change," David said while scrunching his nose. "Everyone read up on this netsim thing?"

"Fascinating technology. The Mifreen society appears to be based entirely around it," Hayworth replied, seemingly happy to move on.

"The brief I read suggests it's a seamless virtual environment."

Hayworth nodded. "They claim it's indistinguishable from reality and allows everyone in their civilization to experience life however they desire."

Calvin snorted. "That's about the stupidest thing I've ever heard. Computer simulations are just that—fake. Who cares how many fake houses, fake money, helicars, or women, for that matter, you have? I'll take the real world, thank you very much."

Leave it to the Marine to put things in black-and-white terms. But the more David thought about it, the more he agreed. Plenty of people played hyperrealistic holovid games back home. He'd enjoyed such things, at least when he was younger. *But the idea of playing a hologame all the time? That seems wrong somehow.* David recalled that many rabbinical texts argued against synthetic-reality products replacing what was real. Typically, the argument went that what was in the physical world was what HaShem had given, and the simulation was a human creation. Therefore, you were worshipping an idol over HaShem.

"I'd like to try it out myself," Hanson said in the lull. "Always enjoyed the latest hologames."

"Yeah, says the engineering nerd," Calvin made a show of rolling his eyes. "The Marines have experimented with using VR for training. You know what we found? Nothing beats live-fire, real-life training exercises because in the computer, when you die, you just reset. Meanwhile, back in reality, when you die, you're *dead*."

"Without a neural interface, we can't experience the full range of virtual reality anyway," Hayworth snapped. "Which we'll never have because the God-botherers in the Coalition have made it virtually impossible to research."

"Not just 'God-botherers,' Doctor. It's a consensus that we should avoid technology that blends man and machine. Neutral worlds where people augment their bodies by cutting their limbs off and attaching artificial ones should be a clue as to why our way is a good idea."

"Does the saying 'Don't toss the baby out with the bath water' mean anything to you people?"

"Get up on the wrong side of the bed this morning?" David asked, forcing a smile.

"I do not like limits on my research." Hayworth crossed his arms. "Maybe if we used VR to fight wars, people wouldn't get killed in them anymore."

"Something tells me if war games became how societies solved their problems, we'd end up with even more death." David grimaced. "War should be the absolute last resort, and it should be horrific. So horrific that no one in their right mind would want to use it as a tool to solve a political dispute."

"Hear! Hear!" Calvin interjected. "Though kicking doors in and putting bad guys down never gets old."

A round of polite chuckles followed.

"Ultimately, what we think of this society doesn't matter. My only objective here is to get some help against the nanites. I hope they've got some hyperadvanced technology in *other* areas."

"And on that, we can agree, General."

David picked up his tablet again to finish the prebrief. They had another fifteen minutes before touchdown, and he wanted the material fresh in his mind.

The shuttle flew on.

———

THE RIDE to the surface wasn't quite as scenic as David had hoped for, as their destination lay outside the confines of what he assumed was their capital city. After a final atmospheric-conditions check, the cargo door slid open, revealing a brilliant blue sky. The star's warmth felt good on his skin as he stepped out with Calvin at his side.

Mifreen in what appeared to be uniforms formed a line

Justice 75

next to a group of vehicles. Their design reminded David of helicars back in the Coalition. *Kind of boxy too.* All the Mifreen had tufts of hair or perhaps fur protruding from their clothing around the neck and wrists. Coupled with exceptionally well-pronounced facial features, they were quickly identifiable as a nonhuman species.

One of the aliens stepped forward and bowed his head. "Welcome, friends. Are you the one named Cohen?" A multisecond delay followed as the translators processed their native tongue into English.

"Thank you. We're glad to be here and meet who we hope are new friends as well. I'm Major General David Cohen, and this is Colonel Demood." He gestured at Calvin.

"The rest are your servants?"

David shook his head. "No, the rest are several of my officers, a Marine escort, and one of our most accomplished scientific minds, Dr. Benjamin Hayworth."

"We are glad to welcome all of you. I am Bal Noran Qisran, and I have been instructed to convey you in peace to our main hall of government. Would you please enter our conveyances?"

Odd manner of speech. Then again, it is a machine translation. "We'd be happy to."

A female Mifreen whispered something into Qisran's ear, and he blinked. "Are some of you carrying weapons?"

"Yes. It is protocol for us not to enter a new situation without proper protection against any possible threat."

"Mifreen is a world of complete peace and harmony. You do not need any weapons here."

"Perhaps in time, we'll see that for ourselves and agree, but for now, my Marine contingent keeps its sidearms," David replied. "This point is nonnegotiable."

Half a minute of excited cross talk between the Mifreen ensued. David didn't catch a word, as it didn't translate.

Finally, Qisran turned back toward him. "We agree to your terms in the interest of peace, as long as you give assurances the weapons will not be used."

"They're for defensive purposes only, Bal Qisran. As long as we're not threatened, you have nothing to fear from humanity or the Terran Coalition."

Qisran inclined his head. "Please, allow us to transport you to the hall of government."

"I'm riding with you," Calvin interjected. "Sir."

David nodded and allowed himself to be ushered toward one of the waiting vehicles. He climbed into the passenger compartment, followed by Calvin, Hayworth, and another Marine. Hanson and the rest of the honor guard took the other one. In moments, the door was closed, and they lifted off.

"Hey, on the bright side, they're not shooting at us," Calvin said with a guffaw. "Beats the last few encounters of the hostile alien kind."

Hayworth harrumphed. "Typical human arrogance. You must get outside your comfort zone to take in new cultures."

"I'm a *Marine*, doc. Looking for threats is our thing."

Before Hayworth could reply, David cleared his throat. "I, for one, am happy this first-contact situation is proceeding peacefully." He peered out the window and took in the cityscape below.

"Interesting architecture," Hayworth murmured. "Far more spartan than I'd expected, given what we saw on the vidlink."

"True."

Neat, grid-like streets and structures constituted the urban area they flew over. Most of the buildings appeared similar to one another, with coloring and materials that matched. It reminded David of a newly constructed subdivision of tract homes back on New Israel. *The kind my mother always hated. She said they lacked character.* He wasn't sure what conclusions to draw except that the Mifreen didn't seem to have an abundance of exterior decoration specialists.

"Hey, did you see that?" Calvin asked.

David snapped his head around. "See what?"

"Robots on the street down there." He pointed.

It took David a moment to shift his position to see where Calvin had indicated. *Huh.* "Yeah, that... Hey, wait a minute. There are hundreds of them."

Calvin raised an eyebrow. "But I don't see any Mifreen."

"There is an obvious answer as to why," Hayworth interjected.

"Which is, Doc? I just kick doors in, remember."

"If most of their population is in a simulation, it makes sense for a species to turn to robotic labor to handle simple tasks."

David kicked Hayworth's comment around in his mind before nodding. "Yeah, you're right, Doctor."

Suddenly, the vehicles gained altitude rapidly. The reason became apparent as they maneuvered between skyscraper-like buildings. One in particular stood out because it was more decorated and had more color than everything else in the city.

"I think our destination is ahead."

As they came to a stop, Mifreen in brightly colored clothing rushed forward and opened the doors on both sides of the helicar.

David stepped out, followed closely by Calvin. Those around them bowed their heads and gestured toward an entrance a few dozen meters away. *Most interesting. The building continues up another... well, by our standards, fifty or sixty floors, but it's inset and only occupies a fraction of the total area of the structure.* He remembered there was a word for such a design but couldn't pull it from the recesses of his mind.

"Welcome to our hall of government, General Cohen," a Mifreen female who had just walked up to him said. "Please follow Qisran and me to our meeting place."

David motioned the others over. "Lead the way."

The trek through the interior wasn't as long as David had expected. After getting into a gravlift, they exited at what appeared to be the top floor or at least very close to it. More Mifreen, again in brightly colored clothing, lined the hallway.

I suppose they've never seen an alien before. The walls were decorated with images of locales teeming with brightly hued skies, unique wildlife, and rugged landscapes. David found the pictures odd in that none matched the biomes seen on Mifreen. *The one with two stars specifically.* They must somehow be connected to the simulated reality.

Qisran paused in front of a set of tall double doors before pushing them inward.

David and Calvin strode into what seemed like a meeting chamber that was fully enclosed by either glass or transparent material of some sort, and five more Mifreen stood within.

So they take precautions too. Two of the aliens had holsters on their waists and wore attire consistent with a uniform.

David stood a step forward. "Major General David Cohen of the Terran Coalition. I'm honored to be here as a guest of your people. We look forward to a mutual exchange of culture and greetings."

The male Mifreen in the middle inclined his head. "Thank you, General Cohen. I, Tal Carewn Quosan, greet you on behalf of all our people in both the physical and virtual realms."

"I've brought some of my senior officers with me—Colonel Calvin Demood, Terran Coalition Marine Corps, Major Hanson, the *Lion*'s chief engineer, and Dr. Hayworth, our top scientist."

Quosan nodded. "These are my cocouncilors, Tal Garnan and Tal Fasran." He gestured to two female Mifreen easily distinguished by their long hair and shorter stature.

David pursed his lips. "Do you not also use the title Hes?"

The councilors exchanged glances before Quosan spoke. "No, that is reserved for those who govern us in the netsim."

"I see," David replied. *What's that line from* Alice in Wonderland? *Curiouser and curiouser.*

"Would you care for refreshments?" Quosan indicated an array of foods and liquids.

"Ah, we'd have to run that by the *Lion*'s chief medical officer first to see if our bodies are compatible with them."

"We took the liberty of scanning your biosignatures and processing the information through the netsim. I assure you they are quite safe and will provide sustenance to your bodies."

"Let's start with some water." David smiled. *Don't want to insult them, but I'd rather have our people confirm those results.*

"Your simulated reality functions as more than a simulation, then?" Hayworth asked as he adjusted his lab coat.

"It is the nexus of our society, Doctor," Quosan replied. "Most research is performed there."

Hayworth furrowed his brow but didn't respond.

"Shall we get started?" David asked.

"Yes. Please, sit." Quosan gestured at the table. The Mifreen sat on the side closest to the windows, and the doors to the hallway closed, leaving only three leaders, their protection officers, and the *Lion*'s personnel.

"You don't seem to be that surprised to meet an alien species," Hayworth remarked as he stretched out in a chair.

"Why would we be? It's well-known that intelligent life exists elsewhere in the universe. We've detected signals and transmissions that are proof of this."

David blinked. "So you've made contact with others?"

Quosan shook his head. "No. Replying was debated, but ultimately, our society is happy with what we have here. However, humans mark the first time someone has *shown up* at our planet. I have to admit I'm baffled. Are you some kind of explorer?"

"Humanity as a race has many explorers. We"—David spread his arms out and touched Calvin's and Hanson's shoulders—"are, however, not among them. We're military officers, sworn to protect our worlds. It's a simple matter of bad luck or perhaps fate that brought us to Sextans B."

"What is Sextans B?"

"Our name for your galaxy." David grinned. "Humans love to assign unique identifiers to things."

"You couldn't pronounce what we call it," Quosan replied. "How did you end up here?"

"Our faster-than-light drive malfunctioned."

Quosan nodded. "An unfortunate circumstance."

"Very. But since we've arrived here, it's become clear there are threats to be faced. We seek allies to stand with us."

"Against what?"

"Intelligent nanites bent on gaining power and

destroying every solar system that contains minerals used for replication."

Suddenly, a holographic projector of some kind came to life. The image of the idyllic beach David had seen in his previous conversation with the Mifreen council members inside the netsim came into focus.

"General Cohen, we meet again," Hes Sansan said. "Your comments are alarming. Do you mean to threaten us with these nanites?"

David held up his hand. "Not at all, and we have no indication they're headed anywhere near Mifreen. We only seek allies." *Slick. Listening in but not revealing their presence. I don't suppose I blame these guys for being suspicious of us.*

"Beyond the obvious question of why, how could we possibly help you?"

"Your society has mastered antimatter power. Our sensors confirm it's what you use for your entire civilization's energy needs."

"And? Your vessel is powered by the same technology."

"We are but one ship and a few smaller escorts. More space-borne assets are needed to have any hope against a force the size of a moon."

"Mifreen has no star-faring vessels, General. We've no need for them."

"But—"

"We do not explore because our planet provides everything our society needs. Our citizens live in complete peace and harmony. Given that threats may exist somewhere in the universe, our world has a defense system that you undoubtedly observed in orbit."

"It was noted, yes. However—"

"Not expanding to other worlds puts your civilization in a precarious position," Hayworth said. "Such as what happens if a comet hits and destroys everything? That's not without precedence."

Sansan narrowed his eyes. "Our technology would allow us to defeat such a threat, Doctor."

Hiding from threats doesn't make them go away. David opted not to share that thought. "Then perhaps you could assist us in developing something to keep the nanites at bay."

"A weapon?"

"Of a *defensive* nature." *Might as well swing for the fences.*

"And if a species you'd never met or heard of showed up asking the Terran Coalition for assistance in weapons research, how would your civilization respond?" Sansan asked. While his tone was perfectly reasonable, the underlying bite was impossible to miss.

"It would depend on the situation, but to be fair, there would be quite a bit of trust but verification involved."

"Trust but verification. A unique saying, General. Yet it will be even more challenging for us to accept your claims because of your unique culture. Without a netsim, how does your society even function?"

David blinked. "Uh, I'm afraid I don't follow."

"Have you found some method to remove resource scarcity?"

"Well, we have abundant energy provided by fusion reactors that's very cheap along with advanced 3-D printers to fabricate things quickly. But no, our society isn't postscarcity. Our citizens have jobs, and our lives have a certain cycle. Once we complete our secondary education, we either enter the workforce or obtain more advanced education in a given area. Then we work for some period of years and eventually retire."

Every Mifreen's face blanched.

Justice 83

David quickly took note. "Uh, does that in some way offend you?"

"What you describe is what we worked for hundreds of years to eradicate. It is distressing that a space-faring race of great technology would still use these methods," Sansan replied.

"Hes, it works for us." David weighed every word that came out of his mouth. *Can't offend these guys the first time out.* "It is our culture, and just as I do not judge yours, I would respectfully suggest that without experiencing it, you cannot judge ours fairly."

Sansan snorted. "There is wisdom in those words, General Cohen."

"How does your society deal with poverty and starvation?" one of the councilors in the room asked.

"The Terran Coalition has a certain floor for everyone's standard of living, if you will. If an individual human or a member of another species that lives among us has issues, we help. That's a combination of our government and private charities. We tie that help to fixing the root cause of a person's problems, such as drug addiction, mental or medical issues, or whatever it is."

"Do you use specie?"

It took David a moment to recall the word's meaning. "Money? Yes."

Several of the Mifreen suppressed a shudder.

"Our system removes the need for such things," Sansan replied smugly. "There is unlimited bounty in the netsim. You may do anything you want, anytime you want. Without regard for anything but your imagination."

"It sounds intriguing." David glanced between several councilors, trying to read their expressions, but found them inscrutable.

"How much of your population is inside the simulation?" Hayworth asked.

"About seventy percent," Sansan replied.

"And the rest?"

"They keep the system going. The biosupport facilities and our computer farms must be maintained. As I'm sure you can imagine, it takes an immense amount of computational power to support a shared reality that encompasses our entire world."

"Surely some want to live in..." David forced himself not to say, "the real world." "Our physical reality."

"The goal of every Mifreen is to enter the netsim," Sansan replied. "There is no other reason for life. Those who aren't lucky enough to be chosen at birth may earn their way through service to the greater good."

"Wait. You don't get a say in it?" Calvin interjected.

"There is... I'm sorry, I am struggling to put this into proper context," Sansan said. "The netsim is all. And everyone is united in a desire to join it."

Every alarm bell in David's mind went off at the same time. But the pragmatist in him forced it down. *It doesn't matter what their system or culture is. All that matters is getting help to fight the nanites.* "Ladies and gentlemen, we look at the universe through different lenses. It's a tenet of my people that we listen to any rational viewpoint and treat it respectfully. There will be things our species don't agree on, but both of us doing our part to stop a galaxy-wide scourge is something we should be able to come to a consensus about."

Sansan regarded for him a moment. "Would you be willing to link with the netsim? To experience it?"

The alarms sounded even harder. "My chief medical officer, Dr. Tural, would have to clear the technology for

Justice 85

human use." David kept his expression as neutral as possible. "Beyond that, you would have to have a temporary interface, because I'm not going into a biosupport system anytime soon."

"Oh, of course. We have all manner of ways to interconnect, General." Sansan smiled in a manner that would've made him look like a serial killer if he'd been human.

"We'll need complete specifications and direct discussion between our medical people and yours," David continued. "Is that acceptable?"

"As long as you consent to not being allowed to remove those documents from our world or copy them to your data devices. Our technology is not to be shared."

David inclined his head. "We have similar rules, Hes."

"Then it is decided." Sansan tilted his head. "Perhaps we can meet in the flesh in the near future."

The way he said it was so jarring to David. *The virtual world is more real to him than, well, the real thing. Again, not for me to judge.* "There are many possibilities."

"We will adjourn for today, in that case. I wish you all long life and peace in the simulation, General Cohen."

The holoprojected image snapped off, leaving them alone with Quosan and the other Mifreen.

"Thank you for taking this important first step with us." Quosan stood. "We will await your return. In the meanwhile, if your people need food or water, let us know, and I will personally ensure resupply of your vessels."

David found the man sincere and noted the distinct difference in how those in the netsim and the few out of it behaved. *Some sort of deep observation about life there, probably.* "Thank you, Tal Quosan." He stood, as well, as did the rest of the delegation.

"We wish you long life and peace, that you may know the simulation."

It's almost a religious phrase. David nodded. "Shalom."

They said little on the walk out. David decided to keep his mouth shut, on the probable chance they were being monitored at all times. *And let's hope they don't have mind-reading devices.*

They'd almost gotten back to the entry area and the air-skimming craft when a worker of some sort fell forward and brushed him. The Mifreen made a number of apologies before stepping back.

David had been born at night but not *last* night. He checked his pockets without drawing attention to himself, and his hand closed around an object that hadn't been there before. His heart rate climbed as he realized someone had just executed a nearly perfect exchange. *This just went from odd to strange.* He both dreaded examining whatever it was and looked forward to learning more about the Mifreen.

8

ANOTHER DAY WAS in the books for Master Chief Rebecca Tinetariro. They'd finished the first week of recruit training, which was affectionately known as Hell Week. Virtually none of the Zeivlots or the Zavlots had a problem keeping up with the physical training. As top members of their military forces, all were in excellent shape. *It's nice to see that training standards are consistently high, including before we arrived.*

Where Tinetariro felt like she'd run into a brick wall was getting the two species to buy into full integration. Only by the brute force of PTing recalcitrants, screaming at them, and generally forcing the issue could she and the other DIs even get them to exist in the same area—to say nothing of actually working together.

So far, eleven of the one hundred twenty they'd started with had either been discharged or quit. Given the drop-out rates of CDF and especially TCMC recruit training, it wasn't a big-enough number to worry about yet but more than she'd hoped to see.

"Seem like you've got a lot on your mind, Master Chief."

Tinetariro glanced at Freeman as they strode through the tents. "I do."

"Care to share?"

"Grappling with techniques I haven't explored yet to get these people to overcome their biases. Has anyone had more success?"

"Not really. I certainly haven't, beyond making them eat the dirt until every muscle in their miserable bodies hurts."

"We'll figure it out."

"I hope we do before my knees give out," Freeman replied with a chuckle. "I forgot I'm actually getting up there. At least the sun doesn't bother me as much." He had darker skin as well.

Tinetariro snorted. "Don't *ever* let me hear you say that within earshot of a recruit."

But Freeman wasn't wrong. Even she had felt aches and pains in places there shouldn't be any. That could be dealt with upon return to the *Lion of Judah*, by Dr. Tural. *Until then, pain is weakness leaving the body.*

"Wouldn't think of it, Master Chief." He blew out a breath. "Did I hear right that a Marine chaplain is coming through next week?"

"Yes, as well as both Zeivlot and Zavlot ministers. We'll rotate through services at the mess tent." Tinetariro was a devout Christian, and she wore the red, blue, and white Christian flag proudly under the African Union symbol on her uniform's left sleeve. "I specifically vetted each religious representative and asked them to speak on breaking down barriers."

"How'd that go?"

"It was difficult to find any who wholeheartedly supported the idea."

Justice

Freeman snorted. "At least you found someone."

"If we can just prove it works with one group. That's the hardest part. After that, it'll fall into place."

"You really believe that, Master Chief?"

Tinetariro stopped. "Yes, I do. It's been that like that throughout human history. It's easy to hate another group in the abstract, until you actually have to get to know them. When you do and discover they're not unlike you, the hate becomes impossible to justify for most."

"You make it sound so simple."

"It is. But it's not easy." She noticed a pale light emanating from one of three tents that housed the recruits. "Am I seeing things, or are we past lights out?"

Freeman checked his handcomm. "Definitely past lights out, Master Chief."

Tinetariro snarled. "Let's see what mischief they've gotten themselves into now." She turned on her heel and marched quickly across the parade ground. Pushing the flap aside, with Freeman following right behind, she found several lights on and a group of recruits out of their bunks.

A group of Zeivlots stood opposite an equal number of Zavlots. Tinetariro could barely tell them apart, except that Zavlots had slight facial characteristic changes from the Zeivlots. They spewed obscenities in their native tongues at one another, their voices growing louder with each passing second.

"Attention on deck!" Tinetariro screamed.

When the recruits didn't move, Freeman jumped into action and got a couple of centimeters from the nearest Zeivlot, screaming in her ear. "Get your ass in line now, maggot!"

Before Tinetariro could do the same, they jumped forward into a line.

"Everyone else, out of your rack now!" she yelled. "Move it! One, two, three!"

The rest of the occupants made a mad dash to comply and line up at the end of their two-tier bunk beds, one on either side of the small trunks in front of them.

Tinetariro strolled up and down the center of the tent, projecting her voice as much as she could. "You can't work together. You can't sleep together. If you can't even do that, how will you ever *fight* together?"

No one answered.

She turned around and marched back down toward the front. "Since you clearly do not wish to sleep before the next grueling day of training, you will start early." She whipped around to face the room. "Shoes on, then disassemble the racks, carry them outside, and reassemble them two by two."

"What for?" one of the Zeivlots dared to ask.

"Shut up, maggot! Move! Move! Move!" Tinetariro roared in reply.

Everyone dashed to their beds and struggled to take them apart. Someone eventually figured out that they lifted out of place after removing a single pin. After that, the recruits quickly hauled the pieces through the front of the tent.

Tinetariro and Freeman provided loud, direct motivation for them to complete their task as quickly as possible. The mattresses were left inside, leaving only the frames of the double racks, which were reassembled and placed on the ground.

Once they were down, Tinetariro addressed the group of forty recruits. "Now, you will pick up those racks and march around my parade ground." After a few of them stole glances at one another, she bellowed, "Now, maggots!"

The recruits rushed for the bunks and lifted the contraptions to balance them on their shoulders.

"One, two, three, four, left, right, left, right," Tinetariro rasped. Then she decided to have a little fun as the formation got underway. "Time to sing, ladies!"

She made her way to the front and set a pace that was fast enough that it would be difficult but not so fast that it would tire them out too early. "Here we go again!" Tinetariro yelled. "Same old stuff again!"

After each line in the cadence, the recruits repeated it.

"Marching down the avenue! A few more weeks, and we'll be through!"

Freeman took up the song. "I won't have to look at you!"

"You won't have to look at me, so I'll be glad, and so will you!" Tinetariro boomed.

They kept it up, hour after hour. She changed the cadence, rarely allowed the recruits to rest or to drink water, and generally made life hell for them until the first light of the star orbiting them peeked over the horizon.

"Halt!" Tinetariro screamed. "Place those racks on my deck now!"

The ragged group slowly put the two-tiered bunks on the ground and adopted a parade rest stance. They looked awful. Sweat, tears, and dirt caked their clothes and underwear, as she'd made them march without their uniforms on.

"You came here because you volunteered. You wanted to be a part of something bigger than you and do great things for your respective worlds." Tinetariro's voice was even raspier than it had been a few hours earlier, as she had pushed herself to the limit. "This is supposed to be brutal. I will not allow in anyone who would sully my beloved Coalition Defense Force's name and honor. Remember why you are here, especially when it gets tough. Now, shake hands with the man or woman opposite you, and hit the showers. Your day begins now."

"Ma'am, yes, ma'am!"

"Move out!"

The first Zeivlot and Zavlot tentatively shook hands, followed by everyone else in the group. Most did so begrudgingly, but a couple almost seemed to have some respect behind the gesture. It was a start.

As the recruits headed toward the group shower tent, Freeman came up beside Tinetariro. "Rough night, Master Chief."

"I hate to admit it," she replied quietly, "but I'm not quite as young as I used to be."

"No shut-eye for another sixteen hours."

"At least we have some coffee."

"Ah, the joys of being a member of the goat locker." Freeman grinned.

Coffee had been strictly rationed for months and was in short supply across the fleet. But the chief petty officers had ways of ensuring some things still made it to the senior enlisted personnel, as it had always been in the CDF.

"When we do the gas chamber and ropes obstacle course next week, we have to ensure that only teams of two execute and that each team has one Zeivlot and one Zavlot."

"Yes, Master Chief." Freeman raised an eyebrow. "Think we're getting through?"

"If frog-marching them around the parade ground all night didn't cause something to sink in, we're probably wasting our time."

Freeman snickered. "Touché."

"Let's get on with it." As Tinetariro strode away, she realized that despite how tired her body was, she enjoyed pushing the recruits to the limit. *Never gets old. If I can guide and instruct them to be something more, then I will have done my duty and some good.*

9

DAVID HAD KEPT to himself during the return trip from Mifreen, since he found the note in his pocket. The maintenance worker who'd placed it there had done a masterful job on the handoff. *The Coalition Intelligence Service would've been impressed with that level of tradecraft.* A tug-of-war had played out in his mind as he debated what to do. Part of him wondered if it was best to just leave well enough alone, but the more he pondered it, the less he was inclined to do so. *Something else is going on here. And I need to know what it is.* His less-than-stellar impression of the Mifreen's netsim and how it functioned reinforced it.

So he'd called for a staff meeting in the deck-one conference room, limited to Aibek, Hayworth, Taylor, and First Lieutenant Toshiaki Yoshino, the *Lion's* intelligence officer. *The fewer who know about this wrinkle, the better right now.*

David pushed the hatch open to find them all assembled early. *Moderately surprising.*

"General on deck!" Taylor barked as he stood and came to attention.

Aibek and Yoshino followed. Hayworth stood but appeared bored.

"As you were," David said as the hatch shut behind him. "Let's get started."

They all returned to their seats and stared at him with a mixture of expressions, except for Aibek, who was as inscrutable as ever.

"We have a situation." David pulled the small piece of polymer-like paper out of his pocket and placed it on the table.

"What's that?" Hayworth asked.

"It's a note that's written in English and was slipped to me by a Mifreen during our meeting."

Everyone, even Aibek, appeared shocked. "Not from a government official?" he hissed.

"No. I think it was a maintenance worker who gently bumped me on the way out, though I'm not entirely sure. Excellent tradecraft, by the way. It's a request for communication with a series of numbers and letters afterward. I can't make heads or tails of it."

Hayworth threw up his hands. "Throw it away."

"Why?" Aibek asked.

"Because we cannot involve ourselves with yet another alien species and its internal problems! For all you know, this could be some criminal or a government test. Perhaps they don't trust us. Our objective should be single-minded. Determine whether they will help with technology against the nanites and *move on*."

David pursed his lips. "I spent half an hour trying to tell myself that, Doctor. But there is a component here we cannot ignore. The Mifreen government wants us to plug someone into the netsim to get a feel for it before they'll discuss any technology exchanges."

"And?"

"What if there's something dangerous about the system?"

Before Hayworth could reply, Yoshino cut in. "It's more likely that there's some sort of antigovernment or insurgent group that sees us as a way to get help for their cause."

"I'm well aware of that possibility. And I'd put credits down that it's what's happening."

"May I see the note, sir?" Taylor asked.

David shoved the piece of paper down the table. "Have at it, Lieutenant."

"Hmmm. It looks like old-school paper, but it feels like a polymer. 'Netsim isn't what it claims to be. Do not believe them.' That's a pretty direct message."

"And it folds too," David replied. "I thought it was interesting. What do you make of the numbers?"

Taylor stared at it for a few seconds. "That's hex, I think."

"Hex?" Aibek asked as he raised an eye scale.

"Hexadecimal. Base sixteen math."

"Let me see that," Hayworth interjected before standing and peering over Taylor's shoulder. "It could be, anyway."

"I wager that it's a network address of some sort, sir."

David tilted his head. "So... what? It's how we reach this person or organization?"

"Possibly. I'd have to run some tests and see what I could find. Cryptology is my specialty, sir."

"So you've said once or twice," David replied with a grin. "But we haven't had a lot of call for that out here."

"It would appear we do now."

"To what end?" Hayworth asked.

"To gather information," David replied. "It would be helpful to understand the lay of the land before we plug *any* of our people into this device."

Justice

97

"I'm willing to do it and avoid all this mess."

"You're the last one who can, Doctor."

Hayworth crossed his arms. "Why?"

"Because you can't be replaced," David replied. "If the worst happened, we'd be stuck here. *You* are one of the only people on the *Lion* who can figure out how to get us home. And frankly, I'm unwilling to stick myself inside some alien technology without the facts... which brings up basic leadership. If I'm not willing to do a thing, I cannot order one of my soldiers to do it."

"Oh, you could." Hayworth smirked. "Plenty of others do."

"I don't."

"No." Hayworth blew out a breath. "I beg you all to consider what comes next. If there is some hidden danger, what then?"

"Then we leave."

"General, I know you well enough to realize you're incapable of leaving if innocent people of virtually any species are being harmed. You have a pathological need to improve things as you see fit."

"Is that so bad, Doctor?" David pursed his lips. "We go from planet to planet here, finding injustice after injustice. There are apparently no FTL-capable races to keep the peace like we have in the Milky Way."

"You have no idea what these interventions will do in the long run. I have repeatedly warned you that someday, your collective good intentions are going to blow up in your face. Whatever you do here, *do not get involved*."

"I make no commitment to what we will do after making contact with... whoever this is, but I believe we're not doing our jobs, Doctor, if we don't pursue it."

"Not like you're going to do what I tell you." Hayworth

shrugged. "But you ought to war-game it out, as you military types are wont to say."

The doctor had a point. David was eager to help. Sometimes, perhaps too eager. But he also believed in the strongest possible terms that those who had the capability to right wrongs and correct injustices had a duty to do so. "I'll take that under advisement, Doctor. Until we have more information, I want this kept quiet. Consider it TS/SCI, Codeword classified."

"Yes, sir," Yoshino replied.

"I'll get it on immediately, sir," Taylor interjected.

"Very well. Dismissed."

———

ON MIFREEN, everyone wore a mask over their soul. Some—namely, those in the netsim—were open about it. They could change their appearance at will, and most constantly did. But it was more than a physical image. Virtually no one showed their inner self. At all times, a careful presentation must be maintained to avoid any appearance of dissent.

Tal Riwald Markul was well versed in the subject. By day, he worked as a data analysis engineer. *I'm confident my coworkers would describe me as perfectly in tune with the requirements of the netsim and its citizens.*

Once the door to his small apartment slid shut, the real Markul came out. He stripped off his business suit and put on a T-shirt before stepping into the tiny walk-in closet in the bedroom. Markul stuck his hand behind several pairs of pants and pressed his palm onto a reader that only he knew was there. A moment later, a panel slid open.

It revealed an even smaller workplace that consisted only of a desk and a chair. He booted up a computing device with a series of biometric unlocks, a passphrase, and a small token hidden under his palm's skin. If the precise sequence wasn't followed, charges built into the computer would trigger and burn down the apartment.

Markul had been breaking into the netsim and government systems for years. For reasons he didn't fully understand, he'd never accepted the official teaching that the netsim was the salvation of the Mifreen species.

The arrival of the strange alien vessels marked the first time they'd been visited by people from another world. *It wouldn't do for our guests not to get the entire truth.*

After the machine completed its initialization sequence, Markul checked the hexadecimal connection he'd established the previous day. Everything the net was saying so far about the humans indicated they were curious and inquisitive creatures. He'd counted on that to win out.

Yes, I've got a nibble. Markul grinned and typed in a long string of commands. His fingers flew across the keyboard, which was old school compared to most VR interfaces, but he preferred the tactile response of the polymer keys.

Possibly, the cutout he'd used to deliver the message to the human leader had been compromised, and the person on the other side of the screen was an agent looking to send him to the education center.

But acting out of fear won't get me the desired result. For all his years of searching for the truth, Markul knew he was only one mistake away from being hauled out. He was playing a dangerous but ultimately intoxicating game of predator and prey.

On the monitor, replies came back to his queries, and Markul led whoever was pinging him on a chase across the Mifreen net. After several bounces off satellite nodes, he felt impressed. *Better than any government chaser I've seen in a while.* However, there was something different about the method in which the connection was made.

Markul stealthily initiated a look-back application and ran into an automated protection system. The code was utterly foreign to him. *It must be the aliens.* It took several tries to evade, and eventually, he obtained access to what was on the other side of the firewall. He spent hours searching through files, trying to avoid raising an alarm. For all their advanced technology, Mifreen cryptography and decryption systems were far more effective than their human counterparts.

When he'd seen enough, he had only one thing left to do: make contact. *First Lieutenant Robert Taylor. What an interesting name.* Markul grinned, hoping he'd found what they needed: help. It would make every sacrifice worth it.

10

DAVID STARED into the eyes of the Mifreen on the other side of the viewer. Taylor had summoned him urgently only a few minutes ago, and his rushed explanation indicated that the man on the screen was what he'd found after exploring the hexadecimal address they'd been provided. Half of David's brain felt like he was walking into a trap. The other longed to know *exactly* what was happening, because the government's hard sell on Mifreen society didn't pass muster.

"Are you ready to go live, sir?" Taylor asked.

They were in a secure area within the *Lion's* intelligence operations compartment, which had been cleared of all personnel. The result was extreme quiet, aside from the whirring of computers.

"Yes. Video and audio."

Taylor tapped a button and nodded.

"This is Major General David Cohen, commanding the CSV *Lion of Judah*. To whom am I speaking?"

"We'll avoid using my name for now, General. Apologies for that, but I must take precautions, as I'm sure you can appreciate." The male Mifreen forced a thin smile. "There is also the small matter of time. We have precious little of it."

David narrowed his eyes. "Look, Mister... whoever you are. I have no reason to trust you. You've got some little spy game going here, and I bit because it was unusual enough that, being a seasoned military officer, I know not to go into something without having all the details."

"Undoubtedly, you were put off by our netsim-focused society. Humanity seems rather focused on individual freedom, or at least the Terran Coalition is."

"And how would you know that?"

"My government's computers aren't the only things I can break into, General. And before you become outraged with me, I'm taking an obscene risk contacting an alien species and asking them for help against my own people."

"Let's be very clear. My fleet isn't getting involved in any internal conflicts. I only seek to understand the lay of the land and decide whether continuing diplomatic dialogue is worthwhile." *He must've penetrated our computer systems.*

The Mifreen stared at him for a few moments. "They told you it allowed all of our people to achieve whatever they dream of, yes?"

David pursed his lips. "Aside from the ones who run the computers and keep up the machinery, yes."

"They were more truthful with you than their own citizens, then," he replied with a scoff. "Yes, that's about right. But I bet they didn't tell you how those outside the simulation live. We are no better than slaves. We are told what to do, how to do it, when to do it, and we cannot decide to go and experience our lives as we see fit."

"Do you have any proof?"

"Scan the surface of our planet with those fancy scientific sensors, and you will see that Mifreen only live in a few cities. Clustered around the infrastructure of the netsim."

"That's not proof—"

"It's a start. Then come down here, and I'll show you what's really happening."

"Even if I was inclined to do so, our shuttle might be detected, and such a thing could be considered an act of war. Which... I'm not interested in another conflict."

The man stared into the screen for several seconds before biting his lip. "I'll give you the proper authentication codes to evade the detection grid and a specific route that flies where their sensors are weakest."

"Why?"

"Because if you don't realize the truth now, they'll start reeling you in. Maybe even export this monstrosity to your society."

David furrowed his brow. "That'd be hard to do, since we're 4.4 million light-years from home and cut off from our people."

"You want something from the government, don't you?"

"I'm pretty sure you already know what we want and what we're dealing with out in the void."

The man smirked. "Yes, I do. The government isn't the only entity that can get you what you desire on our world. I'm sending the codes and instructions. Think on it. If you want to talk, be there at the appointed time. Otherwise, leave this place. And do not return. Your lives depend on it."

Before David could reply, the screen went black. He pushed back from the terminal.

"A bit dramatic," Taylor said. "Though concerning."

David eyed him. "In more ways than one. I want you to go through our systems with a fine-tooth comb. Pull everyone in the department in, and wake up the third shift if you have to."

"Yes, sir. What about the Mifreen, though?"

"The choice seems to be between going along with their government or trusting the word of a hacker who easily got through our defenses. I frankly don't like either of them because the entire situation stinks." David let out a sigh.

"No easy day, eh, sir?"

"You can say that again." David chuckled as he stood. "Get as far as you can in the next three hours. I want something ready by the time I get the senior officers together to discuss this."

"Yes, sir."

David headed out the hatch and back toward his day cabin on deck one. *HaShem, help me to make wise choices.* The weight of the galaxy seemed to descend on his shoulders once more.

———

BINARY CHOICES WERE SUPPOSED to be the easiest ones to make. Yet what loomed in front of David was anything but easy. He'd run it through his head over and over before ordering the *Lion*'s most senior officers to join him for a strategy session. *Sometimes I sorely miss the counsel of General MacIntosh.*

David strode into the conference room on deck one.

"General on deck!" Taylor said as he jumped from his seat.

"As you were." David slid into the chair at the head of the table. He made eye contact with each person present— Aibek, Calvin, Amir, Hanson, and Hayworth, and the comms officer.

"I want to be the first on record as saying that making a trip down to Mifreen is exceptionally risky, sir," Calvin interjected.

"Foolhardy. Unjustified. Idiotic." Hayworth crossed his arms.

"Point made, Doctor." David gestured with his hands. "I don't particularly like this, on any level. However, I also think something else is afoot here."

"Of course there is," Hayworth snapped. "We're examining an alien culture. It's bound to be odd until you get used to it."

"Doctor, this gentleman was quite persuasive. And you did the scans. He's telling the truth—their population is almost entirely urban. Robots and automated systems harvest their food."

Hanson made a face. "Not sure I'd call what I saw pictures of food. Most of the population seems to subsist on some sort of organic paste."

"Is it green? Next, you'll tell me it's people," Hayworth said with a snicker.

Furrowing his brow, David said, "I don't think that joke landed, Doctor."

"Ah, a pity. Such a lack of reading good literature among the youth these days."

"Look, we're talking about working with these aliens. They want us to put a human into their simulation. We want them to give us technology, and it sure looks to me like they're more advanced than us in some areas."

Hayworth blew out a breath. "They undoubtedly have superior computers. Most likely of the quantum variety. So yes, we could get a lot done with them. Maybe even predictive models to determine what might work against the nanites."

"Then I think we need to explore what this hacker's said and meet with him." David crossed his arms. "Lieutenant, did you get to examine his intrusions into our systems?"

Taylor nodded. "Yes, sir. Highly sophisticated. I only detected small traces, and frankly, if I hadn't gone through a couple of network nodes, reviewing the logs line by line, I wouldn't have found anything. Either he or his tech is good enough to easily avoid our automated defenses."

"What if it is a trap?" Aibek asked in a hiss.

"By who? The hacker? That seems unlikely. The Mifreen government? Perhaps a more serious question there."

"Sir, we can modify an assault lander a bit to get stealthier," Hanson said. "Limit its LIDAR signature, for one, and make sure all the sensor-deadening tiles are perfectly intact. It's still not going to be as good as a purpose-built tier-one stealth pod, but it'll do."

"I could fly a stealth recon bird down," David replied.

"You are not rated for such a craft, sir." Amir shook his head. "And the cockpit isn't big enough for two."

While David knew that was true, he figured he could probably wing it. "I can fly a shuttle."

"It's not the same, sir."

"Okay, let's say we do the lander, and it's not a trap. What's the risk level?" David glanced around the conference room.

"We have no idea what type of sensor technology the Mifreen have," Hayworth interjected. "For all we know, they could use something different from the accepted technology standards in the Milky Way. Meaning"—he pointed his finger for emphasis—"none of your fancy CDF stealth technology means diddly...squat."

"It's a calculated risk."

"For whom? Stop interfering in other cultures, General,

for the last time," Hayworth replied, his voice rising. "It doesn't matter what this government is doing. It's none of our business."

"It's our business if we're going to work with them and put one of our people into that netsim."

"If you believe the Mifreen are dangerous, *leave*."

"And pass up useful technology that might help us get a weapon against the nanites? From what you've said, Doctor, this quantum computer is a game changer."

Hayworth stood. "Are we at a point where the ends justify the means?"

"Of course not," David snapped. "You know I detest that sort of mindset."

"Then why employ it?"

"Because there's nothing morally wrong with meeting with this hacker."

"And if the Mifreen discover your shuttle and shoot it down?"

"That's a risk I'm willing to take!" As David uttered the words, he knew his decision was made.

Hayworth returned to his seat. "This is madness. Will we interfere with every alien species we encounter?"

"Yeah, well, we're in a mad galaxy." Calvin chuckled. "I mean, come on. Dueling species trying to blow each other apart with nukes, a race of trial lawyers, void-dwelling aliens willing to commit mass suicide over a weapon, and now *these* guys?"

Several of them snickered.

"When you put it like that," David replied.

"Fine. What do I know," Hayworth said. "At least ask this hacker about his insights into their quantum computer systems, then."

"I plan on it, Doctor."

"I want a full squad of Marines with you, sir," Calvin interjected. "In power armor."

David shrugged. "Fine by me, Colonel."

"A shame I cannot join you," Aibek hissed. "I would like to get off this ship, at least for a little while. The void becomes oppressive to my people after too much time has passed."

"I'll sign you up for shore leave, XO." David grinned.

"Not on this world." Aibek raised an eye scale. "But back on Zeivlot, I will gladly accept it."

David chuckled. "Anything else, people? If not, let's get at it. I want that assault lander ready to go tomorrow morning in time for the transit window."

Silence was the only reply.

"Dismissed."

After they'd all walked out, David took a few minutes to reflect. Hayworth had a point, but he felt unable to turn away. The confluence of events made it such that only one outcome was acceptable, and that was getting the help needed to fight the nanites. If the Mifreen could do that, he felt duty and honor bound to see it through. *Going through the hacker or the government doesn't matter. As long as the price isn't too high.* He would absolutely not allow a human to go into the netsim if the hacker's warnings had any meat to them. *But I have to be careful not to prejudge this.* David closed his eyes. *I miss fighting the League.*

11

AFTER THE DISTURBING events of the day and the major decisions David had been forced to make in regard to the Mifreen, he looked forward to rest. The situation tugged at his heart and mind, as he still wasn't quite sure what the right choice was. Hayworth's enjoinment against interfering with every species they encountered was always present, but so was a sinking feeling that the Mifreen society had something very wrong with it. *At least by human standards.*

But David was determined to set it all aside and focus on his time with Bo'hai. He'd invited her to join him for dinner in his quarters belowdecks that morning. Since he'd decided to keep it simple, dinner had been delivered thirty minutes ago and would be warmed up in the heating unit when she arrived.

Watching the clock and waiting for her, David experienced something he wasn't used to: anticipation coupled with uneasiness. *Is this what the kids call butterflies?* The notion seemed absurd to him, but he supposed it was proof that like everyone else, he had emotions. *Not that I'm allowed to show them, for the most part, as a flag officer.*

The harsh sound of the hatch buzzer filled the cabin.

"Come!" David yelled loudly enough for her to hear and the computer to process it as an unlock command.

Bo'hai walked in with a big smile on her face. "Hello."

It took David a few moments to realize she'd dressed up, and he still had on his khaki service uniform with a black space sweater.

Her dress was black as well, but she wore a flower he didn't recognize in her hair, which was curled in a way he'd never seen her wear it before. "You, ah, look lovely tonight."

"Thank you," Bo'hai replied as her face reddened. "There is little occasion to be fancy on this ship, but I thought tonight warranted it."

David glanced down at his sweater. "I didn't get the memo. Sorry."

She approached him and put her arms around his waist. "I believe the English word is handsome... to describe how you look in your uniform."

David's cheeks heated. "Not quite the word I'd use, but thank you, nonetheless." He embraced her before pushing off and walking toward a small dining area. While his quarters on the *Yitzhak Rabin* and virtually every other ship he'd served on had each been the size of a postage stamp, on the *Lion*, the CO's quarters were massive. They were really more of a small apartment. Still, David didn't spend much time in them. He was usually on the bridge, walking the ship, or in his day cabin on deck one.

"Are we eating here?"

"If that's okay, yes. There's already scuttlebutt that we're seeing each other, and... I do not want to feed the RUMINT mill."

"RUMINT?" Bo'hai tilted her head.

"Rumor Intelligence." David grinned. "Which is rarely accurate or intelligent."

She chuckled. "Is it a bad thing that your crew knows we're dating?"

"No." The conversation in the shuttle flashed into his mind. "Let's just say I'm a private person."

"And this ship is very small. Yes, I've learned that as well. There are no secrets here."

"There can't be." David opened the small refrigeration device, pulled out the two ready-made meals, and stuck them in the induction heater. A few moments later, they were both piping hot. He gingerly laid them on the dining table. "I had two VIP rations pulled from cryostorage."

"What are those?"

"Supposedly, they're in there if we're entertaining a head of state or high-ranking diplomatic envoy. That sort of thing." David flashed a grin. "Out here, though, I figure it's okay for us to indulge for one night. This meal consists of a filet mignon, pureed potatoes, and mushrooms."

"What is a filet mignon?" Bo'hai asked, butchering the pronunciation.

"It's a type of steak, which is the meat from an animal called a cow. Many humans consider it a delicacy. As do I."

"Then I will try it."

David pulled out her chair and adjusted it after she sat then slid into his seat across the table. "May I bless the food before we begin?"

"Of course."

He took her hand and spoke in Hebrew. "Blessed are You, Lord our God, King of the Universe, by Whose word all things came to be."

"That was beautiful." She picked up her fork and knife

and sliced off a small piece of meat. "Even if I didn't understand a word."

David chuckled. "That prayer is called the *Shehakol*."

"You have names for your prayers?"

"Some of them, yes." David took a bite of mushroom mixed with potato puree. "We have a lot of rules around specific prayers, for specific situations, times, et cetera. Even for food, there's six different main prayers we use and rules around what order to say them in when food types are combined."

"That is oddly specific." Bo'hai chewed her steak, then a bright smile filled her face. "This is amazing. I have never tasted anything so good."

"Told you."

"Please don't take this the wrong way, but your religion has many rules."

Shrugging, David munched on his filet. "There's a reason why we call ourselves practicing Jews. It's not easy, nor is it supposed to be. One of the ways we show devotion to HaShem is by obeying His laws. All of them, all the time, whenever possible."

"When is it not possible?"

David's face clouded. "More times than I'd like, especially in the service. CDF grooming standards keep me from growing a beard or having curled sidelocks. We're out of kosher food, and there won't be any more until we get back to the Milky Way. To be fair, we usually run out of it after a couple of weeks post resupply anyway. Those are compromises I've had to make in my faith."

Bo'hai set her fork down. "The Maker sees your heart. That is what counts."

"I think you're right, but not *everyone* sees it that way."

"May I ask a question?"

Justice 113

"Always." David sipped his water.

"Why is your cabin so sparse? There is almost nothing in it that defines you. My home is filled with mementos of life, images captured from when I was a child until now, my family, and friends. I can barely tell you reside here, much less *live* in this space."

"I'm not a stuff guy," David replied. "Never had much use for it, and I have a small family, which is a bit odd for an Orthodox Jew. But nevertheless, it is so."

"There must be more to it."

"When you've been in the void for as long as I have, you learn to move around with a minimum of things to tie you down. I, for instance, have a small apartment in Lawrence City. That's the capital of Canaan. I rarely sleep in it, even though the *Lion of Judah* is homeported out of Canaan's primary military space installation."

"Do you behave that way for the same reason you haven't mated?"

David blinked and considered her words. "I'd never quite thought of that." He bit his lip. "I suppose you might be right. I wouldn't want someone to have to clean up after me."

"May I make a suggestion?"

"Something tells me I couldn't stop you if I wanted to."

Bo'hai giggled. "Have a wall painted. Add some color. Anything."

"Like what?"

"How about painting..." She pointed at one of the living room walls. "That one a nice deep shade of purple."

David forced himself not to burst out laughing, though he couldn't help but smirk. "It would be against good order and discipline to do such a thing. I must maintain military standards."

"And your apartment?"

"Is just as bland."

"You lead a regimented life, do you not?"

"That's kind of the military's thing. In some ways, it's the point. From boot camp all the way up. The idea is to ensure in a stressful situation, we know what to do because it's muscle memory."

Bo'hai tilted her head. "Does that not stifle free thought?"

"You get your ability to think back, one rank at a time." David had often heard the joke from Marines but had never had the occasion to deploy himself.

"I see." She chuckled before taking another bite. "This meal is delicious. Thank you."

"Thank *you* for joining me and making it memorable."

She finished off her filet with a flourish. "When can we have this again?"

"Next month."

Bo'hai giggled. "Is something wrong?"

"That obvious, huh?"

"No, but I can tell when you are troubled. I assume something with the Mifreen?"

David blew out a breath. "We've developed some new information about them, and their netsim. I'll be... examining it in person tomorrow morning."

"Without the government's knowledge?"

"Yes." David put his hands on the table. "Risky, but I decided it's worth it."

"Are you going to tell me the particulars?"

David shook his head. "No. Not until I know more. Act like nothing has changed with their people, should you interact with them."

Bo'hai peered at him. "Isn't it unusual for you to leave the *Lion of Judah*?"

"It's rare, but I don't think I'd say unusual. Some things call for my direct involvement."

She frowned. "You are making light of the risk."

"Risk is everywhere," David replied quietly. "It's part of being a soldier. It's who I am. But I try to manage the risk, for what it's worth."

Bo'hai put her hand on top of his. "I sense something wrong here too."

"I'm trying not to let my natural unease with the idea of wiring sentient beings into simulations get the better of me. Regardless of whether we agree, the Mifreen have every right to do what they want on their planet."

"Then why the clandestine meeting?"

David met her eyes. "Because I need the whole story. I don't believe the government has been completely honest. The individual I'll see tomorrow likely won't be either. Perhaps if I put those two accounts together, I can triangulate the truth or at least get closer to it."

"Are you contemplating something more?"

Sitting back, he ran his teeth over his lip. *Am I?* He wanted the knowledge of what was going on down on Mifreen but wasn't sure what came next. *Well, aside from we won't be getting our people involved in their netsim if there's something nefarious about it.* "Not yet."

"You believe in acting against injustice."

David sighed. "There's a debate back home about what role the Terran Coalition should play on the galactic stage, if you will. It's usually framed as whether or not we should be the galaxy's policeman. Some believe we should stick to our own problems. Others say we should involve ourselves whenever there is injustice, be it on human-controlled worlds or one of the various alien races."

"What do you say, David?"

"As you put it, I detest injustice. Whenever I see it, my first instinct is to correct the problem. Part of the challenge is that human perspectives don't apply to every other species. But some things I believe are universal. And if it were up to me and me alone, I would act against injustice wherever I found it."

"Have you done this in the past?"

David nodded. "Almost got myself court-martialed too."

She stared at him, transfixed. "How?"

"We came across a planet systematically executing people of faith who wouldn't renounce their beliefs. The government planned to join the League of Sol. That was a requirement." David's face twisted. "I joined an unconventional military effort along with several of my officers to help end that abomination."

"And you disobeyed your orders?"

"Yes."

"Would you do it again?"

"Absolutely." David set his jaw. "And without hesitation. It was the right thing to do. When you find innocents being dumped into mass graves... There is one thing a soldier *can* do. Use whatever force is required to stop the slaughter."

Bo'hai smiled. "I adore that about you."

Surprised, David blinked. "Why?"

"Because doing what's right, even when it costs you, is such a rare quality on my world these days."

"Sadly, it's a rare quality on *any* world. But don't put me on a pedestal, dear. I'm just as capable of making mistakes, even horrible ones, as anyone else."

Justice 117

"Perhaps." She squeezed his hand. "Shall we go sit together before I must leave?"

"How about a walk through the observation area on deck three instead?"

"I'd love to." Bo'hai stood.

David did as well and put the empty plates back in the kitchen area. "Shall we?"

She intertwined her arm with his. "Yes."

As they strode out of his cabin, David already dreaded their parting. He felt drawn to her and enjoyed every minute of their time together. *Is this love?* While he wasn't quite sure, it sure seemed to be heading in that direction.

———

IN HIS CUBBYHOLE of an office in Marine country, Calvin let out a yawn. Master Gunnery Sergeant Reuben Menahem, his senior enlisted Marine and right-hand man, had joined him to pick a platoon of their best for the upcoming mission to the planet's surface—that and shoot the breeze. It felt nice to share time with other Marines, especially those who'd seen a lot of combat.

"Can't believe I'm about to say this, but I miss our partner forces on Zeivlot," Menahem said after taking a sip of the dark-brown whiskey Calvin had served when they'd started more than an hour ago.

"Yeah, I've been wondering about them too. That commando we worked with... Ozkek. The real deal."

Menahem snickered. "Couldn't drink brandy for anything, though."

"None of them could." Calvin roared with laughter. "But being back on the *Lion* is nice. No worrying about some two-bit asshole suicide bomber taking us out, at least."

"No, now the dangers are nanites and random alien species," Menahem replied. "I didn't sign up for the Far Survey Corps, sir."

"You know the drill, Master Guns. Water isn't flexible enough for this job."

"Quite aware," Menahem grumbled. "Got any thoughts on this sim thing? All the snipes won't quit talking about how cool the tech is. I had to go to a different mess to get away from the blathering."

Calvin laughed again before taking a swig of brandy. "Now, you know those comms geeks. They love that stuff. Probably figure they could actually talk to women or something in a sim."

Menahem nearly spit out his drink. "Yeah, I'm sure. Still, it's an interesting concept, you know? Something so real that it *is* real, at least to your mind."

"Not my cup of whiskey."

"I can see why it would be appealing to some." Menahem shook his head. "Frankly, sir... I'm ready to go home. This see-the-new-galaxy stuff is not my cup of whiskey, to borrow your line."

"Trust me, Master Guns. I get it. I've got a child at home that I don't even know the name of." Calvin bit his lip. "Dammit. Too old for this crap."

"But as long as we're here, the general seems to be intent on doing what's right."

"I get the sense you might disagree with his actions."

"You know there's a lot of debate about interventions in other worlds' affairs back home. I tend more toward wanting to watch out for Terrans first, and I have a healthy distaste for politicians who waste the lives of Marine and soldiers without understanding the cost of war."

"Cohen doesn't have that problem."

Justice 119

"No, and frankly, the only reason I respect his decisions so far is that of all of us, the general has borne the cost more than most men or women alive today."

Calvin pursed his lips. His friend made a good argument. At times, the grunts on the ground seemed to pay the price, while the political types and the brass took the glory. That never mattered in a war for survival, but with the League conflict out of the way, times were different. *I wonder how they're doing back home. Has the peace held?* "I need to know you're at one hundred twenty percent for this mission."

Menahem eyed him before setting his drink down. "Whatever I may think about our actions, when I'm in the field, the only concern I've got is for the Marines to my right and to my left. In the end, that's what we fight for. Our brothers and sisters. Period."

Calvin grasped Menahem's arm. "Amen to that, brother. Whaddaya say we get some shut-eye?"

"Sounds like a plan, sir." Menahem grinned. "Us old men need beauty sleep before shooting up aliens or whatever else comes our way."

Calvin snickered. "I hate hearing it, but you're right, Master Guns."

12

MASTER CHIEF REBECCA TINETARIRO took a long drink of coffee in the crisp morning air of Zeivlot. It tasted good, even though it was standard-issue CDF brew. She had a minimal supply remaining and savored every drop of it. Her bones and half the muscles in both legs hurt. *I forgot how demanding boot camp is, not only for recruits but even more so for the instructors.* At least they'd seemed to learn their lesson about making noise and fighting after lights out.

But even with the harsh discipline imposed by Tinetariro and her compatriots, the twin species of trainees had yet to jell with one another. Even one helping the other was a minor miracle. So she'd reconfigured the main obstacle course while they slept. An evil grin crossed her face. *Let's see them do that without help.*

Once reveille sounded and the drill instructors loudly woke their charges, it took another half an hour for the recruits to form up, following showers and a quick breakfast. They assembled in the parade ground, and Tinetariro marched up and down the neat rows.

"It is clear to me that you have not yet accepted the

Justice 121

lesson I am attempting to teach. You *will* learn it, or none of you will leave this boot camp as a member of the Coalition Defense Force." She stopped and got two inches from a female recruit's face. "*What is that lesson?*"

"To work together, ma'am."

"If you understand that's what I want, why aren't you *doing* it, recruit?"

"Permission to speak freely, ma'am?"

"Sound off!"

"Because Zavlots cannot be trusted, ma'am!"

It took every ounce of self-control Tinetariro possessed not to slap the woman. "Until you break this disgusting mindset, you will not succeed. Nor will you be able to defend your home worlds from the imminent threat of destruction!" Raw fury coursed through her veins.

Tinetariro paused before taking a step backward. "Fall in! Morning run, ladies!" she barked, painfully aware of how close her voice was to giving out. *I suppose I'm still rusty and have gotten too used to life in the fleet.* A smile wanted to creep onto her face, but she suppressed it. *That will change.*

Over the next hour, Tinetariro and the rest of the DIs led a run over ten kilometers with full packs on. The trek was designed to be as grueling as possible. The endpoint was directly in front of the obstacle course, which began with a wooden tower with the CDF logo emblazoned on it. Under normal conditions, a recruit would be expected to climb over the tower by him- or herself.

Not today.

Tinetariro's nighttime modifications removed the ability for anyone to get onto the planks by themselves. Instead, a boost from another recruit was required. She waited for the stragglers to catch up before positioning herself in front of the structure.

"You will start this morning with a climb. Notice it *will* take assistance to begin. You will only take help from a different species. No Zeivlot will help another Zeivlot. Only Zavlots, and vice versa. Now *move!*"

The drill instructors lined each species up and barked orders at them to advance, one from each queue, to begin the course.

Each line stared at the other like they had the plague. Despite screaming and shouting in both ears from multiple sets of DIs, the recruits froze in what was among the oddest sights that Tinetariro had seen. Treating others differently because of their race, gender, skin color, or creed made no sense. Observing sentient beings do it was even more puzzling.

Tinetariro held up her hand, silencing the other CDF soldiers. "All right. Since you won't even *touch* one another, anyone unwilling to help a nonmember of their species begin the course, fall out!"

Immediately, dozens of Zeivlots and Zavlots melted out of the line.

"Commence course!" Tinetariro screamed, and the handful of recruits who remained in the queue gamely moved forward.

Not even bothering to watch, she turned her attention to the milling aliens, who separated into two groups—one Zeivlot, one Zavlot. "Since you refused to follow my orders, now you will be punished," Tinetariro rasped.

She took a few steps forward and positioned herself roughly in the center between the two masses. "Two hundred pushups starting now! Drop down!"

As the recruits rushed to comply, Tinetariro continued, "Once we finish this, you will complete another ten-kilometer run. If you will not work together after that, we will *keep* doing this until you comply, or I will throw you out of my boot camp. *Do you get me?*"

"Ma'am, yes, ma'am!"

"Start pushing! One, two, three, four, I love the Coalition Defense Force!"

It's going to be an exceedingly long day.

13

SLEEP HAD BEEN SURPRISINGLY easy to fall into once David parted from Bo'hai in the *Lion of Judah*'s observation deck. The space was part garden, part deep-space viewing area in the center of the vessel on deck three. He'd always wondered why it had been installed on a military vessel and figured Dr. Hayworth or another highly placed civilian had something to do with it. And while he rarely visited the garden, it was one of the most popular places on the ship for off-duty personnel to congregate.

The next morning, David had risen bright and early, completing his usual exercise-and-hygiene ritual before reporting to the hangar deck. They'd timed the launch for a period where tracking by the Mifreen would be at a minimum level, based on the *Lion*'s orbit and the specifications provided by the individual who'd previously made contact. *Whose name we still don't know.*

As the shuttle hurtled toward the greenish-blue orb at an angle of approach and speed that pressed everyone into their seats with the force of at least three Gs, David gritted

Justice 125

his teeth. "We need some better inertial dampers on these things."

"Aw, this is the fun part," Calvin replied from beside him. "The pain is how you know you're *living*, sir."

"Let me guess. Pain is weakness leaving the body, right, Colonel?"

"Got it in one, sir."

David smirked. "There's a reason I'm not a Marine."

"We've got a rifle with your name on it anytime you're ready to upgrade, sir."

Calvin and a few of the other Marines laughed.

"I'll keep that in mind."

Talking became even more difficult as the g-force ticked up higher, right before the craft pulled out of the steep dive and executed a textbook nap-of-the-planet approach vector.

David admired the warrant officer's skill in piloting the shuttle and let out a breath as they finally leveled off.

"I believe our tray tables can be put down, and it's time for the in-flight meal," Menahem said, prompting another wave of chuckles.

"Don't get too comfy, Master Guns," Calvin replied. "We've got ourselves yet another alien planet to explore."

With an entire platoon of Marines, including a heavy-weapons element, David noted they had left nothing to chance. They all wore full power armor as well. If he was walking into a trap, at least they had a decent amount of firepower.

It took another twenty minutes before the shuttle settled down with a thud. The rear cargo hatch opened, and sunlight spilled in.

David started to push off his seat, but Calvin put his hand on his shoulder. "Sir, let my team sweep first. Just to be safe."

"Of course." David inclined his head. Though he knew Calvin was looking out for him, he still hated to bring up the rear.

"Let's go, ladies!" Calvin yelled.

The Marine platoon smoothly disengaged their restraints and, like a wave on the ocean, flowed out of the shuttle. Eight went right and the others, left.

A few minutes later, David's commlink beeped. "All clear out here, sir."

He stood and exited the craft.

The scene before him was one of pure beauty. The contrast to the drab cityscapes was so startling that David wondered if they had somehow been transported to a different planet. A massive forest stretched out about a kilometer away. The trees in it towered over the landscape while the call of animals echoed. It reminded David of the vast forests and fields back on New Israel.

"Gotta admit this isn't a bad-looking place," Calvin said as he appeared at David's side.

"It's so different from their capital."

"That place was dull and lifeless. I've seen League worlds with more character." That said something, given that Calvin had participated in the liberation of multiple border planets settled by the League of Sol in the Orion spur.

"Colonel, we've got something over here," Menahem called over his commlink.

David, while not wearing power armor, had an integrated earpiece to plug into the Marine's tactical network. He and Calvin moved over to where the senior NCO was standing. "Whatcha got, Master Guns?"

Menahem held up a piece of printed paper.

To David's amazement, it had English block writing on

it. *Proceed west, 3.1 kilometers.* A string of numbers was listed after that.

"Those coordinates feed into our GPS system perfectly," Menahem said. "And match up with a location about three kilometers away."

Calvin grunted. "Okay, am I the only one who finds this a bit spooky?"

"Whatever tech level the Mifreen have, it's clearly superior to ours when it comes to offensive and defensive network intrusion." David blew out a breath. "Well, we're taking a hike, gents."

"Sir, I don't think that's a good idea," Calvin replied. "At least let us scout the area first then come get you."

David shook his head. "No. We're on the clock. You know that as well as I do. Any second, Mifreen forces, whatever those are, could appear here. I have no interest in causing a military incident. Leave two Marines to post security at the shuttle, and the rest of us will go to the indicated coordinates."

"If something happens to you—"

"Colonel Aibek will carry on," David replied quietly, as he didn't want the entire platoon to hear him. "And if you think I'm planning on dying in some ambush on an alien planet, all I can say is they'd better have brought an army, because we'll fight our way out."

"You seem to have forgotten that flag rank, sir, because you're still doing the John Wayne stuff."

David chuckled. The Marines had something of a fascination with an actor from old Earth called John Wayne. He starred in numerous films called Westerns that, again for reasons David didn't quite understand, were considered mandatory viewing for all members of the TCMC. "Let's move out."

"Privates Rubenstein and Suthorn, take positions on either side of the shuttle. Alert us to any movement, and you are fully authorized to engage anything that looks remotely suspicious. Clear?"

"Sir, yes, sir!" Suthorn barked.

"Squads, bound overwatch," Menahem said. "Move forward."

Power-armored Marines fanned out, four to the front, four on either side, and two taking up the rear. David knew enough about infantry tactics to realize they were trying to avoid bunching up. *And making themselves an attractive target for heavy or indirect weapons.*

The small formation took less than five minutes to enter the forest. When they did, it seemed like someone had turned down the lights. The canopy was incredibly dense and cast long shadows over the ground, which was highly overgrown with scrub brush.

Though there wasn't much of a path, it was better than nothing. David and Calvin kept to it, while the Marines pushed ahead.

On they went for another kilometer before Calvin raised a fist. "Sir, I'm showing we've lost all tactical links to the shuttle."

"Any signs of nonanimal life?"

Calvin shook his head. "Nothing on our movement sensors, and everything on infrared is clearly nonhumanoid."

"Okay. Let's keep going, then. More than halfway there."

"Yes, sir." Calvin pumped his hand forward twice, and the advance resumed.

David felt as if each step he made was measured. A twig snapping in the distance echoed loudly. *There could be a hundred hostiles in here, using some sort of stealth tech.* Rumor

Justice 129

was that CIS and other clandestine agencies had access to such things back in the Milky Way. *Regardless,* we *don't have it.* Onward the Marines trudged through the thick undergrowth before finally cresting a small ridge.

A tent and the remains of a fire sat in a cleared area no larger than ten square meters.

David went up to the tent to find it empty. "Hmmm." He turned three hundred sixty degrees, observing. "Okay! We're here!" he yelled. "If you're present, whoever you are, now's the time. Otherwise, we're heading back."

———

BAL RIWALD MARKUL felt a sense of power as he stood five meters away from the alien beings in their alloy armor and black-coated rifles, unseen and unheard. It was similar to how sneaking into networks and nosing around undetected felt, except for the adrenaline rushing through his body. *I suppose it's time to end the charade.* He touched his wrist, and the shimmer field fell away.

Moments later, fourteen weapons pointed at Markul's center mass.

"Hands up! Reach for anything, and you're dead!"

Markul smiled as he turned his palms outward and slowly raised them. "I mean you no harm, Colonel Demood."

The power-armored figure took a step forward. "How the hell do you know my name and rank?"

"Header files on your transmission packets contain all that and more." He shifted his gaze to the only human not wearing the brightly polished alloy armor. "Major General David Cohen, commanding officer of the CSV *Lion of Judah*?"

"The one and only," David replied with a grin. "Demood, search this individual."

"Yes, sir."

Calvin took a step forward and roughly patted Markul down. "No weapons I can see."

"I actually don't believe in violence."

David tilted his head. "Oh? And why not?"

"Because it's so inelegant. If I resort to hurting people with physical force, I haven't thought hard enough about how to defeat them otherwise." Markul smirked. "Besides, I enjoy seeing defeat on my foe's faces."

"Do you have a name?"

"You can't pronounce it. But in English, what my friends call me roughly translates as Riwald Markul."

"So we're friends?"

"We could be." Markul waved his hands. "May I put my arms down now?"

David nodded. "Now, start talking, and tell us why we're here."

"Oh, that's simple, General. The government toadies can't hear what we're saying all the way out here, and if you followed my instructions, they don't even know you're here. You did follow them?"

"To the letter." David crossed his arms. "Keep going."

"Have you entered the netsim yet?"

David shook his head. "No. Your government has suggested we should try it out, though."

"I'd strongly recommend you avoid that."

"Why?"

"Because it's... What's the word you use? Ah, yes, addictive. People who enter the netsim rarely break free of it." He shrugged. "Why would they want to? It's perfection, especially compared to our horrifically dreary existence."

Justice

"Not according to your government."

Markul snickered. "Why would they tell the truth? Everything they do is centered around keeping the netsim functional. Life outside it is made to be so awful that no one in their right mind would want to do anything else but get to the promised land."

David gestured to the trees around them. "This forest doesn't seem to be awful, nor did the field we landed in."

"Did you not notice there were no Mifreen around in any direction? No buildings, no people, no infrastructure at all."

"Well, yes, but..." David shrugged. "It hit me as a sparsely populated area."

"They don't allow us outside the city walls for our own *protection*." Markul narrowed his eyes. "I don't know how it got started, and I suspect that whoever developed the netsim had decent, perhaps even pure motives. But it ended up as a mechanism to enslave my entire race. Seventy percent of us live in life-support pods, plugged into a never-ending simulation. The rest toil away to keep the others alive and the netsim functional."

"And you?"

"A small number of us know the truth. Those who question authority, seek out unpopular truths, and peer behind the veil. We are hunted and, once captured, killed or adjusted in an education center."

"Adjusted?" Calvin asked.

"Something I wouldn't wish on the most despicable person in the universe. Our technology allows altering the brain on a level that overrides personality. The government uses it to maintain control. The device was initially developed to treat those with severe mental illness and violent criminals."

"There must be those who have no desire to enter the simulation. I fail to see how an entire population could be brainwashed into this." David crossed his arms.

"I examined some of human history, General. Quite colorful. You know what propaganda is. You have all sorts of different words for it, yes?"

"We do."

"My world lives under an oppressive quilt of nonstop propaganda. Anyone who deviates from what is expected of them is an enemy of the state. Individuals and small groups sneak out of the cities and away from the agrifarms. They're tracked down and altered. Their very existence is used to justify the continued state of fear we live in. It is a vicious cycle."

David licked his lips. "There's an ask in there somewhere. You didn't bring us all this way just to explain how awful your government is."

"Quite perceptive, General Cohen. But I wouldn't have thought anything less after examining your service history. It's pretty simple. I want the Terran Coalition to help us leave this world. Me and anyone else who wishes to be free. I examined your database and know there are other habitable worlds we can exist on in this galaxy."

He stood back, awaiting the reply. In truth, Markul had little reason to believe the humans would help them, but he still had a few cards to play in the great game. *Ones that only I hold. Let us see who is the better player.*

14

———

FEW TIMES in David Cohen's life had he been genuinely surprised. Standing in the middle of a forest on an alien world, being asked for what amounted to political asylum by a member of said alien race, counted as one of them. He stared at the humanoid being. Mifreen were far hairier than humans and had unique facial features. The indentations between their eyes made him wonder if they'd had three eyes at some point.

"You can't be serious."

"It's a perfectly reasonable request under Terran Coalition law. Your species seems to have robust protections for refugees."

David thought briefly of the debates around immigration and how they still raged within the Coalition. "For those fleeing persecution, yes."

"Is what I described not the very definition of that word, General?"

"Perhaps. But I cannot take one man's word, even if the argument comes off as sincere. We've seen no evidence of *anything* you claim except that the cities are drab. And frankly, the government officials we met with came across as believable. If you want anything from us, I need *proof*."

What troubled David more than anything was he sensed Markul was being truthful, at least from *his* perspective. *But so did Hes Sansan. They all think they're right.* He wondered how an alien species unknown to the Milky Way would've viewed the Coalition-versus-League war.

"Yes, of course," Markul replied. "I can take you to underground settlements where Mifreen live their lives as best as they can freely. Lots of subsistence farming and many controls to avoid government patrols. Perhaps you could bring a doctor to help treat injuries?"

David stared at him, pondering whether involving himself and the *Lion*'s crew in a situation that sounded like a low-level civil war was a good idea. *If I'm not willing to help innocent people caught up in what has been described or at least figure out what's true, I don't deserve to wear my uniform.* "Can you get us in without being detected?"

Markul nodded. "Yes, I believe so."

"You *believe* so?"

"The government forces get lax. They think they're smarter than the rest of us because of the netsim."

David chuckled. "And you can get lax too."

"Never. I have to execute to perfection every time."

"They only need to be lucky once." David bit his lip. "Okay. Send instructions to the *Lion of Judah*. We'll do the same thing—come down in a stealthed Marine assault shuttle with a nap-of-the-planet approach."

"Thank you, General."

"Don't thank me yet. You've got a long way to go. I'd also work on some hard, data-driven proof if I were you."

Markul pursed his lips. "I'll bring some of my personal

database with me when we meet again. Though you haven't asked what we're willing to do for you as of yet."

David raised an eyebrow. "I don't tie asylum to payment."

"Ask Dr. Hayworth if use of the netsim quantum computer would help speed up his current line of research."

"I'll do that. Now, we're getting out of here before your government figures out something's up."

"A most prudent thought."

David chuckled. "I assume you have your own transport?"

"Quite."

"Then I bid you a good day, Markul."

"May you remain safe on your journey." Markul turned and took a few steps into the forest before the cloaking field reengaged.

Calvin grunted. "That's freaking spooky, sir."

"The whole thing is," David replied. "Let's keep it buttoned up and get back to the shuttle."

"Yes, sir."

Their trip out didn't take as long as the hike in. While the Marines kept alert for any threats, the combat anticipation had lowered. The entire time, David's mind raced with different scenarios and solutions to what had transpired. *Is it possible the Mifreen government is testing us somehow?* He also considered that Markul had lied about everything and was a terrorist. The lack of data prevented much in the way of conclusions.

Once everyone was back on the shuttle and strapped in, it quickly lifted off and matched the course and speeds of before.

Calvin flipped up the faceplate of his helmet. "So, whatcha make of that, sir?"

"I've been thinking on it the entire walk back." David shook his head. "I hate not knowing all the variables of a problem. In mathematics, it makes things nearly impossible to solve. The same is true for real life. You can often fill in the blanks, but that requires guesswork. Now, what did you think of Mr. Markul?"

"Anyone with a freaking personal stealth field is suspicious." Calvin blew out a breath. "I find the concept of plugging yourself into a computer for life insane, though. So I'm probably more inclined to take him at face value."

"Filtering out how we view the universe when dealing with a new species with different cultural norms than us is... difficult."

"I don't care what species you are. Intermeshing organic beings with machines opens Pandora's box," Menahem interjected.

"The Mifreen clearly don't agree," David replied dryly.

"Are we going to help them, sir?" Calvin asked.

David licked his lips. "It's not that simple, and you know it. We need more information before *any* decisions can be made."

"But if he's telling the truth?"

"Then I couldn't look at myself in the mirror in this uniform without doing something about it," David replied. "But that doesn't mean we have to jump to an invasion. There are diplomatic options. Perhaps the Mifreen would be happy to let us take the problem off their hands."

Calvin nodded. "I guess we'll see."

David didn't reply as the shuttle pitched upward, heading nearly vertically into the atmosphere. The g-force pressed him back into his chair, and he counted the minutes until they returned to the *Lion of Judah*. Another series of unpleasant meetings awaited.

Justice 137

———

Meetings and discussions were daily facts of life, ones that David didn't care for. He appreciated action and wasn't interested in endless bloviation about a topic. However, since they'd gotten to Sextans B, he'd spent more time talking than at any point in his career. *I suppose it goes with the territory. We're no longer prosecuting an interstellar war.*

So the afternoon had gone once he'd returned from Mifreen. After a few hours and a sparse dinner, David ended up at the shul.

Chiding himself for not making the evening prayers, he was heartened to see the light on in Rabbi Kravitz's cubbyhole of an office. David knocked on the hatch after making his way over.

"Come in!" Kravitz boomed.

David stuck his head in to see it just as cluttered as ever. "Good evening, Rabbi. Got a minute?"

"For a fellow Jew? Always." Kravitz smiled and gestured to the one chair that wasn't covered in papers, scrolls, or electronic devices.

"Thanks." David slid into the seat and tugged his uniform down.

"What's on your mind?"

"I assume you heard about my trip to the surface?"

"The clandestine meeting?" Kravitz cracked a grin. "There's all sorts of theories floating around."

David snorted. "I'm sure the RUMINT mill is in high gear."

"As always."

"Remember that joke about how the only thing two Jews can agree on is what a third should give to charity?"

Kravitz chuckled. "A classic."

"That applies to the *Lion*'s senior staff right now." David blew out a breath. "I'm not used to this level of discord and turmoil. Dr. Hayworth, as always, has valid points about staying out of other societies' business and minding our own."

"But?"

"But something is off here. I feel it in my bones. And at the end of the day, only one person makes decisions around here. Me."

"I'm glad you understand that and the responsibility that comes with it."

"Yes, I own the mistakes too." David grimaced. "I wish there were some way for me to *know* what the right call is. Because there are so many ways this can go sideways. And at the same time, these Mifreen have technology that could help us defeat the nanites. I'll give Markul credit—he planted the exact right seed in my mind by letting that slip."

Kravitz tilted his head. "In what way?"

"The quantum computing technology that underpins the netsim thing. It can crunch insane amounts of data. And one of the problems the doctor is having is developing a weapon to disrupt the bonds between the nanites, which being able to run millions of simulations in a short time would help solve."

"And let me guess—the price for access is our help?"

David nodded.

"Sounds like blackmail to me."

"Or a desperate man using anything he can to help his people."

Kravitz pursed his lips. "That, too, is possible."

"I'd give almost anything to know what HaShem wants me to do."

"Well, you're asking the right question. But you don't

Justice

need me to tell you that God doesn't send us bright-neon signs with directions."

David shook his head. "No. That'd be easy."

"So it's incumbent upon us to seek His word and scour it for guidance. Remember, where no counsel is, the people fall, but in a multitude of counselors, there is safety."

"Proverbs, chapter eleven, verse fourteen."

"You were paying attention when you attended your rabbinical studies for a few months."

"More than that, Rabbi. I seek to emulate that verse in my leadership style. No yes men, and diversity of thought in every important decision." David sighed. "I still feel like I'm flying by the seat of my pants here."

"So are we all. If I may say so, you've made the correct choice far more than the wrong one."

"Yet I need to be right every time. Otherwise, my crew pays the price."

"Only HaShem can do that. You are fallible."

I know I am. But I can't show it, not right now. Rather than argue the point further, David only smiled. "Of course."

"Would you like to pray with me?"

"Very much so, Rabbi."

"Then let us."

As they both spoke in Hebrew, peace washed over David in what was one of the few times lately he could still experience the feeling. *That and when I'm with Salena.* He thanked God for the blessings of both.

15

CSV *Salinan*
Low Zeivlot Orbit
22 October 2464

MAJOR JOHN WILSON lifted his coffee mug, which was emblazoned with the CDF logo as well as the *Salinan*'s, and took a sip. Every fiber in his body wanted to immediately spit it out, as whatever the stuff was called, it wasn't coffee. A concoction of some Zavlot plant that supposedly tasted like the real thing, it had made its way across the quartermasters of the fleet. *I suppose I should count my blessings because however bad it tastes, it's got a chemical in it equivalent to caffeine.*

They had spent the last week training Zeivlots on the finer details of zero-G construction techniques as fabrication plants spit out truss materials. Wilson had been impressed with how quickly the government and private industry came together to retool manufacturing systems and assembly lines. It helped that they had 3-D printers, though they were far more rudimentary than Terran Coalition designs. He understood transfer of technology there was in progress too.

"Conn, Communications. Ground control is reporting the first shuttle is headed up from the surface."

Wilson nodded and turned to his executive officer, Captain Binota Khattri. "Make sure our new friends and Senior Chief Stokes are ready."

"Aye, aye, sir."

The first step would be to offload the shuttle's cargo while exposed to the vacuum of space and lock the truss sections into place. With sixteen personnel forming two work crews, thirty minutes ought to be enough time to install one load, but Wilson had budgeted an hour for the first run, just in case. His schedule was ambitious but necessarily so. The goal was to create shipyards capable of serving as drydocks for a vessel the size of an Ajax-class destroyer. To get there in any reasonable amount of time, they would construct several feeder platforms to fabricate alloys in orbit rather than ship them up from the surface. Those alloys would form the outer shells of the shipyards and, later on, the hull of the ships they meant to build.

Wilson watched through the external cameras and sensor systems as the shuttle appeared on their scopes before coming in for a picture-perfect approach to the small platform. Its cargo pod opened right on cue, and the soft-suited teams went to work.

"They almost look like they're doing it properly," Khattri said with a chuckle. "I see the chief has been drilling his knowledge in."

Wilson snickered. "That's one way of putting it." Stokes

had a well-earned reputation as a hard-charging, direct, and colorful man.

After forty-five minutes, the truss pieces were mostly out of the shuttle, to Wilson's great surprise. One of the teams pulled the last one out and slid it into place. One worker used a plasma torch to quickly weld the structure tight. *Not bad for their first run.* He pressed a button on his chair. "Wilson to Stokes."

"Read you loud and clear, sir."

"Shorter time than I expected, Senior Chief."

"Give me till the end of the day, and we'll beat your precious little Gantt chart, sir."

Wilson smirked. "I'll hold you to that. Having the next shuttle sent up ahead of schedule."

"We'll be ready."

The commlink turned off with a click. Wilson adjusted himself and stretched his neck. "Any critique of their technique?"

Khattri shook his head. "No, pretty textbook. I'm shocked, actually. Maybe this harebrained scheme will actually work."

Wilson snorted. "I suspect the real work is going on down on Zeivlot. Don't envy Master Chief Tinetariro."

"At least we're not down there."

"Amen." Wilson hefted his tablet and marked one line off the project plan. "Comms, tell ground control to get the next shuttle going."

"Aye, aye, sir."

Wilson was sure it was going to be a good day.

Justice   143

DAVID WENT cross-eyed as he stared at a personnel report on his tablet. It had been a little more than a week since the clandestine meeting with Markul on Mifreen. He'd spent much time ruminating on the situation and consulted with his senior officers and Dr. Hayworth. The fact remained that using a quantum computer would accelerate their research. The science team had described it as a game changer.

Competing ethical considerations came down to highly subjective decision points. *But it remains that a government that oppresses and enslaves its people, as Markul described, has no moral legitimacy. But is that the truth? Or are we being played?* Little evidence supported either one, beyond blind statements and a general feeling of unease that David attributed to his bias against putting technology in charge of too many things.

They waited for another contact from Markul, who'd promised to show proof of the situation on Mifreen. At the same time, the government was exerting a great deal of pressure for a human to enter the netsim. So far, he'd kept pushing it off, but the stalling tactics were wearing thin.

David was about to stop and go get a snack when the entry chime for his day cabin went off. "Come!"

The hatch swung open to reveal Ruth. "Do you have a moment, sir?"

"Always," David replied with a smile. He gestured to the seat in front of his desk and adjusted himself, pulling down the black space sweater over his uniform.

Ruth sat, and a frown creased her face. "Sir, I..."

"What's on your mind?" David asked in the most soothing tone he could muster.

"This is going to sound so silly." Ruth twisted her head to look away. "It's about my and Robert's wedding."

"Go on."

Her eyes came back to meet his. "I feel stupid even saying this, with everything that's going on. There're far more important things on our plate than... us."

David shook his head. "Not right now. Now, out with it. You two aren't having trouble, are you?"

"No." Ruth closed her eyes for a second. "I don't know how to go through with a wedding when we're facing the destruction of twelve billion people. It's selfish to even consider."

"Why did you say yes when Taylor proposed?" David thought of his developing relationship with Bo'hai. He'd had some of the same feelings.

"Because I love him and want to spend my life with him. And marriage honors God's word. It is... What's that you like to say, sir? The order of things."

David smiled. "Drop the ranks." He blew out a breath. "All those reasons are valid, good, and positive. None of them are impacted by the ongoing crisis with the nanites or anything else. We can't stop living our lives because of whatever calamity hits today, tomorrow, or two years from now."

"What right do I have to be happy in the face of all this hell?"

"No one has the *right* to be happy. But we do have the right to pursue happiness. I think you both found that in each other, and you have *every* right to be."

"So you think we should go ahead?"

"Absolutely. And while we're on the subject of what others think, I propose that any occasion for joy would give the rest of the crew hope. Certainly not a reason to get married, but it's still a net positive for all of us."

Ruth nodded after a few seconds. "Good advice, sir."

"Tell my mother that one of these days."

They both laughed.

Justice **145**

"Are you... talking to anyone?" David asked.

"As in a counselor?"

"Yes."

Ruth sighed and pushed a stray strand of hair out of her eyes. "Yes... No... Sort of. Ugh. There's a rather long wait—"

"And you want people hurting worse to go first?"

She nodded.

"Nothing wrong with getting some help when it's your turn. None of us are overjoyed about the situation. I think each member of the fleet has to make peace with our lot in his or her own way."

Before Ruth could respond, the desk-mounted intercom buzzed, and Taylor's voice emanated from it. "General, flash traffic, sir, from Markul."

"Put him through."

"Can't, sir. It's text only. Took me a while to figure out the hash. The message is a time and coordinates for what's labeled as a settlement. I plotted it with Lieutenant Hammond's help. Shows a forested area with no life signs within a thousand kilometers."

David gritted his teeth. *I'd have preferred synchronous communication over "Come here."* "Understood, Lieutenant. Pass it on to Colonel Demood with my instructions to prepare two shuttles, Marine forces, and a medical unit."

"Yes, sir."

He touched the disconnect button and pursed his lips. "I'm afraid I'm going to have to cut this short, Ruth. But once I get back, I'm available any time you'd like to talk further."

"Thank you, sir." She stood. "I guess I'd better hunker down and start planning, eh?"

"I know at least one person who will be delighted to hear that." David smiled.

146   DANIEL GIBBS

Ruth seemed to let some of the worries fall off her face. "Me too."

As she exited, David leaned back. *I wish I had more time to offer.* But he had only so much and a correspondingly limited amount of mental energy to give. *At least I have a relationship too. That is a blessing from HaShem.* He put his head down and got back to work.

———

"I DON'T LIKE that you're going back. It was dangerous enough the first time." Bo'hai pushed a strand of purple hair out of her eyes.

David grinned. "And nothing happened."

"You act oblivious to the risks." She took a sip of water. "It's hard for me to understand that."

"Because you're a civilian. And that's okay." David put his hand on hers.

They were in the officers' mess after hours. As usual, he was in the one closest to deck one, which was tradition-ally known as the CO's wardroom, even though that meaning had changed over time. Almost no one was there, and he felt comfortable enough to show some affection in public.

"Does it get easier?"

"For you or me?"

Bo'hai licked her lips. "Both."

"I was trained on how to ignore fear, and I've spent a career honing that training. Because when things get hard, stressful, or when someone is trying to kill me and my crew, I have to react instantly." David squeezed her hand. "It's hard to be the girlfriend, boyfriend, or spouse back home, not knowing if the person you love is coming home. I have

Justice 147

to imagine it's even more difficult, given the close quarters here. It certainly is for me."

"What do you mean?"

"I mean that..." David bit his lip. The subject was one he didn't like to discuss. "I have to think about you too. How do my actions affect you, and as much as humanly possible, I have to push that out of my head."

She put her other hand on top of his. "It is difficult."

"There's a reason why relationships with a deployed serviceman are hard."

"I think we are worth it," Bo'hai replied with a bright smile. "Don't you?"

"Yes." The depth of his feelings for her surprised him. Ever since admitting he had them, David felt as if they were turning into a flood. It was the most unusual sensation and one he had to push down at times, because the mission came first.

"Will you tell me one thing?"

"If I can." David winked. "No classified info."

She made a show of rolling her eyes. "Why do you insist on going down there?"

"Because I need to know."

"What will knowing if what Markul told you is true do?"

"I'll have to figure out if we're going to help them. And it will be challenging to walk away if what he said to us is accurate. Dr. Hayworth believes the quantum computer the Mifreen use to run their netsim is vital to our efforts to figure out a weapon to use against the nanites. I think Markul is aiming to do a trade. We evac his people in exchange for a back door into that system."

"What will you do?"

"I don't know yet. There's too much unknown to make a moral decision." David shook his head. "On a lighter note, did Ruth teach you how to roll your eyes even more outrageously?"

Bo'hai giggled. "She might have helped." Her smile faded. "I don't envy your position."

"It's a lonely one."

"Perhaps not as much as it was."

"No." David stood and switched sides of the table to put his arm around her. "Nowhere near."

She snuggled into him. "I will pray for you and the others."

David kissed the top of her head. "Thanks. We need all the help we can get."

16

DA'HAF HAS'RAD WIPED his brow and felt wetness across his entire palm. After three hours of exhausting nonstop PT, he and every other recruit were about to collapse into the mud. It had rained overnight, and the dusty trails had become a swirling mass of soft brown soil that caked everyone's boots all the way up to midcalf.

The experience reminded Has'rad of his first trip through boot camp, which had been grueling and many cycles long, more than ten rotations ago. He'd signed on to the CDF for one reason: to defend their home world against the approaching nanite threat. The decision had been easy because after ten years of continuous military service, he was dedicated to protecting his people and their way of life.

But he was suddenly questioning the choice. After weeks of human-led training, he was still treated like a raw recruit. Though that was galling, far more serious was how the Coalition Defense Force seemed to expect them to work side by side with Zavlots.

After all, they had tried to destroy his planet within the previous year. They'd wiped out Zeivlot several times before, so it was challenging to look at one and see anything but the enemy. Has'rad didn't actively hate every Zavlot, but he certainly didn't want to have to put his life in the hands of someone from the race that would kill them all if they could.

How the humans couldn't accept that the two groups were better off not mixing was a surprise to Has'rad. Surely they had encountered another species that was not worth associating with. Yet all he heard from Master Chief Tinetariro was how the Terran Coalition treated everyone respectfully and that humanity had few divisions based on religion, race, color, or creed. It sounded like a fairy tale.

Has'rad stared at the small, squat building in front of him. Made of the same sort of polymer as most of the training camp, it had no markings on the outside to denote what it was used for.

Tinetariro and the other DIs had marched them to the location after completing another leg of the obstacle course. She stood at the front of the formation. "All right, ladies! After shaking out your legs and getting warmed up this morning, you have a new activity. We're going to show you how to use standard-issue CDF protective gear to begin your training for on-ship incidents. Any hazard is critical on a warship in the void and *will* threaten the entire vessel. Even something as simple as a nonflammable gas leak. In this chamber, you will be trained on the proper use of CDF respirators. You will not leave until you pass. Fall out!"

It took a while for each group of ten recruits to cycle through the building. Has'rad was in the fourth group and figured it would be a cakewalk. After all, such things were done by their militaries as well. Learning how to use protective gear and sustaining MOPP—Mission Oriented Protective Posture—levels for an extended period was required during basic training.

Has'rad entered when his group was called, two human DIs screaming "encouragement" in their ears as they jogged into the chamber. They all wore full-face-encasing gas masks with red tubes attached to either side, and the devices also covered both ears.

"This is a standard-issue CDF R-38 respirator. I know what everyone in here is thinking. 'I've served for decades. I can use a gas mask.' This is no regular gas mask, ladies," Tinetariro rasped. "This device is designed to protect you from smoke, toxic chemicals, and complete pressure loss in a spacecraft."

Over the next five minutes, she drilled them on how to use the device and had a DI demonstrate toggling the modes twice. Then Tinetariro held up two small oblong-shaped grenades. "These contain CS gas, a tearing agent that will cause immense discomfort if inhaled or gotten in the eyes. Don masks!"

Has'rad reached for the R-38 respirator and strapped it over his head, carefully ensuring a hard seal over his ears and face. Clouds of white gas dispersed, making it difficult to see. He breathed in and out, thankful that he'd gotten the use of the device right.

The Zavlot next to him wasn't so lucky. The man bent over, coughing and heaving.

Serves him right for not paying attention.

"Help me, please!" he called between coughing attacks. The Zavlot tried to refit the mask several times but couldn't seem to get it right. His cries became more erratic.

Has'rad stared at him and knew that taking joy in the man's pain simply because of his species was horrible. All the bitterness and rage poured out of him. *I talk about how awful they are for destroying our world. But if I won't help a man whose lungs are burning, the Maker would also condemn me to the fiery pit.* Has'rad knelt and quickly refitted the respirator. One of the rubber pieces had flipped on the mask's interior, breaking the seal. He snapped it back into place and toggled the O2 purge.

The Zavlot, whose name he'd never bothered to learn, stared up at him in shock and relief. "Thank you, brother."

"Get away from that recruit!" one of the DIs screamed. "Address your own equipment only!"

Tinetariro made a small gesture with her right hand. Immediately, the human stepped back.

As if following Has'rad's example, several others helped their fellows, and shortly, every mask in the chamber was fitted correctly.

"Now! Some of you have already experienced the gas. The rest of you will learn how to put your mask back on and purge it in an emergency."

Has'rad prepared to carry out the next set of orders, which would undoubtedly involve removing the respirator. But that wasn't at the top of his mind. Instead, the feeling that had come over the chamber puzzled him. For the first time, it was as if they saw one another as fellow brothers-and sisters-in-arms. *Why didn't we do this before? Why now?* Perhaps the past didn't matter as long as they got another chance. And while maybe only the ten soldiers in the building would be affected, Has'rad hoped that whatever had happened would spread. *It needs to. Somehow, we have to get over our hate.*

17

THE TRIP down from the *Lion of Judah* through the Mifreen atmosphere was about the same as the first. It resembled an amusement park ride designed to make the participants vomit over the side. David felt glad when it ended, and they rested on terra firma once more. Once the ramp dropped and both shuttles disgorged their contents, he took a moment to take in their surroundings.

Instead of plains abutting a dense forest, the landscape was different. They were in a clearing, and the surrounding trees weren't anywhere near as close together as the area where they'd met Markul. Instead, vegetation was sparser, and it hit David that perhaps limited numbers of crops could be grown as long as the soil was suitable. *As much as it can be, halfway up the side of a mountain.*

As far as the eye could see, only nature was visible. *I'm sure they want it that way.* David strode over to Markul. "We're on the clock. Care to lead the way?"

"With pleasure, General. I want you to see what I've been telling you is the truth."

Something told David that there were multiple layers of the truth regarding that particular individual.

"Got our squad ready to move out, sir," Calvin announced as he advanced, cradling a standard-issue TCMC battle rifle. "Posted a few guys on overwatch, and the other unit is escorting Dr. Tural and his medics."

"Let's go, then. I don't want to be here longer than we need to." David felt the mission was on borrowed time. *Getting caught with our hands in the cookie jar wouldn't be fun.*

"This way," Markul interjected, pointing roughly toward the northeast. "I recognize the tells here."

David gestured. "Proceed." He fell in behind the Mifreen along with Calvin, a couple dozen Marines, and Dr. Tural's group, who joined him and Calvin at the front. "Enjoying the view, Doctor?"

Tural grunted as they began to walk through the underbrush. "I don't get to leave the ship often, so this is a double blessing. First, I'm allowed an opportunity for Allah to use my hands to heal. Second, I can see evidence of His handiwork all around me."

While the *Lion's* chief medical officer and David hadn't become incredibly close friends, he trusted the doctor with his life. David also found his simple, humble nature to be endearing and an ideal to strive for. "Amen to that."

It took them almost an hour to trudge through a virtually unmarked path, following Markul's lead, until signs of a settlement became obvious. Throughout that time, the Marine contingent found no hostiles or electronic monitoring devices. They lost all comms and sensor uplinks to the *Lion of Judah* about halfway in.

The shelters cleverly constructed around trees and natural high spots in the forest were quite ingenious. *They're taking advantage of the geography to avoid water washing out the structures.* Small retaining walls added to the effect along with tiny spinning devices that David assumed generated electricity from the wind. Strategically placed camouflage netting was everywhere.

A female Mifreen appeared from behind a tree, triggering an immediate Marine response. Several of them raised their battle rifles before Markul yelled, "Friendly! Friendly! Don't shoot!"

David raised his hand and made a fist, which Calvin quickly copied. The Marines lowered their weapons, though they kept them at the ready.

The Mifreen woman slowly approached with her hands clearly visible. She wore simple clothing, nothing like the fancy attire seen in the netsim, nor did it resemble what the Mifreen government officials and office workers had worn. The effect reminded David of the Amish or perhaps ultra-Orthodox Jews—very simple, with only two colors and one type of fabric.

"I am Sanwen Ranjan. I lead this settlement."

She spoke in the Mifreen tongue, and David's in-ear device translated. He took a few steps forward and extended his hand. "Major General David Cohen, Coalition Defense Force."

Ranjan inclined her head. "We offer you thanks for agreeing to speak with us. Markul has promised you would help us."

David cleared his throat and glanced at Markul. "That's not entirely accurate, Ranjan. I'm here to assess the situation, and we brought medical supplies to treat your people. Beyond that, the Terran Coalition and my fleet will not involve ourselves in an internal conflict between you and your government. I would have your side of the story, as if were, however. And I'd like to know your take on the netsim."

"Please walk with me." Ranjan gestured farther into the clustered structures.

"Of course. Colonel, post security, and ensure Dr. Tural has a proper escort."

"Yes, sir. Permission to join you afterward?"

I think I can handle myself with a few civilians, but I appreciate his looking after me. "Of course." David turned to Ranjan. "I'll gladly take the nickel tour."

She stared at him. "Nickel tour?"

"Human expression," David replied with a smile. "Lead on."

As they walked through the settlement, it became apparent the inhabitants led a hardscrabble life that was barely above subsistence. Ranjan took great pains to point that out along with the lengths they went to in order to avoid capture by the authorities. She showed him a small stand of crops interspersed among the trees. "We grow enough to feed ourselves and supplement that with animals caught in the forest."

"Why go to all this trouble?" David asked. "The cities I saw didn't appear to be horrible places to live."

"You saw what they wanted you to see, General Cohen." Ranjan clasped her hands together. "The truth is we are...." Whatever word she tried to use didn't translate. "All are forced to maintain the netsim."

David furrowed his brow. "Are you telling me the mass of your population is enslaved?"

"I do not know this word, but we are told what jobs we will work, placed in assigned housing, and given meager rations to eat, and any deviation from our duties is punished harshly."

"Sounds like slavery to me."

"We are told if we work hard enough, we will gain entry into the netsim. Some do. Most don't. But that doesn't matter because it isn't real!" Ranjan's eyes blazed. "All I want for my people and me is a chance at a life where we have the right to make our own choices."

David pursed his lips. "In the Terran Coalition, we place our citizens' freedom above nearly all other considerations. We hold these truths to be self-evident, that all men are created equal, that they are endowed by their Creator with certain unalienable Rights, that among these are Life, Liberty, and the pursuit of Happiness."

"What does this mean?"

"It means you're free to pursue whatever you want out of life, as long as you adhere to the laws of our society."

"Your job isn't dictated to you?"

"No."

"You can take a mate and form a family as you wish?"

"Yes. The food's pretty good too."

Ranjan stared at him. "I cannot conceive of such a place."

Juxtaposing the utopia the Mifreen government promoted as their society and the first-hand account of Ranjan was challenging. However, David detected no deception in her, and that they lived in the middle of a forest, on the side of a mountain, was a strong point in her favor. *I can see how this all went wrong too. It probably started as a positive before morphing into what it is now. History is littered with people who thought if they just had some more power, they could do more good. And the horrible results of that supposed good.*

"How do you manage to avoid the government if it's looking for you constantly?"

"We move every few seasons. Our shelters are made

from an intelligent polymer. It is a simple matter to break them down and reerect elsewhere."

The Coalition doesn't even have that. Liquids that can morph to hold a shape? "Forgive me, but I remain astounded your species hasn't gone into the stars. You have technology that outstrips us... and humans inhabit hundreds of worlds."

"The Mifreen are insular. The only concern we have is the netsim. It is our entire purpose for being." She gestured to the trees. "Rather than come and spend time in a place like this, most of my species would rather be in a simulation of the same. They find it superior."

"Forgive me, but while my first reaction is to say that's insane, it's also not my place to tell the people who prefer the sim that they're inferior." *This entire situation is beyond sticky, to Hayworth's general point about noninterference.*

Ranjan set her jaw. "If it were only a preference, perhaps you'd be right, General. But it isn't. We are forced to either be in the sim or be slaves to those in it. Those are the only two paths you have on Mifreen."

David opened his mouth but didn't find words to come out.

"Follow me." She turned on her heel and marched away.

After a short walk, the two of them ended up at a small structure that resembled an A-frame house. Ranjan pushed the door open and went inside.

David stepped in and glanced around the sparsely decorated room. The entire house, if it could be called that, consisted of two rooms he could see and perhaps a small bathroom area. "You guys don't believe in locks, eh?"

"There is nothing to steal, General. And if someone did such a thing, I would immediately cast them out of the settlement." She stuck her head into what appeared to be a bedroom. "Dabran, come here, please."

Justice 159

A young girl who, by human standards, would've been no older than fifteen, came to the door and peered out at them. Her face was drawn, thin, and discolored, from what David had observed of other Mifreen. Hair poked out of her clothing, and it was all gray or white. Most concerning was the stare in her eyes. She reminded him of a combat veteran who'd been through hell and lived to tell about it.

"She doesn't speak," Ranjan continued. "Or really communicate beyond a few grunts."

"Why?"

"Because this is what happens when the *education* process goes wrong. When the government catches up to us, and it will... they run us through a simulation designed to promote reintegration into society. I haven't experienced it yet, but in a strong-willed individual, this is what happens."

The implications were horrific to David. He'd heard stories of the League experimenting with mind-control devices and knew their reeducation camps were nothing more than torture chambers. But what he was seeing was worse than anything the cruelest commissar could think up. "I... This is disgusting."

"Then help us."

David locked eyes with her. "It's not that simple. I can't declare war on your government. And even if I did, we only have a few ships. I don't know what kind of military force your planet has, but because of your advanced technology, I have a hard time believing we could effect regime change."

"Then take us somewhere else. Anywhere but here."

"No promises, but I'll consider it."

Ranjan inclined her head.

"Let's find Dr. Tural. I'd like to see how he's doing."

"He should be at the clinic. Dabran, you may return to

your room." She gestured toward the exit before walking out.

With a final glance at the girl, David followed. His heart felt heavy, and more than anything, he wanted to do *something* to help.

The medical clinic was yet another polymer structure that again resembled an A-frame. A small crowd of Mifreen stood outside it along with Dr. Tural. As they walked up, he was in the midst of running a bone knitter over the knee of a young boy.

"How's it going, Doctor?" David asked.

Dr. Tural smiled and set the youngster down. "Thankfully, our technology is compatible with their bone structure. I've been able to cure several broken limbs and regenerate a few tendons and ligaments."

David would've thought the doctor was a pop star or something, the way they crowded around him. "Glad to hear it."

"We have blood samples, and I'll be able to tell in a few days if our medicines can be used safely. At least some should be, considering this species is carbon-based and mammalian and has basic characteristics in common with humans."

Calvin jogged up as the doctor finished speaking. "Perimeter is secure, sir."

"How long before we're ready to pack it in?"

"Another thirty minutes should be fine," Dr. Tural replied.

David turned to Ranjan. "Then let's wrap up. I don't want to draw any undue attention to your operation here."

"There's not much left beyond our school and a few other general amenities." Her eyes flashed. "We don't have any weapons, and you're welcome to scan the settlement if you don't believe me."

"I appreciate the openness." David gestured to Calvin. "Be thorough."

Ranjan seemed to pull her head up as high as it would go. "Follow me."

———

THE *LION of Judah*'s bridge was unusually quiet. Most of the time, it bustled with activity as enlisted ratings exchanged information in the combat-information-center portion of the compartment. But it was currently as silent as a tomb. Those who spoke did so in whispers that barely carried a meter.

Ruth focused on her tactical console and its bird's-eye view of Mifreen. She'd overlaid the scientific sensor suite with the standard data generated by the *Lion*'s LIDAR arrays. While the system couldn't pinpoint specific individuals' life signs, it did differentiate between species. The group of humans was unmistakable.

She glanced back at Aibek, who sat in the CO's chair like a statue. Sometimes Ruth wondered if he ever moved while on watch. But she detected tension coming from him. *Like he's waiting for the other shoe to drop. I suppose I am too.*

A minute turned into ten as Ruth studied her console. An off-track Mifreen aircraft caught her eye. *Hmmm.* Focusing on the errant craft caused a realization that there were more than one. They moved in a sweeping circle. It reminded her of the tacking concept on a sailboat. She drew out the endpoint of the pattern, and her eyes widened. "Conn, TAO. Possible inbound on the general's position, sir."

"Possible? Explain further," Aibek replied in a low hiss.

"Better if I show you, sir." Ruth tapped a few buttons and sent her console view to the holoprojector in the center of the bridge. "That grouping of Mifreen aircraft is generally tracking toward our people and the site of the unauthorized settlement. Or I'm putting two and two together to get twenty-two when it's not warranted."

Aibek hissed louder. "Can you determine whether the craft are civilian or military?"

"Not without upping our scan resolution and probably tipping them off."

"We cannot leave the general and his team exposed. Execute the higher-intensity scan, Captain."

"Aye, aye, sir."

Ruth manipulated her controls, and a few moments later, far more details were filled in. While it wasn't like they had a guide for Mifreen aircraft, the presence of conical-shaped objects under the wings of several of the contacts was a dead giveaway. *Missiles. Probably air-to-air or air-to-ground.* "Conn, TAO. Confirmed weaponry on indigenous craft. Capabilities unknown."

As she spoke, the mass of dots swung around and accelerated. "Sir, they've dropped the pretense and are headed straight for our people." Ruth's heart skipped a beat.

"What is the human expression? That answers that?" Aibek brought a finger down on the ship-wide intercom known as 1MC. "Attention, all hands. This is Colonel Aibek. General quarters. General quarters. Set material condition one throughout the ship. Man your battle stations. I say again, man your battle stations. This is not a drill."

The lights dimmed to blue and bathed the bridge in shadows. The color was supposed to help with seeing their console screens better, but Ruth wasn't sure it accomplished

Justice 163

that goal. On one of her control panels, lights indicating vital areas implementing the XO's orders clicked green in sequence. "Conn, TAO. Material condition one set throughout the ship."

"Raise shields. Charge the energy-weapons capacitor."

"Aye, aye, sir," Ruth replied.

"Communications, contact General Cohen immediately. Warn him of possible hostiles inbound."

"Aye, aye, sir." Taylor paused for a few seconds. "Sir, he's in a dead zone. We can't reach anyone with him. Suggest warning the shuttle pilots. Perhaps they could send a runner."

Aibek raised an eye scale. "What a decidedly low-tech approach, Lieutenant. But it is seemingly the best we can do. Execute."

After a pregnant pause, Taylor replied, "Confirmation received, sir."

While that played out, Ruth calculated the speed and trajectory of the Mifreen vessels and how the planet's atmosphere would attenuate the *Lion*'s neutron beams. "Conn, TAO. I think we shoot them down from orbit, sir. Especially in a straight-line formation."

"We cannot initiate hostilities," Aibek replied.

"Sir, they're clearly—"

"Have they attacked our people?"

"Well, no—"

"Then we will not do so first. It is what General Cohen would want. I know this."

"Even if it makes it harder for us to save him and the others when they *do* attack?"

"If I were acting as a Saurian warrior, I would strike them down before they could ever attack my blood brothers and sisters," Aibek hissed. "But I am acting as a member of the Coalition Defense Force and must obey the rules of engagement. In this instance, by behaving in a strictly moral manner, we are making it more difficult for ourselves. That is true. But General Cohen is fond of reminding me, as I suspect he has done for you as well... doing right is often difficult. That is somewhat the point because if doing good were easy, it wouldn't be such a rare occurrence."

Ruth didn't like it, but she had to admit Aibek was right. *And the general would agree.* "Yes, sir."

"While we wait, look for a way to lock on if they begin combat maneuvering."

"Aye, aye, sir." Ruth smirked. *Not an impossible task but hard. A better place for my mind to be, for sure.* If she stopped to think about it, the Mifreen's reaction made sense. Ruth doubted the Terran Coalition would put up with alien powers making contact with underground dissidents on its worlds. *But we don't run creepy simulations with more than half our population inside. I hope General Cohen can avoid bloodshed. Somehow.*

"Communications, signal the air boss to launch the Phantom squadron on alert five, and ensure the Marine QRF is ready." Aibek's voice had lowered. Every word held more of a hiss than usual.

He's getting ready for battle. Ruth ran more math in her head. *So am I.*

18

As Ranjan continued the tour, David felt increasingly impressed with how much ingenuity the residents showed. They had systems to collect rainwater and store it for later use, essential infrastructure to direct sewer water away from habitable dwellings, and tiny wind-driven turbines to produce electricity. All of it was done under protective canopies of camouflage netting and comms disruptors that prevented scans.

"This is our school," Ranjan said proudly, pointing at one of the larger tentlike structures. It appeared as if it could hold at least twenty. "Learning must continue, even if we are cut off from our technology."

Markul cleared his throat. "It's more of a challenge than my friend lets on. Most Mifreen learn through primitive versions of the netsim. Here, they have to teach by example and through books."

David raised an eyebrow. "That's how we do it too. There have been many experiments on interactive holoprograms, tablet apps, et cetera. But we've consistently found that children are best stimulated in a classroom, with as little screen time in their formative years as possible."

"You instruct your young without technology?"

"Not quite, Ranjan. We limit it, though. And admittedly, there's a lot of debate on the subject. I don't have a child yet, so I haven't fully formed my opinions." David flashed a grin. "But since I come from a family of Orthodox Jews, I'll probably veer more toward the old ways versus whatever is new and shiny."

"You would fit in well here, General. We do not eschew technology. Only things that would control our mind, body, and spirit."

David was about to open his mouth to respond when a loud scream erupted from his commlink.

"Private Roche to General Cohen. Do you read me?"

"I read you, Private. Sitrep?" Unease erupted from David's stomach.

"We've got inbound Mifreen military aircraft, sir. *Lion of Judah* requests you evacuate immediately."

If David were the sort of man who swore, a string of oaths would've shot out of his mouth. Instead, he turned to Calvin. "Did you get that?"

"I did, sir."

"What's wrong?" Markul asked.

"Mifreen inbound. Going to bet they're not paying a social call."

Ranjan and Markul exchanged glances.

"Do you have an escape plan?"

"We don't have heavy-population movers, General," Markul said. "There are a few vehicles, but we're resigned to being found someday. It's worth it for any measure of freedom, no matter how temporary."

As he spoke, a series of sonic booms sounded.

Justice 167

"Sir, we won't have much time." Calvin stared at Markul. "What's coming?"

"Probably a snatch-and-return unit. They use overwhelming force to round up and bring back dissenters."

David bit his lip. "Military forces? What kind of tech are we looking at?"

"Similar to what you're carrying," Markul said as he gestured at Calvin's battle rifle. "Without the fancy armor suits. I think the word you would use is auxiliary units. They're not quite formal military, nor are they entirely civilian." The translator seemed to struggle with some of the Mifreen words.

I should've had a plan for this. We were sure our stealth approach would hold.

"We need to drop the comms blackout immediately," Calvin interjected. "So we can communicate and get help if this goes sideways."

Ranjan shuffled her feet. "It's possible the government doesn't know exactly where we are. My people can still hide."

Calvin snarled. "Hiding doesn't work."

"As I've said, we have no weapons, Colonel Demood." Ranjan spread out her hands. "There is nothing we can do *except* conceal ourselves."

David quickly processed the available options. He and the Marines could hoof it as fast as possible back to the shuttles and escape, though if that was the call, it had to be made immediately. The other was to bring down additional shuttles and evacuate the Mifreen rebels. *Though are they really rebels? They have no weapons aside from bows and arrows for hunting.* The gnawing unknown was what sort of ground kit the incoming hostiles would have. *If it's anything like equal weapons and training, we're screwed.*

Yet the right and wrong of the situation couldn't be ignored. The use of force against innocents was something that David could never set aside. While it was indeed possible that there were armed insurgents or even terrorists among the Mifreen, he saw no evidence of it in *that* encampment. Add a healthy number of children to the mix, and the situation tugged on every heartstring he had.

"Ranjan, what's the exact number of people here?"

"Sixty-two."

David licked his lips. "Two shuttles?"

"Yeah, especially considering the kids," Calvin replied.

"Okay." Again, David weighed the cost. He couldn't bring himself to turn his back on their plight. *If you save one life, you save an entire world.* The Jewish maxim was never far from his thoughts.

"Sir, whatever you're thinking, we've got to do it or go *now*."

David set his jaw. "Ranjan, get everyone together and accounted for immediately. Demood, set a perimeter as best as possible. And drop the comms jammer."

Her mouth opened, but no sounds came out, before she finally recovered. "You... would fight for us? But I thought..."

"I'm hoping it doesn't come to that. The Mifreen and the Terran Coalition have no reason to initiate hostilities. We'll try talking. Now get moving."

Markul pulled out an unfamiliar device and entered some commands. "Our blanker is disabled. You should have full communications abilities again."

"I'll never forget this." Ranjan turned and hurried off, shouting commands.

Women began rushing to corral children while the rest appeared bewildered.

Calvin leaned in and whispered, "Whoever built this

Justice 169

place is an awful tactician. It's not defensible." He pointed at a ridgeline fifty meters to the east. "All they have to do is post up there and pick off anyone that moves."

"I noticed that too." David bit his lip. "Okay. We muster them up, make our way back to the clearing, and wait for the calvary to arrive. While we're at it, look for better terrain to stage a defensive stand."

"With respect, sir, that's a shit plan."

"You got a better one, Marine?"

"Nope."

"Then move out."

"Yes, sir."

———

THE LAUNCH TUBE rushed by as Amir punched his Phantom's throttle to maximum. A few seconds later, he entered open space and arced away from the *Lion of Judah*. Eleven more space-superiority fighters followed him, each showing as a blue dot on his HUD. He adjusted his grip on the flight stick and rolled right toward the planet. "Reaper One to all pilots. Break into finger-four formations. Stand by for rapid orbit insertion."

"Wilco," several pilots echoed.

Amir checked the squadron-status screen to ensure everyone showed green across all systems. Once he'd confirmed all was nominal, he pulled up a direct commlink access to David's headset. "CAG to General Cohen."

A burst of static filled the cabin before David's voice came through. "Go ahead, Colonel."

"Good to hear your voice, sir."

"Likewise. Aibek said he put you guys into the void for contingency operations."

"Yes, sir. Request permission to close on your location to provide overwatch and maintain air superiority."

"Negative, Amir. I want to avoid provoking the Mifreen any further in hopes of preventing bloodshed. If I need you, what's your ETA?"

"Depends on timing, sir. Right now, we're directly over your position, but as we orbit the planet, that will be wildly out of sync. Worst case, thirty minutes. Recommend we proceed now."

David sighed. "No, I won't risk it with these civilians all over the place. I'll try talking first, and we'll see where it goes."

"We'll try to maintain orbit over your coordinates, sir. If you won't let me down there, can I at least get a few more squadrons on alert five, including the Marine Hawkers?"

"Approved. Better to be prudent than sorry." Shouts sounded in the background. "I've got to cut this short. Godspeed, Colonel."

"*Allah ma'ak*, old friend." *May God be with you.*

The commlink cut off with a click, and Amir felt uneasy. Every fiber of his being wanted to disregard David's orders and perform a full-power dive through the Mifreen atmosphere. He set those thoughts aside and instead changed channels to hangar control. "Amir to air boss."

"Go ahead, CAG."

"Move three squadrons of Phantoms to alert five along with our Hawker squadron. Tell the crew chiefs to move it. I believe we may need them. Once that's done, get everything else to alert fifteen." That would cause every pilot on the *Lion of Judah* to report to their ready rooms, and all small craft moved to the flight line, including bombers.

"Wilco."

Amir rolled his fighter again, following the flight

Justice

computer's instructions as he configured it to maintain a geosynchronous orbit over David's position. He whispered a prayer for the safety of all those below, including the civilians. *May Allah protect us.*

———

It took close to fifteen minutes to round up the civilians, even with Calvin and other Marines assisting. Toward the end, Calvin took to some rather direct motivation that included bellowing commands. It got results, and they finally started moving out. David had the Marine who'd come to warn them post up in the trees, right outside of the landing zone. As such, they got real-time reporting on the incoming Mifreen.

The situation wasn't good. On the common operating picture displayed on his tablet, numerous Mifreen units had entered the woods, as if dropped from hovering aircraft. They were enveloping the settlement, and contact was imminent.

Calvin touched his arm. The two of them led the column. "Sir, you seeing what I'm seeing?"

"Couple hundred hostiles closing in? I think they fast-roped in."

"Yeah. Thinking we should hunker down here." He pointed at a nearby group of fallen trees. "Could hide the civvies in there, and we take whatever cover we can."

"We're still at least a kilometer from the landing zone."

"I get that, sir, but if an active firefight starts with these kids in the open, there's gonna be *a lot* of blood spilled."

"If this goes south, we're screwed, to use your parlance," David replied.

"Ah, but we'll take a few of the bastards with us," Calvin replied almost jovially.

Some things about the Marine mindset didn't compute for David, but that was okay. *Space-warfare officers probably don't add up for them either.* "Okay. Get them into position. No one shoots until I say so, or we take incoming. Clear?"

"Crystal, sir."

The next few minutes involved a mad rush to move the scared and skittish civilians into as much cover as possible, taking advantage of the massive tree trunks. All the while, hostiles closed steadily on their position from all directions.

David had called for additional shuttles to be prepared along with a QRF, but he was loath to have them commit to landing more forces on Mifreen. *We'll be perceived as a threat. If I were one of them, I'd be furious that a foreign power had landed military units on my planet. And if we double down, it'll probably eliminate all chances of a peaceful resolution.* Something in the back of his mind told him that getting out of the situation without shooting was unlikely.

"Halt! Halt!" a new voice rang out. It was deep, and it took a moment for David's earpiece to translate. "Humans, we know you are here."

"Shit," Calvin muttered.

David slowly leaned out from behind the tree he and Calvin were standing behind. A rough line of maybe twenty-five Mifreen in camouflage uniforms and carrying what appeared to be rifles of some design stood thirty meters away.

He screamed, "Hold your position! We'd like to talk!"

"How do you propose we do that, interloper? This is our world!"

"You and one other advance. We will do the same to try

to settle this without killing. We have no desire to harm you."

"Any attempt at subterfuge will be met with overwhelming and lethal force."

"We understand." David touched Calvin's arm. "Head on a swivel, and keep your guys on a tight leash."

Calvin grimaced. "Don't worry, sir. We won't start it." His voice turned into a growl. "But we'll finish it."

"Amen to that." David gingerly stepped out from behind the tree, showing both hands. Calvin followed moments later and let his battle rifle fall into its one-point sling.

They advanced about ten meters in tandem with two Mifreen. Both groups came to a halt, perhaps five meters apart.

David stared down the man he assumed was the leader because his uniform was more ostentatious and had additional insignia. "Major General David Cohen, Coalition Defense Force." He ensured his feet were perfectly spaced apart and his posture ramrod straight.

"Commander Parin Nawrad, Mifreen Special Constabulary." Vestiges of thick hair resembling fur stuck out of the neckline of his uniform. He stared at Calvin's power armor for a moment before returning his gaze to David. "Why are you here, human?"

"Your government asked us to allow one of our scientists to enter the netsim. We were contacted by those on your world who have... differing views of the technology. To make an informed decision, I decided to hear them out."

Nawrad balled his hands into fists before relaxing them. "These terrorists have killed hundreds of loyal citizens. Consorting with them is an act of violence against the Mifreen Combine. You are *all* subject to arrest."

"Nobody's arresting us, pal," Calvin snapped. "Unless

you want a fight with the Terran Coalition's misguided children."

The humor didn't land with the Mifreen. "I don't see what children have to do with it."

David jerked his thumb at Calvin. "He's a Marine. Different branch of service, primarily ground combat. Let me translate: we won't be going anywhere with you voluntarily."

Silence followed as all four humanoids stared one another down before Nawrad spoke. "I am authorized to allow you to walk away, return to your landing craft, and leave without violence."

"We'll need to bring down two more shuttles to evacuate the civilians," David replied and crossed his arms.

Nawrad's face contorted into a snarl. "Perhaps you do not understand, General. The criminals you're protecting will be taken to a rehabilitation center and dealt with. They will *not* accompany you."

"These people have done nothing wrong. They harm no one."

"They're terrorists."

David gestured with his hands. "I just inspected their camp. There's no evidence of weapons, explosives, or anything beyond simple tools and bows for hunting wild game."

Nawrad shrugged. "It doesn't matter if they specifically have such materials, General. They represent a threat to Mifreen security, and the special constabulary deals with these threats."

"I give you my word as a Coalition soldier that if your government presents evidence of their guilt in serious crimes, I will return them. But I will not allow you to haul off innocent people who simply want to be left alone."

Justice 175

"This is our world, human. You do not get to decide what we do. You do as you're told. I seek no contest with you, but unless your forces withdraw, we will do whatever it takes to secure our objective."

David glanced at Calvin, whose expression was inscrutable behind the visor of his power armor. *What would General Pipes do here?* The specter of being 4.4 million light-years from home was always in his mind. They had limited resupply and no backup. *Then there's the question of asking my people to lay down their lives for others on a planet we'll likely never see again.* Yet he couldn't ignore what would happen if they marched on.

Throughout the recorded history of the universe, authoritarians of all stripes have used force to make others do their bidding. I can't save them all. He pursed his lips. *But I can save a few.* "Commander, with respect, we will not stand down. I suggest you contact your superiors and ask for instructions because I'd wager your government has no interest in hostilities with the Terran Coalition."

"You have thirty-two power-armor units in this forest, General, and we outnumber you ten to one. If you fight us, you will lose."

David grinned. "I like those odds, Commander."

19

TIME SEEMED to slow in the forest. While animals had been chirping and calling one another, even they seemed to sense the approaching danger. It became deathly quiet. David counted the seconds, waiting for Nawrad to make the next move. He was betting everything on the commander being instructed to avoid hostilities at all costs.

"We will not allow you to take these criminals," the Mifreen finally replied, spit spraying from his mouth.

The continued threat confirmed to David that Nawrad had limitations. "Again, I give you my word that if your government presents clear and convincing evidence of guilt for anyone here, we'll return them. No one wants a war or a simple misunderstanding to get out of hand."

Silence seemed to reverberate between the trees.

David flipped a mental coin. *Maybe I can get a reaction out of him.* "We're going to head to our shuttles now and await the additional transports."

Nawrad snarled but said nothing. The crack of a branch breaking echoed, followed by the thud of someone hitting the ground.

Justice 177

As David turned toward the sound, several sharp reports registered. They were too high-pitched to be from TCMC battle rifles, but the noise was unmistakably metallic.

Then pandemonium broke out. Dozens of shots echoed in different directions before the Marines returned fire, and the forest became a shooting gallery.

Calvin slammed into David, pushing him down while discharging his rifle into Nawrad and the Mifreen next to him. "Shit! You okay, sir?"

Nothing broken, I think. "Yeah. But you weigh a ton."

"All that Coalition tech." Calvin grunted and rolled over. Bullets flew over their heads and shredded a tree only a few meters behind them. "Gotta move, sir."

"Excellent idea except for having the crap shot out of us." David drew his energy pistol from its thigh holster and sent several pulses toward the nearest Mifreen, hoping to force their heads down at least momentarily.

Calvin put a burst of rounds into an advancing Mifreen, only to have the enemy soldier hit the ground, bounce up, and keep firing his odd-looking ballistic weapon, which they all carried. "Stun rounds ain't working, sir!" he shouted as incoming fire only got worse.

As if to underscore his point, the commlink came alive with the voice of another Marine. "We're getting lit up over here, Colonel! Request permission to switch to lethal ammo." The transmission was punctuated with a series of pops followed by screams.

"Do it," David said without waiting for the question.

"Demood to all units. Reload with AP, and waste the mother—"

David adjusted the setting on his pistol. "No need to censor yourself on my account, Cal." He took aim and fired at an onrushing Mifreen and succeeded in punching a hole through the paramilitary soldier's armor. The man collapsed and quit moving.

Calvin ejected the magazine from his battle rifle and slapped in a new one. "I'll keep that in mind, sir." He raised his head slightly and sent several bursts downrange. Multiple Mifreen dropped, and all around them, the other Marines did the same. Momentarily, it seemed as if the situation was stabilizing.

"We should think about moving," David said between rapidly shooting his pistol to suppress the hostiles to their front. His mind raced with tactical possibilities as he tried to reason the best way out of the situation.

"Your lack of power armor is an issue, sir." Calvin grunted. "I don't like the idea of trying to extract you or the civvies in this hostile an environment."

"What choice do we have?"

David cursed himself for not having more Marines and additional air support standing by.

The respite was suddenly interrupted by a series of whooshes, explosions, and fireballs shooting into the air. He curled into a ball as they got closer, and the roar of some mechanical vehicle echoed.

"Son of a... Damn aliens have CAS."

It took David a moment to process the acronym. "We're probably not the only people in the universe to have figured out how to properly fight a war or basic combined-arms theory."

Calvin smirked. "No, but dumb opponents are nice. Like, say, those terrorists back on Zeivlot who had no fire discipline and rushed headlong at you, screaming."

A fresh round of explosions forced them both to hug the dirt while the commlink lit up with Marines yelling.

Justice 179

"One of my guys got caught in the blast radius of that last one."

David blew out a breath. *Get out of the moment. Focus on the big picture.* "Keep them occupied. I'll get us air support. And warm up the QRF."

"On it, sir."

———

AN EMERGENCY GOLD-LEVEL broadcast cut through all comm-link traffic and blasted through Amir's helmet.

"Broken Arrow! Broken Arrow! All CDF stations. Repeat, Broken Arrow!" David's voice sounded more frantic than Amir had ever heard.

"This is the CAG. I read you loud and clear, sir."

"Battalion-strength hostiles engaged, Colonel. Immediate air support needed."

"Wilco, sir. Grim Reapers moving to intercept. ETA... five minutes." *Thank Allah we were able to stay over the target area.*

"Roger that," David replied as the distinctive report of Coalition battle rifles intermingled with screams echoed over the commlink.

"CAG out." Amir switched his commlink to the squadron channel. "Grim Reapers, we are cleared to commit. Set atmospheric insertion on my flight path, and push to max thrust."

He adjusted his Phantom into a nearly parabolic heading and redirected all energy-weapons power to the shields. Technically, what Amir was doing was against CDF protocols, but when seconds counted, he wouldn't play around with his fellow soldiers' lives. The formation of space-superiority fighters moved as one, with all of them taking position around him as they accelerated.

As Amir checked the squadron-readiness screen just prior to losing their tactical network connection because of the heat effects of atmospheric reentry, he saw that they were only a few minutes away from getting four more squadrons on alert five. *May Allah protect us however He sees fit.*

The sight of twelve fireballs shooting through the sky would've been awe-inspiring to anyone watching on the ground. Inside their protective screens, the hull temperature on each Phantom grew dangerously high. Amir pressed on, unwilling to adjust his approach angle and trusting in superior Coalition technology to be overengineered enough to survive.

Outside his canopy, the red flames faded against the deflectors, and blue sky shone through. A quick check of his HUD showed everyone else had made it too. Amir breathed a sigh of relief. "Reaper One to all fighters. Echelon formation. Max thrust on heading zero-eight-seven. Maintain altitude of five thousand meters."

"Wilco," the other pilots replied.

Amir checked the sensor display and realized they weren't alone. The computer classified many contacts as fast movers, and they were headed their way. *Those speeds... Mach three, four?* Whatever they were, he assumed the incoming was hostile. CDF rules of engagement typically required active confirmation of a contact before attacking it, but Amir wasn't taking any chances.

"Bogies! Bogies bearing zero-two-one, range, five hundred kilometers and closing fast." One of the other Reaper pilots beat Amir to the tally-ho call.

"Break to new heading zero-two-one," Amir replied. His threat indicator lit up. The computer couldn't tell what the

Justice   181

target lock was, only that there was one. *It doesn't appear to be LIDAR.* That concerned him because their chaff system was explicitly designed to thwart LIDAR-directed warheads.

"Reaper Six to all. I'm being spiked by multiple bogies."

"Negative on bogie determination. Incoming craft are bandits," Amir replied. "Weapons-free status for all Reapers."

"Wilco," Major Viktoria Chekan, Amir's primary wing-man, said between bursts of static.

With an in-atmosphere range of close to three hundred kilometers, the LT-47F Vulture was Amir's weapon of choice in an air-to-air engagement. He lined up the nearest Mifreen fighter and waited for the tone. "Everyone, lock up a bandit. Ensure we don't overlap."

"Wilco" echoed over the commlink as the range between the opposing forces decreased rapidly.

The missile-lock tone buzzed in Amir's cockpit. "Reaper One, fox three."

"Reaper Five, fox three."

"Reaper Eleven, fox three."

Twelve warheads roared away from the squadron toward the enemy. The contrails were quickly lost in the horizon while icons representing counterfire appeared on Amir's HUD. *Now we find out how well our technology matches up against theirs. May Allah protect us.*

———

DAVID GRITTED his teeth as twin explosions rocked the skies above their position. Two fireballs, visible even through the canopy of the forest, streaked toward the ground several kilometers away. *Not ours. Good.* He and Calvin had fallen back toward the main group of civilians. So far, the combat had been brutal, possibly the worst he'd ever seen.

A Mifreen woman and two small children who hadn't made it to the fallen logs in time crawled forward as best as they could. The kids, a boy and a girl no more than six, cried. The sound carried in the forest and seemed to attract a considerable amount of incoming fire.

Bullets smacked the ground and trees, sending splinters and dust flying in all directions.

Through it all, Calvin was cool, calm, and collected, as if he'd done it a thousand times before.

Probably because he has. David grunted as he sent several pulses from his energy pistol downrange. At the distance from which they were engaging, it was doubtful he'd hit anything, but suppressive fire had its benefits. Out of the corner of his eye, he saw one of the children stand and start to run.

Too late, Calvin and one of the other Marines realized the same thing. They tried to put enough rounds into the groups of Mifreen paramilitary troops to keep them occupied, but it wasn't enough.

David's heart stopped as bullets ripped through the boy and left him facedown in the dirt. The child's mother abandoned cover and took off toward him, only to be cut down in a Mifreen fusillade. Anger ran through David as he snatched up a battle rifle dropped by a wounded Marine.

The fire-selection toggle had three settings: semiauto, three-round burst, and full auto. David switched to the latter and sighted down on the nearest four-man squad of Mifreen. Rage flowed through his veins as he squeezed the trigger and held it.

Dozens of full-alloy-jacket bullets erupted from the

rifle's barrel and flew through the aliens as if they were tissue paper. It only took a few seconds to empty the weapon's magazine, and the smell of propellant filled the air. The anger abated, though he had no way of knowing if those Mifreen were the ones who'd fired the lethal shots. *What kind of people kill children? Even the League was generally better than that.*

While David had shot down the enemy paramilitaries, Markul crawled out of cover, took the remaining child's hand, and dragged her back to the safety of the fallen logs. David felt impressed by the display of bravery and noted that Markul had obtained a Marine sidearm from somewhere.

Calvin swapped magazines. "You okay, sir?"

"Yeah."

He put his hand on David's shoulder. "Getting a little payback?"

David gritted his teeth. "Perhaps."

"Nothing wrong with that, sir."

"How are we looking?"

Calvin shook his head. "Like we're in a tactically shit situation, surrounded on all sides by people who want to kill us, and the only saving grace we've got is our armor's better than theirs." He sent a burst of rounds toward the enemy.

"If we stay here, they'll kill us all, or we'll be forced to surrender."

"Not particularly interested in becoming guests of the Mifreen government," Calvin replied.

"Touché." David held out his hand. "Got a spare mag?"

Calvin grabbed one and handed it over. "Yeah, but don't go full auto again unless it's needed, eh? I don't have enough for spray-and-pray."

"Yes, sir," David replied with a snicker. It seemed strange how the battle produced moments of utter despair followed by levity. *Probably a coping mechanism.* "I could try to have the shuttles put down about five hundred meters to the northwest."

"That's not a clearing. Too dangerous."

"We're running out of options," David whispered.

Calvin shook his head. "Better to wait for CAS to get down here, use our superior firepower on these assholes, and extract back where we came from. Only good news right now is the Mifreen don't seem to know where we parked."

"Maybe we just got unlucky."

"Yeah."

David pulled his tablet out of his pocket and opened the device. "Link me to the common operating picture."

"You got it, sir."

The screen came alive a few moments later with a topographical map of their surroundings along with friendly and enemy positions. It didn't look good, as there were many more red dots than blue ones. *We just have to hold for a few more minutes.*

Sporadic fire continued between the Marines and the Mifreen troops, and David felt pretty good about their chances—until all at once, a murderous wave of incoming fire swept the forest followed by dozens of enemies. They used suppressive fire to force everyone to keep their heads down along with judicious use of explosives that resembled TCMC hand grenades.

The tree trunk David and Calvin had taken cover behind suddenly became perforated with bullets, and splinters shot out of it. They both dropped and lay as flat as possible.

As David raised his rifle, Calvin put a hand on his shoulder. "Best thing you can do is get Amir in here, sir. Let me worry about the incoming."

"On it." He keyed the commlink to the squadron-command frequency. *Come on, Hassan. One more rabbit out of that hat of yours.* The grim reality of their situation set in, and David wondered if he was about to die.

20

THE FIGHT against the Mifreen interceptors had progressed and led to a stalemate. Whatever they used to track threats, their missiles weren't quite as maneuverable as Amir would've expected. Chaff was of limited use, but wild maneuvering threw the warheads off. So far, one Phantom had gone down versus three of the stubby hostile craft.

Unfamiliar tracers shot by Amir's cockpit canopy as he pulled back hard on the flight stick. One of the benefits to flying a space-superiority fighter with an inertial damping system in the atmosphere was he could take a lot more of a pounding in terms of g-force. The maneuver he'd just pulled would've killed a pilot without such a system.

"Reaper Two, fox two," Amir's wingman called.

A few seconds later, the icon representing the hostile fighter chasing him disappeared.

"Reaper Two, splash one."

Amir gave a fierce grin. "Nice shooting, Two."

"Anytime, Colonel. Watch your six."

Before Amir could find a new target to engage, David's voice broke through the commlink. *"Where's my air support?"*

Justice   187

"Five mikes out, sir."

"Negative. We don't have five mikes." The harsh crackle of battle rifles echoed through the feed. "Mifreen forces are about to overrun. We need close air support *now*."

"Sir, the Hawkers aren't here yet—"

"Do a run with a few Phantoms."

Amir pursed his lips as he looped his craft around, being careful to maintain situational awareness. "We have no ground attack munitions, sir."

"Strafing pass, then."

"Sir, we'd be just as likely to kill *you* as the enemy under that foliage."

"Hassan, I'd rather have my ticket punched by you than for certain by the Mifreen. We'll mark with purple smoke, and I'll transmit a series of coordinates. Fly that route, and lay down cover."

Amir gritted his teeth. He hated what David was asking —no, ordering him to do. *The situation must be beyond dire.* "Wilco, sir."

"Thanks, old friend. Cohen out."

The way David had said the words struck Amir as more than just a sign-off. *That was goodbye.*

Amir was not an emotional man, by any stretch of the imagination. Twenty years of flying fighters against the League had seen to that. Still, it cut him to his core. *Allah, guide my sword so I may protect those who fight in Your name.* "Reaper One to Two and Three. Break right and head for the deck. We're going to execute a strafing run."

"Did you say strafing run, Colonel?"

"Clean your ears out, Two." Amir smirked. "Time to prove how good a pilot you really are."

"Wilco, sir."

188   DANIEL GIBBS

"Beta and Gamma elements, keep those bandits off our six."

———

"You sure about this, sir?" Calvin yelled as he changed magazines in his battle rifle. "I mean, Amir's got a point. He'll be shooting blind."

David popped up and sprayed bullets in the direction of several Mifreen paramilitaries charging through a cloud of purple smoke, cutting two down before return fire drove him back behind the log. "You got a better idea?"

While the plan was dangerous, at least the plotted coordinates would, in theory, keep them from taking friendly fire. David hated that particular euphemism.

Calvin yanked a grenade off his belt and pulled the pin. "Frag, over!" He tossed the deceptively small round ball at an onrushing group of hostiles.

Three seconds later, it exploded with a violent roar. A shower of dirt obscured the battlefield, and when it cleared, another group had been cut down. Calvin poured rounds into those who remained before they could retreat to cover.

"Not really, beyond avoiding getting into firefights on alien planets. Down to one frag and one plasma. Wish I'd brought more party favors."

"You're nuts. You know that, right?" David replied, somehow grinning despite the hell all around them.

"Well, that's what I get for eating all those crayons, sir." Calvin glanced around the log. "Shit. They've got fifty-plus guys forming up there."

"You don't think I called this wrong, do you?"

"*Hell* no." Calvin grabbed David's shoulder with his armored gauntlet. "I don't know the who, why, what, or how

Justice 189

here, but anyone willing to shoot unarmed women and children in the back deserves what's coming to them. We wouldn't be who we are if either of us could walk away from a situation like this. And you know what? If it's my time, I can't think of a better way to go out than a last stand against impossible odds, doing what's right."

"This is Reaper One. We're beginning our attack run."

"Read you five by five, Reaper One." David switched channels. "All CDF stations, friendly fast movers inbound. Heads down!"

Time seemed to slow to a crawl as he waited for the incoming assist. The distinctive sound of the Phantoms' in-atmosphere engines grew louder, followed by the high-pitched whine of directed energy weapons. Neutron-cannon pulses, moving so fast that they were barely visible in the forest, slammed into the ground. They sent dirt flying in every direction while shredding trees, foliage, and the Mifreen paramilitary troops caught in their path. David was pretty sure he saw body parts sail over his head as the maelstrom continued.

And just like that, it was over. No more than six or seven seconds had elapsed, but it felt like an eternity. When he stuck his head over the log, the scene in front of him was radically different from the one before the strafing run.

Bodies lay strewn across the ground along with giant splinters of wood and small flames from burning plants. It looked as if the hand of God himself had reached down and smashed the trees and everything around them. David gulped. *Glad they're on our side.* "Cohen to Amir. We owe you one."

Silence descended as if everyone—human, Mifreen paramilitary troops, and civilians—were holding their breath.

Calvin tapped David's arm. "I've got one Marine KIA. Pretty sure it was blue on blue. Don't tell Amir, okay? He's got enough on him right now."

That they weren't all dead was a miracle.

David nodded. "Agreed. He probably doesn't ever need to know that."

"Yeah."

"Give me some options here."

"Call in more Marines, trap these guys in a pincer, and extract the civvies. Or we could use this to push forward to the shuttles."

David weighed the ideas. It would take at least fifteen to thirty minutes to get the QRF on deck and in action. *Or we could move out now.* "Seems to me that without the civilians, our best bet would be to push through."

"Absolutely, sir." Calvin grunted. "Amir's little stunt oughtta put our friends over there on their back foot. For a few minutes anyway. Hit hard, hit fast, and grind them down. But with a bunch of women and children they've already shown no compunction against gunning down..."

The sudden whoosh of a missile launch filled the air, and several exhaust plumes rose over the tree cover.

David did a double take. "MANPADs? Seriously?"

"These guys came prepared."

"Roche to Demood" came the quiet voice of the Marine providing overwatch.

"Go ahead."

"Tangos pulling back about fifty meters, sir. They're setting up a perimeter."

David and Calvin exchanged glances.

"You thinking what I'm thinking, sir?"

"Push forward and head for the shuttles."

Calvin grinned. "No time like the present."

Justice 191

"Agreed, but I'm still calling in the QRF."

"Keep your head down, and follow me, sir." Calvin sprang up from behind the log and attracted surprisingly little attention from the Mifreen troops.

I'm really getting too old for this. David clutched his battle rifle and followed.

21

"UGLY ANGEL ONE CLEARING ATMOSPHERE, Reaper One. Ugly Angels on station and ready for tasking."

Amir let out a breath. *Finally, some good news.* "Glad to hear your voice, Captain. General Cohen needs fire support approximately fifty kilometers from your position. Synch with the Marines' tactical network, and engage at will. Weapons free."

"Wilco, Colonel. Ugly Angels breaking to heading zero-nine-six. We'd be much obliged if you'd keep the bandits I see populating the battle space off our tails."

"With pleasure." Amir checked the sensor display and, to his satisfaction, found far fewer craft than there had been even five minutes prior. He suspected the Mifreen had better tracking technology, but compared to his battle-hardened veterans, their pilots were rookies. *It's one thing to beat sims. Quite another to defeat a foe who knows his business.*

He lined up another of the snub-nosed interceptors in his forward LIDAR cone. The missile lock-on tone buzzed. "Reaper One, fox three."

A Vulture dropped from his Phantom's internal stores

Justice

bay, and a split second later, its engine ignited. Immediately, the warhead roared off into the blue sky and disappeared into the clouds. Since the target was some eighty kilometers away, it took more than a few seconds to get there, but Amir was rewarded with another destroyed Mifreen craft.

"Reaper One, splash one."

"Save some for us, Reaper One," another pilot called over the commlink.

Amir recognized the voice of Captain Wladyslaw Pilecki, commander of the Top Hats—another Phantom squadron. He checked the board to find twenty-four new friendly contacts. *By Allah, the odds have turned in our favor.* "It's good to hear your voice, Pilecki. Drive these hostiles into a kill box, and we'll finish them off."

"Wilco, Colonel."

The closest grouping of Mifreen fighters suddenly adjusted their heading and climbed, reversing course, and flew back toward the east. Simultaneously, Amir's threat-alert indicators went wild. Masses of red dots appeared, indicating a whole lot of trouble headed his way.

"Sir, you seeing this?" Pilecki asked.

"Can you confirm the number of bandits?"

"I'm showing fifty-plus, sir."

"Same here." Amir blew out a breath. "Too many to pursue. Focus your efforts solely on defending the airspace around General Cohen's landing party."

Acknowledgment signals went up from all squadron commanders, and Amir twisted his Phantom around. While the best defense was a good offense, he wasn't willing to take the risk of getting mousetrapped or worse. "CAG to *Lion of Judah.*"

"Lieutenant Taylor here, sir. What can we do for you?"

"Inform the XO that we're facing down numerous new hostiles, Lieutenant. I need orbital fire support."

Taylor gulped. "Understood, sir. I'll pass it along immediately."

"CAG out."

———

THE WARRIOR in Aibek constantly searched for ways to prove his mettle in combat. The concept was central to Saurian beliefs in that he believed it was his job to use his skills to protect others. Yet the battle unfolding below was a disorganized mess. And Aibek detested not being able to affect it in a more meaningful way.

"Conn, TAO. I've zeroed in on the bogies reported by the CAG, sir. Counting more than a hundred incoming."

Aibek hissed. From watching the tactical plot and Amir's engagement so far, he knew that two- or three-to-one odds were terrible. "What options do we have for orbital interdiction, Captain?"

"Neutron beams, sir. Reduced strength to avoid inflicting too much damage on the planet's crust."

"What risk is there for collateral damage?"

Ruth shook her head. "Virtually none, sir. They're over uninhabited areas."

A fierce grin came to Aibek's lips. "Redesignate those bogies as bandits, Captain. Firing point procedures, all neutron beams in arc."

"Firing solutions set, sir."

"Match bearings, shoot, neutron beams."

CDF ship designers believed in redundancy and battle-tested designs over the newest technology. As a result, buttons, knobs, and intricate controls were a feature of

Justice   195

virtually all military vessels. It gave a tactile response and made unique sounds, such as the click when Ruth pressed the button to fire their primary energy weapons.

Streams of blue particle beams raced away from the *Lion of Judah* at the speed of light, nearly instantly striking her intended targets. While the results were impossible to see from the bridge, except in terms of red dots disappearing from the sensor screen, Aibek imagined that to the enemy pilots, it must seem like the Prophet himself had reached down from the heavens to smite them.

"Conn, TAO. Fifteen bandits eliminated."

"Continue to prosecute the targets, Captain."

"Aye, aye, sir."

Ruth kept sending waves of death into the Mifreen formation. While the first two volleys had spectacular results, the enemies scattered and headed as close to the ground as possible. When they were fifty meters off the deck, it was nearly impossible to get a weapons lock. After failing to connect, she turned. "They took evasive maneuvers, sir. I doubt we'll be able to engage until they climb again, and the proximity to friendlies will make attacking a last resort."

"Nevertheless, a good showing." Aibek steepled his fingers, a mannerism he'd picked up from David. "Do not hesitate to take the shot if an opportunity presents itself."

"Aye, aye, sir."

———

WITH A FIREBALL CONFIRMING another hard kill, Amir did a three-hundred-sixty-five-degree glance. He found it essential to maintain situational awareness, even when the tactical computer did most of the work. With no threats in visual range, his eyes went back to the sensor screen on his HUD. Though it was momentarily clear, a massive force of Mifreen interceptor craft showed at the edge of his scanners.

"Amir to Cohen."

"I read you, Colonel." The rapid-fire reports of TCMC battle rifles echoed in the background. "Still busy down here."

"Not to add to your troubles, but there are overwhelming hostiles massing to attack. The window in which we can maintain air superiority is closing. I strongly recommend you evacuate."

A pause followed. "Understood. If it becomes obvious that we won't get to the shuttles in time, you will retreat to avoid being overwhelmed."

"Sir—"

"That's a direct order, Hassan."

"Yes, sir."

"Until then, buy us as much time as you can."

"*Inshallah*, old friend."

"See you soon."

Amir tightened his grip on the flight stick as the commlink clicked off. Under no circumstances would he abandon David and the others, even if it meant his own death. *The rest is in the hands of Allah.*

22

WITH SIX MARINES to his right, David trudged a few paces away from Calvin as they took point on the trek through the forest. So far, they'd made it about half the distance to the edge of the woods. Only sporadic resistance had been encountered so far, but something about the way the Mifreen were falling back made David wary.

Suddenly, a volley of shots splattered around them, kicking up dirt and wood splinters, and one of the power-armored Marines went down.

"Contact front! Hit the deck!" Calvin bellowed.

They melted into the underbrush and gamely returned fire at the few Mifreen visible while David crawled over to the wounded Marine. His eyes widened when he realized a projectile round had penetrated the power armor and gone out the back. *That shouldn't be possible.* The point of power armor was to protect against small arms and require the use of heavy weaponry or specific armor-piercing ammo.

As the incoming fire continued, David realized that something was off, sound-wise. *That doesn't sound like the reports I heard when the battle commenced.* They were facing a new weapon.

He touched his commlink. "Cal, got a problem here. The aliens have something that can defeat power armor. Private Rubenstein's badly wounded, though his suit injected coagulants into the wound. I see a through-and-through."

"Dammit," Calvin replied, keeping his voice down. "Better call CAS back, then. We'll need them to pulverize the Mifreen positions, which is going to slow us down."

"Better slowed than dead." David switched his commlink to Amir's squadron-command frequency. "Cohen to Amir. Come in."

———

"Ugly Angels, this is the CAG. Commence immediate close support run, grid section eight-six-one. Friendly units marked on COP."

Captain Kerry Duncan checked the incoming directive. "That's danger-close range, Colonel."

"Yes, it is. Direct orders from General Cohen. And now from me."

"Wilco, sir. Theta One out." Duncan clicked his commlink over to the squadron channel. "Okay, boys and girls. You heard the colonel. Now we get to earn our measly pay from the TCMC. Split into assigned elements, and stand by to engage the targets."

Acknowledgment signals and a "Wilco" came across Duncan's HUD as he broke left hard. Brimstones were the weapon of choice, as they would give all of them the ability to make position-guided pinpoint fires. It also meant slowing down dramatically. Thanks to the inertial damping systems, Duncan did so without crushing his

Justice

internal organs and smearing himself against the cockpit canopy.

Unlike a dogfight, which at least in some instances had a visual element, given the overarching forest cover, everything they did was based solely on instrumentation readings. Duncan had accomplished the same sortie many times against League troops in the war. *A little wild to be getting low and slow over some alien planet.* "Theta One to ground element. Ready to light the fire over here. Confirm target selection."

"This is Demood. We're playing the music. Go for release, Marine."

"Wilco, Colonel." One of the unique features of the *Lion*'s aviation group was that she carried two squadrons of AS-9V Hawkers, and all the pilots who flew them were TCMC space aviators, as opposed to the CDF pilots, who flew everything else.

"Duncan to all elements. You are cleared to engage hot."

Slowing to a forward speed of fewer than three hundred kilometers an hour, Duncan lined up for his attack run. The onboard targeting computer lit up with multiple hostiles marked by the Marines, and he set his ground-attack missiles to double launch. A moment later, he squeezed the missile-launch button on his flight stick three times in a row.

Six Brimstone warheads dropped off their wing-mounted pylons and accelerated toward the ground, joined by three other Hawkers. An impressive amount of firepower headed into the Mifreen positions. The pilots added bursts of energy from their nose-mounted miniaturized neutron cannons for good measure.

Explosions blossomed above the green canopy, blasting fire and gray smoke into the atmosphere. Duncan jammed his throttle to max and rapidly increased speed. *Not making myself that easy a target for any MANPADs they might have left.* "Theta One to Demood."

"Demood here. Good hits. We've still got a lot of hostiles, so circle back and give us another run."

"Wilco, sir." Duncan grinned as he reset the targeting computer. *I love this job.*

————

THE *WOMP-WOMP-WOMP* of Coalition air-to-ground missiles were music to David's ears. The cries of Mifreen paramilitaries echoed throughout the forest as explosions lit up a perimeter around the remaining friendlies. As the hostile troops tried to retreat, half of them fell from battle rifle rounds, and until they attempted to surrender, he was content to end their ability to threaten his people and the civilians.

Calvin shouldered his battle rifle and put a precision round into one of the fleeing aliens. "Alpha, mike, foxtrot."

"How's it looking?" David asked as he scanned the battlefield. "With those fancy helmet-integrated optics."

"A lot better than it did ten minutes ago," Calvin replied as he dropped another Mifreen paramilitary. "We should take the opportunity to push forward."

"Agreed."

Calvin barked a series of orders into his commlink, and the Marines moved forward like a wave, using bound over-watch tactics. A group rushed to cover and provided cover fire while another brought civilians with them. It took time but minimized casualties.

Thanks to continued support from the Hawker squadron, the Mifreen paramilitaries faded back into the forest, unwilling to press the attack. Aside from stray bursts of slug-thrower rounds, the enemy ceased to be an effective fighting force.

The Marines got the civilians and the wounded to the edge of the forest clearing, where their twin shuttles waited. David and Calvin ended up fifty meters from safety, sandwiched between many Mifreen women and children.

Markul belly crawled up to David. "I think half of them have wounds of some sort."

"So do our people."

"I haven't had a chance to thank—"

"Stow it," David snapped. "One, we're not out of this yet. Two, if I find any shred of evidence you set us up to cause an incident, 'thanks' will not be a word you use."

Markul bit his lip. "I understand how you feel, General. I'd be suspicious too. But I'm just trying to survive, and I sure as hell didn't organize this."

David nodded. "We'll find out later."

Two more TCMC assault landers came into view and, with a loud roar, settled into the clearing. Their ramps opened, and half a dozen Marines spilled out, taking up covering positions.

"There're our rides, sir. I think it's time to get off this Godforsaken planet."

"Couldn't agree with you more, Colonel. I'm getting too old for this."

"Nah." Calvin stood and made a series of hand gestures.

Squads of Marines rose and started escorting civilians forward. Just as the first group made it to the back of the nearest shuttle, the sound of gunfire echoed through the forest. David watched in horror as several Mifreen went down, pink stains spreading across their clothing. The

Marines returned fire gamely, but the amount of incoming was overwhelming.

"*Where in the flying hell are they getting this manpower?*" Calvin shouted as he dropped back to prone.

"Probably brought in reinforcements while we were waiting for the shuttles. It's only a miracle from HaShem that they didn't overrun our forces here."

"I'd wager they want to kill us in a cross fire." Calvin shook his head. "Better call CAS in, sir."

"On it." David keyed his commlink and wondered if they would make it out alive.

23

AMIR APPRECIATED the respite from combat they'd been blessed with after achieving local air superiority. The remaining Mifreen interceptors had pulled back to link up with a large formation of additional craft loitering just outside of engagement range, roughly three hundred kilometers away.

Of course, they wouldn't remain there forever. Many scenarios went through his mind as he considered what the other side was up to. *It's possible they will let us pull out without further hostilities.* After all, deescalating a bad situation with an alien power made sense.

As Amir waited, he monitored the ground situation. While Calvin and David were getting civilians on the shuttles, they still had a long way to go. Each tick of the clock felt like a countdown to doomsday, and he wished his friend would move more quickly.

Over and over, the Hawker CAS craft made attack runs and kept the masses of paramilitary infantry at bay. Each one grated on Amir's nerves as he feared a blue-on-blue friendly-fire incident.

Then, as he was watching the sensor display, the mass of hostiles turned as one and accelerated directly toward the battlefield. *By Allah.* Amir's face grew warm, and his heart skipped a few beats. "Amir to Cohen."

"Go ahead," David replied.

"Our situation is untenable, sir. Close to two hundred enemy aircraft are headed directly for us. You have fifteen minutes until they make it impossible for your shuttles to launch without a virtual guarantee of being shot down."

"Understood, Colonel. We'll dust off in ten mikes or less. Cohen out."

Amir gripped his flight stick and angled the Phantom toward the blob of incoming Mifreen interceptors. "Amir to all fighters. Stand by for BVR combat. Everyone lock a separate bandit, and make our shots count."

―――――

Explosions echoed only twenty meters away as the Hawkers pressed the attack. David felt the pressure waves and at one point almost fell as the nearly constant bombardment by their close air support kept going. He was sure it was the only thing standing between them and death or capture. They'd almost loaded one shuttle and rapidly filled the second with scared civilians, most of whom were women and children.

A boy in the group, seeming to be no older than ten, at least in how humans assessed it, grabbed David's shirt. "My mother? Where is she?" He seemed near hysterics.

"I don't know, but we'll find her when we get all of you to safety." David knelt. "You've got to be brave and get on the shuttle. Understand?" *I hope this translation thing works.*

"Yes."

"Good man." David shoved him up the cargo ramp, and one of the Marines strapped the child in.

David turned his attention back to the stream of civilians headed toward them. Marines kept suppressive fire on their pursuers, who had once again mostly melted into the forest. "Where's Dr. Tural and the medical team? Did they get past us to the other shuttle?"

"No, sir. Not that I saw, anyway," Calvin replied.

"Cohen to Tural," David said after toggling his comm-link on.

"I read you, General."

"Sitrep?"

"We're about eighty meters out. I'm stabilizing a small girl who took a round to her chest."

David closed his eyes. Seeing such a wound on a soldier was brutal. Inflicted on a child, it brought forth emotions the likes of which David wished he could suppress, starting with an intense desire to kill every last paramilitary combatant in the battlespace. "We're out of time, Doctor. Move as fast as you can."

"She might die—"

"We're all going to perish if we don't get off this planet. Pack it in, and get her back here."

"Yes, sir."

David clicked the commlink off. "When we return to the *Lion of Judah*, I want answers."

"Me, too, sir," Calvin replied.

"Your team has performed superbly."

Calvin sent another burst of battle rifle rounds down-range. "Didn't do too bad yourself, for a space warfare officer, sir. Might want to look into Marine OCS."

David snickered. Calvin had a unique way of dropping

battlefield humor into almost any situation. "Yeah, I think I'll let you keep having most of the fun."

"Goody. More doors for me to kick in."

Keeping his rifle at the ready, David waited for the loading to complete.

———

ABOVE ALL ELSE, Dr. Izmet Tural was a healer. He looked compassionately upon every being he encountered, believing that each was a monument to God's creativity, ingenuity, and above all, His love. But he was also a soldier in the Coalition Defense Force. Precious few times had he needed to defend himself or another, and the last half hour of his life had probably been the worst combat he'd seen in twenty years. He was usually relegated to the aftereffects and tried to save as many as possible.

Tural grasped a gravely wounded Mifreen child in his arms, aware that the jostling of running through the forest while under fire could easily kill the girl. But he had no other choice. The antigrav stretchers were in use by an adult and a child in even worse shape.

"Doctor, move your ass!" Calvin thundered over the commlink. "We're about to have our rear ends handed to us out here, and I'm not interested in sticking around for that party."

"Three mikes, Colonel," Tural snapped. He'd heard David the first time.

While the shuttles and the clearing they'd arrived in were within sight, the going was still slow. Stopping to tend to the wounded along the way and getting separated from the main unit hadn't helped. He resolutely trudged through the undergrowth as the sounds of battle grew louder.

Justice 207

"I'm hit!" one of the medics cried as she twisted and fell.

All around them, pandemonium broke out as a group of Mifreen troops charged from both sides. The Marines gamely returned fire but seemed close to being overwhelmed by the sheer volume of incoming.

Tural adjusted the wounded girl to rest in one arm and drew his energy pistol with the other. He shot one of the hostile soldiers in the shoulder, and the force of the blast spun the man around.

Another fusillade of shots crashed into the small team, and the other medic fell to his knees, blood spreading across a wound in his chest. As Tural aimed at another onrushing Mifreen, he realized there were no fewer than two dozen oddly shaped alien rifles pointed at his chest, with a dozen others aimed at the remaining Marines.

"Surrender, or we will kill you where you stand."

The harsh, almost barking tone of the Mifreen paramilitary soldier came through Tural's in-ear translator. He desperately wanted to keep fighting, but death was only moments away. So he did one of the hardest things in his career as a CDF soldier—he let his pistol fall out of his hand, onto the ground. "Let me save these people. I'm a doctor, and they will die without treatment."

"They're dead already," the man replied.

"It is my oath. Please, more bodies are of no use to you. Living, breathing people are... even as hostages."

After conferring with another Mifreen, the paramilitary trooper nodded. "Fine. Do what you can. We'll kill you all without mercy if you attempt to escape or continue to resist."

Even though Tural hoped that David and Calvin would engineer a miracle, he resigned himself to being taken prisoner. *It is the will of Allah.* He knelt beside the nearest medic and passed a scanner over her wound. *Clean entry and exit, nicked two blood vessels and her liver.* "I'm going to open my medical kit."

"Slowly, human."

Tural slid the soft-skinned case toward him and gingerly opened the restraining straps. It flipped open, revealing a full trauma kit. He retrieved an emergency cauterizer before injecting the woman with a dose of a numbing agent around the wound. "There will be intense pain, but this will hold you until we get to better facilities."

She simply pursed her lips and nodded.

Allah, bless my hands so that I may heal in Your name. He continued helping the others.

24

"WE'VE GOT A PROBLEM. They captured Doc Tural and a few others. Can't tell how many," Calvin said as he pushed another Mifreen civilian into the shuttle.

"*What*?" David kept shoving the fleeing women and children into the cargo shuttle as fast as their legs would carry them. "Where?"

"Fifty, maybe sixty meters out."

"Leave six Marines here for guard duty. We'll get the rest and push forward," David said as the last Mifreen boarded. More than anything, he was mad at himself for letting the situation get so far out of hand.

"Negative, sir."

David spun around. "That's an order, Colonel. I'm not leaving my people behind on this planet."

"With respect, sir, there're at least a hundred enemy combatants out there, probably more. They have good enough weaponry to kill us. Half my men are wounded."

"You're also wearing power armor, and we have enough air support to level a city."

"Did you forget about the hundreds of hostile interceptors inbound? We've got to go *now*."

He was right. *And if Calvin advocates retreat, it's for
survival.* But that didn't make it any easier to accept. They
were so close to exfiltrating. "We *can't* leave them."

Calvin put his armored gauntlet on David's shoulder.
"We'll be coming back, sir. I know you well enough for that.
But if we don't go now, all that will happen is these bastards
will end up with dozens of hostages and us for prisoners.
That won't do our people any good."

For a moment, David considered overriding him and
leading a rescue team personally, if necessary. *No. He's right.
We have to dust off.* He felt like punching the shuttle's hull.
"Get everyone inside."

Almost on cue, a group of Mifreen paramilitaries
appeared at the edge of the clearing, only to be cut down by
battle rifle rounds from Marines still outside their shuttles.

"Wrap it up now!" David shouted.

"You first, sir." Calvin gestured to the aft hatch.

David climbed through, followed quickly by a few
Marines who had been providing cover and Calvin. The
moment they were in, the ramp closed.

Calvin slammed his palm onto the intercom. "Warrant,
get us airborne immediately. That goes for all shuttles." He
let go and spoke into his helmet-mounted commlink. "Hey,
Amir, you're always talking about how great a pilot you are.
Now's the time to put up or shut up, buddy. We're headed
back to the *Lion*, and all four craft are loaded to max takeoff
capacity."

David sat and latched into his harness as the shuttle left
the ground, pitched up, and accelerated. For the entire
ascent into the atmosphere, he prayed in Hebrew for the
safety of Dr. Tural, his people, and the rest of the Mifreen

civilians they'd left behind—and plotted his next move to get them back.

———

AIBEK STEEPLED HIS FINGERS. His battle lust was up, and everything around him slowed down. The feeling came naturally for Saurians, whose instincts had been honed over hundreds if not thousands of generations. He stared at the tactical plot and the mass of blue icons headed back to the *Lion of Judah*. The moment they landed on the flight deck, Aibek planned to jump out, as he saw no reason to stick around there.

"Conn, Communications. I'm getting a text transmission from the Mifreen government, sir. They're ordering us to leave immediately, or hostilities will commence."

"Perhaps they have not noticed that already happened," Aibek hissed dryly.

Several members of the bridge team snickered.

But Ruth's smile dropped immediately. "Conn, TAO. Aspect change. Numerous static satellites show increased power readings, sir."

"Do you classify them as a threat?"

"Unknown, sir, but there're a *lot* of them. Two hundred plus."

"Switch designation from Sierra to Master for all contacts displaying the characteristics described, Lieutenant."

"Aye, aye, sir. Populating the board with Master One through Two Hundred Sixteen." Ruth squinted at her display. "Energy buildup continuing, sir."

Some Saurians claimed they could feel the approach of battle. Aibek had never had such a sixth sense, as his human friends would've called it, but something was clearly about to happen. *It will most likely not be good.* "Communications, warn the shuttles and our fast movers."

"Aye, aye, sir," Taylor replied.

All at once, the darkness of the void came alive. Streaks of purple energy in the shape of spheres with dazzling streamers trailing from them raced toward the *Lion of Judah*. They had no time to evade as the first wave hit.

Aibek watched as their forward and ventral shield cohesion dropped precipitously in seconds. "Navigation, break orbit, and execute evasive maneuvers. TAO, what are they attacking us with?"

Ruth cleared her throat. "Muonic-based weaponry, sir. It's especially nasty."

Aibek raised an eye scale. The Matrinids used such technology back in the Milky Way, and it was considered superior to Coalition and even Saurian armaments. "Firing point procedures, neutron beams, Master..." He checked the tactical plot for the nearest planetary-defense satellites. "Eighty-One through Ninety-Five."

"Firing solutions set, sir."

"Match bearings, shoot, neutron beams."

The *Lion of Judah*'s primary energy-weapon emplacements roared to life, and blue spears of concentrated particles erupted from all twenty emitters. They lashed back at the Mifreen platforms, whose shields, for the most part, held. One satellite, which happened to take the brunt of three separate beams, blew apart.

Ruth turned her head. "Sir, I don't know what's powering those things, but it's strong enough to resist two direct hits from a neutron beam."

"Can you tell if they have miniaturized antimatter reactors?"

Justice   213

"Maybe once we review the sensor data in full, but their shields are blocking our attempts to get higher-resolution scans right now."

Aibek didn't like it. He was used to their weapons being more than a match for near-peer opponents. To run into such resistance from a planet without FTL capability puzzled him. "Suggestions, Lieutenant?"

"Alpha strike, sir, with mag-cannons, Starbolt missiles, and energy weapons. Carve a lane for our people to fly through, on the thought that the Mifreen equipped their planetary defense system with point defense."

It sounded like a reasonable approach. "Make tubes sixty through ninety ready in all respects, Lieutenant. Open outer doors."

"All tubes showing ready, sir. Outer doors are open. Magnetic cannons loaded with EMP shells."

"Firing point procedures, magnetic cannons, neutron beams, and tubes sixty through ninety, Master Eighty-One through Ninety-Four."

"Firing solutions set, sir."

"Match bearings, shoot, all weapons."

A simultaneous exchange of fire occurred between the Mifreen satellites and the *Lion of Judah*. While the purple balls streaked in front of the ship, her weapons spoke as one. The large forward vertical rail launching system for the Starbolts caused the entire vessel to shudder for close to fifteen seconds as one missile after another launched.

Meanwhile, mag-cannon rounds, moving at thirty percent light speed, slammed into the enemy's deflectors and exploded. Flashes of different colors abounded as the *Lion* pounded her foes.

"Conn, TAO. Improved results, sir. Nine contacts destroyed."

"How many more until our fighters and shuttles can safely approach?"

Ruth tapped a button on her console. "That depends on your definition of 'safely,' sir. Right now, we'd need to knock out nearly fifty more to ensure unfettered access to our landing bay without much risk."

Aibek raised an eye scale. *Given the rate of our deflector depletion, we do not have that kind of time. Nor can I expend so much of our weapons stores.* "What about full-power combat landings?"

"We'll take some armor damage at the minimum, sir."

"Target the nearest Mifreen contacts at your discretion. Neutron beams only, Captain." Aibek turned his head. "Communications, signal Colonel Amir to execute a high-speed landing of all craft. Instruct him they must get it done on the first try."

"Aye, aye, sir," Taylor replied.

Though it was a tall order, if anyone could pull it off, the battle-hardened pilots of Amir's wing could. *May the Prophet walk with you.* Aibek peered at the tactical plot as the icons representing the shuttles, Phantoms, and Hawkers got ever closer. An idea dawned on him. "TAO, could you program one of our Starbolts to fly at a right angle to our friendly fast movers?"

Ruth glanced back. "With thrust overloaded to make it look like a larger target than it is?"

"It would not fool them for long—"

"But we only need a few seconds." Ruth gave a fierce warrior's grin. "I suggest using six warheads and keep them guessing as much as possible."

"Do it," Aibek hissed.

"Aye, aye, sir."

Commands and responses went back and forth for

Justice   215

several minutes as the *Lion* maneuvered into position, all the while under fire from the Mifreen muonic-energy weapons. Ruth took out a few more of the satellites but not enough to slacken the incoming sufficiently for them to relax.

"Conn, TAO. Forward missile room reports modifications made and all six Starbolts loaded into tubes one through six."

"Make tubes one through six ready in all respects, and open outer doors. Targeting vectors away from our craft."

"Aye, aye, sir. Tubes one through six ready. Outer doors are open."

"Snap shot, tubes one through six."

The deck plates rattled, and the bright engine plumes shone through the transparent-alloy windows at the front of the bridge.

"All tubes fired electronically, sir."

Aibek held his breath and only exhaled when it became obvious the Mifreen platforms were splitting their fire between the missiles, the *Lion*, and her small craft. "There is our opening. Tell Amir it is now or never. TAO, stand by to drop our shields."

"Aye, aye, sir."

He counted off five seconds and watched as the gaggle of fighters and shuttles accelerated toward the *Lion*. "Drop fore shields *now*."

Whoever or whatever controlled the Mifreen weapons seemed to realize the *Lion of Judah*'s defenses were down. Suddenly, all the newly fired purple orbs headed straight toward them.

Aibek debated what to do. *If I attempt to evade, Amir will have to break off at the last second. That is less than ideal.* In the end, he could do nothing except stay the course. As the purple orbs smacked into the armor plating on the

Lion's bow, small pieces of molten alloy broke off in the void.

The first group of fighters touched down, followed by the shuttles, as the pummeling continued.

"Sir, we've got microfractures across the main hull, deck six through ten," Silva interjected. "Emergency forcefields in place."

"Master Chief, sound collision alarm. Evacuate all sections fore of the hangar deck," Aibek hissed. It was the only mitigation effort he could take without risking the rest of the pilots.

"Aye, aye, sir," Silva replied.

In groups of two, the remaining Phantoms and Hawkers zoomed into the pressurized hangar bay. Aibek felt as if the enemy were holding a blade to his throat as each second ticked by. *Hurry, as your lives depend on it.* He flicked his forked tongue in the air, tasting the fear. "Navigation, stand by for emergency Lawrence jump. Put us behind the primary Mifreen moon."

"Aye, aye, sir."

"Hull breach, deck eight!" Silva called. "Venting atmosphere across deck eight, sir."

Aibek sat unmoving. He didn't breathe. His eyes tracked the final two blue icons as they merged with the *Lion* and disappeared. "TAO, raise forward shields. Navigation, execute emergency jump."

Immediately, the rumbling and shaking ceased. Moments later, a swirling multicolored vortex opened in front of the mighty vessel, and she accelerated through. Aibek hoped there was no irreparable damage. "Senior Chief, away all damage-control parties, and get me a report as soon as possible."

"Aye, aye, sir."

I pray General Cohen is safe. Aibek considered going down to find out, but his place was on the bridge in the event of further emergencies. *David will join us as soon as he is able. Until then, thank the Prophet they are still alive, as are we.*

EVEN THOUGH HE held on for dear life, David pitched forward as his shuttle executed a combat landing on the *Lion*'s flight deck. Marines and wounded civilians crowded around. The ramp opened a few seconds after the craft came to a halt, and medical personnel rushed in. While they moved quickly, no one was panicked.

I suppose we learned how to ignore stress after being at war for a few decades. David pressed himself against the bulkhead to stay out of the way before stepping out after the outward flow of people slowed. All four assault shuttles were parked in a rough semicircle, with dozens of soldiers ringing them. He noted a fair number of masters-at-arms, an overwhelming number of paramedics, and a trauma team from the medical bay.

One of the senior physicians, Dr. Bhatt, rushed up to David. "Sir, I can't find Dr. Tural. Do you know where he is?"

David froze, as if his mouth were unable to function. Finally, he replied, "The Mifreen captured him." As Bhatt's face morphed and his jaw dropped, David continued. "We'll get him back, Doctor. See to the wounded. There are a lot of them."

Bhatt gestured to David's arm. "Including you, sir."

"Flesh wound. Take care of the others first."

"But—"

"That's an order, Doctor. I'll be fine."

He nodded and scurried off, leaving David to his thoughts. It took a moment to realize the last hour was catching up to him. Ground combat was something David had experienced repeatedly, ranging from boarding attempts on various vessels to large-scale pitched battles between League of Sol and TCMC units. But what he recalled observing only a few times was the murder of innocent women and children. *Even the worst Leaguer would generally try not to shoot a kid.* The sheer brutality of such an action hollowed one out. *I suppose I should thank Hashem it still bothers me after all these years. Because if it didn't, there would be something wrong.*

The time would come to count the cost and try to deal with the images in his mind. But for the moment, only one thing mattered: getting Dr. Tural and the others back.

"By the Maker!" Bo'hai's voice pulled David out of his mental reverie as she threw her arms around him. "Are you okay?"

He blinked, processed her touch, and gently pushed her away. "I'm fine."

Bo'hai's eyes filled with tears as she took in his dirt-caked uniform, which was ripped in several places and had fresh bloodstains all over it. "What—"

"I'll explain later."

"But—"

"Salena, I've got a ship to run, and we're in the middle of a combat situation. I know you're scared, but I need you to be strong. If you want to help, go assist the medical teams, and try to talk to these civilians. Keep them calm. Someone who's friendly and not in a uniform would go a long way there."

The hurt at being dismissed spilled onto Bo'hai's face, but she quickly forced a neutral expression. "Yes... I will."

Justice 219

"We'll talk later. Once the emergency is over."

She nodded before turning and walking away.

Calvin had been waiting off to the side, and he approached as she departed. "Don't be too hard on her, sir. Civvies don't understand what we do."

David didn't have time to think about his relationship, Bo'hai's feelings, or *anything* else besides the task at hand. "That's the truth. How bad is it, Cal?"

"Bad, sir." Calvin's faceplate was up, and the ever-tough and seemingly unflappable Marine wore a thousand-meter stare. "Six KIA. Half the rest are wounded, but I'm more concerned that these aliens have weapons superior to our armor."

From a tactical and strategic perspective, they'd still won, but David knew what Calvin was getting at: the TCMC and CDF weren't invincible in that solar system. *And even if we have an edge, losing twenty-five percent of our people isn't an option.* "We need better numbers on how many of those rail-gun rifles they deployed."

"I'll go through the tapes personally, sir."

David nodded. "Have Major Almeida ensure our guests are placed in quarters, under guard. I want Marines patrolling the passageways and masters-at-arms checking on them every fifteen minutes."

"Yes, sir. Permission to confiscate all clothing and personal belongings? We could issue them athletic clothes or jumpsuits."

"No, keep them in their outfits. If they're all in jumpsuits or our style of dress, it would make a breakout easier. Take everything else."

Calvin raised an eyebrow. "Worried about that?"

"We have no way of knowing for sure whether any of them are terrorists, and if they are, what better way to strike back at your government than hijacking a 1.2-kilometer-long warship's weapon systems?"

"Makes perfect sense, sir. I'll see to it."

"Good. Then get Markul up to the conference room on deck one. Oh, and Cal? Put him through a body-cavity search. I don't trust him not to try something funny, and I want to ensure we have every piece of electronics he owns. Also, two armed Marines with him at all times. Including when he takes a leak."

"Roger that, sir." Calvin smirked. "You're gonna ruin his day."

"He can sue us." David blew out a breath.

"What are you going to do, sir?"

David stared into Calvin's eyes. "Find a way to get our people home. I'll see you in the conference room at fifteen hundred hours."

"Yes, sir," Calvin replied before turning and marching off.

Once again, a simple desire to help others and get the *Lion* home had blown up in David's face. He was aggravated with himself for not anticipating that the Mifreen would see through their stealth measures. *Perhaps they played us all along. Or maybe Markul did. Who knows? There's also the possibility of it being blind luck that the Mifreen hit that camp when they did.* The only thing he considered a priority at the moment was the safe return of Dr. Tural and the other medical staff. *Then we'll sort the rest.*

25

THE RECRUITS HAD MOVED on from focusing on raw physical training after they shot expertly with Terran Coalition battle rifles and standard-issue pulse-energy sidearms. Tinetariro had changed up the program slightly once she noticed a few Zeivlots and Zavlots finally willing to help one another. Since Has'rad had done so in the gas-chamber evolution, it had spread to enough of the trainees that perhaps half of them begrudgingly got along.

Though it wasn't anywhere near perfect, considering how things had gone when they started, Tinetariro would take it and thank the good Lord in heaven above for anything approaching success.

They were drilling primarily inside a custom-built structure that housed a re-creation of an Ajax-class destroyer bridge, a primary engine room, a shuttle bay, and a corridor with a simulated hull breach. While "A" schools typically taught the detailed skills required for occupational specialties, Tinetariro wanted to incorporate as much knowledge transfer as possible into the program, especially since they didn't have access to the CDF's training centers, which were spread across a dozen planets back in the Milky Way.

She envisioned a lot of hands-on training once the first few destroyers were built, followed by establishing both A and C schools to get as many recruits up to speed as quickly as possible.

The bridge mockup was by no means perfect, but it was usable. Tinetariro stood in the back as ten recruits practiced manipulating the consoles. Red lights flashed, and the words "Simulation Ended" popped up on the control screen on her tablet.

"Recruit Sey'nati, you have lost yet another destroyer," Tinetariro deadpanned. "Care to explain your reasoning?"

"Master Chief," Sey'nati replied, coming to a ramrod-straight posture. "I sought to use the tools at my disposal to destroy the enemy, ma'am."

Tinetariro glanced at the simulation status screen. "It says here the enemy vessel is still functional, yet you and four hundred sixty-eight soldiers are dead. How is that a victory?"

"We died as martyrs. The Maker will honor our sacrifice and grant our brothers a victory."

"On the battlefield, the only thing that matters is killing the enemy. You kill them before they kill you. Dying some glorious death for God doesn't cut it in the Coalition Defense Force." Tinetariro narrowed her eyes. "To put it succinctly, our job is to live for our country while making the other side die for theirs."

"Master Chief, then what of those in the CDF who gave their lives to save our worlds? First Lieutenant Shmeul Kaplan rammed a missile to keep it from hitting Zavlot," one of those in the back piped up.

Tinetariro gave him a withering stare. "I don't recall

speaking to you, recruit!" She softened for a moment. "There are times when death is unavoidable. And if that time ever comes for me, I won't hesitate to make the ultimate sacrifice for my crewmates and my country. But I will *not* waste my life on meaningless gestures that don't alter the battle and cost others their lives. *Nor will you.*"

Sey'nati opened his mouth a few times, seemingly unsure whether he should speak.

"Out with it," Tinetariro snapped.

"Master Chief, what should I have done?"

"Assessed the tactical and strategic landscape. You had at least one option to destroy the vessel you were fighting... ramming it. There was retreat as well. Given the parameters of the test, a retreat was the best solution."

All the recruits exchanged glances.

Finally, Sey'nati spoke. "That's not how we were taught."

"I don't give a flying rip," Tinetariro replied. "The only thing that matters is how we do things in the Coalition Defense Force because *that's* the uniform you will wear."

"Yes, Master Chief."

"Reset the sim. Different scenario. Try it again. Oh, and Recruit Nar'gol, drop down, and give me twenty. You know better by now." A wicked grin crossed her face. *Finally, I can feel the team jelling. It's taken way too long, and we've lost too many along the way. But it'll do.*

MAJOR JOHN WILSON glanced up from his tablet in time to see a tractor beam jut out from a small space-based platform in Zeivlot orbit and latch on to a sheet of alloy. He grinned. "I believe that's a successful test."

"Yes, sir," Khattri replied.

They'd both been on the bridge for the last seven hours, overseeing the final check-out process for the in-orbit smelting system. The Zeivlots and Zavlots had mined raw ore in their asteroid belt then brought it back by the shipload for refining. Because of their respective planets' few natural resources after multiple cycles of Armageddon, that solution was better than nothing. The platform would allow them to bring small asteroids directly into orbit for refining.

And jumpstart their ability to produce high-quality alloys for my shipyard-building program. Wilson set his jaw. "Any issues?"

Khattri shook his head. "No, sir. Ready to proceed."

"Comms, order the station to vector Sierra Sixty-Eight into position. No time like the present to get this show on the road."

"Aye, aye, sir."

Back in the Milky Way, such a device would get months of testing followed by final inspections before certification. In Sextans B, they didn't have enough time for such red tape. Every minute counted in their race to build enough ships to counter the nanites.

A few kilometers away, one of the short, stubby mining vessels towed an unusually metal-rich asteroid toward the platform. It took about fifteen minutes to move into position, perfectly lining up to the approach window, as the *Salinan* stood watch.

Wilson felt impressed by the professionalism displayed by the other ship and their getting it right the first time.

"Sir, Sierra Sixty-Eight is close enough for automatic refining to engage," Khattri said while staring at his tactical readout screen.

"Very well. Engage at your discretion."

"Aye, aye, sir."

A green-blue tractor field wrapped around the seventy-meter-wide asteroid and pulled it into position. Almost immediately, cutting beams went to work.

"Flawless performance so far, sir," Khattri reported.

"Good." Wilson blew out a breath. "We've got to get caught up on our timeline. The only way to get there is continued alloy generation in orbit. Once this design is proven out over the next few weeks, I want to squeeze out enough production from the 3-D printers to make another dozen or so."

"Let me guess. That fancy chart of yours says that'll solve our problem?"

Wilson smirked. "As a matter of fact, it does, XO. Also, it's a *Gantt* chart."

"Of course, sir."

Oh, the young'uns. They'll eventually learn. Wilson put his head back down and went back to updating the tablet. *This is going to be a very long couple of years.*

26

FOLLOWING his capture by the Mifreen paramilitaries, Dr. Izmet Tural had been stripped of his equipment and uniform before being subjected to a medical examination. The experience had been rough, to say the least. Once they'd finished, he was given a pair of gray pants and a matching shirt before being fitted with a blindfold and sensory-dampening headphones.

Being cut off from most of the physical world was daunting, but Tural took it in stride. He repeatedly told himself that David would never leave him or anyone else wearing a CDF uniform behind. *I must survive long enough to be rescued without dishonoring my uniform or breaking my oaths.*

He wasn't sure how much time had passed or how far he had traveled. What Tural did know was when the blindfold and sound deadeners came off, the light and noises were overwhelming.

Perhaps thirty seconds later, his eyes adjusted. He took in the room and was surprised to see a bed that resembled something from the *Lion of Judah*'s infirmary. It had numerous wires and attachments going into it along with a

Justice 227

close-fitting headpiece. *A neurological interface?* While Tural wasn't sure exactly what it was, the thing looked evil, if a piece of machinery could somehow be imbued with darkness.

"I demand to speak with a judicial representative," Tural forced out, finding his voice. "What charge am I being held on?"

"Silence," one of the Mifreen replied and smacked him across his mouth. "You have no rights."

"As an officer in the Coalition Defense For—"

Another harsh smack hit Tural squarely in the jaw.

"Speak again, and you will regret it, human."

Three rather strong Mifreen seized Tural and manhandled him into the bed. He reflexively kicked and tried to resist, but it was impossible with his hands secured behind his back. Seconds later, they'd strapped him in and slid what Tural assumed was a neural interface over his head.

The prongs dug deeply into his scalp and caused ribbons of pain to radiate outward.

Tural cried out and jerked a leg free before he felt the hiss of an autoinjector. It took a few moments, but he rapidly lost the ability to move his extremities. *What now? Are they going to execute me? Scan my brain?* All manner of nightmare scenarios went through his mind, but he tempered them with his knowledge of medicine. *It is unlikely they will want to kill me, as I am a higher-ranking officer and more valuable alive.*

Bright lights swam before Tural's eyes, and everything became a blur.

One moment, he was in the dark and foreboding room. The next, a tropical island lay before him. His brain seemed to glitch as it processed the sudden change.

Tural reached for a table in front of him and grasped it.

The object felt precisely as a wooden piece of furniture ought to. He recoiled and scanned the horizon. Everywhere around him was a crystal-clear ocean with sand visible at the bottom. The island itself was no more than a few dozen meters across and contained only a tiny hut whose roof was over his head and a table with two chairs.

A figure shimmered into existence. The individual was obviously Mifreen and female, based on her physical characteristics. "Greetings, Doctor." She smiled at Tural.

"Lieutenant Colonel Izmet Muhammad Tural. Coalition Defense Force Medical Division. Serial Number 31X8013-5123. Under the terms of the Canaan Convention on Human and Alien Rights, that is the only information I must provide as a prisoner of war."

"Canaan. Is that your home world?"

Tural narrowed his eyes. "Lieutenant Colonel Izmet Muhammad Tural. Serial Number 31X8013-5123."

"What is a prisoner of war, in your definition, Dr. Tural? Or do you prefer Colonel?"

After a few moments of silence, Tural gazed around the island again. He considered explaining the POW concept to the Mifreen interrogator but decided to remain silent.

"Interesting. You see someone fighting in a declared war as having special rights as opposed to a common terrorist who uses violence. You also view yourself as a healer first and a soldier second. "

Tural's eyes widened.

"Yes, we can detect your thought patterns, Doctor."

"If that is true, you know I committed no crimes."

"You believe that, but the mind often convinces itself of things that are not true." The interrogator smiled thinly. "We will discover the truth, one way or another."

Tural placed his hands on the table, testing it once more.

Amazing how it feels like the real thing. Even the breeze was perfect.

"Why did you go to the terrorist camp?"

"Terrorists? The settlement was mostly women and children. They had no weapons. Your forces shot them in the back as they ran for their lives. I have served most of my adult life as a soldier in the Coalition Defense Force, and even our enemies, as brutal as they are, weren't *that* bad."

"When the social order is attacked, words are violence."

"The only words that are violent are direct calls *for* violence."

"Not on Mifreen. You will tell me about your ship and its weaknesses."

Tural set his jaw. "No. Never."

"We'll see about that."

———

DAVID HAD STOPPED LONG ENOUGH to get medical treatment for the cuts on his arms, legs, and torso then proceeded to the deck-one conference room for the meeting. As the adrenaline of combat wore off, he realized that practically every muscle and bone in his body hurt. *This is where I'm reminded I'm getting older.* The realization would've brought amusement had it not been for the dire predicament they were in.

"General on deck," Ruth called out as David strode in.

Everyone stood. Markul seemed to realize what the custom was a second after the rest and belatedly rose from his chair.

"As you were." David dropped into his seat at the head of the table. "This has... gone sideways."

"An understatement," Aibek replied. "Shall I begin with the damage report, sir?"

David nodded. "By all means."

"We suffered extensive armor melt on our forward quarter. Twenty were injured on the flight deck but no fatalities. The hull breach on deck eight is patched. Two neutron beams are out of commission until exterior repairs can be completed."

All in all, what Aibek described wasn't too bad, even though complete repairs would require yard time. "There's a *but* in there somewhere."

"Yes, sir." He turned to Ruth. "Captain?"

"The Mifreen use muonic weapons, sir. They're stronger than our neutron beams, and each one of those defense satellites has robust shielding."

"I get the sense you two want to tell me something."

Ruth bit her lip. "Rescuing Dr. Tural won't be a trivial matter, sir."

"The six dead Marines clued me in to that already," David snapped. He immediately regretted his choice of words as everyone's eyes widened.

"Don't worry about us, sir," Calvin interjected. "You give the word, and we'll turn that damn planet inside out."

David appreciated the sentiment but felt hollow after what had just transpired. "I aim to avoid that by working out a diplomatic solution."

Markul cleared his throat. "May I, uh, speak?"

This better not be a complaint about being searched thoroughly. "Go ahead."

"You won't be getting anything out of the government. They can't... To give back your doctor and personnel would be an admission of defeat. Our system only works when

Justice 231

there is no question about who's in charge. All power resides with inner and outer committees, and it is absolute."

"So what? If they don't maintain the appearance of complete control, there will be riots?" David crossed his arms. "Forgive me, but most of your people don't hit me as the marching-in-the-street types."

"They're not. But if it became clear that an outside entity can vanquish them, it would inspire more. Eventually, enough to make a difference."

"We're not here to effect regime change on Mifreen, even if that's a cause I'd back personally."

Markul stared at him with lifeless eyes. "Try what you must, General. But the only way to get your people back will be through force. I offer my services to assist in infiltrating the Mifreen networks and to help you beef up your security, because compared to ours, it's pretty lax. Expect them to exploit that."

It took everything in David's power to keep from telling the alien hacker he'd already done enough. *That's not fair, and I know it. There's no evidence to suggest he knew what was coming.* "I have some pretty severe trust issues with you, Markul."

"To be expected. I wouldn't trust me either after what just happened, but I want everyone in this room to know I had no inkling they would be coming. And frankly, what I saw put this all into perspective. We've heard about the death squads, about the round-up gangs that shoot women and children without a thought. I... I hoped it was an exaggeration."

David's mind went back to the Holocaust on twentieth-century Earth and his more recent brush with human-run genocide on Monrovia. "We often think that because it's easier to accept than the reality of how quickly monsters can take over. Humans aren't immune."

"I'll volunteer to have my people watch Mr. Markul, sir. If you decide to proceed," Taylor said.

"What exactly do you think you can find?"

"The general if not exact location where Dr. Tural is confined. Aside from that, we might be able to grab a window to run the simulations Dr. Hayworth would like run. It depends on where your people are being held."

"Simulations for the nanite weapon?"

Markul nodded. "Yes, General."

David sat back. *That's certainly a new wrinkle.* "A secondary objective. Dr. Tural and our medics are the primary and most important. And anyone we can find from the settlement if they're at the same installation."

"And what of the people already rescued?" Markul asked softly.

"Let's get through this crisis then address that subject."

Markul slowly licked his lips. "I understand."

David turned to Hanson. "Major, pull out all the stops to get us one hundred percent ready for combat. I want you to activate the second- and third-shift damage control teams and put as many teams on armor repair as possible."

"Yes, sir."

"Very well. Let's get to it. Oh, and, Markul... one last thing. If you violate my trust and attempt to use your access to the *Lion's* computer system for any nefarious purpose, including hijacking its weapons to make some sort of statement against the Mifreen government, I'll turn you back over to them without hesitation. Do I make myself clear?"

"I understand."

"Good." David glanced around the room. "Any saved rounds?"

Justice

Silence was the only reply.

"In that case, dismissed."

The rest of them filed out quickly, but David stayed behind. His head was still swimming with the scenes from the combat and the suddenness with which it had all gone down. While he was sure the call to protect the settlement's inhabitants was the right one, especially after the ruthlessness displayed by the Mifreen paramilitaries, that wouldn't bring the six Marines back. *More letters on my watch. Sometimes I hate this job.* After a few more minutes, he forced himself up and back to work. He would have plenty of time for retrospection later.

27

DEEP in the bowels of the *Lion of Judah*, David steadied himself. He'd decided to hold his virtual meeting with the Mifreen council in the classified comms space rather than on the bridge or his day cabin, primarily to avoid the blowout argument that was almost sure to happen affecting morale throughout the vessel.

He was alone, having specifically requested a comms rating to configure the call before ordering the young woman to leave.

David pressed the button to connect, and a few minutes later, the video display came alive with a holoprojected 3-D image of the conference room he'd visited on Mifreen. The council was present, led by Tal Quosan. The screen split in two as they connected to the netsim, and a spectacular view of the tropical island the inner leaders seemed to live on came into view.

Hes Sansan cleared his throat and spoke directly into the holoprojector. "General Cohen, I am outraged at your actions on our world. We offered you a hand of friendship,

Justice

and instead, you murdered countless Mifreen with your war machines."

David kept his expression as neutral as he could. *I expected this bluster to start.* "Are you quite done?"

"How long have you been lying to us, General? Since you arrived? Do you have an invasion fleet waiting? Has anything you've told us been true?"

"Again... are you quite done?"

Quosan held up a hand. "Do you wish to offer a rebuttal?"

"I *never* lied to you. The Terran Coalition came as friends, and we do not desire military confrontation with the Mifreen people. Your forces shot first, both at us and at innocent civilians. Clearly, we have different cultures, but as a soldier, who in my society is someone sworn to protect the weak at all costs, including their life, I will *not* stand by as such a thing plays out in front of me."

"Even if that's true, it doesn't excuse the direct provocation of your forces landing on our world. Answer that, human."

David pursed his lips. Sansan had a point. *And if it were me, I'd be hopping mad too.* "We were contacted by a member of your society who offered us additional information on the netsim. That information pointed to a disturbing pattern, which I wanted to vet further."

"By landing military assets on our planet? You could've asked us and saved all this shedding of blood."

"And your government would've been honest about rounding people up and killing them?"

Quosan crossed his arms. "We don't do that. The situation escalated dramatically because of *your* involvement."

"I don't think so," David replied. "Your paramilitary troops acted like they'd done it before and mowed down unarmed men, women, and children without remorse. That's not something you just go and do. The way they acted... I suspect that's how you handle every one of those settlements."

"What you suspect doesn't matter, nor does how we deal with internal issues. Or so you've claimed."

"We will never come to an agreement here. I encourage us to instead focus on the return of my people, at which point we'll be on our way."

Sansan and Quosan exchanged glances through the vidlink.

"The only exchange we're willing to make is for you to turn over all Mifreen citizens to us, and we will return the humans," Sansan finally said.

"Your people have requested political asylum from the Terran Coalition. I will not return them to be imprisoned or killed for their beliefs."

Sansan stood up from his wicker chair and angrily thrust it backward. "How dare you tell us what *you* will do with our citizens? They will be punished for their violence against the state."

"What violence?" David asked incredulously. "There were no weapons there or explosives or anything that could be used as such."

"Any person who resists the state by word or deed commits violence."

David's blood ran cold. *Spoken like a true authoritarian.* "That's not how we look at the universe. Violence is *physical action*. Speaking for or against something is *not* violence."

"In your culture, not ours."

David wanted to scream back at them that it didn't matter what they thought—right was still right, as wrong was still wrong. But he didn't because it would serve no purpose. "We're not turning them over because it's against our laws to surrender refugees to a government that would harm them."

"Then you will not get *your* people back, General," Sansan replied haughtily. "Unless you intend to take them by force, and I promise you the next time you engage us, the outcome will be different."

David narrowed his eyes. "Making an enemy of the Terran Coalition is not something to do lightly, Hes Sansan. Far better for us to part without animosity—especially after you killed nine of my people."

"Return the terrorists."

We're going in circles. David leaned forward. "That's not happening."

"Then we have nothing else to say. Depart our solar system at once," Sansan replied.

It appeared Quosan was about speak, but as he raised his hand, both feeds went black. The room was dark for a few moments before the lights autoadjusted.

David leaned back, aggravated with how poorly the interaction had gone. He replayed it several times in mind, confident that the Mifreen position wouldn't change unless they got the refugees back. *Weak is a regime that is this afraid of dissent. That leaves me with one option.* Yet another conflict bothered David's soul. It seemed all they did lately was fight. But there were times when war was the only way. *This is one of them.*

He keyed his handcomm for Aibek.

A moment later, the Saurian responded. "Yes, sir?"

"Get the senior officers together, and start planning a rescue mission for Dr. Tural. I'd prefer a pinpoint raid with a limited force profile. But whatever Demood and Amir feel is best. Oh, and a secondary objective is to rescue as many civilians who want to leave as possible. Have somebody pick Markul's brain to gain insights on how we do that."

"Yes, sir. Give us a few hours."

"Roger. Cohen out."

———

AFTER THE DISASTROUS conversation with Mifreen's leadership, David decided to take some time walking the decks of the *Lion of Judah*. How everything had fallen apart over just a few hours bothered him, but as he replayed the events repeatedly in his mind, he realized he could've done little differently. *Except walk away.* But that wasn't an option either. To turn away from those in distress would be turning his back on everything he believed. *As a CDF soldier and as a Jew.* Still, it left David with a thorny problem: how to rescue Dr. Tural and his people while not starting a larger conflict. *If that's even possible.*

David ended up in the berthing compartments for enlisted crew members, where the Mifreen refugees had been placed. Numerous masters-at-arms covered the area in blanket security while power-armored Marines formed checkpoints at each bulkhead between sections.

The group he approached all came to attention while the Marines saluted.

"Sir, what can we do for you?" one of the enlisted ratings asked.

"Direct me to Ranjan's quarters. I'd like to have a few words."

"This way, sir."

The young private led him down about twenty meters to a hatch that had another master-at-arms posted outside. It swung open to reveal a nondescript NCO's quarters.

Justice 239

Designed for four chief petty officers, it only held one occupant.

Ranjan stood from a chair in the center of the room. Her right eye was swollen and her hair matted with blood. Still, something about how she carried herself spoke to pride. "General Cohen."

"Haven't you been to the medical bay?"

"Yes, but there were so many who needed serious treatment that I didn't want to burden them. I will be fine." Ranjan's face contorted. "Unlike so many who perished." Pain and shame radiated out of her.

"It's not your fault, what happened down there."

"I should've protected them better."

"May I come in? I'd like to discuss what happens next."

"It is your ship, is it not?"

"Yes, but that doesn't mean I check my manners at the door." David took a few steps in and nodded to the enlisted personnel, who closed the hatch behind him.

"Even with the horror we went through only hours ago, stopping to think that we are flying through the cosmos is astonishing." Ranjan crossed her arms and limped back to the chair. "Have you spoken with our government yet?"

"Oh, yes." David grimaced. "They want to trade you and your compatriots for our people."

Ranjan's face paled even more, and her lip quivered. "Will... are..."

"No. Absolutely not. We don't negotiate with terrorists, and what those soldiers..." David could barely bring himself to say the word, as what the Mifreen had done went against every rule of war. "Did puts them in the vein of the worst I've seen during my time in the service."

"Is this enough for you to act against our government?"

David let out a sigh. "It's not that simple. From a moral

perspective, absolutely. But I lack the military forces to effect a regime change. The best I can do is guarantee your safety."

"Then what will become of us?"

"Would you be willing to live on a different world? Among an alien species?"

"Yours?"

David shook his head. "No. We're far from where humans call home. But we've made allies, and they owe us favors." He forced a small smile to his lips. "And I'll call one in."

A longer-than-usual pause between the words Ranjan spoke in her native language followed before they echoed in English through the translator. "What if they won't accept us? My people will... They'll wipe our minds for this. You cannot send us back."

David pursed his lips. "Listen to me carefully. I'm not sending you or anyone else back. As far as I'm concerned, those we rescued have sought asylum under the provisions of the Terran Coalition charter. First Lieutenant Cuellar, from the JAG corps, will meet individually with your people, and we'll make it official."

"What of your people? I overheard the, ah, Marines, is it? Discussing many who were shot, and some who didn't make it."

"We lost too many. *Any* life lost is too many. But none of us regret our actions."

"Is there anything I... we could do to help?"

David shook his head. "The medical staff has it well in hand. Do you, perhaps, believe in a higher power? If so, prayers would be welcome."

Ranjan tilted her head. "A higher power... I do not know this phrase."

Justice 241

"What humans call God, in various forms and names. The being who created the universe."

"Ah. Some traditions talk of this, but they dropped out of belief long ago." Ranjan made a face. "We are told that because of the netsim, *we're* gods. I may not pray, but I will fervently wish, with the rest of my people, for a full recovery by yours."

"That's all we can do now. Well, aside from one thing. We're going to have to go down there and get our people. I'd be grateful if anyone in your group could provide intelligence."

"I'm not sure if anything we know would help, but question us however you wish. We will answer honestly and openly."

David stood. "Good. I'll keep you informed as to what happens next, but for now, stay in your quarters, and once the crisis is over, we'll give everyone access to the enlisted mess hall and basic recreational facilities."

"Thank you, General."

"Godspeed, Ranjan." David turned on his heel and pushed the hatch open. After a curt nod to the soldiers outside, he moved down the passageway, back toward the gravlift. *Yet another delicate situation I've gotten us into. Hayworth, as usual, is right about interference. So why can't we stop doing it? Or perhaps more importantly, why can't I?* David knew, somewhere deep inside, that he had a need to right things that were wrong. Beyond defending his home, it was why he'd ended up as a career soldier in the CDF. *Now to see if I can pull us out of this without the loss of even more lives. HaShem, I need Your wisdom more than ever.*

28

LIGHTS FLASHED in front of Tural's eyes. He faded in and out of consciousness, or at least it felt as if he was. The experience was unlike any other in his life. A rich aroma hit his nostrils, and he recognized it as a mixture of turmeric and coriander. His eyes blinked open to reveal a table before him. *My home on Arabia Prime? How can this be?* Without thinking, he reached for a piece of pita and used it to scoop up a large bite of *zaalouk*, a Moroccan eggplant dish among his favorites, and shoveled it into his mouth.

The food tasted even better than he remembered. It almost melted in his mouth, and he gasped in shock. *Where am I?*

Tural nearly jumped out of his skin when he felt a familiar touch.

Zaha, his wife, sat next to him, and as he watched, she stroked his arm. "You look as if you've seen a ghost."

"This cannot..." *It must be the netsim. That is the only logical explanation.*

"You're having it again, aren't you?" Zaha asked in a soothing tone.

"What?"

"The feeling of being out of your body. The doctors said it would fade in time. You're home, Izmet. It's okay. You all made it home."

Tural blinked. "The *Lion of Judah* got back?"

"Yes." Zaha smiled.

"I don't remember. The last thing I recall, we were on a planet in Sextans B." Tural groped around in his memory but couldn't quite recall how he'd come to be where he currently was.

"Yes, you keep having flashbacks." She put her head on his shoulder and kissed him. "It's happened to a lot of you. But you are *home* now."

As he was about to open his mouth to ask another question, everything shifted. The room spun then disappeared in a bright flash of light. *What?* It was difficult to process the sudden change. One moment, he was on Arabia Prime. The next, back in the cold, dark room he vaguely recalled and strapped into a bed with various wires and a headset attached to him.

"*Where am I?*" Tural screamed. "Who are you?"

"You are on Mifreen, Doctor. Calm yourself."

"No. I was home."

An alien woman came into his field of view. She smiled. "You were in our netsim."

"No. This isn't real. I was home."

"Tell me what I want to know, and you can go back."

Tural's eyes shifted around the room. *I am a prisoner.* "What do you want?"

"Explain to me how the *Lion of Judah*'s armaments work and its defensive technologies."

I must maintain control. Allah, help me to discern reality from what is fake. He gathered all his energy to force his lips to form the word. "No."

"If you tell me, I'll send you home."

Tural's mind swam. *Not real. Not real. I'm on Mifreen. That's it. Not real.* "No! I will not betray my oath." He coughed violently and thrashed against his bonds.

"Tell me, and I will send you home, Doctor."

"I demand to speak with a representative of the Terran Coalition!" Tural tried to move his head to no avail.

The Mifreen interrogator stepped out of his line of sight. He heard her voice as an echo.

"Put him back in."

Lights flashed in front of his eyes once more, and he felt like he was falling. *Allah, please help me. Let me resist.* Reality was no longer easily discernible.

29

MARKUL TRUDGED through the corridors of the *Lion* with a master-at-arms close behind. While no longer tightly restricted to his quarters, he still had to ask permission to go anywhere besides the enlisted mess or observation deck. *The experience I am having today would've been considered a particularly vivid fiction story not a month ago.*

He still found it difficult not to think that somehow he'd ended up in the netsim. One could use various tests to determine whether they were in the physical world, and so far, they'd checked out—the biggest being Markul couldn't simply imagine what he wanted.

"It's here, sir."

Markul spun around to see the enlisted soldier gesturing at a double hatch with writing he couldn't read on a nameplate next to the opening. "Thank you."

The hatch swung open, and Markul stepped inside. Dr. Hayworth, as always in his white lab coat, and several aliens of a species he didn't recognize were engrossed at their workstations.

"Yes?" Hayworth asked without looking up. "We're quite busy, so make it brief."

Markul had little experience with humans but knew from the tone of the doctor's voice that he was either angry or annoyed. *There appears to be something universal about pissed-off humanoid species.* "Are you upset in general, Doctor, or more specifically with me?"

Hayworth leaned back and grumbled. "I do not have time to discuss your feelings, Mr. Markul. If that's even your real name. There is science to be done here."

"I've been offering to help—"

"You've *helped* enough."

"I..."

"Since I have nothing else better to do," Hayworth said as he pushed off his chair and shuffled forward, "allow me to explain something to you, Mr. Markul. Are you familiar with the concept of noninterference?"

"I am afraid not."

"How about this... When a technologically advanced culture interacts with a significantly less developed species, it generally causes such upheaval in the less advanced race's society as to cause civil unrest and implosion."

Markul licked his lips. "We have never interacted with non-Mifreen in this manner, so no, these concepts are new to me, Doctor."

"They're not new to us," Hayworth replied and crossed his arms. "We know better. Mucking about in your evolution isn't just dangerous—it's *wrong*. That includes armed conflict with even an oppressive alien government, which I will concede that yours is."

"You believe it would be better to allow our government to perform unspeakable horrors on us than to use some of your power to intervene?"

Justice 247

"I don't deny it's a harsh policy and challenging to adhere to, but this is my belief. I'll defend it until the end. Humans and any other species have no business telling other races what to do or how to do it."

Markul had difficulty putting Hayworth's comments into perspective. It seemed a simple matter of right and wrong to intervene the way David and the others had. "We would probably be dead or educated by now without what you claim is wrong, Doctor. Not to mention this doesn't appear to be the policy of the Terran Coalition's government."

Hayworth snorted. "There is no Coalition government here, Mr. Markul. Only a military officer whose God-bothering tendencies come to the fore every other day!"

Several of the other scientists turned to stare.

"I apologize," Hayworth said before anyone else could speak. "This is a matter on which I have strong beliefs, but that doesn't excuse being unprofessional. General Cohen is doing what he believes is right. He and I disagree, though I feel obliged to help limit the fallout from his actions."

Markul bit his lip. "Understand that I didn't want things to go the way they did, Doctor. I know some of you believe I engineered this series of events."

"That is a hypothesis that fits the available facts."

"Yes, I had to undergo a lie detector test to prove I didn't tip off the Mifreen government," Markul replied darkly.

Hayworth shrugged. "And? A better question, Mr. Markul, is why are you in my lab?"

"I think I can help."

"You've done *quite* enough."

Markul held up his hand. "Doctor, please. I want to do something to change the equation for your people and mine. Let me do that. Allow me to make this all worth it."

"How?"

"You need to run advanced simulations against a quantum computer to determine a weapon that's effective against the nanites you're fighting, yes?"

Hayworth eyed him. "Yes. I'd hoped we could make a deal, as it were."

"If you outline the tests, I'll format them into something the netsim interface can read... and volunteer to deliver the payload."

"Can you accomplish that remotely?"

"No, it would have to be a physical connection, and I have to be there. Too much could go wrong and honestly would. The technology is kept in the most secure installations on our world."

"A wonderful senior officer staff meeting is in a few hours," Hayworth replied with a smirk. "Be there as my guest."

Markul raised an eyebrow. "I can't leave my quarters without an escort, Doctor."

"Don't worry about it. I'll handle the military." He waved toward the hatch. "Now, get out of here so I can get some work done."

Markul nodded. "I shall see you later, then, Doctor." He'd heard the human saying enough to repeat it. Hayworth grunted as Markul walked out and nodded to the enlisted soldier standing outside. On the way back to his quarters, he wondered what he was getting himself into. *I hide in the darkness and am in no way a combatant.* Perhaps that was changing.

———

DAVID ARRIVED twenty minutes early to the scheduled staff meeting. Colonels Demood and Amir had already deter-

Justice 249

mined a limited raid was out of the question and instead advocated for a full assault by most of their ground and air assets. David had reluctantly signed off and had them continue planning the requested operation, which took a few hours more.

One of the things he'd had to learn long ago about command was letting his people do their jobs. After all, they wouldn't have their ranks and positions if they weren't professionals. And while some CDF officers were indeed subpar, that didn't apply to anyone on the *Lion of Judah*—at least, not that David knew of. *If I did, I'd have transferred them off. At least, I would've before we ended up in Sextans B.*

Still, the most challenging part of that cycle was waiting. David hated being idle. While he engaged in recreational activities and spent time with friends and family, those options weren't available to him, and even if they were, he had a hard-wired need to contribute while the rest did.

David greeted each officer as he or she came in. Ruth was first, followed by Hanson, Calvin, and Amir. The closer it came to the top of the hour, the fuller the table became. Taylor, Aibek, Merriweather, and Hammond rounded out the senior staff.

Taylor took a few moments to connect the holoprojector and the four Ajax-class destroyer COs in the battlegroup with it.

Finally, Hayworth shuffled through the hatch with Markul in tow.

"This is a classified discussion," David said. "Mr. Markul isn't cleared."

"You'll want to make an exception," Hayworth replied.

"And why is that, Doctor?"

"Because he has vital information, which is why I signed off on his leaving his quarters."

David considered having a master-at-arms escort the Mifreen off deck one but decided against it. *Hayworth is typically spot on. I'll trust this is worth the risk.* "All right, I'll allow him to stay, but, Mr. Markul, mind your p's and q's here."

"Thank you, General," Hayworth replied. He gestured to an empty side chair in the back, and Markul ambled over.

"Let's get started," David said when the hatch slid shut. "Top of the agenda is executing a limited incursion onto Mifreen."

Ruth, Amir, and Calvin exchanged glances as if asking who would go first.

"We have a problem, sir," Ruth said. "To take out enough of the Mifreen defense satellites that we can stage the rescue of Dr. Tural as well as rescue the civilians from a separate point, we'd have to expend a lot of our weapons inventory."

"How much?"

"Forty percent of our missiles and that much or more mag-cannon rounds."

"That would leave us in a poor position to deal with other threats," Aibek hissed.

David licked his lips. That was out of the question, given their current lack of ability to produce more munitions. "Do you have a different solution?"

"As much as I hate saying this, sir, reducing our efforts to saving Tural only is the only way to trim the war materiel costs," Calvin replied.

"How many Mifreen have responded to Markul's appeal?"

"At least five hundred accounted for," Taylor said.

David let his head fall back against the chair. "There has to be a better answer... another way."

Several seconds of uncomfortable silence followed.

Justice 251

"Sometimes we can't have our cake and eat it, too, sir," Ruth finally said.

"Even if we could figure out that problem somehow, the fact remains that our embarked air wing can't be in two places at once." Amir shook his head. "I see no way to accomplish this, sir. By Allah, I am sorry."

Static crackled over the commlink line before Lieutenant Colonel Anton Savchenko's voice echoed. "If I may, General?" He was the commanding officer of the CSV *Margaret Thatcher*, a block II Ajax-class destroyer and the most capable of the *Lion*'s escorts.

"Go ahead. I'm open to *any* sane ideas."

Savchenko's face popped onto the holoprojector along with a view of his senior staff gathered around a table in a much smaller conference room. "Not quite sure this will qualify as sane, sir. But we could jump in right outside the atmosphere then fly down on top of the coordinates where the civilians will gather."

"You wish to enter a planet's atmosphere?" Aibek hissed. "Our vessels are not designed for such an activity."

"An Ajax's hull can handle the stress, and it's the only play we've got to accomplish both objectives," Savchenko replied.

David turned to Hanson. "Major, what's your take from an engineering perspective?"

"The colonel's correct, sir. Block II hulls especially can handle the load, assuming shields are up and at nearly full strength. Though I'd like to caution everyone that jumping in close enough to make this work will likely release exotic particles from the Lawrence drive."

The mere mention of exotic particles was enough to make the blood of any ship's engineer run cold. Catastrophic damage could result if they impacted the wrong pieces of machinery at the wrong time. The *Lion of Judah* had almost been lost to such before, and David was squeamish about situations where they were deliberately released. "This sounds high risk."

Savchenko shrugged. "There is an elevated risk, yes. But it's outweighed by the positive of getting those civilians out. We may argue about interference, and I know Dr. Hayworth leans toward avoiding it whenever possible, as do I. But the truth is we already broke things here..."

"And we owe it to those people to get some of them off," David finished. "Assuming I run with this tactic, can the *Thatcher* hold off Mifreen air assets long enough to retrieve the refugees?"

"Based on my review of their capabilities, I see little danger from those planes, sir. They've got air-to-air missiles, of which it would take dozens if not hundreds to knock our shields down."

That matched David's observation, but hearing one of his tin-can drivers agree was nice. "Okay. Demood, do you have an assault plan?"

Calvin nodded. "I want to send everything we've got. Every assault lander, Marine shuttle, tanks, armored personnel carriers, and even our mag-cannon-based mobile artillery. Pure shock and awe. They won't know what hit 'em. We get in, get Tural, and get out."

"May I speak?" Markul asked with a hesitant wave of his hand.

"If you have something germane to add, go ahead," David replied.

"I believe while you rescue your people, additional information may be gleaned from the netsim. Specifically, simulations of different weapon types and frequencies.

Justice 253

Something to do with your neutron beams. Dr. Hayworth wouldn't fill in all the details."

"Doctor, care to explain?"

"The Mifreen netsim runs on a massive quantum computer. Better than anything we've got. If I had to guess, I'd say it's a hundred, maybe even two hundred years ahead of us."

"That's quite impressive, but how does it help with the nanite situation?"

Hayworth smiled. "It can run numerous high-quality simulations when fed the right parameters. Instead of cycling through thousands of permutations of our neutron beams and other energy-weapon-output types manually and through trial and error, this thing will do it automatically. Without putting anyone's life in jeopardy. Well, at least from the nanites. I'm sure the Mifreen will try their best to kill us."

A smattering of snickers followed.

"They're welcome to try, Doctor," Calvin said. "But I didn't survive three decades of combat with the League of Sol to get sent off by some shitty alien video game fanatics."

Laughter broke out, and even David joined in.

He waited for it to die down before continuing, "Colorful commentary aside, the Mifreen remain a dangerous adversary we must take seriously. Doctor, in your opinion, will running these simulations help advance a weapon effective against the nanites?"

"Without them, I despair of our chances of success. With them, I'll shave months if not years off my research."

"I don't see the harm if we're already there. Configure the sims, and ensure Mr. Markul explains the particulars with a Marine intelligence rating."

Markul and Hayworth exchanged glances.

254   DANIEL GIBBS

"I'll have to be there in person, General," Markul said.

"So will I," Hayworth interjected. "Too much could go wrong."

David's jaw dropped, and his first reaction was to shout no as loudly as possible. Then he processed that for the doctor to make such an offer was extraordinary and likely pointed to a mission requirement. "And why can't a Marine comms rating do the work?"

"Because your experts—no offense to them, General—don't have decades of training on exploiting Mifreen computer systems." Markul smiled thinly. "I do."

"And I can't take any risks of my simulations not running properly," Hayworth said.

"Let's be clear here," Calvin interjected. "This will be a no-shit warzone. I can't guarantee anyone's safety. Strap into a Marine shuttle, and you're putting your life on the line."

Hayworth shrugged. "If I'm going to perish, I'd rather do it making an effort to solve the problem."

Calvin nodded. "I can respect that, Doctor. But it's the general's call."

Every eye in the room turned to David.

"I don't like the idea of putting one of humanity's greatest minds on the firing line."

"Nor do I particularly relish the thought myself," Hayworth replied.

No such thing as zero risk in life. David knew in his gut that trying to get the simulation data was the right call, despite the danger. "I'll authorize it, Doctor. That leaves us with one overriding problem... how do we get word to Mifreen who want off the planet to be at our pickup location, without tipping off the government?"

Markul raised his arm. "The same way we alerted them to the possibility of leaving."

"And you're sure it's secure?"

"As much as possible, yes."

David stroked his chin. "Colonel Savchenko, how many can the *Thatcher* take on without risking life support systems?"

"It'll get real tight above five or six hundred additional people. But given the length of time involved, we're fine even if it blows past that. Don't worry, sir. I'll be prepared."

This is the beginning of a real plan. "Okay. We have to move quickly. I had hoped this would be a bit further along, but the pieces are in place. Finalize the details, drill, and prep. We go tomorrow morning."

"Yes, sir," Calvin replied. "I'd like permission to stage some exercises in the hangar this afternoon. It's the only open space in the ship I can have my Marines practice driving tanks off assault launchers."

"I have no objection," Amir said. "As my pilots will be in the simulators."

"Okay. Anything else?" David ticked off a few seconds. "Very well. Dismissed."

They filed out, leaving Aibek and David alone.

Aibek stood by the hatch and waited for the last person to exit before closing it. "May we speak?"

"Of course. You were uncharacteristically quiet during the meeting."

"I am wrestling with this situation." Aibek sat near David and made a face, showing his teeth.

"As am I." *And here's where my XO tells me we shouldn't interfere with other cultures.*

Aibek's tongue flicked in the air as if he was tasting it. "I am concerned about what we're doing with the Mifreen. To arbitrarily save a few while allowing this monstrosity of a government to continue persecuting its citizens is... disturbing. Have you considered going further and overthrowing their system entirely?"

David's eyes widened. "I wasn't expecting you to go there, old friend. I've thought about it too."

"But?"

"We don't have the forces to effect regime change on Mifreen, so it's out of the question. Beyond that, I don't think I have the command or moral authority to do such a thing. Saving our people and a limited number of those who want to leave because they're hunted and persecuted... that, I can justify before a CDF board of inquiry and HaShem."

Aibek nodded. "What of the innocents? The Prophet charges us to use our blades to defend the weak."

"Once the nanites are dealt with, we can right wrongs. Until then, that must be our primary focus."

"You speak truth and wisdom," Aibek hissed. "Yet it does not soothe my desire to draw blood from these butchers."

"Don't worry, my friend. There will always be some sort of evil in the universe for you to fight. Let's take them one at a time, though."

"I will." Aibek stood. "Someday, we will return here, and this government will rue that day."

"Agreed." David set his jaw. "Now, let's go do our part to get our people home."

30

CALVIN LEANED BACK and rubbed his eyes. He'd been staring at the screen for what seemed like hours. He, Amir, and Menahem were deep in the throes of putting together a unified operations plan. It stretched his mind in ways he hadn't considered over the past six months of low-intensity combat against the Zeivlot insurgents.

"Getting tired, sir?" Menahem asked. "We can let you get your afternoon nap, if you'd like."

"Could you get me a bottle while you're at it?"

Amir snickered. "You two sound like an old married couple."

They both turned and stared.

"Maybe you'd like to break out some pugil sticks." Calvin grinned and shook his head.

"Or you could hop into a simulator and allow me to school you in the ways of the pilot."

"Yeah, yeah, stay in my lane, blah blah blah." Calvin crossed his arms. "Anyone else think we're hurt by a lack of training out here?"

"We got lots of training shooting up jerks back on Zeivlot," Menahem replied.

"Not the same, though. We're gearing up to stage an invasion. When's the last time we practiced that? I'd say at least eighteen months. Maybe more."

Amir shrugged. "And where should we practice such things in Sextans B? With what spare parts? It is challenging enough to keep my air wing going, with our limited operations tempo since our arrival."

"Logistics are a challenge period," Menahem interjected. "But the colonel's right. We lose our edge when we don't practice. Though so far, against overmatched opponents, it hasn't mattered."

Calvin set his jaw. "There's the problem. I don't think the Mifreen are that far behind us. In some areas, it's obvious they're more advanced."

"I am impressed," Amir said. "I thought you had too many crayons today to determine the tech level of an alien species."

"Ha. Ha. Ha." Calvin made an obscene gesture toward Amir. "Aren't you cute."

"Getting soft over there, my friend," Amir replied.

Calvin tilted his head back and laughed. *Suppose I deserved that one.* "So you're telling me you aren't worried?"

"I am concerned about many things. The biggest one right now is the lack of shuttlecraft. Based on your numbers, we can't spare any from the *Lion*'s complement, and the two assigned to the *Thatcher* are both small and would take days to get any meaningful numbers of people off the surface."

"Two assault landers would do the trick." Calvin crossed his arms. He'd run the numbers, and while it would mean a hundred fewer Marines with him, that was life.

Amir pursed his lips. "I have a better suggestion."

Justice

259

"Out with it, Pretty Boy."

"Reassign all shuttlecraft from our escorting destroyers. Eight will get you almost the same number of people transported as two assault landers."

Calvin turned to Menahem. "Why didn't I think of that, Master Guns?"

"Because you eat too many crayons, sir."

All three roared with laughter.

Once it died down, Amir turned serious once more. "I believe we've got this together enough to get some rest. Tomorrow will be a challenging day."

Calvin nodded. "Yeah, you guys run along. I got something to do first, though."

"What's that, sir?" Menahem asked.

"Thought I might drop by the God box."

"Nothing wrong with that."

Amir stood. "Then I shall see you both tomorrow, inshallah."

"Amen," Calvin replied as he jumped up. "With any luck, those Mifreen bastards won't know what hit 'em." Though he grinned, Calvin was apprehensive. Still, there was little more to do except execute and let the chips fall where they might.

———

It had been close to thirty-six hours since David had any meaningful interaction with Bo'hai. He should've visited her sooner, but there had been no opportunities for anything beyond preparing for battle, and the one time he'd comm-linked her, the response had been less than inviting. So David stood outside her quarters' door, albeit at twenty-three hundred hours, and pressed the door chime button.

No response came, and he rang again.

"Coming!" Bo'hai's voice echoed inside. A few seconds later, the hatch swooshed open to reveal her standing there with disheveled hair. "Oh, I'm sorry. I thought someone from the science team wanted a translation checked."

David shook his head. "Nah, no eggheads here. May I come in for a few minutes?"

"Yes."

Once David had sat on the couch, he said, "I was overly harsh yesterday on the flight deck, and I apologize. I have to balance my responsibilities to my ship, the crew, *and* you. It's a work in progress, and while I did have to focus, I could've been nicer in the moment."

Bo'hai put her hand on top of his. "Your crew has to come first. I know this. It is hard to accept, but I understand. This responsibility... Sometimes I don't know how you do it, day in, day out."

"I've got a great team," David replied with a small smile.

"We can learn this together, yes?"

David nodded. "Typically, that's how relationships work. I think."

She giggled. "Did you sleep last night?"

"Not much. Our plan is... high risk."

"Will you join the attack tomorrow?"

David blinked. "I wasn't aware you knew when the operation was planned for."

"When the ship is going into harm's way, everyone changes. It's difficult to explain, but I can sense it in their emotions and how they interact with one another."

"Yeah, that tracks. When you stare death in the face, it prompts some deep thinking."

"Do you plan to join the ground assault?"

"No. I'd like to because I feel this situation is my fault.

Justice 261

Dr. Hayworth told me that one of these days, I'd involve us in something that cost lives, and when it did, the guilt would follow. He was right."

"The Mifreen you rescued would disagree."

"But would the dead Marines?" David bit his lip and fought down emotion.

"I think they would, too, from what I've seen of the men and women under your command. They are all seemingly infected with the same thing as you... a deep sense of honor and an inability to abide injustice."

"Salena, that sounds great in theory. And you know, it's how I think most of the time. But something is different now. Back in the Milky Way, I'm not the ultimate decider. Here, I am."

"You've mentioned this sentiment."

"There's something about it mentally... I've always wondered how President Spencer shouldered the load. Now, I'm in awe of him. I only have to look out for thirteen thousand lives. While he has... seventy-five billion? I can't imagine the mental weight of that."

"You talk of him often."

"He's a good man. One of the best leaders we've had in modern times. And more to the point, he knows the cost of war because he served as a front-line fighter pilot. Spencer got us out of the survival mindset and into the mode of *winning*."

"Perhaps we will get to meet him again."

"We?" David grinned.

"Is there no room in your Terran Coalition for one such as me?"

David blinked. *I hadn't really considered she would want to go home with me.* "Of course there would be. I didn't think you would want to give up your family, friends, and home here."

"What is it you like to say? Time will tell?"

"Yes. My mother constantly said that when I was kid. It stuck." He squeezed her hand. "Are we okay?"

Bo'hai stared into his eyes. "Yes. Why do you ask?"

"Because I don't want to go into battle with something... unsaid." David left off that he didn't want to leave things in a bad place if he were to perish.

"I understand," she replied.

He wasn't sure if Bo'hai really did but was unwilling to push further. "It's getting late."

"It would be nice if you could stay longer."

David smiled. "Not tonight. I need my rest for the day ahead."

"Do you think you're doing the right thing?"

"In what way?"

"By trying to save more Mifreen."

"I think..." David furrowed his brow. "What I saw with people who wore uniforms and claimed to be soldiers shooting children in the back makes me believe that Markul's cause is one worth fighting for. And while it's a small thing to rescue even a thousand of them, it's better than nothing. I can't help them all, but I *can* save some."

Tears came to Bo'hai's eyes. "That is a noble sentiment, and I will pray fervently for your safety and everyone else in harm's way."

David kissed the top of her head. "Thank you. I think the Marines are going to need it. We all will."

"Is there anything I can do?"

"All those people coming up from the surface will need a friendly face. You and the other civilians could provide that as they come over for processing."

"Then I shall do it with a smile."

David grinned. "Let's have dinner tomorrow night. I'll pull out another VIP meal." It would, at the very least, be something to look forward to. *And give her a signal that I expect everything to be okay.*

"I will hold you to that."

They stood and embraced.

"It's going to be fine," David said. "We've done this sort of thing before, and there's no one in the universe I'd rather go into battle with than the men and women of the *Lion of Judah.*"

Bo'hai nestled her head under his chin and didn't reply beyond hugging him more tightly. They spent several minutes like that before finally parting. David found the walk back to his quarters longer than usual but took the time to clear his mind. The next day, there would be no room for any emotion. He had one goal: execute their objectives.

31

ORDERING men and women into battle was something David knew how to do, and he did it well. In many ways, it was the point of his job—to win every engagement with minimum loss while maximizing damage to the enemy. And like almost every other combat of his career, David felt foreboding as he prepared for the fight ahead.

He'd gotten precious few hours of rest during the night after he left Bo'hai's quarters before the alarm blared at oh dark thirty. Once he'd completed his prayers, exercise, and morning grooming ritual, the next stop was the main hangar. David had a gnawing belief that he should offer the Marines the choice to opt into the mission rather than giving the command.

David walked through the massive double hatch and onto the flight deck. The size of the space still awed him. Dozens of shuttles and assault landers were lined up from end to end, and thousands of Marines milled about in loose lines, waiting to board them.

An eagle-eyed senior NCO noticed David's entrance almost immediately. "General on deck!" he bellowed.

Justice 265

The words reverberated through the hangar, bouncing off the alloy surfaces. Everyone came to attention except the aviation ratings fueling the various small craft and the weapons specialists who carted antigrav sleds with missiles on them toward the fighters. The Marines specifically formed neat rows, like a human wave.

David made a beeline for Calvin's command shuttle, where the colonel loudly barked orders and encouraged his people to move faster.

"General, sir." Calvin brought his heels together and stiffened. "Didn't realize you'd be joining us this lovely morning."

"At ease," David replied with a smile. "I wanted to address everyone before you get moving."

"We don't have a mic set up, but if you'd like, use my commlink, and it'll get you through to everyone suited up for the op." Calvin pulled a small device out of his ear and held it out.

"Thank you." David took the piece of polymer and adjusted it to fit his own ear. "As you were, gentlemen."

Moving as one, the Marines all relaxed into a parade rest stance.

David stared out at the gleaming ranks of power armor and the battle rifles and other heavy weapons held at the ready. The sight was awe-inspiring and reminded him of how effective the Terran Coalition was at waging war. *Why is it that every time we turn around in this galaxy, there's another foe?* He didn't remember first-contact situations turning violent anywhere near as often in the Milky Way. *But there are established, older civilizations there. Empires, even.* In Sextans B, no such entities seemed to exist. *And those nanites probably wiped out anyone who tried.* He set his jaw.

"Today, we have three separate objectives. One is to

rescue Dr. Tural. The second is to obtain data for the science team to further develop a weapon capable of stopping the swarm headed toward the system that holds our ticket home. And finally, rescue as many innocents as we can. Back in the Milky Way, this was a lot easier. We knew who the enemy was and how to fight them and could rest easy in the knowledge our cause was worth fighting and, if necessary, dying for."

The sea of faces visible through their helmets stared back at him, unflinching and unmoving.

"What I do know is that anyone willing to shoot an unarmed child in the back is evil. I don't care what your culture is, how it works, or what other context there is. Some things are right, and some things are wrong. I believe we have a responsibility to do something when we can. But I cannot in good conscience order you to carry out an invasion, as brief as it may be, that hasn't been sanctioned by our civilian government. Make no mistake... With every fiber of my being, I believe we should intervene. I only wish we could do more. So anyone who is willing to put their lives on the line for a species we barely know, people we've never met, solely because it is the right thing to do, please take one step fo—"

The sound of more than two thousand Marines' power armored boots clanging on the deck echoed loudly from one end of the hangar to the other.

David allowed himself a small smile. "I wish I were going with you—"

"Don't worry, General. We'll give 'em hell!" some Marine a few rows in shouted.

Others joined in, cheering and hollering.

Someone else shouted, "Just give us some covering fire from orbit, and we'll do the rest!"

Justice

"You'll have it. Now, good luck, good hunting, and Godspeed. Prepare to embark!"

Another rousing cheer went up as David took a step back to Calvin and passed the commlink back.

"I should have you come down here and get them lathered up before every mission," Calvin said with a chuckle.

David closed his eyes and shook his head. "This is going to be a rough one."

"Yeah, but like you said, it's worth it."

"I'd best be getting up to the bridge to oversee deployment."

"Yes, sir. I'll get this rabble sorted, and we'll be ready."

David nodded then turned on his heel. Before he'd taken more than a few steps, Calvin's voice echoed behind him.

"Sir."

David turned to see Calvin standing ramrod-straight with his hand at his brow.

"We'll bring him home, sir."

"I know you will. Carry on, Colonel."

"Yes, sir."

As David exited the hangar, he felt immense pride in his crew. *If HaShem will watch over us, they will carry the day. This, I know.* And even though the next few hours would be difficult, that knowledge put a spring in his step.

32

AFTER DAVID'S impromptu speech to the Marines, it had taken another hour for all the shuttles, assault landers, space-superiority fighters, close-air-support craft, and bombers to be fully prepared. *Probably the first time since the League war that the entire MEU and aviation wing was spun up and about to launch into the void simultaneously.*

He spent the time on the *Lion of Judah*'s bridge, overseeing final preparations. They'd been at material condition one, with battle stations manned and ready, for half an hour. The officers and enlisted ratings had an air of anticipation. *It's odd that combat is something to both dread and want to get on with.*

"General, the air boss reports all craft ready for launch," Aibek said. "As does Colonel Demood and the CAG."

David nodded. *The die is now cast.* Either the Marines would triumph, or a lot of good people would die. *It's possible for both of those to happen too.* He bowed his head and whispered a prayer in Hebrew. "Adonai, if it is Your will, allow those who go to fight to return safely, and protect all members of my crew. Allow us to rescue the innocents with minimal loss of life. Amen."

"Conn, Navigation," Hammond called after he'd finished. "Lawrence drive coordinates triple-checked, per your orders."

"And the *Margaret Thatcher*?"

"Coordinates locked in and confirmed, sir."

"Navigation, activate Lawrence drive. Communications, signal Sierra One to proceed as planned."

"Aye, aye, sir," Hammond and Taylor echoed.

In front of the *Lion*, a vortex opened. The bridge lights dimmed as the immense power requirements sapped all available energy. Because of how close they were jumping to the Mifreen planet's atmosphere, it took even more of a charge than usual.

"Wormhole stable, sir."

"Take us in, Lieutenant."

The mighty vessel accelerated along with three of the Ajax-class destroyers serving as her escorts. Only the CSV *Margaret Thatcher* remained behind. A few moments later, they popped out the other side, and the blue-green sphere of Mifreen appeared through the windows at the front of the bridge.

"No exotic-particle release reported," Aibek hissed.

"Conn, TAO. Sensors back online and no hostiles within range," Ruth interjected.

"Populate the board, Captain," David replied. He flipped his screen to a view of the *Lion*'s primary hangar deck. It was an impressive sight. "Reminds me of an old-school elephant walk on the *Ark Royal*."

"I am unfamiliar with this saying. What does it mean?" Aibek asked.

"The term dates back to Earth and an animal we don't

have anymore, something called an elephant. Rather large things, actually. The size of a small helicar. Anyway, it's slang for maximum sortie surge."

"*That* term, I understand."

David chuckled. "Communications, get me Colonel Amir."

"Aye, aye, sir. He's tied in."

The speaker on the CO's chair crackled with static. "This is the CAG."

"All ready down there, old friend?"

"Yes, sir. All squadrons on deck and ready to engage the enemy."

David set his jaw. "Understood. Good hunting out there, and Godspeed to all of you."

"May Allah watch over you and our Marines."

"You're cleared to deploy."

"Wilco, sir. Amir out."

The only indication of a couple hundred small craft streaming out of launch tubes and the forward-facing hangar doors was the appearance of dozens of new blue icons on the tactical plot. Labeled by squadron and Marine platoon, they spread out like a cloud from the *Lion of Judah*.

David pressed his head back. *Now, we'll see if our plan works.* He cleared his throat. "Communications, send to all CDF command channels... execute, execute, execute."

"Message sent, sir," Taylor replied.

"Navigation, intercept course, Master Eighty-Six. TAO, warm up our weapons, and prepare to engage." David gripped his armrests. All other concerns melted away as he fully absorbed the tactical situation, and time marched on.

———

Justice

ANTON SAVCHENKO HAD PULLED some crazy stunts in his career and been party to many more. Not too long ago, the CSV *Margaret Thatcher* had gone up against ten alien vessels and walked away the victor. That feat paled in comparison to what they were about to try. The bridge team was strapped into their harnesses, while the rest of the vessel was at material condition one. A familiar blue light bathed the bridge to allow human eyes to better process the information coming at them on screens lining every station.

"Conn, Navigation. Lawrence drive coordinates set and double-checked, sir. Ready to activate on your command."

"You sure about this?" Captain Kabar Masoud, the *Thatcher*'s executive officer, whispered.

"No." Savchenko smirked. "But it's still the best option out of many bad ones."

Masoud shook his head but didn't reply.

He's probably tired of risking our lives and limbs for every alien species we come across. In some ways, Savchenko understood. In others, he saw the appeal of doing good, though if it were up to him, they would retrieve their people and move on without tempting further peril.

"Navigation, execute jump."

"Aye, aye, sir."

A vortex through the fabric of space opened directly in front of the *Thatcher*. It steadily increased in size for several seconds as the lights on the ship dimmed from the enormous power draw. Once it reached critical mass and large enough for the Ajax-class destroyer to enter, the ship accelerated.

Savchenko gripped his armrests as the vessel rocked during transit. Moments later, they appeared on the other side. *Now, if we can just avoid a trap.* He feared getting pummeled by the Mifreen defensive satellites before their shields could be raised, as jumping as close as they were to a gravity well required every scrap of power.

"Conn, TAO," First Lieutenant Abigail Miller began in her trademark Houston drawl. "Hostile contacts populating the board."

"Raise shields the moment you have power, TAO."

"Aye, aye, sir. Deflectors energizing... and active."

"Navigation, plot a course to the rendezvous coordinates."

Masoud touched Savchenko's shoulder and pointed at his damage-control readout. "Exotic-particle release detected in main engineering, sir."

"Where exactly?"

"Unknown from here, sir."

Savchenko's blood ran cold. He pressed a button on his armrest for the intercom. "Engineering, respond."

"Go ahead, sir." The voice of Captain Colton Ramos echoed, as did an alarm klaxon. "A little busy down here."

"We're showing exotic-particle release up here. Anything I should be worried about before committing to a planetary atmosphere insertion?"

"The reactor torus wasn't affected, nor were our coolant systems, Colonel. But I've got several faults in the Lawrence drive itself. We're still assessing, but I doubt we could jump out anytime soon."

"Best guess till we could?" Savchenko bit his lip.

"At least forty-five minutes, more likely an hour, sir."

Damn. He considered abandoning the mission and heading to safety behind the nearest Mifreen moon. It could be argued that to proceed was an undue risk to the continued survival of his command. But Savchenko pushed that thought down. *Besides orders being orders, I'm not going to abandon a*

Justice

273

thousand or more innocent civilians to their deaths or a fate worse than what I'd wish on a Leaguer, from what the RUMINT around the fleet is. Even if I wouldn't have agreed to this myself.

"Keep me apprised, Ramos."

"Aye, aye, sir."

"We're not aborting?" Masoud asked.

"No." Savchenko set his jaw. "The iron lady does not turn."

"Conn, TAO. We're getting lit up by the Mifreen targeting scanners, sir. They've figured out we're here and closer than Sierra One. Energy build-up has commenced."

That was only a matter of time. "Navigation, all ahead flank. Take us into the atmosphere." Savchenko glanced around the bridge. "Make sure you're strapped in, people. This is going to get rough."

His words were prophetic. Almost immediately, the *Thatcher* was buffeted as it touched the outer atmosphere of Mifreen and began its descent. Within thirty seconds, the shields glowed red as superheated plasma built up around the protective bubble.

"Outer hull temperature approaching seventeen hundred degrees kelvin, sir," Masoud said as the deck pitched upward from a particularly violent shake.

We're rated for twenty-five hundred without danger. "Two minutes to go."

Onward, the *Thatcher* plowed, pushing the increasingly dense air aside. Without their harnesses, the crew would've been tossed like rag dolls. Several times, Savchenko thought he might dry heave but was able to keep it at bay. Finally, things seemed to smooth out, and a blue sky could be made out through the windows as the red glow dissipated. *That is not a sight one sees every day.*

"Conn, Navigation. Leveling out at twenty-five thousand meters, sir."

"Take us down to five thousand meters, Nav." Savchenko tugged his uniform shirt down. "XO, alert flight control to get our shuttles moving. We're on the clock. Comms, broadcast signal on the encrypted channel that Markul gave us. Tell them to get ready."

"Aye, aye, sir," several officers echoed as they rushed to comply.

Savchenko glanced at the mission clock. *Now, if everything would go right for once.*

"Conn, TAO. Aspect change. New contacts bearing zero-six-three and one-four-zero. Assess as Mifreen inbound fast movers."

"Designate contacts as hostile, TAO. Arm point defense, and engage as they enter range."

"Aye, aye, sir."

Yeah. Highly unlikely. Savchenko counted the seconds until the next curveball arrived and hoped the rest of the fleet was succeeding.

———

CALVIN'S COMMAND SHUTTLE VIBRATED, shaking him in his harness. Master Gunnery Sergeant Menahem sat next to him, while Hayworth and Markul were on the other side of the compartment. They had thirty-five Marines with them, and everyone was loaded for bear.

"How come it's rattling like this while we're still in the vacuum?" Markul asked.

"Because we're in tight formation with close to seventy-five small craft and catching wakes from the others' reactionless drives," Menahem replied. "There's a reason why the g-forces don't crush you when we accelerate. It's because the Coalition utilizes inertial dampening technology to affect gravity. That's also why all our ships have artificial grav plating, and you can walk normally."

Hayworth let out a snicker. "A decent explanation for a layman, Sergeant."

Calvin cleared his throat. "Never address a Marine E-9 as Sergeant, Doctor. Master Guns or Master Gunnery Sergeant."

"You know I'm not one to know all these ranks."

"It's a respect thing, Doctor."

"Oh, like my not appreciating being called Doc?"

Calvin smirked. "Touché." He turned to Markul. "Please tell me you didn't eat before this op."

"No, I was told not to." Markul gulped. "Glad I didn't, because I hate fast movements."

"Oh, let me guess—you get helicar sick?"

"Yes."

It took every ounce of self-control Calvin had not to deploy a brutal quip about nerds in combat. Instead, he monitored the sensor display from his helmet's HUD. Every Marine assault lander, shuttle, and close-air-support asset they had hurtled toward Mifreen. *In a couple of minutes, this ride's gonna get bumpy.*

"Still questioning bringing civvies on this op, Colonel," Menahem whispered. "Hayworth is a 'can't lose' asset."

Before Calvin could reply, Hayworth interjected, "I might be old, but my ears work, Master Gunnery Sergeant." He waved his hand dismissively. "Obtaining the sim data is critical to my research. Without it, we will probably fail."

Calvin eyed the doctor. "Takes a brass set to knowingly go into harm's way. So you have my respect for that, Doctor. Do what my Marines tell you to, keep your head down, and come back alive. That goes for you too, Markul."

"Oh, I'm planning on it, Colonel," Hayworth replied with a grin.

Yeah, he's got balls. I'll give him that. The shuttle jostled, and Calvin glanced at the sensor screen once more. *Here we go.* "Okay, ladies, it gets fun from here. Oh, and, Markul, don't you dare throw up on my deck."

"Uh, yes, sir."

Calvin pointed under Markul's harness. "Barf bag. Get it." *Oh yeah, this is going to be a fun ride.*

33

SANSAN WASN'T USED to being disturbed. In fact, his existence was one of sheer bliss. Inside the netsim, any whim or fancy imagined could be instantly fulfilled. The last two weeks had seen more interruptions than any period in memory. While it had been known for decades that other worlds harbored life, the Mifreen believed any travel between the stars was impossible. Regardless, they built a planetary defense system and focused inward. The advent of the netsim offered a sustainable society where most could live out their fantasies. Sansan believed it to be the culmination of all advancements.

Then the Terran Coalition had arrived. At first, he thought the humans would be a welcome addition to the Mifreen, perhaps even a species they could integrate into the netsim, for the betterment of all—until they attacked the hunter teams who risked their lives to track down terrorists.

Now they invade us. Images of war machines flowing out of spacecraft that landed next to one of their central computing hubs had spread throughout the government, both in and out of the netsim.

Sansan left the historical simulation he preferred living in, set roughly a thousand rotations before the modern era, and appeared on the council's shared island, which was cut off from the rest of the network and solely their domain. The others popped into existence seconds later.

"Thank you for coming," Sansan said. "We have a crisis on our hands."

Quosan snorted. His avatar's movements were off ever so slightly, a product of not being fully enmeshed with the simulation and simply a digital representation. "The humans are overrunning our ground forces."

"What of the air units?" Sansan asked.

"The CDF technology is superior to ours, even though they are less numerous. We took heavy losses in the last battle over Firtala. Additional assets will be in theater within fifteen minutes."

"Good." Sansan exhaled. "What else can we do?"

Quosan stared at him. "Have you not familiarized yourself with the rest of our military resources?"

"Why? That is the realm of the outers."

Quosan's face curled into a snarl before smoothing out. "We should deploy the Guardians."

"That is our last and best weapon."

"Yes, and these humans represent an existential threat. If they're able to penetrate the netsim, they could wreck everything."

"Fine," Sansan replied. "Send them. Perhaps our decision not to create space-based assets was a mistake."

"I've been saying that for years."

So you have. "We'll address it after this crisis is dealt with." Sansan stretched his neck. "Now, if you will excuse

Justice 279

me, I have other important matters to attend to." He'd just reached a critical juncture of the simulation and wished to complete the chapter before moving on. To be interrupted yet again was intolerable.

———

As a young Marine, Calvin had joined several planetary liberation efforts during the League-Coalition war, but as the conflict morphed into a lower-intensity conflict in the late 2440s and early 2450s, those had become fewer. Operations tempo ramped back up in the latter stages before the League's defeat, but even those were smaller because of the lack of planetary-based garrisons on the border worlds the TCMC invaded in the Orion Spur. Therefore, it was a unique sight to see the full might of a Marine Expeditionary Unit engaged against an enemy.

Calvin loved every minute. The aft ramp of his cargo shuttle dropped, and he was the second Marine out, with Menahem taking point. Hawkers roared overhead, and explosions echoed as they put precision-guided munitions on target. The Mifreen compound was nondescript, reminding him of a series of stacked boxes.

The place was nothing like the soaring architecture they'd encountered on other worlds in Sextans B, but Calvin wasn't there to sightsee. His sole purpose was to blow things up, kill the enemy, and accomplish the objectives defined by General Cohen.

A platoon of six Grant main battle tanks advanced to Calvin's right, their primary guns firing. Security emplacements blew apart in balls of fire from high-explosive shells, while squads of Marines advanced behind the armored behemoths. Hover APCs followed, adding their weapons to the mix.

Mifreen forces consisting mainly of a dismounted infantry gamely attempted to resist with little effect. Those who stood and fought were killed by combined arms fire, while those who ran were cut down in droves.

"Nice to see we haven't forgotten how to make war," Calvin said between grunts as he took in the scene before him.

"Lieutenant Jackson is reporting a clear path to the primary target, sir," Menahem replied. "Enemy has virtually no combat effectives in the open. If you want to move the special package forward—"

"Now's the time." Calvin let his battle rifle drop into its one-point sling. "Make sure our boys understand that Hayworth has to survive. We can't lose him."

"Got it, sir." Menahem shook his head. "This is like riding a bike. The training never leaves your muscles once it's ingrained."

Calvin grinned. "A beautiful thing."

"Sir, with respect, you're weird."

"Aw, hell. Who cares? These guys brought hell on themselves, and I'm here to make sure we deliver."

"Yes, sir."

"Who's in charge of Hayworth's detail?"

"That would be Lieutenant Richards, sir."

"And where is he?"

"Twenty meters away, marching over with his platoon, sir."

Of course the Master Guns would have that answer ready to go. Calvin smirked. "Doctor!" he yelled.

Hayworth and Markul advanced, with several power-armored Marines surrounding them.

Justice 281

"I've got forty-three Marines ready to take you into the heart of the beast. You will hold here until we gain control of the first few floors of the complex. Clear?"

"Quite."

Another wave of Hawkers picked that moment to overfly the complex. Fewer explosions echoed, as not many targets were left out in the open.

Another man jogged up with what seemed like a sea of power-armored Marines. "First Lieutenant DeMarcus Richards reports as ordered, sir."

Calvin jerked a finger over his shoulder toward Hayworth and Markul. "Keep these two safe, and exfiltrate whatever tech they want to drag out."

"Yes, sir!"

More APCs pulled up, and Richards shepherded his people and the civilians into them. All the while, the sounds of battle crackled around them. Calvin wanted to be in the thick of the action, not taking up the rear.

"All Coalition stations, this is Lieutenant Jackson, north sector. We're being overrun by—" A loud burst of static interrupted the transmission. "Broken arrow! Broken arrow! Immediate CAS support requested."

Calvin waved down a passing light tactical vehicle while he replied, "Lieutenant, repeat info on hostiles."

The driver pulled over in a cloud of dust.

"You're not going where I—" Menahem began.

Calvin jumped into the passenger seat. "Yeah, I am. Feel free to join the party."

Menahem shook his head before climbing in the back. "There's a reason why the command-and-control shuttle exists, sir."

"Yeah, stuff it, Master Guns. Private, take us to these

coordinates." Calvin fed the driver bearing and range data from the tactical network. "And step on it."

"Yes, sir!" The youngster threw the vehicle into gear and stepped on the accelerator, throwing both of them back in their seats.

The ride only lasted a few minutes, as the area wasn't that big, but the buildings were tall enough to block the line of sight.

"Lieutenant Jackson, this is Demood. Come in. Over." Calvin couldn't tell if communications were being jammed, but the Marine's life-signs monitor showed him as alive, with an elevated heart rate and breathing pattern.

As the small, lightly armored transport curved around the security fence and into the open, Calvin watched as one of the Grant MBTs blew apart when an energy beam hit its turret. Once the orange flames faded, nothing was left except melted debris. Calvin felt like he'd been stabbed in the chest. *What the hell can do that?* Not even League tanks could mount beam weapons capable of penetrating Coalition armor. It had kept both sides using armor-piercing projectiles.

Calvin's jaw dropped as a wave of smoke cleared, and the originator of the beam came into focus. He cued the emergency-override channel to the *Lion of Judah* and hoped they still had time.

34

WAITING WAS the worst part of combat for David. If his people were in harm's way, he wanted to be actively involved. Instead, the *Lion of Judah* hung in the sky above Mifreen. She did little more than strike down enough of the defensive platforms to ensure that when their planet-side forces exfiltrated, a window would be open to escape through.

David also monitored the battle as best he could through Marine helmet cams, sensor displays, and real-time LIDAR tracking from Amir's fighter squadrons. A separate screen had outputs from the Valiant-type heavy bombers, who continued to prosecute their attacks on the Mifreen satellites. All in all, the assault progressed well.

"Conn, Communications. Emergency patch through from Colonel Demood, audio only, sir," Taylor said.

I knew it was too good to last. "Put him on, Lieutenant."

"Aye, aye, sir."

David didn't recognize the sound that filled the bridge. He placed it somewhere between a high-pitched whine and a loud electronic hum.

"Sir, we've got some crazy sci-fi shit down here."

Aibek and David exchanged glances.

"I'll need a bit more than that, Colonel."

"Uh, we're getting our asses lit up by giant robots, sir. At least ten meters tall, with mounted particle-beam weapons. Nothing we've got is having an effect, including our mag-cannon artillery. Whatever they're using, it's cutting through our armor and shields like it isn't there."

If David's people weren't fighting them, the idea of massive mechanized vehicles out of a holovid attacking them in a galaxy 4.4 million light-years from home would be comical. *Except this is no cheesy holo show.* "What about close air support?"

"Our Brimstones aren't getting through their deflectors, sir." The harsh sounds of an explosion emanated from the speaker mounted in David's chair. "Dammit, Private, I told you to swerve when it warms up!"

David worked through possible solutions and arrived at only one. "TAO, orbital strike possibilities?"

"Should be doable if they can paint the target, sir. I wouldn't want to fire without positive confirmation. At these ranges, a fraction of a percent off would be disastrous."

"Demood, did you hear that?"

"Yes, sir. We'll play the music down here. Just make it quick."

"Keep this line open," David replied. "TAO, firing point procedures, neutron beam, ground target."

"Firing solution set and synchronized to Marine target indicator, sir." Ruth turned her head. "Strongly recommend reducing power to twenty percent to avoid blue on blue."

"Reduce power, then match bearings and shoot neutron beam."

"Aye, aye, sir."

Justice 285

A single blue energy spear shot out of the *Lion*'s bow and disappeared into the atmosphere below. From their distance, it was impossible to tell the effects. David held his breath, waiting for a report.

"Good hit! Good hit!" Calvin yelled a moment later. "Ah, shit. Didn't penetrate the shields, General. Dial it up and try again!"

Ruth turned and shook her head. "Sir, we can't do that. The thermal effects from a half or full-power neutron beam impact would run the risk of killing our people. A *significant* risk, I might add."

"And they're in power armor. Add on to it that we're talking about a nearly urban environment." The Canaan Convention on Human and Alien Rights specifically disallowed weaponry that would indiscriminately kill civilians, a guiding principle for the CDF and its rules of engagement. David bit his lip. "I need options, TAO."

"Missiles are out," Ruth replied. She licked her lips. "Wait a minute. We could use EMP shells on the mechs. Whatever they are, deflectors are susceptible to EMP disruption."

David nodded. "We hope, anyway."

"Did somebody up there say to use an EMP on it? Need I remind you that'd fry our tanks, planes, and everything else?"

"Not necessarily, Colonel," Ruth replied. "The small craft can clear out. Everything else should shut down. You don't have to worry about power armor because it's designed to avoid the effects of an electromagnetic pulse. We can follow up the strike with neutron beams, I hope putting an end to these things."

"One hell of a gamble," Calvin grumbled. "Then again, we don't have much choice. It's that or pull out."

"We're not leaving Dr. Tural and our people behind," David said.

Aibek nodded. "The Prophet would approve."

"Demood, get your people to safety as best as possible, and hunker down. We're going to proceed with the EMP strike package."

"Yes, sir."

David pressed himself back in his chair. *I pray this works because the thought of losing hundreds of Marines is more than I can bear to consider.* "Comms, warn Amir off. Get them a minimum of one hundred kilometers from the impact zone."

"Aye, aye, sir. On it," Taylor replied.

Here goes nothing.

———

CALVIN SWITCHED his commlink to the all-Marines channel as they raced away from the Mifreen assault mechs. "This is Colonel Demood. Listen up, people. Pull your vehicles somewhere safe, and break contact with the enemy as much as possible. The fleet's gonna engage from orbit with EMP rounds to disable these stupid mechs. Aside from our power armor, anything with juice flowing through it will get fried. I want you to kill every nonessential system and stand by. Sixty seconds to orbital strike."

"What about us?" Menahem asked.

"Hey, Private, drive over there. We'll get behind cover and play the music."

Menahem stared at him. "You mean I'll be target painting this thing."

"Yeah, Master Guns. When you need it done right, ask a professional."

Justice 287

The fast tactical transport swerved to one side and came to a stop. All three jumped out and quickly got behind a concrete hut. The mechs circled in the distance, firing their beam weapons. The forward unit had scattered as the tanks retreated, and fire teams put antiarmor missiles into the hulking automatons.

I wonder if they have a pilot or are driven by AI or remote control. Calvin stuck his head out. The machines, upon closer inspection, looked like a cross between something out of a holovid and some funky new-age art. A pair of contraptions that appeared to be wings held numerous weapons emplacements, while the mechs' superstructure towered twenty meters into the air. *Be nice if we had those.*

Calvin toggled a manual text message to every Marine and vehicle in his MEU that read *EMP strike in thirty seconds. Final warning.*

"I sure hope the general knows what he's doing."

"Got a feeling he's winging it, just like we are," Calvin replied. "Okay, power it all down."

The seconds ticked down, and he shut off everything except the radiation sensors, basic helmet visual enhancers, and life support. Even with the sound-deadening power armor, the *crack* of the EMP shell was deafening as it pierced the air and slammed into the visible mech unit. Moments later, spears of bright-blue light melted armor off the giant mechanized war machines. The beams cut through the superstructure and left the one mech that was visible split in two. It crashed to the ground, and an enormous explosion issued from the wreckage.

Calvin had just enough time to duck behind the concrete hut before a blast of dust and dirt blew past. "Yeeeah! That'll teach those overconfident assholes not to mess with the Terran Coalition's misguided children." He toggled his power armor fully online once more.

The common operating picture updated, with the Mifreen attackers nowhere in sight. Calvin breathed a sigh of relief. "Looks like we got 'em, Master Guns."

"Yeah." Menahem's voice held an undercurrent of emotion. "Lost another Grant and six more Marines."

"Damn." Calvin was beyond sick of his men dying. He knew his number might be up someday, but that didn't bother him. Losing his Marines made him want to rain hell down on anyone and everyone connected with the Mifreen government. "Are they getting any more reinforcements?"

"Not that the drones or our Hawkers can see. I think we're clear, sir."

Calvin nodded. "Okay. Then I want to join the hostage rescue team."

"Sir—"

"I have a burning desire—no, a *need* to shoot the people responsible for my people dying in the face. You get me, Master Guns?"

"You can't get at the Mifreen government, sir."

"I know, and the poor pukes in that netsim center get the short end of the stick because I can't. Now, Private, mount up, and let's move." Calvin gripped his battle rifle. Payback was coming.

35

"Conn, TAO. Another wave of Mifreen warheads inbound, sir," Miller reported as the *Margaret Thatcher* vibrated and shook.

Savchenko had never felt anything like it. *Which makes sense because the atmosphere makes everything different.* Most of the incoming was shot down by automated point defense, but a few got through and exploded against their shields. "How are we doing on taking people off planet?"

Masoud glanced up. "Getting there, sir. Flight projects two more complete loads."

"That'll make more than a thousand souls. Any idea how many are children?"

"No, sir. Why?"

"Because kids weigh less." Savchenko chuckled. "Which takes less power to propel us back into orbit."

"Ah, I didn't think of that." Masoud grinned.

Other issues came to mind, like life support not being designed to cleanse the air of twice the amount of CO_2 the *Thatcher*'s crew complement would expel. But as long as they got them offloaded within a few hours, the system

290 DANIEL GIBBS

would be stressed but able to keep up. To prepare, Savchenko had additional scrubbers ready.

"Another group inbound, sir," Miller called out.

"Persistent little buggers," Masoud interjected. "We could open up with our mag cannons. Proximity detonate some high-explosive rounds."

Savchenko stroked his chin. "Not a bad idea, but I'd rather save our shells. Who knows when we'll actually need them. PD seems to be doing just fine."

"For now."

Masses of red dots accelerated toward the *Thatcher*'s port side, again smacking into her deflectors. Even though they were little more than air-to-air warheads with small explosives, the sheer number of the things made an impact.

We're a pretty hard target to miss. Savchenko shook his head. "Tell flight to hurry it up. I want to be moving the moment the last group of shuttles touches down."

"Aye, aye, sir," Masoud replied.

Savchenko couldn't shake the feeling they were on borrowed time. He willed everything to go faster, as little good as it would do them.

An insistent alarm filled Amir's cockpit, warning him of a warhead headed directly for his fighter. He pulled back hard on the flight stick, performing a maneuver that the Mifreen interceptors couldn't hope to match, thanks to the Phantom's superior inertial damping system and vectored thrust capabilities. Even their missiles weren't good enough to track his craft through the inverted roll. Both flew a short distance and self-destructed.

Amir had tagged the bandit that fired on him using his

Justice

HUD's sensor display and looped around, prowling for the hostile. The Mifreen pilot had already settled on a new target—one of the slower-moving Hawker close-air-support fighters. *Not so fast.*

"Reaper One, fox two," Amir said into the commlink when he heard the lock-on tone.

A Vulture dropped from the underbelly of the Phantom, its gel-fueled rocket motor came to life, and it accelerated rapidly. Moments later, the warhead slammed into the Mifreen craft and blew it apart.

"Reaper One, splash one."

The debris rained down, burning brightly in the atmosphere, as Amir hunted for a new enemy. He checked the battle-space-awareness system and took in a 3-D depiction of several hundred kilometers around the netsim installation where the Marines were fighting. It showed squadron-strength hostiles remaining.

But we have enough force to handle them. Still, the Mifreen weren't pushovers. They'd knocked down two Phantoms and at least one Hawker so far. Amir felt thankful that the pilots they were fighting seemed less able than those he had fought previously. *It stands to reason they don't have a large air force. After all, why would they? They have only a single government.*

A group of new red dots at the edge of the sensor screen attracted his attention. He zoomed in and used a tactical link with the *Lion of Judah* to parse the data. *By Allah.* "Amir to Demood."

"A little busy right now," Calvin replied. The sounds of battle echoed.

"You are about to be busier, my friend. Numerous enemy aircraft are massing. How close are you to retrieving the package?"

"Not as close as you'd like," Calvin replied.

"Hurry."

"Tell that to these Mifreen bastards who won't quit fighting."

"We'll buy you whatever time we can, but my fear is these interceptors can easily shoot down our shuttles."

"How far out are they?"

"Six, maybe seven hundred kilometers. It appears as if they're still massing for an overwhelming force."

"Okay, so we've got a few minutes anyway. I'll wrap it up down here as fast as I can. We're clearing the sublevels now. Do what you can."

"Wilco," Amir replied. He clicked off the commlink and was about to go after another bandit when something amid the ground clutter caught his eye.

"Ugly Angel leader, what do you make of the surface contacts, bearing three-three-six?"

"Looks like some armored vehicles and transports, Colonel. Good catch."

"Engage and destroy."

"We're observing weapons hold until visual confirmation is complete, sir."

Amir set his jaw. "Negative. Weapons-free status. Take out the incoming. The only things headed toward the installation are enemy troops."

"Wilco, sir."

Another Mifreen interceptor appeared in his sights. With a fierce warrior's grin, Amir moved to engage.

36

IZMET TURAL WOKE up with a start. A nightmare of being strapped onto a table with unidentified medical instruments attached to him flashed before his eyes. He seemed to have the dream every time he closed his eyes. Blowing out a breath, he pushed himself up to a sitting position. Sunlight spilled into his bedroom through an open window.

The Tural residence on Arabia Prime was on the shores of one of the larger oceans. Ironically, while the planet had officially been settled by people from the former Earth countries of Saudi Arabia, the United Arab Emirates, and Oman, the architecture of his home was more Moroccan, as was the general vibe of the city.

The estate had been in the family for generations, and as the oldest male, he'd inherited it from his father, who, like him, had served in the Coalition Defense Force for decades.

"Izmet? Are you awake?" Zaha asked, her voice seeming to float through the air.

"Yes, I just woke up," he replied. Shaking his head to clear the mental cobwebs, Tural walked out of the master suite, down the stairs, and into the giant kitchen.

294   DANIEL GIBBS

Zaha stood next to an elaborate coffee machine. "Your usual or tea?"

"I think I'll do the coffee." Tural smiled. "I know you'd prefer I go back to our black tea blend."

"Yes, it's better for you."

"Says you." He took a mug from her and had a sip. "After almost thirty years in the service, I'm used to it." *Hmmm. That's odd. It tastes like CDF brew.*

"Hello, Father!"

Tural whirled around to see Maryam rush into the room. She embraced him, nearly knocking the mug from his hands.

He hastily set it down and returned the hug. "When did you get here? I thought you were on space duty."

"Oh, I left the CDF six months ago. Don't you remember?" She playfully knocked on the side of his head. "Yosef and I decided it would be better to raise our children with both of us on the same planet and at home for dinner each night, with the war over."

A pang hit him at the birthdays, concerts, school plays, and milestones of all his children's lives that he'd missed. But it was what was required of him, and his hands had saved thousands of soldiers over the decades. *Which is what Allah put me in this universe to do.*

"I understand how you feel," he said finally. "And I thank God we now have peace."

"Yet you still wish to go back to the *Lion of Judah*," Zaha interjected.

Tural tilted his head. "I am afraid I'm still having some memory issues this morning."

She touched the side of his face. "It'll come back."

"Eventually. The nightmares, though... I don't wish those on the worst Leaguer."

Justice

"I meant to ask—how is the *Lion*'s reactor doing?"

As Zaha was a musician, such a question struck Tural as strange. He stared at her. "The same as it always is, taken care of by many engineers."

"How does it run again?"

Tural narrowed his eyes. "Zaha, you know I cannot answer such things."

"Why?"

"Because they're classified."

Zaha huffed. "But I thought the Coalition gave this technology freely to the Saurian empire."

"We'd never give that away. It's the pinnacle of our ability to project power."

Everything in Tural's mind and soul screamed that something was wrong, but he couldn't quite put his finger on what, aside from the unnatural questions from his wife. *Where was I before I got home?* Whenever he tried to push through and retrieve the information, it was as if a mental block had gone up. *This is not right.*

"What's so special about the reactor?" Zaha asked.

"I cannot say beyond what is already public knowledge." *I should call General Cohen. He'll know what to do and can help.* Tural took a few steps toward the stairwell.

"Why won't you tell me? Don't you love me?"

Tural turned back. "My wife would never say that to me. She knows the oath I took. What is this place?"

Zaha only smiled in reply.

A moment later, Tural felt like he was falling through a long, dark tunnel. He screamed as loudly as he could, anticipating a sudden stop at the bottom that would end his life, but it never came.

AT THE CENTER of a squad of power-armored Marines, Hayworth shuffled down a corridor inside the netsim control center. Markul walked beside him, and little was said as they pushed forward as rapidly as possible. Oddly, Hayworth felt no fear. He wasn't quite sure what to make of that, surrounded by men with various implements of death. They'd engaged in little combat, primarily because the main assault force had already swept the area.

Markul held up his hand and pointed at a nondescript door. "This is it," he whispered.

"Stand back," the leader of the Marines, Sergeant al-Benghazi, barked. He reached forward and, using his servo-assisted armor, nearly ripped the door off its hinges. "You're on the clock, Doctor. Colonel says we're out of here in fifteen minutes."

Hayworth waved his hand and stepped inside. "Yes, yes. We go when I say we go. That will be when the data we need is recovered. Not a moment before." Even though he was over seventy, when he wanted it, iron filled his voice.

"Access ports... active," Markul said to himself as he started unloading equipment from the satchel he'd lugged with him. "Give me a few minutes to get the interface set up, then we'll start running your test scripts, Doctor."

"Harrumph."

Markul plugged several cables into unfamiliar connectors on a rack of equipment with a myriad of different-colored lights, all blinking in various patterns.

Hayworth stared. "You're using an analog interface?"

"Yes. It allows us to skip several layers of security." Markul grinned. "So-called security experts make the mistake of believing access control to the facility is so tight that it prevents what we're about to do. Which I suppose it does, unless you have a few thousand warriors with you."

Justice

Hayworth smirked. Something about the younger man's attitude appealed to him. *He's a professional and knows his business. That is something I appreciate in life.*

"I'm in," Markul announced before plugging another cable from his device into a standard CDF tablet. "Doctor, you can get started here."

"You made a custom interface?"

Markul nodded. "It was the only way to get our systems to talk to each other."

Hayworth was more than impressed—he was astounded. "If we survive this, and General Cohen allows you to remain on the *Lion*, perhaps we could discuss your supporting my science team in a more formal capacity."

"Let's focus on the survival part first," Markul replied with a chuckle before his face clouded. "We have a problem."

"What *now*?"

"Unfortunately, I can't disable all of the cybertrips." Markul sighed. "Once you start, it will light up the status dashboard of whoever monitors this node and half a dozen AI systems. I would expect an armed response."

Al-Benghazi grumbled. "You eggheads worry about this crap," he said as he gestured to the rows of machines. "We'll deal with the tangos."

"Fine by me," Hayworth replied. "Mr. Markul, proceed." As crazy as it sounded, he was having fun.

37

WHILE THE MIFREEN ground forces had mostly been subdued, that didn't mean they were out of the fight. Bullets sprayed by Calvin's head, and he snapped his battle rifle up, putting a three-round burst into the attacker. The man slumped backward, blood spilling from multiple holes in his chest. The other Marines around Calvin joined in and dropped two more hostiles.

"Energetic little bastards," Calvin said as he reloaded his weapon.

"And they keep coming."

Since detaching from the armored forces and making his way into the netsim complex, Calvin had seen small groups of defenders at almost every corner. They seemed to realize that because of their lack of power armor, head-on resistance wouldn't turn out well. But the Mifreen appeared determined to fight to the last man and woman. Shooting from cover, they slowed the Marine advance.

On top of that, the complex was a maze. Though it was easy enough to get from the ground level into the first few

Justice 299

sublevels, after that, it became clear the installation was sprawling. Calvin wondered just how much computing gear it contained and, more importantly, enemies. He'd pulled back every Marine he dared to take off the perimeter and sent search teams out by squad into the labyrinth.

An innovation installed into every suit of power armor was a software module for their helmet's optics that would translate written Mifreen into English. So far, it had greatly assisted them in determining where the elevators were and what was on each floor, at a high level.

Calvin raised his battle rifle. "Push forward." As he was on point, he started walking.

Twenty meters later, they came to another bank of lifts. Six of them seemed to provide access deeper into the complex. One of the younger Marines pressed a call button, and a pair of elevator doors opened.

"Okay, why not. We've cleared this level, as far as I can tell." Calvin stepped in, waited for the others, and hit the button for the next floor down. The cables and motor creaked as the cab moved down. Fifteen seconds later, the doors slid open.

Calvin and the rest of the squad had posed in a combat stance, with as many rifles pointing out as possible, yet no incoming fire came. They quickly filed out and posted up on the three corridors heading out of the junction.

"Menahem to Demood. How copy?"

"Good copy. Over," Calvin replied.

"Sitrep done there, sir?"

"No joy on our precious cargo and a whole lot of dudes with ballistic weapons."

"SNAFU, then?"

"That'd be it, Master Guns."

"Do you need additional teams?" Menahem was acting as a glorified traffic controller, sending Marines to wherever they were needed for search and recovery of the POWs.

Calvin imagined his senior enlisted man hated every moment of it too. "Yeah, another squad down here wouldn't be bad."

"Sir, we've got faint human life signs, two hundred meters."

"Wait one, Master Guns." Calvin turned to the private, who had a highly sensitive hand scanner up. "Up or down?"

"I *think* on this level, sir. Southeast quadrant."

"Master Guns, send three squads and medics. We've got human life signs."

"On it, sir."

Calvin raised his weapon, and as he was about to move out, something on the wall caught his eye. He turned and ran the Mifreen script through the translator matrix. *Education Center.* Calvin narrowed his eyes as he tossed the phrase through his mind. *Markul said something about the government running people through education camps.* The sign had two other locations, each in a different color. The floor had three lines running down it, which corresponded to those colors.

"Follow the orange line. That's where our people are. I'm almost sure of it."

A few Marines exchanged glances, but Calvin paid them no heed. "Let's move." He pushed forward, taking long strides with the others. They maintained formation and used bound overwatch tactics to leapfrog ahead, taking care to ensure at least four Marines were in cover at any given time and covering the length of the corridor.

Bursts of automatic weapons fire came from down the

Justice

301

passageway, out of several doorways. Rounds smacked the power armor of several Marines, ricocheting off in showers of sparks. TCMC battle rifles spoke as one, making the smell of propellant fill the air. Several Mifreen dropped to the floor.

"Contact front!" Calvin barked into the commlink. "Get those reinforcements down here ASAP," he said while lining up a hostile in his weapon's sight. He squeezed the trigger and put a round through the Mifreen's head.

Sharp cracks echoed down the hallway, and two Marines pitched backward.

In Calvin's squad monitor, both showed life-threatening injuries. "Smoke! Deploy smoke now!" He ripped a grenade off his belt, pulled the pin, and tossed it forward. "Smoke, over!" Next, he flattened himself to the floor, despite the weight of his power armor, and used hand signals to guide the others.

It took ten seconds for him to crawl to the fallen Marines while the others kept suppressive fire directed down the corridor. One was already gone, while the second was surviving only because of the automated medical protocols in his suit. "You hang in there, Santos."

"Yes, sir," the young man answered weakly. Blood dripped from his mouth, visible even through the helmet visor.

Calvin keyed his commlink. "Master Guns, where the hell are my medics and additional squads? We've got heavy enemy presence down here, and at least some of them have those damn miniaturized rail guns."

"Should be clearing the lift any second, sir."

Weapons fire continued. A rail-gun round nicked Calvin's shoulder armor, causing him to rotate and aim down the passageway. The infrared sensors built into his helmet visor helped him identify at least one Mifreen. *Come on. Stick your head out, you bastard.* Calvin squeezed the trigger on his battle rifle when the hostile leaned forward to shoot. *Alpha, Mike, Foxtrot.*

A split second later, the familiar *whomp-whomp-whomp* of an automatic grenade launcher loosing its deadly payload filled the air. Explosions at the far end of the corridor produced a pressure wave and a blast of flame that died out quickly.

"Sorry, sir. Got held up on the last level," a power-armored Marine said as he scooted to a stop near Calvin.

"All that matters is you made it." Calvin glanced back to see a few dozen friendlies and corpsmen rushing forward to tend to the wounded. "We got heavy weapons back there, beyond a mark forty-seven grenade launcher?"

One Marine stepped forward, cradling a minigun. "This work for you, sir?"

Calvin grinned. "I'm done playing with these bastards. Next roadblock we hit, you plow the road. Got it, son?"

"Yes, sir!"

The reinforced Marine group pressed forward in leaps and bounds. Brushing aside all resistance, they drove over the Mifreen. Calvin kept on point, leading them down the orange line on the floor. Twice, hardened positions called for the heavy weapons squad. The enemy didn't stand a chance between the minigun spraying bullets at a rate of five thousand rounds a minute and their grenade launchers.

Finally, Calvin stood before a pair of reinforced doors marked Education Center. "Demolitions! Get this thing wired up."

"Yes, sir!" a Marine replied as he started affixing det cord. Less than a minute later, he stepped back. "Ready!"

Justice 303

As the TCMC contingent retreated to a safe distance, Calvin yelled, "Fire in the hole!"

When the explosives went off, the entrance fell backward, revealing another passageway with dozens of doors lining the walls. A few sentries raised their weapons but were cut down by battle rifle fire from the Marines.

"Fan out! Clear every room!" Calvin bellowed.

Marine fire teams stacked on two doors on either side of the corridor before kicking them down. Each held Mifreen civilians strapped to what appeared to be medical beds. The process was repeated over and over until finally, a Marine screamed, "We've got him! Dr. Tural's alive! We need a corpsman over here!"

Calvin breathed a sigh of relief. *Thank you, God.* He cued his commlink. "Demood to *Lion of Judah.*"

———

"Conn, Communications. Flash traffic from Colonel Demood, sir. They've passed Checkpoint Epsilon and have secured Dr. Tural."

Relief washed over David before he pushed it away. *Now we just have to get our people out of there.* "Any word on his condition?"

"Not beyond seriously wounded, sir. The colonel also reports they've rescued a number of Mifreen prisoners."

"Tell him to collect his people and return to the *Lion of Judah* posthaste."

"Aye, aye, sir."

"I sense your worry," Aibek said. "Do we not have the advantage?"

David pointed at his tactical plot, which he'd configured to show the common operating picture on the ground around the Mifreen netsim complex. "Enemy forces are massing just outside the range of our indirect fires. I'd wager whoever's commanding their military isn't sure what our capabilities are and plans to use overwhelming force. The fact that we only conducted orbital strikes against their mechs probably leads him or her to believe we have some limitations on using those weapons."

Aibek raised an eye scale. "They are, ah... How do humans say it? Fish in a box?"

"Barrel. Fish in a barrel." David grinned. "Yes, they are. But we still can't use indiscriminate bombardments because that's against our rules. Even if I'd like to."

"Lucky for the Mifreen, this is not a Saurian Royal Navy vessel." He showed his teeth. "Otherwise, I would raze half their city to the ground."

David knew his friend wasn't exaggerating. "Let's hope it won't come to that." His eyes went back to the tactical plot. *Come on, Calvin. Wrap this up, and get our people home.* A split screen showed the CSV *Margaret Thatcher* was under heavy fire. David whispered a prayer in Hebrew for both teams' safety, as that was all he could do besides wait.

———

SPARKS SHOWERED from an overhead electrical line and fell to the deck on the *Margaret Thatcher*'s bridge. Nothing ignited, which was to be expected, as the vessel was constructed to strict military standards, and the alloy plating was specifically formulated to be fire resistant. But it was still a disconcerting experience.

Savchenko held on as the deck pitched upward. "Shuttle status, TAO?"

Justice 305

"Forty-five seconds, sir," Miller replied. "Shields near collapse on port, forward, and dorsal quadrants."

"Nav, confirm orbital insertion trajectory plotted."

"Ready to execute, sir."

"Sir, aspect change on hostile fast movers. They're breaking off," Miller interjected.

While Savchenko wanted to believe it was because of a mauling the single-seat fighters had taken from the *Thatcher*'s point defense, he had an uneasy feeling the other shoe was about to drop. "XO, tell the shuttle bay to hurry. Disregard safety protocols if they have to, but *land those craft*. Every second counts."

Masoud nodded. "Aye, aye, sir."

"Conn, TAO. New contacts inbound. Assess as hypersonic, land-launched missiles, sir."

And there's the other shoe. A knot formed in his stomach as he stared at the tactical plot. The red dots representing the Mifreen warheads tracked quickly across the screen. Several were shot down by the automated PD system. Still, one stubbornly evaded everything the *Thatcher* threw at it until a glancing blow sent the rocket plowing into the ground only a few kilometers away from the ship.

Without warning, a brilliant white flash burst through the windows at the front of the bridge. Automatic filters snapped on, saving them from permanent eye damage, but it took several seconds for the watch standers to fully recover. When the pressure wave hit, it sent everyone flying in their harnesses. The restraints held, but the ride was quite rough.

Shit. "TAO, confirm radiologics." While there was no question in Savchenko's mind what the payload was, he wanted to be sure.

"Fusion reaction confirmed, sir." Miller turned. "One of those would be strong enough to blow part of our bow off."

"Last shuttle docked, sir," Masoud interjected.

"Seal the shuttle bay, XO. Nav, all ahead flank. Get us into orbit." Savchenko gripped his armrests as the *Thatcher* accelerated. Through the windows, the view turned blue as the vessel pitched upward.

"Conn, TAO. Twenty-plus hypersonic missiles inbound, sir."

Savchenko did some quick math on the closure rate plus their acceleration gradient. *Our delta-V is too low. We won't outrun these things before making orbit.* When he ran the scenario through his mind, he found few solutions. Overstressing the reactor for more speed might work, but then they ran the risk of torus failure on the trip back to Zeivlot.

Then a light bulb turned on in Savchenko's head. "TAO, firing point procedures, tube one. Manually target the formation of warheads headed toward us, and detonate a single Hunter as close to the center as possible."

"Sir, I must remind you that the Canaan Convention on Human and Alien Rights prohibits the use of strategic weapons inside an inhabited planet's atmosphere."

"I'm well aware of the convention, Lieutenant! They negated that provision by releasing a fusion bomb on us. There are no cities or major urban areas within the blast radius. So kindly carry out my orders before we're reduced to our constituent atoms."

"This is the XO. I concur with the release of strategic weapons within a planetary atmosphere. Execute, Lieutenant," Masoud said.

"Acknowledged, sirs," Miller replied. "Firing solution plotted."

Justice 307

"Make tube one ready in all respects, and open the outer door."

"Aye, aye, sir." Miller pressed several buttons on her console before continuing. "Tube one ready in all respects. Outer door is open."

"Match bearings, shoot, tube one."

Such was the rumbling and the shudders ripping through the *Thatcher's* hull that the launch didn't even register. In the void, it would've shaken the ship. Instead, the only indication they'd loosed a Hunter missile was another blue dot appearing on the tactical plot.

"Tube one fired electronically, sir. Unit running hot, straight, and normal. Ten seconds to intercept."

Savchenko watched his display like a hawk as the distance between the warhead and his ship increased. The rate of closure with the onrushing Mifreen hypersonics was mind-blowingly rapid, and within seconds, the contacts overlapped.

"Time on target detonation *now*, sir."

A few seconds later, a wave of turbulence slammed into them so hard that Savchenko's first thought was that it would send the *Thatcher* flying into the planet below them at maximum speed. Then, as quickly as it had begun, it was over.

This is one of those rare times I wonder if there is a higher power up there, looking out for us in some broad sense, because we ought to be dead. The plot showed no incoming contacts, and Savchenko allowed himself to relax just a hair. He turned to Masoud. "Too close for government work."

"This entire evolution was too close a thing. But we rescued a lot of innocents. That's worth it."

Savchenko wasn't sure if his XO was saying that for his own benefit or for the bridge at large, but he agreed. *If I were in charge of this fleet, we'd make fewer pit stops to assist aliens in need. But I'm not, and Cohen seems to know how to pick 'em.* He hoped the benefit was worth the cost.

"Conn, Navigation. Clearing the Mifreen atmosphere, sir."

"Lay in a course for the nearest Lagrange point, max thrust."

"Aye, aye, sir."

38

A watched progress bar does not fill, Hayworth thought as he stared at his tablet. They'd been hammering away at the Mifreen intrusion-prevention systems for what seemed like an eternity, but the alien tech was infernally effective. Every time Markul got through one firewall, some other defense appeared.

Progress was slow, but they'd gotten more than half the simulations run and exfiltrated from the netsim servers, even as the sounds of combat echoed around them. So far, security forces had made several attempts to storm the server room, which was held off by the Marines, who'd taken multiple wounded. Bullets had whizzed by Hayworth's body and hit several of the enormous computing devices. But so far, everything still worked. How long that would continue, he wasn't sure.

"This is growing exponentially more difficult," Markul said as he pounded away on a keyboard.

"Your species seems to have significantly advanced its computing technology."

Markul nodded. "Yes, Doctor. It's the pinnacle of our

research, in most ways." He hit a final key with a flourish. "Try now."

Hayworth triggered a restart, and the graphic moved with purpose. "Much better."

A sudden burst of gunfire was coupled with a cry from one of the Marines, who stumbled into the room. Blood dripped from a hole in his power armor, and a medic rushed to help.

First Lieutenant Richards stuck his head in the door. "Wrap it up in here."

"We're not leaving until we have the data!" Hayworth replied. That the words erupted from his throat so quickly surprised even him.

"Doctor, I can respect your wanting to complete the mission, but we will be overrun here. Hostiles are pushing forward with superior numbers and weapons capable of piercing our power armor. Leave the fighting to the professionals, and wrap this up."

"Lieutenant, you are no doubt aware of the threat posed by the nanite swarms encountered a few weeks ago?" Hayworth replied.

"Of course—"

"Then hear this: what I'm doing here is directly related to our ability to fight effectively. Your job is to hold off the Mifreen while I finish the science, and you'll have to shoot me to get me to leave before it's done."

Another simulation was completed and copied to the portable data transfer device as he spoke.

"Seventy percent, Doctor," Markul interjected.

Richards appeared surprised and even flustered by Hayworth's forceful response. He touched the armor on his arm and fiddled with a control surface. A moment later came the echo of an explosion followed by a blast of dust through the door. Simultaneous reports from a dozen Coalition battle rifles on full auto added to the cacophony. Richards turned and brought his own weapon up, adding its fire to the mix.

For all his bluster, Hayworth knew the jig was almost up, but he was determined to press on to the bitter end. *I helped loose this monster on the galaxy, and I'll do my part to end it. Whatever the cost.*

"Doctor, Colonel Demood has ordered me to remove you by any means necessary, including stunning you and dragging your unconscious body back to the shuttle!" Richards shouted over the din of battle. "For your sake and mine, I strongly suggest you do not let it get that far."

Markul grabbed Hayworth by the shoulder. "The protection system reset. It'll be five to ten minutes before I can break through. We need to go."

With great reluctance, Hayworth pulled the cable from his tablet. "*Dammit.* Fine."

It only took Markul a few moments to scoop up the rest of the gear and put it back in his sack. "We're ready, Lieutenant."

"Good. Wait one." He turned back toward the door and barked a series of orders. Pulse grenades flashed at the end of the corridor, followed by more sustained bursts of battle-rifle rounds. "Move it! Now!"

Not needing to be told twice, Hayworth and Markul shuffled through the blown-apart doorframe and into the middle of a small Marine detail. They moved swiftly for the rear, toward the elevator to the surface. *We should've stayed longer. I don't know how I'll complete the work without all the simulations.* The entire way, he cursed himself for not coming up with a better solution.

As far as Calvin could see, rows of TCMC assault landers sat in neat lines as the Marine force collapsed its perimeter. Support vehicles, the mag-cannon self-propelled artillery pieces, wounded, and the rescued civilians were loaded first. From time to time, groups of Mifreen attempted to push forward, but their efforts were disjointed at best. Dr. Tural was already aboard a medical transport along with the other survivors.

The sporadic enemy fire was enough to force everyone to keep their heads down, especially personnel not wearing power armor. *My biggest fear here is they attack us as the pocket closes in.* "Demood to Amir. How's it looking up there?"

"Still running out of time, Colonel. How is your load-up going?"

"Not fast enough," Calvin replied. "Give me a five-minute warning, would you?"

"Wilco."

Hayworth appeared with a group of Marines making their way to one of the shuttles. Markul seemed to follow the scientist around like a lost puppy while lugging a sack of equipment. Marines in power armor surrounded the small group.

"Nice work down there, Doctor."

"It would've been nicer if I had been allowed to finish," Hayworth replied.

"Doc, security forces were overrunning your team."

Hayworth paused and turned on his heel. "We needed those simulations, Colonel. *All of them.* I was more than happy to risk my life to obtain the optimal result."

"And I wasn't willing to see all of you killed by over-whelming force. We had to blow the entrance to keep those

Justice 313

assholes bottled up. There had to be hundreds of people down there."

"Getting a weapon to use against the nanites is the only consideration that matters."

Calvin crossed his arms. *I don't have time for this.* "You know what, Doc? I respect anyone willing to put their life on the line for a cause. Why don't you enlist in the TCMC, get some training, and get back to me."

"I don't need my individuality bred out of me to fight—"

"Get the doctor and his people strapped into a shuttle ASAP," Calvin said, jerking his thumb backward. "We're dusting off as soon as the last Marine is aboard."

Hayworth turned and marched off, still grumbling as the squad around him kept pace.

"Sir, got a problem," Menahem interjected over the commlink between bursts of static from Mifreen jamming.

"Go ahead, Master Guns."

"Several tanks had their hover units and tracks disabled. I don't think we're getting them going anytime soon. Request permission to destroy them in place and step up our withdrawal."

Calvin bit off a string of curses. Each one of the Grant MBTs was precious, as they couldn't exactly resupply. *Nothing we can do, though.* "Burn 'em to the ground, Master Guns. Nothing survives. Thermite plus an airstrike."

"Yes, sir. On it."

He switched to the all-Marines channel. "Keep moving. I want to be airborne in ten mikes, and I'm going to PT any puke who holds me up."

The orderly withdrawal continued.

DAVID STEADIED himself as more muonic energy slammed into the *Lion*'s port deflector quadrant. They'd reentered weapons range to blast a new hole in the defensive satellite network, as the risk to the fighters and shuttles was too severe to leave to chance. Using their neutron beams as well as pinpoint strikes from the Valiants, they'd cut a decent-sized hole without expending too many precious Javelin, Starbolt, or Hunter missiles. *I'm acutely aware of how hard it is to get more weapons out here.* In time, however, the Zeivlots and Zavlots would produce at least some CDF hardware, excepting their most advanced tech.

It had been a few minutes since Calvin signaled they were about to dust off, and David felt apprehensive as time ticked by.

"Conn, TAO. Aspect change. Numerous Sierra contacts clearing the Mifreen atmosphere. Sierra One has reached a safe distance."

The Thatcher *is out of harm's way, at least.* "Maintain covering fire for the fast movers at your discretion, Captain."

"Aye, aye, sir."

"Do you plan to recover them within the gravity well, sir?" Aibek asked with a raised eye scale.

"No. As we discussed, we'll pull back beyond weapons range of the planetary defense system then grab our people and go." David stared at the tactical plot as outgoing fire from the fleet erased more of the Mifreen platforms from the universe. Each tick of the clock saw another blue dot representing a Marine assault lander populate on the board.

While the muonic weapons were potent, they seemed to have limited tracking capabilities against smaller craft. It also helped that Amir had the good sense to recognize the enemy's limitations and order the air wing to manually jink and juke as they raced away from the blue-green orb.

David spent every second of the next few minutes on the edge of his seat, willing his people to survive with no losses. When the last shuttle passed through the optimum-weapons-range envelope of the Mifreen satellites, he finally breathed a sigh of relief.

Giving the small craft another ten minutes to ensure no stray shots would get lucky, David decided it was finally time to move. "Navigation, come to heading two-six-five, break orbit, all ahead flank."

"Aye, aye, sir," Hammond replied.

"XO, coordinate with the air boss. I want our people landed ASAP."

Aibek swung his screen around. "We took additional hull damage." He pointed at several areas flashing red.

"Does it affect our ability to jump?"

"Major Hanson recommends we complete temporary repairs."

David shrugged. "Not like the Mifreen can do anything about us hanging out for a day. Once we pick up the shuttles, we'll swing around to the far side of their nearest moon."

"I will prepare additional damage-control teams," Aibek said as his forked tongue flicked in the air. "As our stay should be a short one."

"Agreed."

39

In the hours since the recovery of the *Lion*'s small craft and Marines, time had rushed by in a blur for David. He'd toured the hangar to see the damaged fighters, bombers, and shuttles then visited the medical bay once things calmed down. The crew's spirits were high, and in talking with enlisted ratings, it was clear they viewed the Mifreen society as something to stand against morally.

That did little to assuage David's guilt. Dozens of Marines were dead along with several pilots. Ten fighters had been lost in battle against the Mifreen. All of them were irreplaceable. That none of the shuttles had been shot down on their way out of the atmosphere was a miracle from HaShem, and it seemed as if the entire fleet was on borrowed time. More than anything, David wanted to encounter a species with which they could coexist. *But have we really ever done that? Maybe the Matrinids, but even the Saurians we had to fight a series of wars with to get them to stop trying to conquer the Terran Coalition.* Ultimately, he had to rise to the occasion of whatever God wanted from him. *And perhaps someday, we can rest.*

Justice 317

But that wouldn't happen anytime soon.

David walked into the conference room on deck one, and the officers and civilians sprang from their seats. Virtually the entire senior staff, Hayworth, Bo'hai, and a few other scientists were present.

"As you were."

Dr. Tural was also there, which amazed David. He appeared as if he'd been through hell, with bruising around both eyes.

David took his seat at the head of the table as the rest returned to their chairs. "I will start by thanking everyone in your respective departments and commands for your outstanding performance in this dire hour. It remains the single greatest honor of my life to serve with such committed soldiers. Doctor, it's good to have you back."

"Thank you, sir. And to all the Marines and pilots," Tural said. His voice sounded weaker than usual, but it was clear. "I thank Allah you were able to save me from a fate worse than death."

"Just doing our job," Calvin replied. "Besides, I'll kick bad guys' doors in no matter what galaxy we're in. Pulling a friend out of prison was a bonus."

The ability to look at the universe the way Calvin did was appealing, and David had thought similarly on many an occasion.

He smiled as everyone else chuckled. "XO, repair status?"

"Hull breaches are mostly patched, sir, but Major Hanson has concerns about our Lawrence drive," Aibek said with a hiss.

"Uh, yes, sir. A few of those Mifreen energy discharges hit too close to our primary driver coils for my taste. I want to ensure we run complete diagnostics and put eyes on every inch before signing off on an FTL jump."

Sticking around this solar system is the last thing I want to do. "Okay. Has there been any sign of Mifreen spacecraft?"

"No, sir," Ruth replied. "I think we'd have already seen them if they had such vessels."

"You're right, Captain. But who knows with these guys."

Aibek held up a finger. "We will need extended time in a shipyard facility to fix our armor damage, sir. Right now, the only thing available is temporary patching."

One more problem. "Then we'll have to hope those are up and running back at Zeivlot and Zavlot soon. More importantly, how are our casualties doing?"

Dr. Tural leaned forward. "One hundred eighteen are still in the sick bay. We transferred the wounded from the *Margaret Thatcher* to the *Lion of Judah*. All are expected to recover."

"And the Mifreen civilians?"

"We spread them out in overflow quarters on the *Lion*," Aibek replied. "All are under heavy guard."

"Good. When we get back to Zeivlot, we'll find a more permanent home for them. Let's hope one where they can integrate into Zeivlot society and become productive members of it." David leaned his head back. "Dr. Hayworth, have you been able to analyze the simulations you ran against the netsim?"

"Some of them," Hayworth replied. "I wasn't able to get everything done, which will greatly hamper our efforts."

"Better than nothing, Doctor," Hanson said. "You reduced the possibilities to a manageable number."

"Even if we can isolate the right frequency in a simulation, that's far from being a real weapon."

Justice 319

"I'll take any small victory we can achieve. Do you have a timetable for completing your analysis, Doctor?"

"Soon."

David decided to leave him alone and proceed. "Major Hanson, I'd like to be underway tomorrow morning. Is that an acceptable timeframe to complete your drive tests?"

"Yes, sir."

"Then I have nothing else. Saved rounds, ladies and gentlemen?"

Silence answered him.

"Very well. Dismissed." David's eyes went to Dr. Tural. "Doctor, please stay behind. I'd like to talk for a few minutes."

He nodded and waited patiently for everyone else to exit.

David gave Bo'hai a small smile as she passed, which she returned.

After the hatch slid shut, he said, "I was shocked to see you here, Doctor. Are you sure you're well enough for duty?"

"I need..." He put his hands on the table while blowing out a breath. "I *must* be around others and engage my mind, sir. There's little physical damage to me... a few drugs that were quickly flushed out. But the mental aspects, that will take some time."

"If you recall, I was tortured by the League. I know what it does to your mind and body."

"The netsim is something else entirely. I was certain... absolutely certain that I was back on Arabia Prime with my wife and children. Reality became something else." Tural licked his lips. "It was so jarring to be pulled out that my mind couldn't process it. Sometimes, I thought the real world was a nightmare and vice versa."

David shuddered. "That sounds horrific, Doctor."

320 DANIEL GIBBS

"This technology isn't something a human should ever use. You must see to it that it never reaches the Terran Coalition." His eyes blazed.

"Agreed. I'll never use it or allow it to be exported to our nation. Or anywhere else, if I can help it. Something that messes with the mind so much that it makes it think a simulation is real has the power to destroy a civilization."

"Part of life is striving to be better and overcome adversity. I knew this on my home world."

"As did I." David grinned. "We grew up pretty close to each other, from a cosmic perspective."

"True. Through our attempts to be better, humans learn and become stronger in character as long as they seek Allah. Or HaShem, as you call Him, or just plain old God as many others do."

"We live in hope, Doctor." David put his hand on top of Dr. Tural's. "If you'd like to talk to someone who went through hell and lived to tell about it, I'm always here."

Tears came to his eyes. "I may take you up on that, sir. For now, though, I need to use these hands to heal. That is what God called me to do, and it brings comfort."

"In that case, I hope it brings you healing."

He stood. "As do I."

"Godspeed, Doctor. I'll be praying for you."

"Thank you, sir. Godspeed to you, as well."

David remained seated as Dr. Tural walked out, and the hatch slammed shut behind him. While he was intensely proud of his people for pulling off the rescue and saving a thousand innocent civilians, he still questioned whether it was right to interfere. Hayworth's words about regretting the loss of life when David's action blew up in his face confronted his soul. *I could've walked away, and no one would've died. Nothing that followed would've occurred if we'd never gone down to meet with Markul.* Yet the other side of him pushed back just as hard. *If I don't take a stand for what's right, who will? As the commanding officer of this fleet, I have an obligation to do something with the power we have.* The question remained, however: at what cost? The moment David thought of another thirty-six dead Marines, soldiers, and pilots, his heart sank. *I did that.* He decided to get out of the conference room and go do something else. *Otherwise, I'm going to go down a bad road.* Heading to the shul to pray for forgiveness seemed a good place to start.

40

—————

It had been less than twenty-four hours since the *Lion of Judah* and her battlegroup engaged the Mifreen, yet David could've sworn it was more like a month. They'd completed emergency repairs to the *Margaret Thatcher* along with the *Lion*'s forward and port quarters to ensure as little risk as possible from the series of Lawrence drive jumps before them. Finally, they were underway. David sat in his usual seat on the bridge, glad to be putting the planet behind them.

"Sir?"

David snapped his head around. "Sorry, XO." He smiled.

"Thinking of other matters?"

"Yeah."

"Our fallen comrades?"

Aibek had a good way of focusing on the issue, whatever it might be.

"Yes, among other things."

"They walk with the Prophet now." Aibek's voice was Zenlike. "A fitting end to any warrior's life, to use his blade to defend the weak. It is the proper order of things."

Justice 323

Saurian culture believed in honor above all, and their religion was an interesting mix of Christian-like beliefs and ironclad directives to use power to defend the innocent. At times, David had trouble putting it together, but he respected their faith. *And my friend Talgat, above all.*

"Well, to paraphrase Colonel Demood, who joins a long line of Marines ripping off the Roman poet Horace... It's better to make the other guy die for his cause."

Aibek raised an eye scale. "On this, we agree."

"Navigation, Lawrence drive status?"

"Charged and ready, sir. Five minutes to the outside Lawrence limit."

Despite the losses, since they'd rescued more than a thousand civilians, David knew that, as usual, the *Lion* and her crew had performed superbly. And it made him proud.

"Conn, Communications. I'm getting an audio-video transmission from Mifreen, sir. They're requesting you by name."

David pursed his lips. "Won't kill us to see what they want. Put it on my viewer, Lieutenant."

"Aye, aye, sir."

An image of Hes Sansan appeared on the screen. The backdrop was the same as before, an idyllic tropical paradise that practically beckoned for one to jump into the ocean. But unlike the last times they'd spoken, Sansan did not wear a smile. His face was taut, his lips pressed together.

"We show you leaving our solar system, General Cohen."

David nodded. "That's correct. We'll be jumping to FTL soon. What do you want?"

Sansan's face contorted. "What do I want? You've destroyed our way of life, General. I want you to pay!" Spit flew from his mouth.

"And how exactly did I do that? We didn't harm your

precious netsim. My Marines only extracted our people and innocents who wanted to leave."

"*Innocents?* They are not innocent! They stand against the unity of the Mifreen people. This disease you helped them spread is moving throughout our planet. There were protests against the netsim by outers this morning!"

David, try as he might, couldn't keep the smirk off his face. "And how exactly is that a bad thing? Sentient beings everywhere, regardless of their species, have a right to self-determination. If your citizens are demanding basic freedom, good for them."

"It doesn't work unless all agree. But these miscreants will destroy our society... because you helped them!"

David considered closing the channel after telling the Mifreen leader to enjoy his comeuppance but decided not to. "Your netsim has a fatal flaw, Sansan. It's similar to something called communism, which humans tried for hundreds of years back in our galaxy. You see, there are those among humanity who believe that everyone should work together, receive the same rewards, and have the state dictate who does what. Sound familiar? In exchange, since all are compensated the same, everyone is in a utopia."

"Why would that be bad? It sounds like a reasonable way to live," Sansan replied.

"The problem is that the utopia only exists for some. There is no way to cancel out the laws of nature. Minerals must be mined to feed our fabrication plants and 3-D printers. Food must be grown. And *work* must be accomplished. What communism is left with is a society where some at the top enjoy the utopia, while most of those at the bottom are little better than slaves. Which is exactly what *your* society is."

Justice 325

"Most of our people enjoy utopia," Sansan shot back. "Almost all *want* to and are willing to do what it takes."

"It doesn't matter what percentage of people are on board. That you're using coercion, propaganda, and a police state to force compliance is morally wrong. Such ideas belong on the trash heap of civilization. Humanity and many other races have tried it. It ends the same way."

"We have the right to do what we want on our world!"

"And if you hadn't attacked us, captured our people, and massacred women and children in front of me, this fleet would've kept on going. You brought this on yourselves, Sansan."

"Hundreds of years of progress could be lost." Sansan's eyes blazed. "Because... why?"

"Turning your population into slaves isn't progress. It's an abomination. I have no regrets for my actions or those of my crew. I only rue that we can't take everyone who wants to leave."

"Work of any type is slavery, human. Only in the netsim are we free."

"And there's the flaw in your logic," David replied as he leaned forward. "Yes, humans have to work. It brings purpose to our lives. But we can change what it is we do. In the Terran Coalition, you can have any job you want, if you're willing to train for it. If you'll apply yourself, anything is possible. What you won't get here is cradle-to-grave provision and care by our government. Because any system large enough to do that ends up like yours—controlling every facet of each person's existence."

"Come back to our world, General Cohen, and I promise to erase your precious ship from the universe. Do you understand me?"

"*Far* better men than you have tried, Sansan." David

grinned. "Someday, we'll be back. That's a promise. Ask the League of Sol. I keep my promises. And when I return, anyone who wants to leave will have the chance. Unless, of course, your citizens overthrow this diabolical system you've got going. In that case, I'll return as a friend. *Lion of Judah* out."

The screen cut off, and it took David a moment to realize everyone was staring at him.

"Well said, sir," Aibek hissed.

"I hate the cost," David replied. "But there are times when evil must be confronted and defeated. This was one of them."

"Do not discount that Dr. Hayworth was able to retrieve valuable data."

"With Markul's help."

Aibek raised an eye scale. "I noticed you added him to the duty roster."

David shrugged. "He's quite adept at computers, and we need all the help we can get. Until Markul gives a reason otherwise, he'll have a place on the *Lion*."

"Still, he is one who skulks in the shadows."

"Sauria has an intelligence service, yes?"

"Yes, but that does not mean I embrace their methods." Aibek adjusted in his seat. "I prefer to match my blade with the enemy."

He does have a bit of a one-track way of looking at things, but I find it refreshing. One always knows where they stand with Talgat. "It takes all kinds to win a war."

"Perhaps," Aibek hissed.

"And now we head back to Zeivlot." David steepled his fingers. "I'm counting on Dr. Hayworth to achieve a breakthrough with the simulation data."

Justice 327

"What about the obelisk? Vog't still does not allow us complete access."

That fact stuck in David's craw. "We'll see. I've got a few more cards to play there. The increasingly high likelihood that we're on our own to deal with the nanites is certainly one of them."

"I could always take a more direct approach." Aibek grinned, showing off both rows of incisors, which were one of the trademarks of a Saurian.

"We'll keep that one in reserve." David chuckled.

"As you wish."

The *Lion* flew on toward the Lawrence limit. While David believed they'd done something positive for Mifreen, he couldn't shake the hole in his soul that the continued losses of his crew caused. He had a myriad of other concerns, not the least of which were the pounding the ship continued to take and the severe damage to the *Margaret Thatcher's* outer hull. It all added to a continued *drip-drip-drip* of pressure. *All there is to do is press on. One foot in front of the other, and trust that HaShem will see us through.* It sounded good in David's mind, and he knew it was the right thing to do. Yet actually *doing* it... that was something else entirely.

———

JOHN WILSON PEELED off his black space sweater, revealing the khaki uniform shirt underneath, then tossed the garment toward his bunk. He'd worked another sixteen-hour day, and they'd made significant progress toward completing a third orbital shipyard. The automated alloy smelter had made it far easier to 3-D print truss segments, which sped up their efforts.

As happy as he was to be making progress, the ache of

being millions of light-years away from his wife and children was ever-present. He glanced at an image of them on a digital picture frame before turning away. *At least the work keeps me busy and not thinking of home.*

The entry chime buzzed.

Pretty late for somebody to come by my stateroom. "Come."

The hatch swung open, revealing Khattri. "I hope I'm not disturbing you, sir?"

"Never, Binota." While it might not show on the bridge, they were quite close. "Come in."

Khattri took a few steps inside and held out his tablet device. "Have a look."

"Good news?" Wilson asked as he accepted it and skimmed the screen. "They've already got the heavy cargo shuttles running? That's astounding."

"I thought so." Khattri grinned. "The Zeivlots and Zavlots, when properly motivated, are quite resourceful. They've even improved things a bit from our original design."

Wilson gestured to the small couch and chair. The stateroom was cramped, almost absurdly so. But given the *Salinan's* size, he was lucky to have a two-room suite at all.

Dropping into the chair when Khattri sat on the couch, Wilson shook his head. "Can you believe this?"

"Sir?"

"We're outfitting an alien race with a couple hundred Ajax-class destroyers in hopes of stopping a civilization-ending threat from *nanites.* Tell me that doesn't sound like a plot on *War Patrol.*"

"Eh, not really. *War Patrol* was more beat the Leaguers week in, week out. Less hard sci-fi."

Wilson threw his head back and laughed. "Leave it to you to point *that* out."

Justice 329

"Well, I have to be a stickler for accuracy, sir. It's part of my religion. We cannot lie." As Khattri spoke, he adjusted his *kirpan*.

"How's the crew doing?"

"Well, I think. There is no shortage of activities to engage in, with extra duty assignments out the wazoo for all. An idle mind being the devil's playground, as it were. I will confess, sir, at times, I question what we're doing."

"How come?"

"The Zeivlots still won't give us access to the obelisk. That's what brought us here, right? Maybe we should be forcing the issue. Figure out how to reverse the process and evacuate them rather than try to fight a force that appears overwhelming."

Wilson shook his head. "Even if we could, I'd wager it's a one-way street back to the Milky Way. And call it virtually impossible to send twelve billion people back. The number of ships needed..."

"Any more impossible than defeating a planet-sized hostile?"

"Cohen and his people think it's the best way. If they get an effective weapon together, it's probably our only chance of success. To your point, the chance is small."

"But still worth doing?"

"I think so. Don't you?"

Khattri nodded. "It is difficult to contemplate death in a faraway galaxy, helping a race that isn't ours, with my loved ones never knowing my fate. Yet when I consider the symmetry of it, perhaps it is what is demanded of us."

"Some good has come out of this," Wilson replied.

"By all that's holy, *what*?"

Wilson grinned. "Haven't heard about any bombings,

asteroids being tossed at planets, or attacks on schools, places of worship, or hospitals lately, have you?"

Khattri blinked a few times then laughed. He shook his head. "It shouldn't take what this world has had thrown at it to get them to see the light."

"Some of us need repeated object lessons. Like Senior Chief Stokes." Wilson held out the tablet. "If you don't mind, I'm going to hit the sack."

"Of course not, sir." Khattri stood. "You should take a day off."

Wilson shook his head. "No time. With the impending doom hanging over our heads, stopping for five minutes seems like sacrilege."

"Making yourself sick from exhaustion won't help anyone," Khattri replied as he swung the hatch open. "And it's obvious you're the glue holding this effort together, John."

"Thanks, Binota. Sleep well."

Khattri inclined his head before departing and leaving the small cabin in silence.

With a tired sigh, Wilson finished stripping off his uniform and collapsed into his bunk with a final look at the image of his wife, daughter, and two sons. *I'm getting home. Somehow. Just got to do this thing first.* Within seconds, he was out like a light.

41

Dr. Benjamin Hayworth stretched his neck to one side and was rewarded with a *crack*. The move felt good, as he was quite stiff from staring at the holomatrix projectors for hours. As the *Lion* headed back to Zeivlot, the doctor had spent most of his time in the lab, combing through the data they'd retrieved from the netsim's quantum computer. The process was slow-going and tedious.

"Careful with that, Doctor. If you twist your neck too hard, you'll end up in the medical bay."

Hayworth harrumphed. "I've been doing that since before you were alive, Eliza."

"Yes, so we *all* know." Merriweather chuckled. "It's getting close to time to call it a night, rest our minds, and give this another shot tomorrow."

"The incompleteness of the data is an issue. I should've insisted we stay longer and finish more simulations."

Merriweather set her spill-proof CDF coffee mug beside her workstation and turned toward him. "Heroics look good on you."

"Not heroics, my dear. Just doing my job."

"Which is what someone who does something above and beyond the call says when it's for the right reasons." Merriweather touched his arm. "I'm proud of you."

Hayworth pursed his lips. "Thank you." He determined he would not show emotion, as that wouldn't do. His armor had to be complete at all times.

"Let's hope the team working at the obelisk on Zeivlot will have made progress."

"With the parameters set by their government and religious leadership, I doubt we'll *ever* make progress. The best thing we could do is drill a hole in the side of it."

"If that's even possible. The alloy is unlike anything else."

"And?" Hayworth shrugged. "The only way to gain knowledge is to push the limits of science."

Before a debate could break out, the double-sized hatch to the lab swung open, and Markul walked in. His colorful clothes were in stark contrast to the military uniform Merriweather wore and Hayworth's white lab coat. "Ah, good evening."

"Good evening," Merriweather replied. "No escorts?"

Markul smiled thinly. "General Cohen gave me my, uh, parole, I think it's called. At least until we get back to Zeivlot, is it? Depending on what the government there says, I believe we'll be relocated to that planet, for the time being, at least."

Hayworth snorted. "Yes. I heard that too. What can we do for you?"

"I... just want to help. Wherever and however I can." Markul took a deep breath. "What you collectively did for me and those you saved is a debt that will probably never be repaid. But I can try."

Justice   333

"Feel like crunching some numbers? I could use a better algorithm to parse this data."

Markul nodded. "Sure. I'm good at that."

It took Hayworth a few minutes to reconfigure one of the workstations to lock out access to more sensitive systems and files within the science lab. He finished then stepped back. "You may use this one. And only this one. If you try to access restricted information, I'll know it, and I'll have no problem tossing you out on your rear. Clear?"

Markul smirked. "Quite, Doctor. Are you always this blunt?"

"Yes."

"Dr. Hayworth is trying to say that we're trusting you, but don't abuse it," Merriweather interjected. "And he was mightily impressed with your abilities on the surface. Though don't expect him to ever repeat it."

Markul licked his lips before taking a few steps across the lab to sit at the terminal. "Thank you both."

Hayworth harrumphed and went back to his work. He easily lost track of time, combing through advanced mathematics, looking for the proverbial needle in a haystack.

Merriweather's voice dragged him out of his thoughts. "Doctor?"

"What?" Hayworth snapped. "I was in the middle of working through a problem."

"Markul has something for us."

"It's only been a few minutes."

"More like an hour and a half, Doctor," Markul replied smoothly. "But numbers are like that, aren't they? I lose myself in them too."

"Hmm. Yes. Well, continue."

Markul pressed something on his touch screen, and a stream of numbers displayed across a few of the larger holo displays. "From your notes, I gather you focused research on the upper electromagnetic spectrum."

"Yes." Hayworth eyed the information. "Extremely high-energy EM bursts. We were able to disrupt, at least somewhat, the nanites' bonds by pushing our shields into those higher EM bands."

"This is what spit out from a culling of the netsim data. Frankly, I'm not sure what it means."

"It means we're on the right track. The nanites appear susceptible to high-energy electromagnetic radiation."

"I'm no physicist, but if I read these numbers right, the power output is beyond anything manmade. Even with an antimatter reactor," Merriweather said as she gestured to the display. "A magnetar, maybe?"

Hayworth shook his head. "It would have to be a particular type of magnetar—one that was also a pulsar."

Merriweather stared at him. "Is that even possible?"

"Yes but rare. There're a few dozen in the known universe."

It dawned on Hayworth as he stared at the numbers that perhaps they'd stumbled on the answer. *Yes, we can't recreate a magnetar, but we could devise a way to harness high-energy photons in a focusing field. Though there's still the matter of the proper frequency.* A rare smile came to his lips. "This is very promising. I suspect the quantum computer would've solved this for us if we'd only had more time. But... there's enough here to finish the job."

"Perhaps we should pick this up tomorrow, Doctor," Merriweather said. "It's after midnight CMT."

"The night is young, my dear!" Hayworth stood. "All we need is some more coffee and to let the science flow."

She shook her head at him but suppressed a laugh. "Okay, it's your world, Doctor. We're only living in it."

"About time someone realized that." Hayworth winked and stretched. "Let us proceed to the nearest mess then return to the work."

Hayworth shoved his hands into his lab coat as they left together. He felt buoyed by the new line of inquiry, and while the road ahead would be difficult, he was confident in the process and his people. *And one of these days, I'll show the military just how valuable science is over brute force.* The thought brought another smile to his lips.

———

SSI Headquarters
Churchill – Terran Coalition
12 November 2464

Kenneth Lowe glanced up from the document he was reviewing as his intercom came to life. During most afternoons, he had two hours blocked off to sign agreements, review reports, and track performance against their various contracts. Most days, it was like watching paint dry, but the job was a vital and needed part of the business. That time was known as a do-not-disturb period, which made the interruption odd.

"Yes?" he asked.

"Sir, I have Dr. Saunders for you. He says it's urgent."

Kenneth glanced at the stack of requests still to be gone through. "Tell him I'll give him a vidlink back in an hour."

"Uh, he's here in person."

I'm never getting out of here today. "Okay. Send him in."

Moments later, the double wooden doors swung open,

revealing the outer portion of the CEO's office suite. Kenneth's executive assistant held her hand out, gesturing for Saunders to enter.

"I'm sorry for barging in, Mr. Lowe," Saunders said excitedly.

"You look like a man with something on his chest," Kenneth replied. He nodded toward his assistant. "Thanks. Please hold all calls until Dr. Saunders is finished."

"Yes, sir."

The doors closed behind her, and Kenneth gestured to one of the chairs in front of his sizeable mahogany desk. He crossed his legs and stretched his neck. "Truth be told, Doctor, giving my eyes a break from the screen probably isn't the worst thing I could do this afternoon. Now, care to tell me what's so important that it warranted an in-person visit?"

"I've had a significant breakthrough. In those PASS-CORE reports we were able to obtain and the classified data from the Far Survey Corps, I believe I've identified evidence of a precursor civilization. Some of the artifacts and buildings dated to more than a hundred thousand years ago."

Kenneth's eyes widened. "That's a long time. Why haven't these findings been made public before?"

"As best as I can tell, FSC doesn't want rogue archeologists jumping the line. There have been limited excavations done at one site, but the advent of the war with the League of Sol... put an end to it. Now the planet resides just inside neutral space."

"Close to one of the neutral human colonies, then?"

Saunders nodded. "Yes, New Cornwall."

Kenneth's stomach turned over. New Cornwall had a reputation for hating the Terran Coalition. "Is it within their space?"

Justice

"No, it's considered part of the Systems Alliance territory."

"Well, that's positive, at least. What attracted your attention?"

"The power-wave analysis I performed that showed dark energy present... well, it matches up with trace readings at this dig site."

Kenneth's jaw dropped. "That's one hell of a coincidence."

"I thought so too. I've put out some feelers, and getting an expedition there will be costly. Poor patrols by New Cornwall means more pirates than usual, and you know how that makes independent spacers skittish."

"Yeah." Kenneth stroked his chin. "Except I know a guy. How much are you thinking this will cost?"

"Two, perhaps three million Coalition credits."

Kenneth winced. "And assuming good security is provided?"

"Half that."

"Okay. I'll make a call."

"You can just wave a magic wand?"

Kenneth grinned. "It's possible I'm on good terms with the fleet admiral for the Independent Systems Federation. And he might, in turn, have some good feelings toward General Cohen and the *Lion of Judah*. More importantly, what do you hope to find, Doctor?"

"Ideally, a mechanism by which whatever this technology is works. If it even exists." Saunders shrugged. "Frankly, I don't know. But it's the best lead we've got."

"Sounds like the only one."

Saunders offered a thin smile. "Yes."

"Let's say you find something. What then?"

"Depends on what exactly we locate. If it's a discrete

338 DANIEL GIBBS

piece of technology that somehow influences or expands a normal Lawrence drive wormhole, we could back-engineer it in time and focus our drives. Then we get an even bigger needle in a haystack, looking for where the *Lion* ended up. If, indeed, it survived."

Kenneth quickly realized that the breakthrough, as big as it might seem at the moment, was still so far from a successful recovery of General Cohen and his fleet that it barely warranted mentioning to General MacIntosh. *I have to keep trying, though. On the trillion-to-one chance that they survived.* "All right. Send me all the details, and I'll work my magic with Admiral Henry."

"Already in your inbox." Saunders stood. "I'll get back to it."

"Thank you, Doctor."

After he left and the big mahogany doors closed again, Kenneth leaned back and stretched. *I hope this isn't a wild-goose chase.* With all the incidents happening all over the Terran Coalition, waves of League refugees showing up and taxing their already scarce rebuilding resources, the mighty symbol of their victory returning might be enough to pull the Coalition back together. *Sounds good on paper, anyway.* He returned to his tablet. *Ah, the refit for the CSV* Oxford *is almost done. Colonel Sinclair's ship. I'll oversee closeout on that one myself.*

———

Recruit Training Depot Sextans B
Zeivlot
19 November 2464

Justice

Master Chief Rebecca Tinetariro wiped her eyes, which were bloodshot and tired, and every joint of her body hurt. Muscles she'd forgotten existed sent impulses of pain, and each step was difficult. *Thirty years of service are catching up.* Still, *she* decided when enough was enough. And Tinetariro was far from through. She'd led a grueling training event for the remaining Zeivlot and Zavlot recruits for the last twenty-four hours. Meant to push them to their absolute limits, the exercise saw them tested on CDF hardware, shipboard operations, and physical fitness.

It also pushed the instructors to their limits. Most senior noncommissioned officers on the *Lion* hadn't pushed boots in a decade or more, just like Tinetariro. But none of that mattered because neat rows of polished recruits stood in front of her.

They'd finished the test, and every last one passed. They were only a little more than half of their original number, but she would take it. *At times, I didn't think we would graduate a single soldier.* She was amazed by how quickly the animosities between the two species had dropped after an act of kindness by one Zeivlot for a Zavlot in the gas hut. *Perhaps sometimes, just one or two people can make a huge difference.*

After twenty-eight hours of being awake, it was shocking that any of them could form a proper line and maintain ramrod straight posture, but that was the effect of CDF training. It would instill muscle memory that never let go.

Tinetariro moved down the first row of recruits, stopping and shaking the hand of each one. Though it was a marked departure from standard procedure, she was incredibly proud of them. Not only had they taken everything the drill instructors could throw their way, but they'd learned to overcome a lifetime of hatred also. *That* was something worth being proud of.

She finally reached where Has'rad and Sey'nati stood. "At ease, recruits!"

Both of them relaxed into parade rest posture.

"Recruit Has'rad and Recruit Sey'nati, you placed first and second in your company." Tinetariro smiled. "I expect nothing less from two leaders who helped set the tone for all."

Has'rad responded, "Yes, Master Chief."

Tinetariro made eye contact with several others as she stepped back. "A few days from now, there will be a formal ceremony for your graduation from CDF recruit training. After that, in recognition of your time served in your respective planet's armed forces, you will be granted step-up promotions and sent to proper A schools for additional training in your military occupational specialties. I hope to see at least some of you volunteer for officer-candidate school and pursue a commission in the Coalition Defense Force." She paused, looking around at them. "It has been an honor to serve as your senior drill instructor, and I fervently hope that in the months and years to come, together, we will save your worlds from the nanite threat. Until then, I expect each of you to discharge the oath you took to the Terran Coalition. Godspeed to you all. Company... dismissed!"

As the recruits dispersed back toward their barracks, Tinetariro finally let herself relax. While the work was far from over, proving it could be done had been the first and most crucial step. The next batch would be easier, until it became muscle memory. *Like everything else in the CDF.* For the moment, sleep awaited.

EPILOGUE

SALENA BO'HAI HAD SPENT the last forty-five minutes trudging through the passageways of the *Lion of Judah*, hunting for David. Since he was a flag officer, she didn't have high-enough clearance to use the crew-locate feature for him in the *Lion's* computer. Instead, Bo'hai had to do things the old-fashioned way. *Well, he's not in his quarters, either mess frequented by the senior officers, or the observation deck.*

She felt dejected as she stood outside a gravlift, waiting for it to arrive. The doors swooshed open, revealing an anti-grav sled loaded with supplies and a young man who, presumably, was moving them. "Oh, I'm sorry. I'll take the next one."

"Nonsense! There's plenty of room. Step right in."

His smile and demeanor were warm and comforting.

"Okay," she replied and squeezed in.

"Which deck?"

"Eight, I think."

"You think?"

Bo'hai had made it a point to study how the humans wore their clothing, especially the uniforms. She discovered she could learn much about each individual from their markings. The young man had the insignia of a private and another patch she recalled was from the logistical corps. *Which would explain why he's hauling boxes.* "I'm looking for someone, and I'm not sure where he is, Private... Waters."

"Hey, you got the pronunciation right on the first try." Waters grinned. "Why didn't you use the computer to find whoever it is?"

"I, ah, lack the appropriate permissions to use your computer."

"Oh. Looking for the general, huh?"

Bo'hai blinked. "How did you know?"

"Simple process of elimination. You have to have special clearance to geolocate flag officers. But you're in luck, ma'am. Because I saw him not half an hour ago heading to cargo bay four. That's deck twenty-six."

"Then that's where I'm going." Bo'hai smiled.

"You got it, ma'am." Waters smacked one of the buttons on the control panel, and the gravlift took off. "Mind if I ask why you're looking for General Cohen?"

Bo'hai shrugged. "I'm worried about him."

"Know what you mean, ma'am. He looked like he had the weight of the universe on his shoulders."

"I was hoping to help carry some of that."

"My Bible says that's the best way to do things." The lift came to a halt, and the doors slid open. "Your stop, I think."

"Thank you, Private."

"Anytime, ma'am."

Bo'hai scooted between the gravsled and the right side of the box-like cab. The doors to the lift closed behind her, and she stared at a helpful directory screen to determine where she was headed next. *Cargo bay four... left, three hundred meters.* The *Lion of Judah* was nothing if not massive. She still marveled at how the Terran Coalition had been able to construct vessels of such size in the void.

It took a few minutes to get there, and some crewmen and -women were still present, even at the later hour. For a long time after Bo'hai had come aboard, the other humans paused or did a double take at her alien features. That time had passed, it seemed. Most didn't give her another look after flashing a smile. She, too, had long grown accustomed to the different types of humans. They seemed to come in all shapes, sizes, and colors, which wasn't unlike her people, but they were vastly less homogenous. As a scientist, she found humanity a fascinating study.

Once Bo'hai arrived at the double-wide and -tall entry hatch for the cargo bay, she paused outside it. The massive bay was dimly lit, and it took a moment for her eyes to adjust.

David stood at the far end, in front of a flag-draped coffin. He brought his hand to his brow and crisply saluted before touching the cloth and whispering something in a language she couldn't make out.

As Bo'hai watched, David moved to the next coffin. She realized there were dozens of simple metallic boxes with an electronic display at the end. *Stasis chambers. Should I leave?* She couldn't decide whether she was intruding on a profoundly personal moment, or if she should approach him.

As David reached the end of the line of coffins, he again spoke in a whisper.

Hebrew. He's praying in Hebrew. Bo'hai was about to turn to go when an anguished cry caused her to whirl around. Everything else overrode her reluctance, and she rushed to his side. As she took long strides across the deck, David held himself up with one hand.

Bo'hai put her arm around him. "It's okay."

David acted like he'd been struck by lightning. He jumped back, and his jaw dropped. "I'm sorry. I didn't hear you come in," he finally got out.

"You don't have to hide it from me."

He blinked. "What do you mean? I was just saying a prayer for..." David couldn't finish the sentence. Instead, tears streamed down his face, and he rotated away so that she wouldn't be able to see him.

Bo'hai embraced him from behind. "I can't imagine what you're going through, but I am here for you."

At first, David tried to resist, but she wouldn't let go. Then his efforts to push out of the hug turned into gut-wrenching sobs. "I couldn't save them. They're dead because of *me*."

"No." She worked her way around to see his face and cupped it in her hands. "The Mifreen did this. Not you."

"They were there because of me! I made a choice to get involved."

"It was worth it."

David bit his lip as tears continued to flow. "You don't know that."

"Yes, I do. And so do you. There are over a thousand people that you and all the others saved crammed into this ship."

"Is that worth forty-three lives?" David asked, anguish in his voice.

"Were the tens of millions lost defeating the League of Sol worth it?"

"This is different. We're not defending our homes. I intervened in an alien civilization's inner workings."

Bo'hai stared into his eyes. "You can't blame yourself."

"I'm in charge. I made the ultimate decision. There's no

one else to pass the buck to. No orders from command. Only mine. And I don't know if I did the right thing. Part of me thinks I did, but when I look at this..." He gestured to the rows of deceased soldiers and Marines.

She clung to him and desperately searched her mind for something, anything to say to make it better. "You did what you had to. I couldn't have walked away either. None of us could."

David put his head on her shoulder. "It's not something a civilian can understand. Only someone who's been there."

"Then talk to Colonel Aibek or Dr. Tural—"

"*I can't.*"

"Why not?" Bo'hai asked him, tears in her eyes. "You can't let this destroy you from the inside."

"Because they're counting on me to get them home, and if I shatter that hope, this entire fleet falls apart. And with it, any possibility of defeating those nanites. So I have to man up and shoulder the burden myself." David turned his head. "I never wanted you to see me like this."

Bo'hai clicked her tongue. "Having feelings isn't bad, but bottling up pain until it consumes you is."

"If I were back home, I'd talk to a therapist I used to see. But she's a few million light-years away."

"Then you're stuck with me."

"Salena—"

Bo'hai put her finger to his lips. "I may not know what it's like to carry a weapon and fight in a war. But I do know what it feels like to think you're moments away from death and to be lost, alone, and scared. Let me in. Don't push me away."

David seemed to be trying to formulate a response.

"I love you."

"I... love you too." The words fell out of his mouth as he stared at her.

She rested her head under his chin. "Not how I expected us to say that to each other."

David chuckled and wiped his eyes. "Cute, dear."

"We can get through it together."

"I'll be okay."

Bo'hai grabbed his uniform lapels. "We do it together. Promise me."

For a few moments, David didn't speak or move. Then he nodded slowly. "Okay."

She took his hands. "What were you doing?"

"Asking HaShem to take their souls into paradise and to forgive me for pride and hubris."

"Then I will pray for them as well."

David took a deep breath and composed himself. "Thank you. We should probably get out of here, before someone comes in and notices."

"A smart idea." Bo'hai held out her arm.

He paused and wiped his eyes again with his uniform sleeve before tucking her arm under his and leading the way out.

———

NEITHER DAVID nor Bo'hai noticed a figure standing in the shadows of the cargo bay, watching them. Once the doors closed, Waters stepped into the light and knelt where David had fallen on the deck. Wetness was still visible.

Waters touched it and shook his head. "A good man is never alone, David ben-Levi Cohen. I wish you'd remember that."

A tear slid down Waters's face as he walked away.

The Lost Warship: Book 5 – Resolve:

As Major General David Cohen and the *Lion of Judah* continue their search for allies and technology to fight the nanites, the arrival of an artificial life form changes everything. But is the being the friend he portrays himself as, or a foe? The stakes have never been higher for the *Lion* and her crew.

Now available on Amazon!

Tap HERE to read NOW!

THE END

ALSO AVAILABLE FROM DANIEL GIBBS

Battlegroup Z

Book 1 - Weapons Free

Book 2 - Hostile Spike

Book 3 - Sol Strike

Book 4 - Bandits Engaged

Book 5 - Iron Hand

Book 6 - Final Flight

Echoes of War

Book 1 - Fight the Good Fight

Book 2 - Strong and Courageous

Book 3 - So Fight I

Book 4 - Gates of Hell

Book 5 - Keep the Faith

Book 6 - Run the Gauntlet

Book 7 - Finish the Fight

The Lost Warship

Book 1 - Adrift

Book 2 - Mercy

Book 3 - Valor

Book 4 - Justice

Book 5 - Resolve

Book 6 - Faith (Coming in 2023)

Breach of Faith

(With Gary T. Stevens)

Book 1 - Breach of Peace

Book 2 - Breach of Faith

Book 3 - Breach of Duty

Book 4 - Breach of Trust

Book 5 - Spacer's Luck

Book 6 - Fortune's Favor

Book 7 - The Iron Dice

Deception Fleet

(With Steve Rzasa)

Book 1 - Victory's Wake

Book 2 - Cold Conflict

Book 3 - Hazards Near

Book 4 - Liberty's Price

Book 5 - Ecliptic Flight

Book 6 - Collision Vector

Courage, Commitment, Faith: Tales from the Coalition Defense Force

(Anthology Series)

Volume One

ACKNOWLEDGMENTS

This is probably the hardest afterword I've compiled as an author.

On May 23rd, my father passed away after being diagnosed with stage four cancer on May 1st.

Those three weeks were all at once sad but also filled with bittersweet memories as I moved in with him to help ensure he had good care through the end of his life. My father was an institution. A true human superman, who seemingly could do anything, and did. Even a few months before the end, he was painting his house – try doing that at 40, much less 93.

He was able to read this book as I printed it out in an unpolished state and put it in a three-ring binder for him.

It was the last thing he read.

And now, he is gone – to a better place, I am sure of that.

Thank you all for reading, and to all those who sent me emails, Facebook messages, etc – thank you for the prayers. They were, and continue to be, vital.

For now, I march onward.

Godspeed,
Daniel Gibbs

Printed in Great Britain
by Amazon